Half Hidden

Half Hidden

EMMA BLAIR

LITTLE, BROWN AND COMPANY

A *Little, Brown* Book

First published in Great Britain in 1996
by Little, Brown and Company
Reprinted 1998

Copyright © Emma Blair 1996

The moral right of the author has been asserted.

A CIP catalogue record for this book is
available from the British Library.

ISBN 0 316 87773 5

Typeset in Adobe Garamond by M Rules
Printed and bound in Great Britain by
Clays Ltd, St Ives plc

Little, Brown and Company (UK)
Brettenham House
Lancaster Place
London WC2E 7EN

Prologue

'Why are you crying, Mummy?'

Elspeth Le Var dashed away her tears, unaware up until that moment she'd been weeping. Beyond her, St Aubin's Bay lay blue and sparkling in the summer sunshine. Overhead a flight of gulls cried and swooped in their never-ending search for food.

She glanced at her concerned nine-year-old daughter. 'Sorry, silly of me.'

Holly laid a tentative hand on Elspeth's arm. 'Is something wrong? Aren't you feeling well?'

'No, I'm fine, darling. I was just thinking . . . remembering.'

The young girl frowned, knowing it was most unlike her mother to get into such a state. Elspeth never cried, at least not to her knowledge. 'Remembering what, Mum?'

Elspeth opened her handbag and took out a small, lacy handkerchief which she used to dab the large soft tears still flowing from her eyes. 'Oh, things,' she prevaricated.

Holly wasn't to be put off, distressed to see her mother so upset. 'What things?'

Elspeth smiled at the raven-haired girl, thinking how pretty she was, how like her father. 'The war, darling. I was thinking about the war.'

'You never talk about that, Mum. Dad does, sometimes. But never you.'

The war, Elspeth thought bitterly. That awful time when Jersey had been occupied. Five long years during which there had been terrible hardship. She inwardly shuddered at the memory.

'No, I don't,' she admitted in a whisper.

'Why not?'

How did you explain to a child the awful experiences they'd all been through? The pain, hunger, despair and deaths. And fear, oh yes, the fear that gnawed inside each and every day that the hated enemy goosemarched their beloved streets.

She sighed, fumbled again inside her handbag, this time for a cigarette, and lit up. 'Do you know why I called you Holly?' she queried softly.

The girl shook her head.

'It was after my best friend, Holly Morgan.'

Elspeth took a deep drag, noting at the back of her mind that her hand was shaking. 'It would have been Holly's birthday today, which is why I suppose I got to thinking about her,' she explained.

The young Holly was intrigued, this being first she'd heard of her namesake. '*Would* have been?'

Elspeth nodded. 'She's dead. She died . . .' Elspeth broke off and gulped in a deep breath, a vision of Holly Morgan dancing before her eyes. Dear Holly, sweet Holly. How she still missed her, achingly so.

'Was she killed by the Germans?' young Holly asked.

Elspeth stared out over the bay, a kaleidoscope of images flashing through her mind. 'No, my darling,' she replied quietly.

'Did Daddy know her?'

'Very well. Four of us used to go out together. Daddy, myself, Holly and a chap called Martin, a Jerseyman like your father. He would have married Holly if it hadn't been for the war.' Elspeth smiled thinly. 'But then the war changed a lot of things, a lot of lives.'

She glanced across at a concrete fortification built by the Germans during the Occupation, a myriad of which were dotted all over the island. Those and the many tunnels dug by slave labour.

'Jemima was originally her cat. I've never told you that.'

Young Holly's eyes widened. 'Really!'

'Yes. I adopted her after . . .' She trailed off, and swallowed hard. 'Would you like to hear about Holly Morgan?' she asked, her voice crackling with emotion.

Young Holly nodded.

'Then sit here beside me.'

When Holly had sat as instructed Elspeth took one of her daughter's hands in hers and gently squeezed.

'Holly Morgan and I went to school together . . .'

Chapter 1

What a lovely smile, Holly Morgan thought of the chap striding purposefully in her direction. Good looking too.

'I think he's going to ask you up,' Elspeth whispered to her, the pair of them at a local Saturday night dance.

'Maybe it's you he's got his eye on.'

Elspeth briefly considered that. 'No, it's definitely you. I'll betcha.'

The chap stopped in front of Holly, his smile widening. 'Would you care to dance?'

Elspeth shot Holly an 'I told you so' look.

Holly rose. 'That would be nice. Thank you.'

They walked on to the floor where they waited for the band to strike up the next number. 'I hope it isn't a polka. I'm useless at that,' the chap said.

He was only fractionally taller than her, Holly noted. But that was all right, just as long as he wasn't shorter. Twinkling brown eyes, she further noted. She decided she liked him.

'My name's Martin by the way,' he declared.

'And I'm Holly.'

'Holly,' he repeated. 'Sort of Christmassy.'

She laughed. 'No one's ever said that before.'

'Well, they have now.'

He took her into his arms as the band began playing a waltz, the two of them moving easily, fluidly together. He wasn't one to tread on her toes, she reflected with satisfaction.

'It's the first time I've been to this particular dance,' he stated, making conversation.

'I thought I hadn't seen you here before.'

'You come a lot then?'

She matched his smile. 'Hardly a lot. From time to time, usually with my pal Elspeth. That was her sitting beside me.'

Sounded like she didn't have a current boyfriend, Martin thought, which pleased him.

'Martin what?' she queried.

'Voisin. And you?'

'Morgan.'

He nodded. 'Can I say something?'

'Go ahead.'

'You not only look gorgeous but smell it as well.'

With someone else she might have been offended by his being so forward, they'd only just met after all. But his voice rang with sincerity. He meant it. It was no superficial chat-up line.

'Why, thank you.'

'My pleasure.'

He suddenly removed his hand from her waist and waved. 'My mate Terry,' he explained. 'He's shy.'

'Unlike you,' she teased.

Martin shrugged. 'That's never been a problem with me, I admit. I've always been fairly outgoing.'

'Which is Terry?' she queried.

'Over by the door there. Dark hair and glasses.'

Holly spotted him. 'You're right, he does appear the shy type.'

'It wouldn't be the first time we've gone to a dance and he's never asked anyone up. Even a few pints of Mary Ann lager inside him doesn't help. Daft idiot.'

The number ended and they applauded. 'Another?' he asked.

She'd been hoping he'd say that. She wanted to know more about Martin Voisin. 'Fine.'

He positively beamed. 'Smashing. I enjoy dancing with you.'

And I with you, she thought.

He groaned, and she laughed, when the band broke into a polka.

'What happened?' Elspeth demanded when Holly eventually rejoined her. 'I thought you two had "got off" together.'

'It seems we have. Martin, that's his name by the way, has gone to search out his mate. He'll be back shortly.'

'Is he nice, Martin I mean? He certainly looks it.'

'Very.'

'The pair of you make a good couple.'

Holly laughed. 'Let's not go overboard, I've only known him half an hour.'

'What I meant was the pair of you look so natural together. As if you'd known each other for ages.'

'He's extremely easy to be with,' Holly admitted.

'Are you going to let him take you home?'

'He hasn't asked me yet,' Holly protested.

'But if he does you will, won't you?'

Holly pretended indifference. 'I might.'

'You'd be a mug to let that one escape.'

Holly silently agreed. 'What about you, have you been up?'

Elspeth pulled a face. 'A couple of times but not with anyone anywhere near interesting. I haven't been lucky like you.'

She had been, Holly further silently agreed.

'What does he do?' Elspeth inquired eagerly.

'He's an apprentice mechanic at a garage in Byron Street.'

'Oh yes. Sounds OK. Did you tell him you're a trainee nurse?'

Holly nodded. 'He made a joke about bed pans.'

Elspeth pulled another face. 'They're no joke as both you and I well know. They're disgusting items.' She also was a trainee nurse at the General Hospital.

'Here he comes,' Holly declared, having spotted Martin coming over with Terry alongside.

'That's the mate,' Holly explained, nodding in their direction. 'His name's Terry and he's shy.'

Elspeth giggled. 'Shy!'

'Apparently wouldn't say boo to a goose.'

3

'I wonder if he's going to ask me up?' Elspeth mused. Why else would they both be coming over?

'Could be.'

Terry wasn't only shy but nervous to boot, that was clearly obvious when he and Martin halted before the girls. Martin introduced Terry who, reddening, mumbled how pleased he was to meet Holly. Then she did the same with Elspeth.

'Well, on you go,' Martin urged Terry who reddened even more. 'I eh . . . I eh . . .'

Elspeth decided to take matters into her own hands and save the poor soul further embarrassment. 'Why, I'd love to dance, thank you very much,' she declared to him.

Relief flooded Terry's face. 'I'm not very good, I'm afraid.'

'That won't be a problem, neither am I,' Elspeth lied, for she was an expert dancer. 'The two of us can just stumble around together, eh?'

Rising, Elspeth grasped Terry by the arm and led him on to the floor.

'Shall we?' Martin suggested to Holly.

During the last waltz he asked if he could see her home and she readily agreed.

Elspeth, who'd taken a shine to the shy Terry, had to suggest the same thing and he, too, readily agreed.

"A car!' Holly exclaimed. This was indeed a luxury.

'It's not mine, I only wish it was. It's my dad's. He lets me use it on occasion.'

'Very posh,' Holly commented, surveying the sleek black vehicle that was older than it appeared.

'Runs like a dream. I make sure of that,' Martin declared proudly, opening the front-seat passenger door and politely helping her inside.

Nice manners, she thought, something that always impressed her. 'Has Terry got a car?'

' 'Fraid not. Those two will have to walk.'

'You should have offered them a lift.'

Martin grinned at her. 'I wanted you all to myself. Now what's the address?'

'There's nothing like being honest,' she replied, then told him where she lived, which wasn't all that far away.

'I know it,' he said, starting up the car.

Let him kiss me or not? she wondered. Who was she kidding! Of course she would.

'Do you like the pictures?' he asked.

She knew what that was leading up to and a thrill ran through her. 'Depends what's on.' She didn't want to seem too eager.

'How about a comedy?'

'Uh-huh.'

'Does that mean yes or no?'

'Yes or no to what?'

'Next Friday. We could have a drink first and fish suppers after. What do you say?'

Not too eager, she reminded herself. 'Friday,' she mused. 'Hmmh.' She pretended to think.

'Maybe you're seeing someone else?' he queried casually.

Holly smiled in the darkness; the casualness of his voice hadn't fooled her one little bit. He was as anxious to meet up again as she was. 'No.'

'You don't want to go then, is that it?'

'I never said that. But there's my job, you know.'

Realisation dawned. 'Of course, nurses do shifts.'

'Exactly. But as it so happens I'm free next Friday evening. Where and when shall we meet?'

Martin grunted with relief. That had been a nasty few moments. 'Six-thirty all right? I'll pick you up at your house.'

'Fine. I'll be ready.'

Martin hummed jauntily as he drove the remainder of the short distance to where Holly lived.

'Friday then,' he said as he brought the car to a halt.

'Friday.'

He reached across and took her hand. 'Goodnight.'

'Goodnight.'

Holly hesitated, then reached for the door handle, only to stop when his other hand came to rest on her shoulder.

'Can I kiss you?'

She had begun to think he wasn't going to. 'If you wish.'

They were parked at the kerb for a full fifteen minutes before a breathless Holly finally emerged from the car.

Dan Morgan glanced up from the exam papers he was marking as his daughter entered their sitting room.

'You look pleased with yourself,' he commented wryly.

'Do I?'

'I would say so.'

She ran a hand through her hair hoping it wasn't too dishevelled, or that her lipstick wasn't smudged. She would have gone straight to her room to repair the damage if she'd known her father was still up. Dan was normally an early go-to-bedder. She'd forgotten about the exam papers.

'It was a good night,' she said.

He raised an eyebrow. 'Do I take it from that, and the stars in your eyes, that you met someone?'

'That would be telling,' she teased.

'Which means yes.'

'Could be,' she prevaricated.

Dan laughed softly. 'You're positively glowing. He must be some lad.'

'His name's Martin and he's an apprentice car mechanic. We're going out next Friday night.'

Dan laid down his pen and studied his daughter more closely. It wasn't easy bringing up a child on your own, particularly a daughter. But he thought he'd done a fairly good job of it.

'Going where? Or shouldn't I ask?'

'A drink to begin with, then the pictures with fish suppers afterwards.'

'My my, the full works eh?'

'The full works,' she agreed with a smile.

'He must be keen.'

'That was the impression I got.'

'There again,' Dan mused. 'He'd be stupid not to be. A beautiful, intelligent, charismatic girl like yourself.'

'Dad,' she laughed. 'I think you're just a teensy bit biased.'

'Not me,' he protested. 'Just because you're my daughter has nothing to do with it.'

'In a pig's eye.'

How like her mother she was at times, Dan reflected. Not so much in her looks, though you could see Gill in her, but more in personality. His Gill would never be truly dead while Holly was alive.

He'd been young enough when widowed to have married again but that had been out of the question as far as he'd been concerned. There was, and always would be, only one woman for him and that was his beloved Gill.

He glanced across at her photograph standing on the sideboard, remembering how it had been between them, the love, warmth, caring. All ended by a blood clot that had taken her suddenly one evening. They'd been talking at the time, discussing his day at the school when, completely out of the blue, it hit her. Just like that, no warning, nothing. One moment she'd been fine, her normal self, the next . . .

Dan swallowed hard and brought his attention back to Holly who was rattling on about the dance.

He forced himself to listen.

'So how did you get on?' Elspeth demanded eagerly when she and Holly met up the next day at work.

'We're going out on Friday. How about you?'

'The same.'

Both of them giggled.

'Did he kiss you?' Holly asked, sure of what the answer would be, knowing Elspeth.

'*I* kissed *him*.'

'I thought you might somehow.'

'Well he'd never have made a move. I had to take the initiative. What about you?'

'We snogged in his car before I went in.'

They giggled again.

Holly abruptly broke off. 'There's Staff. We'll chat later.'

'You betcha.'

And with that they hurried off in different directions, each looking forward to exchanging notes and having a right old gossip about the previous night.

'How's your fish?'

'Scrumptious,' Holly replied.

'Mine too. You're not cold, are you?'

'Not in the least.'

'Pity.'

'Why?' she queried with a frown.

'It would have given me an excuse to squeeze even closer to you.'

Holly laughed. 'Do you need an excuse?'

Martin shuffled his bottom till it was tight against hers. 'You and the moonlight, who could ask for anything more?'

'Don't forget the fish and chips,' she teased.

'OK, you, the moonlight and fish and chips.'

Holly gazed up at the full moon shining overhead, its silvery reflection lighting up the bay. In the distance was the dark, shadowy outline of Elizabeth Castle.

'I've never sat on the esplanade wall at night eating fish and chips before,' Holly murmured, thinking how romantic it all was. The suggestion to eat there had been Martin's.

'I have.'

She turned to stare at him, her expression hardening a little. 'I see.'

'A number of times in fact.'

She'd appreciated he must have had previous girlfriends but the last thing she wanted to hear was the fact confirmed, or about them.

'Is that so?'

'Oh yes.'

A silence ensued during which they both continued to eat. 'I was here last week actually. Only I had scampi then, not cod,' Martin said eventually.

'Really?' she responded, a brittle edge to her voice.

'Lovely scampi they were too.'

She could have sloshed him. What was he doing! What had been a marvellous evening out up until then had become, within a few short moments, completely spoilt.

'I've never tasted better now that I come to think about it,' he went on.

Bloody scampi! Bloody man! she inwardly raged.

Martin sighed. 'I could sit here for hours.'

'Oh, could you?' she said caustically.

'Hours and hours.'

She wanted to say, and did you with your other females? But didn't. What a let down, what a rat. And she'd thought . . .

'Terry insisted we go for a walk after the scampi. He was drunk you see. We both were.'

'Terry!' she exclaimed.

'Of course, who else?'

She knew then she'd been had, that he'd been deliberately misleading her.

'You didn't think I was with a woman, did you?' he mocked.

'You bugger!' she hissed, and hit him on the arm.

Martin roared with laughter. 'Got you there. Good and proper.'

She attempted to punch him again but this time he caught her wrist, pulling her round and into him, a number of chips flying away to fall into the water below.

Then his lips were on hers, his tongue probing deeply into her mouth. She felt herself melt inside.

'Oh, Martin,' she whispered when the kiss was over.

'I know, I feel the same way.'

'Do you?'

'Very much so.'

What remained of their fish and chips was forgotten, and stayed forgotten, as his mouth closed again on hers.

Dan struck a match and applied it to his pipe. 'It seems to be getting serious between you and this Martin,' he said through clouds of blue smoke. 'How long have you been going out together now?'

'A little over three months,' Holly answered from where she was ironing.

'Hmmh!' Dan murmured through the haze.

Holly upended her iron, thinking she'd take a few minutes' break. 'Would you like a cup of tea or coffee?'

Dan shook his head. 'About Martin.'

'What about him?'

'Don't you think it's time we met?'

Holly shook out the shirt she'd just ironed and put it on a hanger ready for the wardrobe. 'You have met.'

'At the door, Holly, only that. Saying hello isn't exactly meeting someone.'

She'd been meaning to bring Martin home for some while now but, for various reasons, had simply never got round to it. 'What do you suggest?'

'How about him coming to supper?'

She nodded. 'Fine. When?'

'Any night you like.'

She thought about that. 'Wednesday?'

'Right.'

Holly left the sitting room and went off to make herself a pot of tea, already planning what she'd cook for the coming Wednesday evening.

Holly was amused to see Martin so unsure of himself, quite unlike his normal confident self. She had no doubt it was her father's authoritative schoolmasterish manner that was unsettling him. She'd seen that happen before.

'Whisky or sherry, Martin?' Dan asked affably.

'Eh . . . whisky, I think.'

'Soda?'

'Yes, please.'

'Why don't you sit,' Holly suggested to Martin as Dan crossed to the sideboard.

Martin rolled his eyes at her, Dan's back being to him, which made Holly smile, then sat.

'I'll just go and check on how supper's doing,' Holly declared and, still smiling and amused, strolled from the room.

Martin shifted uncomfortably in his chair, wondering what on earth he was going to talk to a schoolmaster about.

'You're an apprentice car mechanic, I understand,' Dan said, handing Martin a generously filled glass.

'That's correct, sir. I love cars. Always have. Ever since I was a little boy.'

Dan nodded and sat facing his guest, as aware as Holly of the effect he was having on this young man whose character he intended to assess. Holly was his responsibility after all and he wasn't a man to take his responsibilities lightly. Particularly where his daughter's welfare was concerned.

'Do you like cars, sir?'

'Never been interested in them, never owned one. The internal combustion engine is a total mystery to me,' Dan replied.

Damn! Martin thought. That line of conversation, his favourite, had just gone out the window.

Dan decided to have a little bit of fun. 'Etruscan art is my hobby. Do you know anything about that?'

Martin gaped at him. 'Etruscan art?'

'You must have heard of the Etruscans. They were around at the same time as the early Romans.'

Martin hurriedly searched his memory. Trying to come up with something, anything, intelligent. 'Didn't they fight the Romans in the Punic wars?'

Dan produced his pipe and tapped it into an ashtray. 'You're thinking of the Carthaginians, different people entirely.'

'I'm afraid history has never been my strong point,' Martin admitted sheepishly.

'Won't be long,' Holly announced, breezing back into the room. She collected the sherry Dan had poured for her from the sideboard. 'So what are you two talking about?'

'Etruscan art,' Dan informed her, a mischievous glint in his eye.

'Dad!' she admonished. 'You're not at school now.'

'But it's my hobby,' he protested. 'School's got nothing to do with it.'

'Well, if you go on about Etruscan art you'll bore the socks off Martin. So that's the end of that subject,' she stated firmly.

Dan lit up while Martin gazed beseechingly at Holly.

'Dad enjoys listening to big band music,' Holly declared, know-ing Martin also to be keen on it.

'Really!' Martin exclaimed. 'So do I. I'm a great fan of Glenn Miller.'

Holly sat and sipped her sherry while Martin and her father fell to discussing the relative virtues of various bands, British and American.

After supper Dan played some of his extensive record collection to an enthusiastic, and now thoroughly relaxed, Martin.

'What did you think?' Holly queried after Martin had gone.

'Nice chap.'

'You approve?'

He regarded her knowingly. 'Would it make a difference if I didn't?'

'Of course.'

But Dan knew better. Holly was a headstrong girl who might respect his opinion but would not necessarily go along with it. If he'd disapproved of Martin she might well have continued seeing the lad despite him.

Holly was delighted the evening had been such a success, Martin and her father having become firm friends by the end of it. And all thanks to big band music!

She mentally awarded herself a gold star for cleverness.

As he did every week, Dan had come to his wife's grave to talk to her, which he always did aloud if there was no one else within hear-ing distance. In his mind he visualised her listening.

'I finally met this young man of Holly's; he came to supper the other night, and I was most impressed. Clean-cut chap with excel-lent manners, intelligent too, of course, which our Holly needs.

'They really are quite struck on one another, that was apparent, and I wouldn't be at all surprised if the relationship didn't become a permanent one in time. It had that sort of feel about it. You know, like it was between you and me?'

Dan smiled. 'Do you remember our courting days? Seems so long ago now, and at the same time might have just been yesterday.

We used to go for those long walks along the shore together chattering away like a couple of magpies. And every so often we'd stop and . . .' He broke off to smile at the memory.

'Those were wonderful days, Gill, but then all my days with you were wonderful. Truly so. Our entire marriage was that.

'By the way, Holly bought a new dress for a dinner dance she's going to at The Grand with Martin. It's red satin with a skirt that's pleated at the back. She put it on for me when she brought it home and I thought she looked gorgeous in it.

'She and Martin are going with Elspeth and her beau Terry who's a friend of Martin's. The four of them go out gallivanting quite a lot together.

'Another thing, I . . .'

On the way home from the cemetery Dan bought a newspaper which bore banner headlines proclaiming that Hitler and his Nazis had marched into Austria.

'No, Martin, no!' Holly protested, squirming out from under him. 'I won't go any further, I've told you that before.'

Martin gazed at her longingly as she smoothed down her skirt. 'I'm sorry, I just got carried away.'

'What if I ended up pregnant? What then? Think of the humiliation, not only for myself but Dad. Anyway, I'm simply not that sort of girl.'

'I know,' Martin breathed, shaking his head.

Holly knelt beside him, grasping his knee. 'Don't think I don't want to, because I do. Just as much as you. But it wouldn't be right.'

'I know,' Martin repeated.

'I love you,' she stated with a smile.

A smile he matched. 'And I love you.'

'With all my heart.'

He did love her, he thought. Desperately. A love that had grown and grown during the year since they'd met. 'Why don't we get engaged?' he proposed abruptly.

She stared at him, relishing those words she'd been waiting to hear.

'Well?'

'Oh, Martin!'

'We couldn't get married for a bit yet. I've my apprenticeship to finish and you your training. In the meantime we'd have to save up for what we'd need when we get a place of our own.'

He was suddenly filled with excitement, as was she. 'You haven't answered me yet,' he said.

'The answer's yes. Of course it's that.'

'I'll take you out on Saturday and we'll buy the ring and make it official.'

She moved back on to the couch alongside him. They had her house for the evening to themselves, Dan out visiting an old crony whom he regularly played chess with.

'How do you feel?' Martin queried.

'Thrilled to bits. All sort of bubbly inside. And you?'

'I don't know about bubbly but . . .' He hesitated. 'Somewhat scared as well. It's a big step.'

'Huge,' she agreed.

'But I've no doubts, Holly. None at all.'

'Me neither.' She went into his arms, laying her head on his chest. 'I won't until we're married though. You must understand that.'

He groaned.

'I won't, Martin. Not until our wedding night. I've always promised myself that would be the case and I'm not changing my mind now. When I put on that white wedding dress I'll be the virgin it implies.'

'Puritan,' he teased.

'Lecher.'

They both laughed.

When Dan returned home he was the first to be told the news. Exactly as he'd expected, he thought, as he warmly congratulated them both.

Chapter 2

'War,' a grim-faced Dan breathed, shaking his head in despair. This was awful, a tragedy. He rose from his chair to stare at an equally grim-faced, and shaken, Holly.

'I need a drink. What about you?'

'No thanks, Dad.'

Sighing, he crossed to the sideboard where he took out a bottle of scotch and poured himself a hefty one. 'God help them all,' he murmured, and gulped down half the contents of his glass.

'It's all so . . . . frightening,' Holly said. 'We'll be all right here, won't we?'

'I don't see why not.' At least he hoped that would be the case.

'Czechoslovakia, Poland – Hitler's a maniac,' Holly declared.

'I couldn't agree more. And with the forces at his disposal probably the most powerful and dangerous maniac the world has ever seen.'

Dan had another gulp of whisky, and shuddered, thinking of the millions killed in the previous conflict with Germany. Now it was about to happen all over again.

'What are you doing tonight?' he asked.

'Meeting Martin.'

Dan nodded.

'In fact I'd better make a move or I'll be late.'

'Give him my regards and tell him I've got some new records I'm sure he'd like to hear.'

'I'll do that, Dad.'

Holly went to her father and kissed him on the cheek. 'I shouldn't be late.'

'I'll probably be in bed when you get back. If I can sleep, that is. It isn't every day war is declared. Gives you a lot to think about.'

As Holly was leaving the room Dan refilled his glass, deciding to take the bottle with him to his chair which he slumped into.

'War,' he repeated as the front door slammed shut. They'd all hoped, prayed that it wouldn't happen. But it had.

'Christ!'

'We heard it at work. Charlie De Gruchy popped out for fags and came charging back with the news, having been told at the newsagents. He says he'll join up.'

Sudden alarm seized Holly. Reaching across the café table she grasped Martin's hand. 'You wouldn't do that, would you?'

'The thought never entered my head,' he quickly assured her. 'I have no intention of getting myself shot.'

Holly exhaled in relief.

'If Charlie wants to be a hero, let him. He was always a daft sod anyway.'

'Which you're not?'

'I hope I'm not.'

She caressed his hand, then released it. 'People are speaking about nothing else, which is only to be expected, I suppose.'

Martin glanced round the crowded café, noting that all the customers were talking animatedly. He had no doubt the general subject of conversation was that of the war.

'Of course I'd have to go if the Islands brought in conscription as they've done on the mainland,' he went on. 'But that's highly unlikely.'

'Highly,' Holly agreed. She had a new thought. 'Will this affect our marriage plans?' The date for their wedding had been set for the following July, 1940.

'I don't see why. There's no reason for us to change anything, with the exception of the honeymoon that is. We may have to have it on Jersey, but that's hardly a hardship.'

'I don't care where we honeymoon. Or even if we don't have one at all. Just as long as we get married.'

'I can't wait for that either,' Martin stated, brown eyes twinkling.

Holly knew precisely what he meant by that, and laughed.

'Roll on,' Martin said. 'Roll on.'

Holly sipped her coffee, the love she felt for him welling up inside her. If they'd been alone she'd have kissed him. How integral a part of her life he'd become, she reflected. He meant everything to her.

'Charlie says he's for the navy,' Martin went on. 'Told us he's always fancied going to sea.'

'Can we forget about Charlie. Please?' Holly pleaded softly.

'I was only mentioning.'

'I don't want to hear any more about him.'

'OK, OK, keep your shirt on.'

Martin dropped his gaze to stare into his coffee cup, wondering what type of ship Charlie would be assigned to. There had been a time when he'd rather fancied going to sea himself, but that had been before he'd met Holly.

Now all he fancied was her.

Rotten.

'Look!' Terry exclaimed excitedly, pointing skywards. 'A flight of Spits.' He turned to Martin. 'They are Spits, aren't they?'

Martin shaded his eyes. 'They're Spits all right. Headed for France I would guess.'

'Would you like another cuppa?' Elspeth asked Holly, reaching for the Thermos. It was a Sunday in early October, and they'd motored to Quaisne Bay for a picnic. Despite the time of year the weather had so far proved remarkably kind.

'Please.'

'Aren't they beautiful,' Martin murmured as the planes came rapidly closer.

'Smashing. I wonder what it's like to fly one of them,' Terry mused.

'I wonder,' Martin echoed, imagining himself at the controls, thinking it must be a hundred times more exciting, and exhilarating, than driving a car.

'I'd love to have a dekko at a Merlin engine sometime,' he stated.

'Complicated piece of machinery I should imagine.'

'No doubt. But from what I understand they're quite something.'

Both young men stood staring in awe as the Spitfires roared overhead.

'Wow!' Terry further exclaimed.

'Give 'em hell!' Martin shouted to the now receding planes.

Terry sighed and flopped down beside Elspeth. They were also engaged, having become so shortly after Martin and Holly. Their wedding was scheduled for the following August.

'Any more sandwiches?' Terry inquired of Elspeth.

'Some ham ones left. That OK?'

'Hmmh.'

'I don't know where you put it,' Elspeth commented. 'You've already eaten enough to satisfy a horse.'

'Healthy appetite, that's all,' he retorted.

'How about you?' Holly queried of Martin as he rejoined her on the tartan travelling rug.

He shook his head. 'But I wouldn't mind another cup of tea if there's any left.'

'There is,' stated Elspeth, handing Holly the Thermos.

'Did you read the *Evening Post* last night?' Elspeth asked Terry.

'No, I missed it, I'm afraid.'

'There was a hair-raising article about what the Germans are doing to the Jews.'

'Oh?'

'Apparently they've got things called concentration camps.' She frowned, searching her memory. 'Dachau and Buchenwald I think they were called. Anyway, they've been sending Jews there where they're being horribly tortured.'

A silence settled over the group. 'Tortured?' Terry repeated at last.

'So it said. And it's young Germans, according to the article, doing the torturing. Seventeen- to twenty-year-olds. Same age group as us.'

'That's appalling,' Holly murmured.

'I felt quite sick when I'd finished the article,' Elspeth went on.

'I'm not surprised,' Martin commented.

'There are lots of Jews in Poland,' Terry informed them. 'Lots.'

The picnic had been a lighthearted affair up until then. But not any more. They were still in a sombre, reflective mood when they arrived back home.

Martin set a pint of Mary Ann lager in front of Terry and sat down.

'What's wrong with you?' Martin inquired. For something clearly was.

'I've made up my mind.'

'About what?'

'Elspeth's going to go berserk.'

'About what?' Martin persisted, tasting his own pint.

'I'm going to join up.'

Martin stared in astonishment. 'You're what?'

'Going to join up.'

'Holy shit!' he breathed.

'Women and children. They machine-gunned women and children. The sort of bastards who do that have to be stopped.'

'What are you talking about?'

'It was on the news. The SS *Lancashire* was torpedoed and sunk by a U-boat. It was transporting a considerable number, they didn't give the actual figures, of servicemen's wives and children. Some managed to get into liferafts, others just jumped into the water. The point is, the U-boat surfaced and machine-gunned everyone. Men, women and children.'

Martin was profoundly shocked.

'Children,' Terry repeated softly. 'How in Christ's name could you machine-gun them?'

Martin didn't know what to say. What could be said?

'That's what made me decide to join up. I'd been thinking about it anyway, but that made me decide.' He paused, then added, 'Don't think me soft but I cried when the newscaster finished speaking.'

'I don't think you soft,' Martin said, a catch in his voice.

'I'm going along to the recruiting station on Saturday morning and was wondering . . . Would you come with me for moral support?'

'Of course,' Martin replied instantly.

'Heaven help me, I'm not a brave man. Far from it. But there are times when I just feel you have to stand up and be counted.'

Martin nodded his agreement.

'I thought we might go and get pissed afterwards. I'm going to have to be that to tell Elspeth. I mean, what with the wedding planned and all. That'll have to be postponed now.'

'You won't tell her beforehand then?'

Terry shook his head. 'It's got to be a *fait accompli.* She'd do her damnedest to talk me out of it otherwise. And that is one strong woman, I can tell you.'

Martin knew that to be a fact. 'What time on Saturday?' he queried.

'Elevenish?'

'Fine.'

'You're a pal, Martin. Thank you.'

'Women and children,' Martin muttered, and shook his head. It was beyond belief.

'Martin, Terry, how are you!' Bob Dorey cried. Rushing over, he shook them both by the hand. Bob was an acquaintance of long standing.

'Are you here for the same reason as me?' he demanded. They were standing outside the recruiting station.

'Terry is, I'm just here to get pissed with him afterwards,' Martin replied.

'Good idea. I'll tag along if I may?'

'Sure,' Terry enthused. 'The more the merrier.'

Inside they met up with someone else they knew who declared he too would accompany them to the pub.

Pub*s*, it transpired.

Holly was aghast. 'You what!'

'Signed on the dotted line for King and country,' Martin slurred. He was seeing two of Holly and wondering which one was really her. God, he was drunk.

Her hand flashed to crack against his cheek, sending him staggering backwards. 'Here, hold on,' he protested.

Tears sprang into her eyes. 'How could you!'

'It was the women and children, I couldn't bear the thought of that. They machine-gunned them, Holly, the lousy bastards, they machine-gunned them in the water.' He explained about the SS *Lancashire*.

'I see,' she muttered. 'So this was all Terry's doing.'

Martin giggled. 'That's the funny part, the joke. They turned him down, said he was medically unfit. Bad eyesight, flat feet, you name it.'

He swayed, and had to lean against a wall for support. 'I'll be off in a week. They take you over in batches apparently.'

Holly dashed away her tears, reality not having really sunk in yet. 'And you had no intention of joining when you went there?'

'None at all. But then we met up with Bob Dorey who was taking the shilling, and inside . . .' Martin broke off and shrugged. 'It seemed the right thing to do, Holly. I got to thinking about the women and children and . . .' He trailed off this time.

'You're a fool, Martin Voisin,' she choked.

'Maybe. But I don't believe so. As Terry said, there are times when you have to stand up and be counted and this is one of them.'

'And what about our wedding?'

'That'll have to be postponed. I'm sorry.'

She wanted to take and shake him, to slap him again, harder than before. She wanted . . .

'You'd better get off home to bed. You're in a terrible state,' she said instead.

'Pissed as a rat,' he hiccuped. 'Ten rats.'

'Will you be all right? Do you want me to come with you?'

He shook his head. 'I'll grab a taxi. I came here in one.'

A week! she thought in despair after he'd gone. Such a short time really. Nothing at all. And the wedding postponed.

Still weeping, she made her way to her bedroom.

Dan stopped outside Holly's door and listened to the sound of her crying. It was several hours now since he'd come in to find her like this.

Best to let her get it out of her system, he thought for the umpteenth time. There was nothing he could do or say that would help.

Perhaps another cup of tea. Though the last one he'd made her had gone untouched.

'I received notification this morning, I'm leaving Monday,' Martin informed Holly.

She was on an early shift that day, but perhaps she could change with someone. Sister would understand.

'Will you come and see me off?'

She explained about the early shift. 'If I can.'

'My folks will be there to say goodbye.'

Holly nodded.

He took her into his arms, relishing the scent of her newly washed hair. 'I'm going to miss you like you wouldn't believe.'

'It'll be the same for me.'

'Who knows? The war might not last that long. And there will always be leave. I don't know how much I'll get but I'll be back every opportunity I have. I swear.'

She laid her cheek on the crook of his neck. 'What was it you said about Charlie De Gruchy? Let him be a hero, he was always a daft sod.'

'I suppose I deserved that.'

'You won't be a hero, will you?'

Martin laughed. 'No fear! You won't get me sticking my neck out unnecessarily. I'll do what has to be done and no more. You can rest assured of that.'

'And you'll write?'

'I promised you, didn't I?'

'I'll treasure and keep every letter.'

'Don't expect too much, Holly, I'm not exactly the best letter writer in the world. That sort of thing doesn't come easily to me.'

'As long as you write, that's all that matters.'

He lifted her face and kissed her, not passionately, his lips resting lightly on hers. But it was enough to arouse him, which she felt.

'God, I love you,' he whispered.

'And I love you.'

'I know.'

'I'll miss you so much, Holly.'

'Then you shouldn't have bloody well joined up!' she retorted sharply which made them both laugh.

He dropped a hand to stroke the swell of her buttocks. 'Christ, I want you.'

'You should have thought of that.'

'Now you're being cruel.'

'Serves you right.'

His other hand sought, and found, a breast which he gently kneaded.

'Damn Hitler and his Nazis to hell,' Holly murmured.

Martin couldn't have agreed more. 'Do you have a picture I can take with me? I haven't got one.'

'We'll have one done together, how about that?'

'Perfect.'

'In fact we'll have two. One for you. One for me.'

She shivered inwardly at the hardness pressing against her thigh. The great mystery she'd so often wondered about. The act of truly becoming a woman.

She sang softly, 'Lavender blue, dilly dilly, lavender green. When you are king, dilly dilly, I'll be your queen.'

'You'll always be my queen, Holly. No matter what happens.'

'And you my king.'

She mustn't keep crying, she chided herself. She mustn't. And this time, miraculously, the tears stayed away.

'Can I have the key to your parents' caravan without them knowing?' Holly asked Elspeth.

'The caravan! Whatever for?'

'Strictly between you and me?'

'Strictly.' Elspeth made the sign of the cross over her heart. 'Word of honour.'

'I want to take Martin there to give him his going-away present.'

Elspeth's eyes opened wide as the penny dropped. 'Holly Morgan!'

Holly reddened. 'I was wondering what to give him and then it struck me what he'd appreciate most.'

'But you've always insisted you never would until you were married.'

'I know. And don't think I haven't wrestled with my conscience, I have. But the circumstances are exceptional, Elspeth, he's going off to war, for goodness' sake. I want to give him something to really remember while he's away.'

'I understand.'

'Do you think I'm doing the wrong thing?'

'Not at all. I'd probably have done the same with Terry if he'd been accepted. Just take some Durex with you, you don't want to fall pregnant. You can get them from the hospital.'

Holly giggled. 'I've already got some. A packet of three.'

Elspeth giggled also.

'The evening before he leaves, I thought.'

Elspeth grasped her friend's wrist and squeezed. You'll have the key by then, I promise.

'I wish you'd tell me what this surprise is, I'm dying of curiosity,' Martin said, changing gear going into a bend.

'If I told you, it wouldn't be a surprise.'

His eyes flicked sideways at her. 'Torturer.'

Twice during the day Holly had almost changed her mind, her conscience nearly getting the better of her. But they loved one another, she'd reminded herself. And, as she'd said to Elspeth, the circumstances were exceptional.

A few minutes later she instructed him to turn up a lane, and shortly after that they were parked in front of a smart caravan.

'Here?' Martin frowned.

'Here,' she confirmed. 'Come on.'

Holly opened the caravan door, took a small torch from her coat pocket and flicked it on. The oil lamp, which she now lit, was where Elspeth had said it would be.

'Well, what's the surprise?' Martin queried, gazing round in bewilderment.

'Haven't you guessed?'

He shook his head.

'Here's a clue,' she declared, fishing in her other coat pocket.

His expression was such when she handed him the packet of Durex that Holly burst out laughing.

'How do you feel?' Martin asked later as they lay snuggled up in the caravan's main bed.

She considered that. 'I honestly don't know.'

'But you did enjoy it?' he queried anxiously.

'Oh yes, of course. It was just . . . different from what I'd expected, I suppose.'

'You don't regret it, do you?'

She reached across and gently stroked his face, thinking this time next day he'd be gone into who knew what dangers. A shiver of anxiety for him ran through her. 'No,' she whispered.

'Sure?'

'Absolutely.'

'I feel guilty in a way. You'd always insisted . . .'

She silenced him by laying a finger across his lips. 'It was my decision, darling.'

He noticed then for the first time that she was wearing a gold band on her left hand. 'Where did that come from?' he asked, touching it.

Holly smiled. 'It was my mother's. I wanted to feel . . . married to you when we did it.'

He didn't know what to say to that.

'I wanted to pretend we were already married. Which we will be when it's possible.'

He kissed the ring and the finger it was on. 'I take you as my lawfully wedded wife. How's that?'

'And I take you as my lawfully wedded husband. For ever and ever.'

'Amen,' he concluded.

'As good as the real thing, eh?'

He stared at her, his heart thumping with emotion. 'There were three in that packet,' he murmured huskily.

'And we don't want to waste any, do we?'

Nor did they.

*

It was a wet, blustery day with a wind blowing in off the Channel that was sharp as a butcher's knife. Holly had driven down to the quayside with Martin and his parents, the four of them now standing together, Martin with a suitcase by his side.

Martin glanced at his watch. 'You'd better not hang around in this weather, Mum. You know how chesty you can get.'

'It's time then,' Mrs Voisin said hollowly, a strained smile on her face.

'It's time,' Martin agreed.

Mrs Voisin's lower lip trembled as she embraced Martin. 'You take care now. Look after yourself.'

'I will, Mum.'

Her eyes were suddenly brimming as she pecked him on the cheek.

'Goodbye, son. Good luck. See you when you get a spot of leave,' Mr Voisin said, sticking out his hand which Martin shook. Then Mr Voisin embraced Martin.

'We'll wait for you in the car,' Mr Voisin declared to Holly.

'I'll walk back if you don't mind. I'd prefer that.'

'Suit yourself.'

'Goodbye, Martin,' Mrs Voisin whispered tearfully.

This was awful, Martin thought. Worse than he'd expected. He wished they'd just go.

'Right then,' sighed Mr Voisin, taking his wife's arm. Together they walked forlornly away.

Martin smiled at Holly whose loose hair was blowing in the wind. He'd never loved her more than he did at that moment.

'I'd better join the others,' he said.

'OK.'

'I'll write first chance I get.'

'I'll be watching the post.'

'Try not to worry, Holly. I know that might be difficult, but try all the same.'

She nodded.

'I've got my photograph,' he stated, patting his right breast.

'I'm going to buy a nice frame for mine and put it beside my bed.'

He swallowed hard. 'Thank you for . . . last night. It was wonderful.'

Suddenly she couldn't stand it any more. Grabbing him she kissed him fully and deeply, then broke away.

Abruptly, turning on her heel, she hurried along the quay, tears streaming down her face.

She never looked back.

Chapter 3

Sister A'Court waited patiently till the last nurse was seated, Holly and Elspeth among the gathering, then began to speak.

'As you're all aware, I'm sure, the evacuation takes place in three days' time. It has been decided by higher authorities that many of our patients should be moved to the mainland, which means I'm going to need volunteers to accompany them.'

Holly glanced at Elspeth who imperceptibly shook her head. Holly felt the same way, she wished to remain on Jersey with her father who'd already said he had no intention of being evacuated. He would stay with his school and pupils.

'Those nurses who go may or may not return, that depending entirely on events. It might be we could be invaded before they could do so.'

Sister paused and took a deep breath. A great deal had to be done in the next few days, a lot of organising, and she wanted to get on with her part of it.

'So, volunteers?'

A number of hands went up and she noted on a pad who they belonged to.

'That should be sufficient I think,' she declared when the last name had been jotted down. 'We'll need others to assist in getting the patients aboard. They'll be taken down to the quay in a fleet of ambulances, and once embarked will have to be settled down for the journey.'

Her finger flicked, indicating various nurses including Holly and Elspeth. 'You lot will do the assisting, returning to the hospital to carry on with your normal duties afterwards.'

'Any questions?'

There weren't.

'Right, that's all.' And having said that, Sister swept from the room.

'Do you think we will be invaded?' Elspeth asked Holly as they rose from their seats.

'It's quite possible now the Islands have been demilitarised. There again, because we have been they might decide to ignore us. It's anyone's guess.'

A short while previously the decision had been taken in Britain to remove all forces personnel from the Islands, leaving them entirely unprotected. If the Germans did decide to invade they wouldn't meet any opposition. A fact the Germans were as yet unaware of.

Elspeth shook her head. 'I just can't imagine German soldiers here. Can you?'

'Not really. The very idea seems so unreal somehow.'

'Anyway, I'm off. See you at lunch.'

'See you then.'

'Are you sure you don't want to go? I'll be perfectly all right on my own,' Dan said.

'I'm staying with you, Dad, and that's that.'

'It might well be the last opportunity for anyone to get off the Islands. The Germans are getting closer by the day. I'm told you can now hear the guns over in France when the wind's in a certain direction.'

'Who would have thought the French would have been so easily overrun,' Holly mused.

'It's only a matter of time for them now. Poor buggers,' Dan commiserated. 'And the Germans won't stop at France, you can bet on that. It'll be Britain's turn next. At least Churchill's now Prime Minister. If anyone can stop them he can.'

'And what if he can't?' Holly queried quietly.

'That doesn't even bear thinking about,' Dan said equally quietly. A subdued Holly set about making their evening meal.

She couldn't sleep. She tossed and turned, her mind in a turmoil. If only she'd heard from Martin but it had been months now since his last letter which had been all too brief, merely stating he was fine and in good health and spirits. Because of censorship there had been no clue as to his whereabouts or what he was up to.

She rose up on to an elbow and switched on her bedside lamp to gaze at the photograph they'd had taken just before he'd gone off, a photograph now resplendent in a silver frame.

What would he be like when he returned? Bound to be different, she thought. That was only logical.

'Oh, Martin,' she whispered. 'I miss you so.'

He'd told her not to worry, but she did. Terribly. How could she not after hearing about the awful happenings at Dunkirk. A miracle they called it, but miracle or no a great many men had been left on the beaches. Men who would never see their homes, families or sweethearts ever again.

Perhaps some warm milk would settle me, she thought, then decided against that, not wanting to wake her father who was a light sleeper. If he heard her moving about he'd get up to find out what the trouble was, and she didn't want that.

She snapped out the light and settled back, thinking of Martin, remembering the good times they'd had together. Smiling in memory of that last evening in the caravan.

Eventually, to the accompaniment of the dawn chorus, she fell into a fitful sleep.

The scene that greeted them at the quayside was one of sheer bedlam. People of all ages were milling and jostling everywhere, the harbour filled with ships for the evacuation. Many of these ships bore the marks of their recent errand of mercy to Dunkirk.

'This is going to take ages,' Holly commented to Elspeth, the pair of them having contrived to be in the same ambulance.

The lead ambulance began to sound its horn as the driver attempted to force his way through. Slowly the convoy inched forward.

'Water, nurse, water,' Mr Jones pleaded from his bunk. He was a man in his late eighties.

Elspeth set about giving him some while Holly continued staring out of the window.

She spotted a number of people she knew. There were Mr and Mrs Le Quere who lived in the same street as herself and Dan, and there Mary Poole who'd been at school with her and Elspeth.

A fat woman lost her balance and pitched over, shrieking when someone trod on her. She looked thoroughly shaken when helped again to her feet.

At the entrance to the quayside and along the harbour wall many cars had simply been abandoned by their owners, even a brand new Bentley that had particularly caught Holly's eye.

A warship hooted as it left the quay, slowly steaming out into the harbour and Channel beyond. Two smaller vessels that had been patiently waiting took its place.

The ambulance rocked slightly from the press of bodies bearing against its sides causing Holly momentary alarm. 'I hope to God this mob don't have us over,' she said anxiously, glancing at Mr Pinel, another frail old man who was desperately ill indeed and whom Holly personally thought shouldn't be travelling.

'Talk about pandemonium,' Elspeth commented, rejoining Holly.

The driver of the lead ambulance was on the lookout for the SS *Argyle*, which was expecting them. The ship had been commandeered by the Royal Navy and had a doctor on board.

'There she is,' he muttered to his driving companion, nodding at a large ship ahead. Ratings swarmed down the gangplank as they drew alongside.

'Not long now and we'll have you nicely settled on board,' Holly said to Mr Palin, giving him a warm smile. There were six patients altogether in their particular ambulance, all men.

The first ambulance began unloading its human cargo, moving

off when that was completed, the second ambulance in the convoy now occupying the spot where the first had been.

'Can I have a cigarette, nurse?' Mr Jegou asked.

'I shouldn't allow it really,' Elspeth replied, going to his side.

'Oh please? I'm gasping.'

'OK then. Where are they?'

'In my right-hand jacket pocket.'

Mr Jegou couldn't get them himself because he had two broken arms, the result of an industrial accident. Elspeth found the cigarettes and helped him light up.

'Magic,' he smiled as he exhaled.

Time passed and then it was their turn at the gangplank. Their driver stopped, hopped out and opened the rear doors. Several burly ratings swarmed in.

'Let's be having you, gents,' one of them declared in a thick Brummie accident.

Holly brought up the rear with Mr Palin, having decided to leave him till last. At the top of the gangplank they were met by more ratings eager to assist. All of them couldn't have been more friendly or helpful.

'Holly! Holly Morgan!'

Holly was about to enter a hatchway when she halted at the sound of her name being called. She frowned as a rating hurried towards her, the frown turning to a smile when she recognised him to be Charlie De Gruchy.

'Hello, Charlie. How are you?'

'Not bad, Holly. And yourself?'

'A bit harassed at the moment as you can see. But fine otherwise. This is your ship, I take it?'

He nodded. 'We were at Dunkirk.'

'That must have been awful,' she sympathised.

He eyed her speculatively. 'Have you heard of Martin?'

She missed his use of the word of, and not from. 'Not for some while.'

Charlie's expression became grim. 'I see,' he muttered.

'Why?'

He glanced about, took her by the arm and moved her to a quiet spot a little further along the deck. 'I spoke to Bob Dorey at Dunkirk. He was one of those we ferried back to England.'

Charlie paused, then said, 'I'm sorry to have to tell you, Holly, but Martin was killed at Dunkirk. Bob was there when it happened.'

She suddenly had a tight pain in her chest and was having trouble breathing. 'Killed?' she echoed.

'I'm sorry, Holly. Truly I am. They can't have notified his parents yet.'

She shook her head. 'That can't be right. It can't be. There's been a mistake.'

'No mistake, Holly. Bob was there.'

'No!' That came out as an anguished, strangulated croak.

Charlie's face was filled with pity as he stared at her. Damn his luck at having run into Holly. But having done so he couldn't not have told her.

'We'd better get you below, girl, get you sat down.'

'How?' She wanted the grisly details. Had to know them.

'Strafed by a plane. According to Bob it got four of them in that single pass.'

'Was he . . . did he . . .?'

'Killed instantly, Holly. Outright. There wasn't any pain or suffering.'

That was something, she told herself.

At which point she collapsed in a dead faint.

It was Elspeth who got her home. Settling her in front of the fire, which Elspeth lit as it was already made up, and putting on the kettle. Holly, white as a sheet, sat staring straight ahead, numb with shock and grief. Elspeth had sent a message via one of the other nurses to inform Sister what had happened.

Over and over Elspeth kept thinking it could easily have been her Terry. If he'd passed his medical he too could be lying dead at Dunkirk.

'Drink your tea,' Elspeth urged, the cup lying untouched at Holly's feet.

Holly didn't reply.

'How about some spirits, then? Are there any in the house?'

Again Holly didn't answer.

Elspeth bit her lip. She could have used some spirits herself but didn't like to go searching unless Holly joined her.

'At least we had that evening in the caravan,' Holly said suddenly. 'At least we had that.'

'Yes.'

'I'll never forget it.'

'No.'

Holly bent forward and put her head in her hands. Her entire body started to shake.

Elspeth went to Holly and put a comforting arm round her. The pair were still like that when the outside door clicked shut, announcing Dan's arrival home from work.

'Holly! I'm back.'

'In here, Mr Morgan,' Elspeth called out.

Dan breezed into the room, then came to a halt in consternation at the sight which greeted him. 'What's up?'

'Martin's been killed,' Elspeth informed him.

Dan sucked in a deep breath. 'Oh no,' he sighed.

Elspeth explained about Holly bumping into Charlie De Gruchy aboard the *Argyle* and how he'd spoken to Bob Dorey who'd been there when it happened.

Going to Holly he took one of her hands in his. 'I really am terribly sorry, darling.'

She looked up at her father, eyes red and staring. He stared back, heart bursting for her.

'Charlie also said apparently that the Voisins couldn't have been notified yet. They would surely have told Holly if they had,' Elspeth went on.

'Then they're the ones who'll have to be told. I'll go myself.'

'No,' Holly whispered. 'I'll go.'

'You're in no fit state,' Dan protested.

'I'll be all right. Honest. I just need a little bit longer to pull myself together. I'll cycle over.'

Dan knew his daughter well enough not to argue further. Her mind made up on the matter, there would be no changing it.

'I could use a scotch,' Dan declared, releasing Holly's hand. 'What about you, Holly?'

She shook her head.

'It might calm you down,' he advised, for she was still shaking. Again she shook her head. 'I'd throw up if I tried.'

'Well, how about you, Elspeth?'

'Please, Mr Morgan. I'm pretty upset myself. Martin had become a good friend.'

'Of course.'

Dan poured liberal-sized whiskies and added soda to them both. 'To Martin,' he whispered before drinking.

Holly put a thumb into her mouth and bit it.

'Why, Holly, how lovely to see you,' Mrs Voisin exclaimed.

'Can I come in?'

As she stepped into the Voisins' bungalow Holly knew that, when she left, their lives would have been irrevocably shattered.

'I still can't believe it,' Terry said to Elspeth, the pair of them strolling hand in hand along the beach.

'I know.'

'Poor Holly.'

'It took guts for her to go and tell the Voisins. You have to admire her for that.'

'When is she going back to the hospital?'

'Sister's given her a week off.'

They walked a little way in silence. 'I feel so guilty,' Terry said eventually. 'If it hadn't been for me, Martin would never have joined up and he'd be alive today. If only I'd never asked him to go with me to the recruiting station.'

Elspeth squeezed his hand. 'You mustn't torture yourself. What's done is done and can't be changed.'

'That doesn't make it any easier,' Terry sighed. 'Martin was always so alive and full of fun. You couldn't have asked for a better or more loyal mate. And now he's gone. What a sodding waste.'

'Just thank your lucky stars they turned you down otherwise you too might have bought it at Dunkirk.' Elspeth shuddered. 'It doesn't bear thinking about.'

Terry suddenly stopped, bringing Elspeth up short. 'Planes,' he stated, pointing skywards.

'Ours?'

'Can't make out yet.'

The planes droned nearer.

'Six of them. And they're theirs. Heinkels.'

They stood watching as the Heinkels headed for St Helier, Elspeth giving a sharp intake of breath as bombs began to drop.

Even at that distance they heard the explosions followed by swiftly rising palls of dense black smoke.

'They're bombing the city,' Terry said unnecessarily. War had finally come to the Islands.

Later they discovered the planes had bombed lorries on the quay-side that were filled with potatoes, mistakenly thinking them troop carriers.

Having dropped all their bombs the German pilots had then opened up with their machine guns, killing a number of people.

Three days later, on 1 July 1940, the Germans arrived in force.

The long Occupation had begun.

'The bastards are everywhere, strutting through the city, arrogant beyond belief as only Germans can be,' Dan fumed to Holly.

'I know. I've seen them.'

'There's been a run on the shops ever since they got here. They're buying everything in sight. Particularly luxury goods.'

'At least they're paying for them instead of looting.'

'There is that,' Dan grudgingly admitted.

'And they haven't hurt anyone. At least not that I've heard.'

'Not yet. We'll see in time.'

'They're flying a bloody great swastika over the town hall,' Holly said.

Dan nodded.

'Will the British try to recapture the Islands, do you think?' she asked.

'If they're considering recapturing them, why demilitarise in the first place?' Dan shook his head. 'No, I doubt that very much. Or, if they do try and recapture it won't be for quite some time. Not after Dunkirk. They've got the mainland to worry about, that'll be their prime concern.'

'I was wondering,' Holly mused. 'Do you think we should stock up on food? You never know.'

Dan briefly considered the suggestion. 'A good idea.'

'I'm on a late tomorrow so I'll do it in the morning.'

Dan removed all the notes he had in his wallet and gave them to her. 'There. Buy as much as you can.'

Later in bed Holly did as had become her nightly custom since learning of Martin's death. She kissed the photograph kept by her bedside, then held it to her breasts.

A single tear slid down her cheek.

Holly stopped to stare at the swanky American Oldsmobile, black with a hood in dark cream, that roared past. Inside were several high-ranking Germans and a girl roughly her own age, all of them laughing.

It hadn't taken her long to fraternise with the enemy, Holly thought bitterly, wondering who the bitch was. She thought the girl beneath contempt.

Dismissing the incident from her mind she hurried along the pavement in the direction of her favourite grocery shop which had the added advantage of doing free deliveries. Ahead of her was an elderly lady whom she recognised as Mrs Vasse, a neighbour. Mrs Vasse, a habitual sufferer from arthritis, was hobbling.

Coming towards them, four abreast, were a group of Luftwaffe officers, walking with their usual swagger and air of insufferable arrogance.

Mrs Vasse could see they weren't going to make way for her and was damned if she was going to step aside. 'Ignorant pigs,' she muttered.

The next moment she'd been roughly elbowed off the pavement to fall heavily into the gutter.

'Dear God!' Holly exclaimed in horror, breaking into a run.

The Germans had stopped to stare, from their expressions clearly thinking this highly amusing.

'Are you all right?' Holly queried, squatting by the fallen woman.

Mrs Vasse was not only all right, she was livid. 'Help me up,' she instructed, voice tight with anger.

Once more on her feet Mrs Vasse rounded on the German officers and glared at them, their expressions becoming even more amused. One spoke to another, and slapped his thigh.

That was too much for the spunky Mrs Vasse. Her clenched fist lashed out, much to the Germans' astonishment, to land squarely, and very professionally, on the jaw of the officer who'd elbowed her.

With a cry he pitched backwards, landing with such force he split the back of his skull. Blood spurted, quickly soaking into his collar and back of his smart uniform.

'Serves you right, you supercilious lout,' a delighted Mrs Vasse told him, brandishing the same fist in front of his face.

Holly watched appalled as two of the other officers grabbed the elderly lady while the third spoke rapidly in German to his comrade on the ground.

'Leave me alone, you buggers. Leave me alone!' Mrs Vasse yelled, struggling to try and free herself.

'Let her go. She's an old woman,' Holly pleaded with them. The reply to that was something spat at her in German.

There was a clatter of boots and two members of the Feldpolizei, ordinary military police, came rushing up. A rapid exchange took place between them and the officers. The one who'd been injured, now standing again and clutching the damaged area of his head, was snarling and repeatedly jabbing a finger at Mrs Vasse.

'It was all their fault. Really it was,' Holly declared to the Feldpolizei who, not understanding English, dismissed her protestations with a wave of the hand.

Holly stared in dismay as, after another rapid exchange in German, Mrs Vasse was hauled away.

So this was how it was to be, Holly thought. Well, none of them had expected any better of the Germans.

Nor did she make any move to help the injured officer who was, by the sound of it, complaining volubly to his companions.

Holly was quite shaken as she continued on to the grocery shop where she recounted the whole episode to those there.

'Seven days in prison for a woman that age. It's a disgrace!' Holly fumed to her father, referring to Mrs Vasse.

'I quite agree. But there are those who might say the sentence was lenient in the circumstances. She did strike a German officer after all.'

'Only after he'd knocked her over.'

'That's hardly the point. You must remember whom we're dealing with. Nazis, the self-styled master race. Or so they'd like to think.'

Holly's face suddenly broke into a smile. 'The way she hit him, if I hadn't seen it I wouldn't have thought it possible. Smack on the chin and him flat on his back as though he'd been hit by Joe Louis himself!'

Dan started to laugh. 'It is funny when you think about it. Good old gel.'

Holly joined in the laughter. It *was* funny when you thought about it. Good old gel indeed.

When Mrs Vasse returned to the street she was given a heroine's welcome, she declaring to an admiring audience that prison had been no bed of roses but that punch had been worth every minute of it.

Chapter 4

'**D**o you take this man . . .'

Holly, chief bridesmaid at Elspeth and Terry's wedding, dropped her gaze to stare at the church floor, her happiness for the couple clouded by the thought that she and Martin should have been married themselves the previous month. Originally she'd been asked to be matron of honour, but that changed to bridesmaid after Martin's death.

In her mind she was visualising what her own wedding would have been like in this very church. She in white, as Elspeth was, Martin in morning suit, as Terry was.

Stop it, she chided. Why torture herself over what might have been. Martin was dead and gone, they'd never be wedded now.

'The groom may kiss the bride.'

Holly looked up again and somehow forced a smile on to her face. But it wasn't Elspeth and Terry she saw kissing, but Martin and her.

She in white, he in . . .

'It's not much of a reception but the best we could manage in the circumstances,' Elspeth's mother Linda said to Holly.

'I think you've done very well, considering.'

Linda sighed. 'Isn't she a pretty bride?'

'Beautiful,' Holly agreed.

'And Terry, ever such a nice lad. They get on so well together.' Linda beamed. 'A real love match.'

'I'd better circulate,' Holly said, wanting to get away from this line of conversation.

'Oh yes, do.'

Holly moved off.

'Hello. We haven't met. I'm Tony.'

He was tall, dark and had the unmistakable look of a farmer. She judged him to be in his early twenties.

'I'm Holly.'

'I know. I asked.'

She raised an eyebrow. 'I noticed you in church and thought I'd like to meet you. And so here I am.'

'Here you are,' she agreed.

'I'm a cousin of Terry's. We live on the other side of the island just outside St Mary's village. Do you know it?'

'I've been there.'

'The family have lived in the area for generations. Potato farmers on the whole.'

'How interesting,' Holly commented, ever so slightly sarcastically, a fact that went unnoticed by him.

'And what do you do?'

'I'm a nurse.'

'Really!'

'Same as Elspeth. We're both at the General Hospital.'

'She's never mentioned it, but then I don't know her all that well.'

'Elspeth's my best friend. We were at school together.'

Tony had a sip of beer, noticing that Holly's glass was almost empty. 'Can I get you a refill?'

She shook her head. 'It's terrific they managed to lay on some whisky. It's hard to come by nowadays since the Jerries banned the sale of spirits.'

Holly thought of her father who'd been complaining about exactly that only the other day. He wasn't a heavy drinker but did enjoy a dram of scotch.

'It was nice talking to you,' Holly smiled, intending to move on.

He swiftly reached out and grasped her arm. 'Don't go. We're just getting to know one another.'

Holly groaned inwardly, realising what was coming. 'I have to see to Elspeth. Help her get changed.'

'I was wondering . . . how about us meeting up sometime? I quite often get into St Helier on a Saturday.'

'No thanks, Tony. It's kind of you to ask, but I'm afraid not.'

His face fell. 'Oh come on, give me a chance. Don't turn me down out of hand.'

She could see he was the persistent type. Well, that was just too bad.

'Is there someone else?'

'No,' she whispered.

'So what's the problem?'

He obviously knew nothing about Martin. 'I'm simply not on the market at the moment, Tony. It's nothing personal.'

His disappointment was obvious. 'Too bad.'

She smiled and walked away, leaving him staring after her.

'Did Tony ask you out?' Elspeth queried, now in her going-away outfit, a smartly tailored grey suit and dazzling white blouse, the latter made in France. Her shoes were grey to match the suit. The entire ensemble had been bought before the Occupation.

'You knew about that?'

'Terry said he'd been asking about you and I put two and two together.'

'Well, he did as a matter of fact. I turned him down, of course.'

'He's quite a catch apparently. His family are wealthy.'

Holly shook her head. 'I'm not interested. Not in him or anyone else.'

'I understand,' Elspeth commiserated quietly.

'And don't think I will be ever again.'

'Don't say that, Holly. Surely in time?'

'I doubt it. Martin was . . . special. *It* for me.'

Elspeth sighed. 'You're too young to be saying things like that, Hol. You've your whole life ahead of you. There'll be someone else eventually. Time heals everything, you know. At least, so my mother always says.'

Holly didn't believe that for one moment. The ache inside her would never go away, or the profound sense of loss.

Terry popped his head round the door. 'You ready yet? I'm champing at the bit.'

'She's ready,' Holly informed him, glad their conversation had been interrupted. The last thing she wanted was to put a dampner on Elspeth's big day.

'Have a good time,' Holly said to her friend, who kissed her on the cheek.

When she'd waved Terry and Elspeth on their way, Holly returned for her coat intending to go home. The reception would continue for some while, but she'd had enough.

Besides, she didn't want to bump into Tony again, having the distinct impression that if she did he'd have another go at asking her out.

Going out with someone other than Martin was simply inconceivable.

It was the height of the Battle of Britain, as it had become known, and Churchill was speaking on the wireless, broadcasting to the nation. Holly and a group of nurses were eagerly listening.

'Never, in the field of human conflict, was so much owed by so many to so few . . .'

Viv Radmore, a highly emotional girl, overcome by the moving oratory sobbed loudly.

'Sshhh!' several of the others hushed.

Churchill went on to disclose that Britain was to give the United States 99-year leases of naval and air bases in Newfoundland and the West Indies. This transaction, he further said, meant that these two great English-speaking democracies would be entwined to mutual advantage for a hundred years.

He continued. 'No one can stop it. Like the Mississippi it keeps rolling along. Let it roll on in full flood, inexorable, irresistable, to broader lands and better days.

'Britain now bristles with two million soldiers, rifles and bayonets in their hands, ready to resist invasion . . .'

All eyes in the room were shining when Churchill finally finished.

'Maybe that'll knock some of the arrogance out of those Jerry swines,' Helen Mason commented, a choke in her voice.

The rest, as one, nodded their agreement.

'What the. . . .!' Dan exclaimed when there was a thunderous knocking at the front door. This did not bode well, so late in the evening.

'It's past curfew, Dad, so it has to be Germans,' Holly said anxiously.

His thoughts precisely. 'You stay here.'

Three Germans confronted him when he opened the door. An Unteroffizier and two privates.

'We are searching for hoarding,' the Unteroffizier barked in heavily accented English.

'You'll find no hoarding here,' Dan retorted.

'*Ach so*,' the Unteroffizier said, and swept past Dan, pushing him aside. The two rifle-carrying privates stamped along in his wake.

'Hey, hold on a minute!' Dan protested, to no avail.

The Germans found the kitchen and began ransacking through its cupboards. Luckily they discovered nothing untoward.

'Hmmh!' the Unteroffizier snorted, eyes darting everywhere, ensuring there were no nooks, crannies or hidey-holes they'd missed.

'Thursday, *jah!*' he said to Dan, watching them.

Dan nodded.

'Is any meat in house?' Thursdays and Fridays had been ordered meatless days. On those days the consumption of meat became a penal offence, the exceptions being horse flesh, birds and rabbits. There was already a thriving black market in existence throughout the island, rabbits, for example, changing hands for from twenty-five to thirty-five shillings apiece. Rationing had been in place since shortly after the Germans' arrival.

'None,' Dan assured him.

'Search the rest of the house,' the Unteroffizier ordered in German.

Dan clenched and unclenched his hands as the privates brushed by, quickly following when they went into the room where Holly was.

They located the little scotch Dan had left from the last bottle he'd been able to buy. Scotch he'd been saving.

'Aha!' the Unteroffizier exclaimed, putting his hands on his hips.

'For a rainy day,' Dan explained.

The Unteroffizier frowned. 'What is rainy day?'

'Special occasion. An emergency.' Dan wished he spoke German. 'Offer.'

'I beg your pardon?'

'I think he wants you to give him some, Dad.'

'Oh!' If that was the case he'd have to comply, Dan thought bitterly. The alternative was probably being dragged off on a trumped-up charge.

'Certainly,' Dan smiled. And poured half of the bottle's contents into a glass.

The Unteroffizier accepted the glass, sniffed the whisky, then saw the lot off in one swallow.

'Good,' he pronounced.

Dan was about to put the top back on the bottle when a hand restrained him.

The Unteroffizier smiled, an unpleasant sight Dan thought. '*Ja?*'

Dan got the message. '*Ja,*' he nodded, and poured the rest into the German's glass.

While this charade was going on the two privates searched the room, nor were they careful about it. When they'd finished, everything had been turned out, in many instances tossed carelessly aside.

Satisfied, the Unteroffizier flicked a finger and the privates disappeared upstairs to the bedrooms where they clumped noisily about.

'You like schnapps?' the Unteroffizier inquired casually of Dan.

'Oh yes.' That was a lie. He considered schnapps to be appalling stuff. Firewater.

The Unteroffizier tapped his glass. 'Better. Scotch whisky better.' He then chuckled, finding that funny.

Bloody thug, Dan thought. And smiled.

Silence descended, the Unteroffizier sipping his whisky, as they waited for those upstairs to complete their task. Finally the two privates reappeared to inform their superior that all was as it should be.

The Unteroffizier finished his drink and banged the glass on to the sideboard.

'So,' he said.

'I'll see you to the door, old chap,' Dan declared.

The Unteroffizier nodded to Holly, then strolled from the room, the two privates coming stiffly to attention as he passed them.

Holly sagged with relief when they'd gone. Lucky for her and Dan they hadn't been hoarding. She knew of others who were.

Holly and a few colleagues were having their tea break, except there wasn't any tea, when Viv Radmore came careering in. Viv came up short, panting.

'Have you heard?'

'Heard what?' Holly queried.

'It's Sister. Sister A'Court. She's downstairs under sedation.'

'Sedation? Why?' Heather Aubin demanded with a frown.

Viv delivered her bombshell. 'She was on her way to work when she was . . . raped in broad daylight!'

The others were stunned. 'Raped?' Meggy Hill croaked.

'A couple of Jerry soldiers grabbed hold of her and dragged her up an alleyway. Apparently they pulled her scarf over her head, forced her face first against a wall and . . .' Viv broke off and swallowed hard.

'Holy shit,' Sally Pallot breathed, eyes wide.

'Is she all right?' Holly asked.

'She came rushing into the hospital in hysterics, babbling about what had happened to anyone who'd listen. She must have been in terrible shock to babble like that, knowing Sister. Anyway it was so bad they had to sedate her. The police have been sent for.'

'Poor woman,' Meggy said.

'Did they catch whoever did it?' Sally queried.

'I don't think so. At least not yet. They ran off when they'd finished, leaving Sister . . . well you can imagine what she was like.'

Holly could certainly imagine.

For the rest of that day it was the talk of the hospital.

'Can I have a word please, Nurse Morgan,' requested Sister Moignard, Sister A'Court's replacement. That unfortunate woman had been given indefinite compassionate leave.

Holly followed Sister into her room.

'You're being reassigned,' Sister announced. 'As from Monday next you'll be taking up duties on ward fourteen.'

'Fourteen!' Holly exclaimed. 'But that's a German ward.'

Sister looked sympathetic. 'I appreciate that, nurse, but they need tending to same as anyone else. I'm sorry, I can understand if it offends you being reassigned there, but there we are.'

'Couldn't someone else . . .'

'No arguing, nurse,' Sister interjected. 'You've been reassigned and that's all there is to it.'

Holly knew further protestations were useless. 'Yes, Sister.'

'The other news is you're going on nights for a month. That should make your task a great deal easier.'

'Yes, Sister. Thank you.'

'You may go.'

A dejected and despondent Holly went.

'Nurse.'

Holly started, not having heard the doctor's approach. 'Yes, Herr Doctor?' she queried.

The man standing beside her was tall with blond hair and piercing blue eyes. Typical Hun, she thought.

'I wish to examine the patient Gleisner. Will you please accompany me.'

'Of course, Herr Doctor.'

Though it was Holly's second week on nights this was the first time she'd seen this particular doctor. She led the way down the ward till they came to Gleisner's bed.

Gleisner, shot full of morphine, was out cold, a faint sheen of sweat glistening on his forehead. According to his notes Gleisner was nineteen years old.

'Could you pull back the bedclothes, please.'

'Certainly.'

The doctor frowned slightly as, having switched on a small light above the bed, he read Gleisner's notes.

Gleisner was a Luftwaffe pilot who'd crashlanded at the airport, his aircraft having been severely damaged in a dogfight. Both his legs had been mangled as a result of the crash.

'Can you unloosen the bandages, please,' the doctor instructed.

'Left or right leg, doctor?'

'Left *and* right.'

Holly did as she was bid.

The doctor partially unravelled one set of bandages, and sniffed them. Then he did the same with the other set.

'You can re-do them now, nurse,' he declared.

While Holly was busy with the bandages the doctor scribbled on the notes. When Holly was finished he snapped off the overhead light.

'It's as we feared,' he said to Holly, en route back to the night nurse's station. 'Gangrene. The legs will have to be amputated.' The doctor sighed. 'And him such a young man too. A tragedy.'

Holly never knew why she said what she did then. 'You lot should have thought of that before starting the war,' she snapped.

The doctor halted and looked at her in astonishment.

'I'm sorry,' she stammered, thinking how foolish she'd been. If the doctor reported her she could be severely punished. The Germans didn't brook criticism, however justified.

'You have a point, nurse,' the doctor said amiably.

'Will you report me?'

He smiled. 'For what? I heard nothing.'

'Thank you,' she breathed.

'Think nothing of it.'

When they reached the nurse's station he informed her he'd be calling back later, though he didn't say what for. And with that he went, leaving the ward as silently as he'd arrived.

Not a bad egg, for a Jerry, she thought, telling herself she must watch her tongue in future. Why bring unnecessary trouble down on her head.

This time she heard the ward door creak open. 'I thought you might like a cup of coffee,' he said, placing a steaming mug in front of her. 'It's real and freshly brewed.'

'Real! I haven't had real coffee in ages. Only that ersatz muck that's doled out.' They were speaking quietly so as not to disturb the patients.

He smiled. 'Awful, isn't it?'

'Dreadful,' she agreed.

She sipped the coffee and murmured in appreciation. 'Sheer nectar. How did you come by it?'

He winked. 'Being a German has its advantages. Being an officer certainly does. There's not much I can't lay my hands on.' He studied her. 'Why, is there something you want?'

Holly struggled with her conscience. How could she bring herself to ask a favour of a German, the enemy, even a nice one. Though it wasn't for herself, but Dan.

'I don't suppose you can get some scotch whisky?' she asked.

'You like that?'

'No,' she said quickly. 'It's for my father. He adores a sup of it now and again.'

'As do I. I became quite addicted to "the cratur" during my sojourn in Scotland. It's a braw bricht moonlicht nicht the nicht, eh?'

She laughed softly. 'Very good. How long were you there for?'

'I went to medical school in Edinburgh.'

Holly was fascinated. 'That explains your excellent English.'

'Thank you. What's your name, by the way?'

'Nurse Morgan.'

'I'm Peter Schmidt. Pleased to meet you.'

'Pleased to meet you, Dr Schmidt.'

He glanced at his wristwatch. 'I must be getting on. I have other calls to make and forms to fill out. I'm on night duty myself for a while so I'll be seeing you again. Nor will I forget about the scotch.'

'I'll pay, of course,' she added hurriedly.

'We'll cross that bridge when we come to it. 'Bye for now, Nurse Morgan.'

She went back to her coffee, savouring it to the last drop.

Sister A'Court answered their knock. She was pale and haggard, her normally well-coiffured hair hanging in rats' tails.

'This is a surprise,' she declared.

'We thought we'd call and say hello and see how you are,' explained Elspeth who'd accompanied Holly. It had been Holly's idea.

'Come in.'

They were ushered through a small hall into a neatly appointed sitting room.

Sister fluttered a hand. 'Sit down. Would you care for a cup of tea?'

'No thank you,' Holly replied quickly, not wanting to take advantage of this kind offer. The tea ration was small enough without sharing.

Sister self consciously ran a hand through her hair. 'I'm such a mess I'm afraid. I meant to wash my hair earlier but somehow just never got round to it.'

'How are you within yourself?' Elspeth asked.

Sister glanced down at the carpet. 'Not so good actually. It's going to take me a long time to get over . . .' She hesitated, and swallowed, 'what happened.'

'That's understandable,' Elspeth sympathised.

'I keep . . . going over and over it in my mind.' She shuddered. 'It was ghastly beyond belief.'

Holly hadn't thought of it before, but now it came to her that Sister, unmarried and one of that breed who totally dedicates themselves to nursing, had probably been a virgin, which made matters even worse.

'When are you coming back?' Holly inquired.

'I don't know. The truth is . . .' She shuddered again. 'I'm not sure I can.'

'But why not?' Elspeth queried.

'The shame, the humiliation. Everyone knowing. I don't think I could ever live it down.'

'It wasn't your fault,' Holly protested. 'You were simply unlucky to be in the wrong place at the wrong time.'

'I keep telling myself that, but it doesn't make any difference. I can just imagine the sniggers, what's been said.' She glanced at them through haunted, tortured eyes. 'How could I ever exercise control again, especially over the younger nurses, with them knowing that I'd been . . .' She trailed off, unable to say the word raped.

'I think you're wrong, Sister,' Holly stated. 'There's nothing but sympathy for you. It might have been any one of us after all.'

Sister wrung her hands. 'I know I'm being stupid, but nonetheless that's how I feel.'

'Bloody Germans,' Elspeth hissed.

'I hate them,' Sister whispered. 'I can't tell you how much.'

'Is there anything we can do?' Holly asked quietly.

Sister shook her head.

'I hope they cut the balls off those bastards when they catch them,' Elspeth declared vehemently. Something she would never previously have dared to say in front of the redoubtable Sister A'Court.

'If they catch them,' Sister said. 'There's no certainty that they will. Two amongst the thousands swarming over the island.'

'Well, I hope they cut the balls off them if they do,' Elspeth repeated.

'I doubt she'll ever be the same again,' Holly commented to Elspeth when they were once more in the street.

Elspeth agreed.

'For you,' Dr Schmidt declared, placing a brown paper parcel in front of Holly.

'Is it . . .?'

He nodded.

'Why, thank you.'

'And there's something in there for you personally. A small gift.'

'For me?' She wondered what it was. 'Can I look?'

'Of course.'

She opened the parcel to discover two half-bottles of Black and White plus a bag of coffee.

'That's wonderful,' she beamed. 'How much do I owe you?'

'I didn't pay for any of it so you don't owe me a thing.'

'But I must pay you,' she insisted.

'As I explained, that's unnecessary. I hope your father enjoys the whisky and both of you the coffee.'

'Oh, we will, I assure you.'

'Then that's payment enough.' His expression hardened. 'We lost Gleisner this afternoon.'

'Yes, I know.'

His eyes took on a faraway look. 'I have a brother exactly the same age also in the Luftwaffe. I worry a lot about him.'

Holly twisted her engagement ring, thinking about Martin. 'And I had a fiancé in the army. He was killed at Dunkirk.'

He touched her lightly on the shoulder. 'I am sorry. It must have been a terrible loss for you.'

'It was. We were very much in love.'

'War,' he whispered, and shook his head. 'What a business.'

What a business indeed, she thought bitterly.

Chapter 5

'You'll never guess,' Sally Pallot said, eyes gleaming.

'What?' Meggy Hill queried, sensing gossip.

'Do you know Pat Le Clerq on ward three?'

Meggy and several of the others present in the nurses' room nodded. 'The little fat girl with red hair.'

'Get on with it,' Elspeth prompted.

Sally smirked. 'She's going out with a Jerry officer.'

'No!' Elspeth gasped.

'It's true. She's been seen.'

'Well,' Helen Mason breathed. 'Who'd have thought she'd become a Jerrybag.' That was the name that had been given to Island women who fraternised with the Germans.

'Is she . . . you know?' Heather Aubin queried.

'Sleeping with him?'

Viv Radmore giggled.

Sally shrugged. 'No idea.'

'Imagine sleeping with a Jerry, the sodding enemy. Ugh!' Meggy exclaimed in distaste.

'It's disgraceful,' Helen breathed.

'He's quite a dish, apparently,' Sally went on.

'If he's such a dish, what's he doing with her,' Meggy commented snidely. 'As Sally said, she's fat and hardly an oil painting.'

'Maybe he likes them on the plump side,' Viv smirked.

'She's *fat*, not plump,' Meggy retorted.

'What do you think, Holly?' Elspeth queried, Holly having so far listened in silence.

'I certainly don't approve if that's what you mean.'

'She should be tarred and feathered. They all should,' Helen declared.

'She'll be well taken care of, you can bet your ration book on that,' Sally said. 'I'm sure that's the big attraction for many of the Jerrybags.'

'Extra food,' Heather sighed. 'My stomach's rumbling just at the thought.'

Holly lowered her gaze, feeling guilty at having accepted the scotch and coffee from Dr Schmidt. Wisely she'd kept the story of that to herself, with the exception of Dan, that was, not even letting on to Elspeth whom she normally told everything. The coffee was gorgeous though.

'Well, I personally won't be speaking to her again,' Sally declared. 'I don't speak to lousy Jerrybags.'

'There's one in my street,' Heather informed them. 'You should hear some of the things that are shouted at her. Would make an Irish navvy blush.'

There was general laughter at that.

'Like what?' Elspeth demanded.

Heather shook her head. 'I won't repeat what I've heard. Too disgusting for words.'

That was greeted with even more laughter.

'I'm just glad I'm not working with her, that's all,' Viv said.

'Difficult,' Meggy agreed. 'I mean, you'd have to speak to her then. Impossible not to.'

There was some further discussion on the matter then they had to break up the conversation and return to duty.

'Sister A'Court's hanged herself,' an ashen-faced Elspeth informed Holly.

'No!'

'The news is racing round the hospital. Sometime yesterday they think. The body was discovered this morning.'

Holly was stunned.

'She just couldn't have been able to live with herself.'

'And they still haven't caught the rapists,' Holly said quietly. 'If they do, they should be charged with murder as well as rape.'

Elspeth nodded her agreement.

'Christ!' Holly whispered.

Dan gazed at his supper plate in dismay. 'I don't know how we're expected to survive on this amount of food,' he grumbled.

'I do my best, Dad.'

'I know, Holly. I appreciate that.'

'At least it's good for the figure,' she smiled.

Dan, a naturally slim man, smiled back. 'That's something I've never had to worry about.'

'There's always the black market.'

He shook his head. 'I'll have no dealings with them. I'm surprised your even mentioning it, knowing my feelings on the matter. It's wrong and shameful. Jersey people exploiting their own folk. I'd horsewhip the lot of them.'

'And yet you accepted the whisky and coffee,' Holly teased.

He glared at her. 'That was quite different, no money changed hands. They were gifts. Even if they did come from a German.' The coffee was now finished, while what remained of the whisky was well hidden against any other unexpected visitations from the Occupiers.

'Sister A'Court's funeral is tomorrow,' Holly stated.

'Yes, that was dreadful. Are you going?'

'A number of us have been given time off to attend. She's being cremated.'

'Very, very sad,' Dan commented. He'd never met Sister A'Court but Holly had often spoken of her.

'London took another pounding last night,' he said. 'It was on the wireless earlier.'

'I'm glad I'm not over there. It must be horrendous.'

'Coventry's a shambles apparently. Blitzed good and proper.'

'At least we don't have to worry about that here,' Holly stated.

'No, we're just being starved to death, that's all,' he jibed, staring wistfully at his plate.

Holly laughed. 'It's not that bad.'

'*Yet*,' Dan added. 'Take my word for it, it'll get worse before it gets better. This war looks like dragging on for years.'

Holly knew that to be true.

'I've been meaning to say something to you,' Dan stated quietly.

She raised an eyebrow.

'Don't you think it's high time you took off Martin's engagement ring? He is . . . dead after all.'

Holly glanced at the ring which had never been off her finger since Martin had placed it there.

'Life goes on, Holly, no matter what.'

She laid down her knife and fork and twisted the ring, a habit she'd fallen into whenever thinking about Martin.

'I really think you should,' Dan went on. 'In my opinion it would be for the best.'

'I'll consider it,' she whispered.

Dan left it at that.

'How are you? I haven't seen you for a while.'

Holly had bumped into Dr Schmidt in the corridor, stopping when he had. It would have been rude to walk on past when he clearly wished to talk.

'Fine, thanks. They put me back on nights for a couple of weeks.'

His face lit up in a friendly smile. 'That explains it then.'

Holly glanced around, nervous at being seen talking to a German, even if he was a doctor and a kind one at that. She didn't want any malicious rumours getting about. Hospitals were notorious for that.

He lowered his voice to a conspiratorial whisper. 'I was wondering, do you want any more coffee? I can easily get some.'

'No no!' she exclaimed in alarm. 'We're all right. Honestly.'

He frowned. 'Are you sure?'

'Yes, I swear.'

'Oh well,' he sighed. 'Any time. Just let me know.'

'I will. Now I must be getting on.'

'It was nice chatting with you, Nurse Morgan.'

She made a noise at the back of her throat that meant nothing at all, flashed him the briefest of smiles and continued on her way.

He stared after her, understanding.

'Why hello, Holly.'

She'd been walking along Queen Street when the Voisins, Martin's parents, had appeared out of a doorway. It was the first time she'd seen them since breaking the news about his death. She'd often thought of calling round but had never been able to bring herself to do so. It would simply have been too much to bear.

'You're both looking well,' she told them.

Mrs Voisin shook her head. 'I don't feel it, I can tell you. What with one thing and another.'

'Oh?'

'She suffers, does the wife. Always has.'

Holly wondered what she suffered from, but didn't inquire. Nor was that forthcoming.

'We have to walk everywhere now,' Mrs Voisin grumbled.

'Can't get petrol for the car any more,' Mr Voisin explained.

Just then a car filled with German officers rattled past. Mr Voisin glared after them. 'There's no shortage for them, though. They can get all they want.'

'Sods,' Mrs Voisin muttered.

'They killed our lad,' Mr Voisin said, the expression in his eyes pure hatred.

'Damn them all to everlasting hell,' Mrs Voisin hissed.

'Amen to that,' her husband added.

Holly felt like saying they weren't all bad, having Dr Schmidt in mind, but didn't think that would be appreciated.

'We'd ask you round to tea sometime, but well, you know how things are,' Mrs Voisin said, turning her attention again to Holly.

'I understand.' That was a relief.

'Everything all right at the hospital?' Mrs Voisin asked.

'Fine. I've been doing a lot of nights recently, but that's part and parcel of the job.'

'Would hate that myself,' Mr Voisin declared.

Mrs Voisin suddenly frowned. 'You're not wearing Martin's engagement ring.'

Holly blushed. 'No.'

'I see. That didn't take long,' Mrs Voisin said, disapproval in her voice.

'I thought it for the best,' Holly murmured, echoing her father's words.

'I'm sure you're right,' Mr Voisin said in the same tone of disapproval as his wife.

'I keep it at home in a little box. It's something I'll treasure always. That and a photograph we had taken together just before he left.'

'Hmmh,' Mrs Voisin murmured.

'Well, it was lovely seeing you,' Holly declared, wanting to get away from the Voisins. She was deeply embarrassed.

'Goodbye then,' Mrs Voisin said tartly.

'Goodbye.'

'Damn,' Holly muttered to herself a little further along the street. She could have done without the encounter.

'What's wrong with you? You've got a face like fizz,' Dan asked her when she returned home.

She explained about the Voisins. 'I can't tell you how guilty it's made me feel.'

Dan put a sympathetic arm round his daughter. 'Taking it off was the right thing to do, Holly, believe me. It was a constant morbid reminder. And as I said, life goes on.'

'I know,' she whispered.

'I'm sure Martin would have agreed. He was a practical lad, remember.'

She nodded.

'Now, what's for supper? What delicious goodies are in store?' he inquired jocularly.

He groaned when she told him. It was neither delicious nor a goody of any sort.

Cabbage soup and what would be a very thin slice of bread.

It was Holly's day off and she'd decided to go for a long walk along the sea front, something she did regularly to help blow the hospital cobwebs away and help keep her fit. Sometimes she rode her bicycle, but today it was a walk.

To go down on the beach itself was forbidden, and impossible in most places anyway due to the huge rolls of barbed wire strung all along the sea wall.

It was quiet, few people about, the last person she'd encountered now a speck in the distance behind her. How she adored this island, she thought. If she'd been allowed to be born anywhere in the world she would have chosen Jersey. Not that she had much experience of the world, a sole trip to London a few years previously being it. But she was certain she'd have chosen Jersey anyhow.

She spotted a solitary, dejected male sitting on a bench staring out over the water. Frowning as she got closer, Holly thought the man looked familiar. Then recognition dawned, it was Dr Schmidt.

'Here's a coincidence,' he said, giving her a strained smile when she halted beside him.

'I'm out for a constitutional,' she explained. 'You?'

He hesitated, then replied, 'I wanted some time to think. Collect my thoughts.'

'Oh? Something bothering you at work?'

'Not that simple I'm afraid, lassie.'

His using the word lassie made her laugh.

'Why don't you join me?'

Now it was her turn to hesitate.

'Don't worry, there isn't a soul about. We're quite alone,' he said drily.

She flushed.

'They can hardly brand you a Jerrybag for having a few minutes' conversation. Besides, I'm in civvies. No one's to know I'm a German.'

That was true, she thought, sitting. 'You know that expression then?'

'Jerrybag? Oh yes. A rather cruel one it is too.'

'That depends on your point of view. Which side of the fence you're on.'

'Touché,' he smiled.

'Personally, and I hope you don't mind me saying this, I think it's disgusting fraternising with the enemy. You have occupied us after all!'

'But we've treated you fairly,' he countered. 'You can't deny that.'

'Well . . .'

'There then.'

'That doesn't alter matters one bit. You've no right to be here, nor France, or Czechoslovakia, or anywhere else come to that.'

'I suspect the Führer might disagree,' he said mildly.

She bit her tongue, not wanting to give him her views on his infamous Führer. That might be going too far. He was still a German.

'Do you agree with what Hitler's done?' she queried instead.

'Nurse Morgan!' he exclaimed, a twinkle in his eye. 'As a serving German officer of course I agree with Hitler.'

'And what of Peter Schmidt the man, the doctor?'

'Ah!' he breathed. 'What of him indeed?'

She waited patiently. 'Well?' she finally demanded.

'Peter Schmidt the man and doctor has learned discretion. A wise thing to learn in the circumstances, don't you think?'

Holly smiled. 'That tells me everything.'

'Everything?' he teased.

'It certainly answers my question.'

'So,' he said, and once more stared out over the water. 'Do you know what we call these islands of yours?'

'What?'

'The Paradise Islands.'

'The Paradise Islands,' she repeated. That was beautiful.

'Can you blame us for wanting such a place?' He was teasing again.

'Of course I can. They're not yours, though, they're ours. You're trying to steal them.'

'Isn't history full of such events?' Adding drily, 'The British themselves are quite good at taking what they want, their empire is testimony to that.'

'But . . .' She trailed off. Damn it, he was right.

'Australian aborigines for example.'

'What about them?'

'I don't believe they invited the British to take their homeland from them. Or . . .'

'OK! OK!' she interjected. 'You've made your point. Except that British colonial rule is far different from what you Germans are doling out. There's no argument about that.'

'Do you smoke?'

She shook her head.

'Do you mind?'

'Not in the least.'

He produced a packet of cigarettes and lit up.

'Anyway, all that aside, why were you looking so glum? You gave the impression of being positively miserable.'

He studied the smoke floating up from his cigarette, debating whether or not he should confide in her.

'I received a letter this morning,' he said slowly. 'What you call a "Dear John".'

Her previous hostility melted. 'Oh, Doctor, I am sorry.'

'She was someone I met in Berlin. Her name was Marlene.'

'As in Dietrich?'

'As in Dietrich,' he confirmed.

'What, eh . . . happened?'

'Simple really, she met someone else. An officer in the Gestapo.' His face hardened. 'For her to go with someone like that makes me very, very angry.'

'Were you engaged?'

'No, Nurse Morgan, but we were extremely close.'

She realised that was a euphemism, he'd been sleeping with this Marlene. 'Do you love her?'

He shrugged. 'I thought I might be in love. I wasn't sure.'

'Then you weren't. If you'd been in love, truly in love, you'd have known. There wouldn't have been any doubt in your mind. Believe me, I speak from experience.'

'Your fiancé killed at Dunkirk.'

'Yes,' she breathed.

'Then perhaps I wasn't.'

'And she obviously wasn't with you otherwise she'd have waited.'

'She could dance wonderfully,' he mused. 'I've never known a woman dance like her.' He turned to Holly. 'Can you dance well?'

'I'm not bad, though hardly spectacular as Marlene seems to have been. How did you meet her?'

'In a night club. She was with some friends, as was I. One of my friends knew one of hers, we came together as a group and she and I hit it off right away.'

'Does she work?'

'Oh yes, a secretary. Very efficient she used to assure me.' He laughed. 'But then we Germans have a name for efficiency, have we not?'

Holly nodded.

'At least she had the decency to write to me. At least she had that.'

'It isn't the end of the world,' Holly sympathised. 'You'll meet someone else.'

'Probably. And you?'

She blinked. 'I can't envisage that. Martin was everything to me.'

'Martin,' he repeated. 'A nice name.'

'I thought so.'

'And what did he do?'

'He was a car mechanic. We were due to get married last July, and then he went and joined up. So we never did, and now never will.'

'The war . . .' he mused.

'What a business.'

He nodded. 'My very words, I seem to remember.'

'They were indeed. And I agree with you wholeheartedly. A terrible, terrible business.'

They sat in silence for a few moments, he grinding the remains of his cigarette out underfoot.

'Will you walk further?' he asked eventually.

'Yes. Another mile at least.'

'And I shall return to the hospital. I'm on duty in several hours.'

He stood, and so did she. He held out a hand and shook hers. 'Goodbye for now, Nurse Morgan.'

'Goodbye, Dr Schmidt.'

'What's your Christian name, by the way?'

'Holly.'

He nodded. 'Goodbye then, Holly Morgan. And I hope that one day you too will meet someone else.'

As she continued on her way she found herself twisting that part of her finger where her engagement ring had been.

Dan's headmaster was called Dr Gallichan and that Friday afternoon, the conclusion of their school week, he had summoned the teaching staff to his study. Fully assembled, he now spoke to them.

'As from Monday the instruction of German to all pupils, I stress that, *all* pupils, will be compulsory. The instruction itself will be conducted by German personnel.'

Dan was outraged, as were many others present.

'What are they trying to do, turn the children into little Jerries?' Miss Dupré, a dragon of a woman, barked.

'I suppose that's the general idea,' Dr Gallichan replied mildly. He hated this as much as the staff.

'Hmmh!' Dan snorted.

'Will these "personnel" be soldiers or what?' Mr Fortesque inquired.

'I really don't know. We'll just have to wait and see who turns up.'

'Pages and pages of blatant propaganda in the newspaper, and now this,' Mr Moody fumed.

'I know. It is a bit much.'

'A bit much!' Dan exclaimed. 'It's more than that.'

Dr Gallichan regarded Dan steadily. 'And what am I supposed to do, Mr Morgan. Say no?'

'We understand your position, Headmaster, of course you couldn't refuse. It's the principle of the thing.'

'I quite agree.'

'Jack-booted Germans strutting through our school, who would ever have thought it,' Miss Mallet sighed.

'It'll take some getting used to I suppose.'

'They'll be wanting us all to learn their bloody language next,' Dan raged.

'Possibly,' Dr Gallichan nodded.

Dan's eyes glittered with fury.

'I don't want any incidents over this matter,' Dr Gallichan warned them. 'It wouldn't do the school or its pupils any good.' His expression softened. 'Besides, I don't want to lose any of you. I like to think we're one big happy family here, let's keep it like that.'

'Deutschland, Deutschland Über Alles. Up theirs!' Miss Dupré declared.

Everyone, including Dr Gallichan, laughed.

The following Monday, nine o'clock on the dot, the Germans arrived and German lessons began.

Dan was hesitant. 'I hate to ask, but do you think you could get me some more scotch?'

Holly glanced up from the book she was reading to frown. 'Dad!'

'I appreciate it might be difficult for you . . .'

'It's not that, Dad. I just don't want anyone thinking I'm fraternising. That girl Pat Le Clerq I mentioned to you before is having a hell of a time. Everyone is being quite beastly to her, she's having to take some dreadful stick.'

'But she's going out with a German, I'm hardly asking you to do that. A quiet word in this Dr Schmidt's ear perhaps. Where's the harm?'

Holly sighed.

'It's entirely up to you, of course. And I insist we pay this time. No more gifts.'

'I thought you detested the black market?'

Dan had been prepared for that, his answer ready. 'From what you've told me about this Dr Schmidt, he won't charge more than he himself pays for it. There'll be no profiteering so it won't be black market.'

He slumped into the chair facing Holly. 'I'll pay in either English sterling, local currency or Occupation Marks, whichever the good doctor prefers. All he has to do is state his preference.'

Holly studied her father. It went totally against the grain for him to make such a request, but then war changed people, she was witness to that every single day. It lowered their standards, in some cases made them plummet.

'A quiet word then when I can manage it,' she said.

Dan smiled. 'Ta.'

It took Holly nearly a fortnight before she was able to get Dr Schmidt on his own.

'That can be arranged,' he said, after she'd stammered out her request.

'Only please don't mention it to anyone. And when you give it to me, do it when nobody else is watching.'

'I understand,' he nodded.

'And this time we'll pay. I won't accept the bottle unless we do.'

'Agreed, Holly Morgan.'

'Thank you,' she whispered. 'You're very kind. Now payment . . .'

'English sterling,' he decided after she'd explained the options, and named a price which was very fair indeed.

Another nurse appeared and Dr Schmidt immediately began discussing one of the ward cases with Holly.

Holly was impressed by this, and grateful.

Chapter 6

There were five of them in the room, all close and trusted friends of Dan who'd called them together.

'We must retaliate in some way, form a resistance movement as it's rumoured the French have done. Our passivity has gone on long enough, it's high time we struck back,' he declared.

Fred Aubert, an accountant, shifted uneasily in his chair. 'And you're proposing that we, the five of us, form this resistance movement, Dan?'

'The nucleus of it, that's correct.'

'Don't you think we're a bit old, past it?' Ronnie March queried.

'We're hardly in the first flush of youth but that doesn't stop us being active.'

Ronnie, who was in his late fifties, sighed.

'What sort of things do you have in mind?' Bob Le Geyt asked.

'Cutting telephone wires for a start. General all-round sabotage, anything that'll give the Germans a headache.'

'Hmmh,' Bob mused, thinking about that.

'Are you considering we arm ourselves?' Fred inquired.

Dan nodded.

'You know all firearms have been confiscated,' Fred went on.

'I'm willing to bet there are still plenty around, secreted all over the place. Especially in the countryside. All we have to do is find them.'

Bob laughed. 'I see!' he exclaimed sarcastically. 'And as we make these inquiries how long will it be before some bugger informs on us? I hate to admit it but there's been considerable collaboration going on.'

A growl of agreement went round the room.

Dan knew that to be true. The extent of collaboration, sometimes for preferential treatment, on other occasions out of sheer spite, a settling of old scores, had astounded him. 'We'd have to be careful of course . . .'

'More than bloody careful!' Fred interjected. 'It's just too risky.'

'I agree,' Harry Laffoley, the local undertaker, nodded.

Dan breathed heavily. 'There are still a great many things we can do without firearms. They aren't essential.'

'It's the collaboration that worries me. You simply don't know who to trust nowadays,' Bob said.

'There's another point,' Fred declared.

'Which is?'

'France is a large country, you could commit an act of sabotage there and be fifty miles away by the following morning. We can't do that on Jersey. We're a small island, a self-contained prison if you like that's crawling with thousands of warders. It would only be a matter of time before we were caught, and shot. And make no mistake, shot we would be. That's a certainty.'

'And what about reprisals?' Harry queried. 'Would you be prepared to keep quiet while your friends and neighbours were rounded up, tortured and executed? I don't think so, Dan.'

'They'd get us one way or the other,' Ronnie March agreed.

'No no, a resistance movement is out of the question,' Bob declared. 'Given our situation, it's quite impractical.'

'Are we to do nothing then?' Dan burst out.

'There's nothing we can do,' Harry stated quietly.

Fred Aubert rose from his chair. 'I concur. All we'd be doing is throwing our own lives away and putting others in jeopardy. You can count me out of such foolishness for one.'

'And me,' said Harry.

The other two agreed, leaving Dan frustrated and fuming.

'If you take my advice, old pal, you'll drop this and forget about it,' Ronnie said, patting Dan good-humouredly on the shoulder.

When they'd gone, Dan poured himself a scotch from the bottle Holly had bought from Dr Schmidt.

There *had* to be something he could do, he told himself. There had to be something.

But what?

'It's the latest food supplementary,' Elspeth declared to Holly who'd dropped in to visit. 'Will you taste it?'

Holly stared at the red liquid in the cup she was handed. 'It looks disgusting,' she declared.

'Try it.'

Holly tasted the cup's contents. 'Ugh!' she exclaimed.

'I suppose we'll get used to it in time. Or so Terry says.'

'What is it?' Holly asked.

'Beet tea. I don't know who thought it up but I was given the recipe only yesterday.' She sighed. 'It's nothing like the real thing but with that in such short supply this makes some sort of substitute.'

'It's certainly different,' Holly smiled.

'I've also heard that some people are doing the same thing with acorns, though I haven't come across that yet,' Elspeth went on.

Acorns, Holly mused. Whatever next?

'I wish I had a nice biscuit to offer you,' Elspeth sighed. 'A Marie would go down a treat right now.' Marie was the name of a biscuit popular on the island before the war.

'I can't remember the last time I had one of those,' Holly reflected. 'There again, there are lots of things I can't remember the last time I had.'

She changed the subject. 'How's Terry? I haven't seen him for a while.'

'Oh he's tip top. Married life suits him.' Elspeth giggled. 'And me. He's just fantastic in . . .' She giggled again. 'You know. He's a holy terror when it comes to that.'

Holly gave her friend an indulgent smile, pleased for her happiness. She glanced around the room which had a warm, homey atmosphere.

'You've certainly settled in well.'

'Oh we love it here. Couldn't be better.'

Holly felt a stab of jealousy. If it hadn't been for the war, she and Martin would have had a home like this where they too would have been incredibly happy. Who knew? She might even be pregnant by now. A condition that had so far eluded Elspeth. Though, from what Elspeth had just said, not from the want of trying.

'Are you all right? You're suddenly looking most peculiar,' Elspeth asked in concern.

'A touch of heartburn,' Holly lied, not wishing to divulge what had been going through her mind.

'More tea? Or is it that which has given you the heartburn?'

'Possibly, so I'll do without a second cup.'

'Terry said only the other day . . .'

From there on it became Terry this, Terry that and Terry the next thing till Holly was quite fed up hearing about the wonderful Terry. Jealousy again, she told herself. Stop it.

V.

Dan stepped back and admired his handiwork. Daubed in red paint the V was about four feet in height and adorned the side wall of a bakery. It was the third Dan had done that night, and he intended doing more.

V for Victory, Dan muttered to himself. The Germans knew what it stood for all right and it would annoy the hell out of them. He smiled, thoroughly pleased with himself.

'Halt! Who goes there?'

The words, barked out in German, startled Dan. A quick glance took in two shadowy figures at the other end of the alleyway. He broke out in a cold sweat when he saw a brace of rifles being raised.

Dan dropped the brush he'd been holding, the can of paint still on the ground, and ran.

Two shots rang out, one zipping to the side of him, the other smacking into the bakery wall causing chips of stone to spatter.

I'm a dead man, he thought in despair.

And then, very quickly, two more shots.

'Christ!' he exclaimed, nearly knocked off his feet.

He'd been hit.

'Holly, wake up! I need your help.'

Holly came groggily awake. 'What is it, Dad?'

'I've been shot.'

She snapped alert. 'Shot? But . . .'

'In the arm.'

She swung out of bed, the light already on. Dan was standing there, clutching his arm, fingers stained with blood.

'How did this happen?' she demanded.

'I'll tell you shortly. Just see what you can do, will you? It's damned painful.'

'First we'll get that jacket off.'

He groaned in agony as she eased it over his shoulder. When the jacket had been discarded she ripped the sleeve of his shirt along its entire length, revealing the wound.

'You're lucky,' she declared after a cursory examination. 'The bullet went straight through the fleshy part of your arm.' She then tested his arm, he groaning again, to ascertain whether or not the bone had been broken. It hadn't.

'Downstairs to the kitchen,' she instructed. 'I'll need hot water.'

Once in the kitchen she filled the kettle and put it on, after which she got out their medical box and rifled through its contents. Fortunately she had everything to hand that she needed.

'You really should see a doctor with that,' she said, unwrapping a bandage.

'Oh yeah,' he replied sarcastically. 'Who do you suggest? Your Dr Schmidt?'

'Very droll.'

'No, Holly, if possible we keep this strictly in the family. Safer that way.'

'So what happened?' she demanded again. There was nothing further she could do till the kettle boiled.

She stared at him aghast when he told her.

'You were out, not only after curfew but painting stupid signs on walls!' she exclaimed incredulously.

'I had to do something, Holly. Only a gesture I grant you, but something at least.'

She was furious. 'You could easily have got yourself killed, and damn well nearly did. And what if they'd captured you? What then?'

'I knew it was a risk . . .'

'An insane one, if you ask me. Honestly, Dad, you're unbelievable.'

'I did what I considered right,' he replied defiantly. 'Everyone on this island has just rolled over, it's disgraceful.'

'But not you, you have to try and be a hero.'

He had the grace to colour. 'Hardly that, Holly.'

'A man of your age charging about at night with a can of paint. If it wasn't so pathetic it would be laughable.'

'I don't view it like that. Anyway, I'm not that old.'

'So how did you get away from them?'

'I know the place like the back of my hand, I was born and brought up here, don't forget, like yourself. And it was pitch dark, the only illumination being moonlight, which helped. I finally lost them by hiding in an outhouse.'

'Like some bloody big kid,' she berated him. She was thoroughly shaken that her father had taken such an appalling risk.

'I don't suppose you thought about me before you went out on your jaunt,' she went on.

He stared at her blankly.

'If you'd been caught they might have come for me as well.'

'But you had nothing to do with it!' he protested.

'The Germans might not have believed that. Then I'd have been right in the mire same as yourself.'

He hung his head. 'Sorry. I didn't think about that.'

'Well, you damn well should have.'

When she picked up the now boiling kettle she noted that her hands were shaking. Hardly surprising, she thought. God, she was angry! How could he have been so foolish?

She poured some water into a bowl which she placed on the table beside a seated Dan.

'Another thing you didn't take into consideration,' she said, dipping a clean cloth into the bowl. 'If you'd got yourself killed then I'd have lost a father as well as a fiancé in this damn war. Losing Martin was more than enough, I can tell you.'

He grimaced as she started to work with the cloth. 'I said I'm sorry,' he muttered.

When she'd cleaned the entry wound she said, 'This is going to sting, I'm afraid.' And with that she poured antiseptic over the wound.

Dan sucked in a deep breath. Sting! Typical medical understatement, he thought.

Holly now placed a thick strip of gauze over the entry wound and instructed Dan to hold it in place.

She repeated the process with the exit wound, slightly larger and messier than the other, then bound his arm, securing the bandage with a pair of brass safety pins.

'That's the best I can do for the moment,' she announced.

'Thanks.'

She stood up and shivered, having not bothered with her dressing gown in her rush to attend to Dan. 'How do you feel?'

'Dreadful.'

'Promise me you won't do anything silly again, Dad?'

'I promise.'

'I mean it!' she warned.

'I'll keep my promise. I swear.'

She put her arms round his neck and kissed the top of his head. Having gone and shrugged into her dressing gown she returned to the kitchen and made them both a cup of badly needed tea.

She poured a large dollop of scotch into Dan's cup before giving it to him.

'Something wrong with your arm, Mr Morgan?'

Dan gently patted the bulge in his sleeve and smiled at Dr Gallichan. It was the morning after his near-fatal escapade.

'Gashed it on a nail,' Dan lied. That was what he and Holly had decided on to explain things.

Dr Gallichan pulled a face. 'Painful, I should imagine.'

'Not as bad as it might have been. My daughter Holly attended to it, she's a nurse as you know.'

'Hope it doesn't turn septic.'

So did Dan.

Holly stopped her bicycle but didn't get off. From that position on the road she could see a corner of the caravan where she and Martin had made love together the evening before he'd gone away.

A lump came into her throat as images of that night flashed through her mind. The pair of them entwined, he stroking her, them moving as one, her cries . . .

Now he was gone for ever, dead, and they'd never make love again. Never laugh together again, never hold hands, a thousand things.

'Oh Martin,' she sighed.

For a moment or two she thought she was going to cry, but tears didn't come.

She knew then she was truly beginning to come to terms with her loss.

Peter Schmidt strolled into the bar of the Grand Hotel, thinking that a couple of beers would go down nicely before bed. He was instantly hailed by a group of fellow officers.

'Peter, come and join us,' Hauptmann Klumpp called out. He was red-faced, having already been drinking for several hours.

'I'll get my beer first,' Peter retorted, going up to the bar.

'Well, this is a merry group,' he declared, sitting on a chair that had been pulled over for him.

'It's Dieter's birthday,' Klumpp informed him. 'We're celebrating.'

'Many happy returns,' Peter smiled to Dieter Hercher who was an Oberleutnant like himself.

'Thirty today. I feel ancient,' Dieter moaned, which raised a general laugh.

Oberleutnant Wolf Sohn tapped one of a number of bottles that were on the table. 'We have some excellent Armagnac here, Peter. Will you take a glass with us?'

Peter shook his head. 'Beer will be fine. I have a heavy day tomorrow.'

'So!' nodded Wolf.

Klumpp winked salaciously at Peter. 'Then you won't wish to accompany us when we leave here shortly.'

Dieter Hercher snorted with amusement.

'Where are you off to?'

'The Hotel Victor Hugo, where our superiors have seen fit to provide entertainment for us lonely men away from home.'

Peter knew what type of entertainment that was. 'The brothel, eh?'

Klumpp nodded. 'That make you change your mind?'

Peter had never been in a brothel in his life, nor did he ever intend to. The idea of going with a prostitute was repugnant to him. 'I still have a heavy day tomorrow so you'll have to count me out.'

Klumpp playfully punched Peter on the arm. 'Come on, let your hair down. Worry about tomorrow when it comes.'

'I doubt my patients would appreciate that,' Peter replied lightly.

'French tarts especially imported. I can't wait,' Wolf Sohn declared, and hiccupped.

Peter had heard on the grapevine that the tarts were all ugly as sin but refrained from saying so as his friends seemed intent on sampling them.

He drained his glass. 'I'd better be going. Enjoy yourselves.'

'Oh we will,' Klumpp assured him. 'We'll make those ladies squirm, won't we.' The latter addressed to Dieter and Wolf who both voiced their agreement.

Peter would have liked another beer but didn't want to stay in that particular company any longer.

'A word of advice,' he said, rising.

'Advise away,' retorted Wolf.

'Speaking as a doctor, and your friend, make sure you use a gummi. Better safe than sorry, eh?'

Klumpp patted a breast pocket. 'Don't worry, Peter, we're well provided in that department.'

Peter wished them luck and left. He was hardly a prude, he thought as he went up in the lift. But tarts!

He'd never be so desperate as to go with one of those.

*

Dan was jubilant. Others had taken up where he'd left off and now there were dozens of V for Victory signs all over St Helier. The Germans, as he'd known they'd be, were furious and now posters were going up offering a £25 reward for information leading to the arrest of anyone responsible.

As for his arm, that was healing nicely. Holly said she was pleased with its progress. Her main worry had been that, despite the antiseptic, it might become infected, but that hadn't occurred. He'd got off relatively lightly, and appreciated his luck.

Sister Zimmer came steaming on to the ward. She was one of a band of German nurses who had recently arrived on the Island. They were relatively few in number as yet, but more were on their way and when the full complement was in place the local nurses would be returned to their original wards. Sister Zimmer's English was almost non-existent but she could make herself understood in medical matters.

Sister spoke rapidly to another German nurse who nodded vigorously, then almost ran from the ward.

What's going on? Holly wondered. She soon found out.

Sister mimed a plane flying to Holly. 'Luftwaffe boom. Many many . . .' She indicated a patient.

'There's been an aircraft crash?' Holly interpreted.

'Yah, boom! Many many . . .'

'I understand,' Holly interjected.

Dr Schmidt appeared on the ward and Sister immediately conferred with him. Then she was hurrying away.

'Did you get that?' Peter asked Holly.

'An aircraft crash.'

'Two troop-carrying Junkers. I haven't got the details yet but I do know we're going to be extremely busy before long. Sister says there are five empty beds on the ward, but we're going to need a lot more than that.'

He paused in thought, then said, 'You stay by my side. I'll use English nurses only as I speak the language. Others will have to muddle along as best they can.'

Half an hour later the first of the crash victims arrived.

*

Holly glanced at her watch. Eight hours now without a break except for going to the lavatory. Moan and groans filled the ward, which was jam packed with beds and trollies.

The operating theatres had been in non-stop use, but because there were so many casualties, many needing attention as soon as possible, minor, and some not so minor, operations were being carried out on the wards.

Peter paused for a moment to catch his breath. He looks exhausted, Holly thought. But then they all were. Only Peter, with the heavy responsibility of surgeon, even more so. Over the hours his face had become strained and lined, adding years to him.

He gazed down at the almost severed foot he was trying to save, and decided it was a losing battle. It would have to come off. He told Holly and the other nurses present at the bedside of his decision.

Twelve hours now and still they were at it. Holly noted that Peter's hands had begun to tremble, which worried her. They all needed a break and a cup of something, especially him, but that was impossible.

Further along the ward a patient suddenly shrieked, a horrible sound that set Holly's teeth on edge. The shrieking ceased as abruptly as it had begun.

'Tell me about yourself, Nurse Morgan,' Peter requested quietly.

'I beg your pardon?'

'I said tell me about yourself. It will help with my concentration.'

Nurse Coutanche, also assisting, shrugged when Holly glanced at her.

If that's what doctor wanted then that's what doctor would get. She started with her childhood.

For a brief moment their eyes locked and Holly saw the pain in his, a reflection of the pain surrounding them. She'd liked Peter Schmidt up until then, now she also respected him. This was no cold, clinical butcher but a sensitive caring human being doing his best against dreadful odds.

Then it was back to work, Peter suturing with all the skill and finesse of a seamstress.

*

When Holly stumbled into the room, Dan quickly stood and switched off the wireless. He helped her to a chair which she collapsed into.

'It was awful,' she said.

'I take it you've been dealing with the survivors of the crash? I heard about it at school.'

'They might be Germans and the enemy, Dad, but you couldn't help but feel sorry for them. Some of the burns cases . . .' She broke off and shuddered.

'As you know, the tea ration is finished but there is that beet muck. Would you like a cup?'

Holly closed her eyes. 'Peter was magnificent,' she murmured. The next second she was fast asleep.

Dan covered her with an eiderdown and left her where she was.

Peter had met up again with his friends in the bar of the Grand and this time there was no talk of the Hotel Victor Hugo. All had agreed that had been a disappointment, the French tarts, as Peter had previously known, ugly as sin.

'The latest order is that the local Jews have now to register,' Wolf Sohn stated.

'And not before time too. It should have been done directly we occupied the Islands,' Klumpp commented.

'Jews. A filthy race,' Wolf went on.

'If it was up to me, I wouldn't bother registering them. I'd simply round them up and shoot the lot,' Dieter Hercher declared.

Peter studied his friend, appalled by his statement. Not a flicker of his true emotions showed on his face, he knew better than that. As he'd once told Holly, he'd long since learned discretion.

'As it is, they'll be deported,' Klumpp said. 'Good riddance to bad rubbish.'

'What do you say, Peter?' Wolf asked.

Peter took his time in replying, first lighting a cigarette. 'I didn't know there were many on Jersey,' he prevaricated.

'One is too many,' Dieter riposted.

'The Führer has the right idea where that scum are concerned. He knows how to treat them,' Klumpp declared, and laughed nastily.

Peter thought of Mr Abelman, one of his tutors at Edinburgh. You couldn't have met a kinder man or a better tutor. He'd had a great affection, and admiration, for the old Jew.

'Some of their women are pretty though. You have to admit that,' Wolf observed.

Klumpp shrugged. 'That's beside the point. They're still Jewesses, pretty or not.'

'I was only remarking. Not that I would go with one myself. Heaven forbid!'

'Of course not,' Klumpp nodded.

Peter changed the subject.

Chapter 7

'It's a scandal, that's what it is. A scandal!' Miss Dupré was declaring in loud ringing, outraged tones as Dan entered the staff room.

'I couldn't agree more, Miss Dupré,' Mr Fortesque said, shaking his head in sadness.

'What's a scandal?' Dan inquired.

Miss Dupré fixed him with a beady eye. 'Two young women were caught chalking up V signs last evening and both were thrown into jail.'

Dan's heart sank.

'The scandal is, both are under twenty and one is heavily pregnant.'

Oh my God, Dan thought.

'What do you make of that?' Mr Moody asked.

Dan sighed, momentarily lost for words. This was dreadful. Of course he was to blame; if he hadn't started the signs in the first place this would never have happened.

'I feel extremely sorry for them,' Dan mumbled.

'Mind you, on the other hand they've only themselves to blame,' Mr Moody pointed out, which earned him a glare from Miss Dupré. 'It was a hazardous thing to do and now they must face the consequences, whatever those may be.'

'Perhaps the Germans will only keep them under arrest for a few days and then let them go,' Dan said hopefully.

'I'll believe that when it happens,' Miss Dupré snorted.

'Let's pray the Germans are lenient,' Dan went on. 'It's hardly a capital offence after all.'

Miss Dupré snorted again.

Dan, weighed down with guilt, wished with all his heart he'd never started the whole nonsense.

'Nurse Morgan!'

Holly stopped as Dr Schmidt came hurrying up.

'How are you? I haven't seen you for over a week.'

Holly was now back on her old ward with Sister Moignard, the rest of the German nurses having arrived to take over their wards.

She glanced nervously around. 'I'm fine, thank you, Doctor.'

He smiled. 'Don't worry. I made sure we were alone before approaching you. I have a proposition to make.'

'A proposition?'

'You enjoy walking and so do I. I would like to explore this island of yours, and who better to show me the sights than a native?'

Alarm filled Holly. 'You mean *me*?'

'Why not?'

'But, Doctor, I . . .' she stammered, desperately trying to think of some way to turn him down without it being a flat refusal.

'We could meet outside the town, and even if we're seen together who would know me to be a German? I'd be wearing my civilian clothes.'

Holly considered that. She was in his debt after all, and wanted to remain in his good books so she could continue to get supplies of scotch for her father.

'I don't know,' she hesitated.

'As an inducement, I'll bring along a picnic.'

A picnic! That was an inducement indeed. For the Germans ate like lords while the islanders were on a starvation diet. This was an opportunity to get some decent food inside her.

'I, of course, wouldn't mention it to anyone.' He smiled again. 'We don't want you branded a Jerrybag!'

She made a snap decision. 'All right.'

'Good. When is your next day off?'

She told him.

'I shall arrange to have the same day off. Now where shall we meet, and when?'

After a few seconds' thought, Holly named a time and place and he assured her he'd be there waiting.

'Nine months!' Dan exclaimed. 'Oh, my God!'

'What's nine months?' Holly queried.

'Those two young women whom the Jerries arrested for chalking up V signs. It's here in the *Evening Post*, they've been given nine months each to be served at a prison in France.'

He looked at Holly through stricken eyes. 'It's all my stupid fault this has happened. And one of them pregnant too!'

It was harsh, Holly thought. But that was the Germans all over. Heavy handed as ever.

'Nine months,' Dan choked.

'At least they weren't informed on. That would have been even worse,' Holly said.

A wretched Dan nodded his agreement.

Thank the Lord it wasn't my father being sent to prison for nine months, Holly thought, which could easily have been the case. Just as he could have so easily been shot dead running away that night.

'I wish . . .' Dan trailed off and shook his head.

'Wish what?'

'That there was something I could do.'

'Don't come up with any further daft ideas for a start,' Holly told him.

'No,' he whispered.

He returned to his *Post* to read the article a second time.

It was a glorious day and from their present vantage point Holly and Peter had a panoramic view of the Channel.

'It really is a beautiful place, this Jersey of yours. No wonder we call them the Paradise Islands,' Peter commented.

'Enjoyed your walk so far?'

'Oh yes, very much so. And the running commentary as we went along. That's something I wouldn't have had on my own.'

'Well, next stop is Spook Wood and Goblin Hollow.'

He frowned. 'I know the word goblin but not spook?'

'It means ghost.'

'Ah!' he smiled. 'An addition to my vocabulary.'

'I must say you really do speak English extremely well.'

'I have a gift for languages and an excellent ear, I'm told. I'm fortunate there.' Peter sighed with pleasure. 'Would you like to eat now? Or shall we wait till later?'

She hungrily eyed the wicker basket he was carrying. 'Now, if you don't mind. I'm ravenous!'

'Then eat we shall.'

He handed Holly the basket. 'Would you like to set things out? Be mother as it's so quaintly called.'

Holly opened the basket and gasped. 'Oh, Peter, this is wonderful!'

'You approve, eh?'

'I most certainly do.'

There were beef sandwiches, pâté, cheese, biscuits, butter, salad, fruit and a bottle of Beaujolais. Also a flask of coffee with a small container of sugar, and another of milk.

'The hotel was most obliging when I requested the picnic,' Peter said, sitting down on the grass. 'They put it together in their kitchens.'

The plates Holly took out were best china, as were the matching cups and saucers. The cutlery was silver plate.

'I'll open the wine,' Peter suggested, producing a corkscrew from his pocket.

There were wine glasses in the basket which Holly placed in front of him.

'Pâté to start?' she queried.

'Lovely.'

He laughed when her stomach rumbled loudly. 'You weren't joking about being ravenous.'

'I most certainly wasn't.'

She fixed him with a steady stare. 'I don't think you appreciate just how little we get to survive on. While your lot are stuffing their faces, we're going without.'

His expression became sober. 'I'm sorry, I shouldn't have laughed. I hadn't realised just how serious the rationing was for you. I knew it was bad but apparently it's even worse than I thought.'

'What we're allowed is pitiful.'

'Here,' he said, handing her a full glass. He then raised his own in a toast. 'Cheers!'

'To the end of the war.'

'I'll certainly drink to that.'

Holly closed her eyes in appreciation. The wine was delicious.

'Now tuck in,' he said.

'Hmmh!' she murmured as she bit into pâté and biscuit.

Peter slowly sipped his wine, watching her eat. She really was a pretty young thing, he thought. There was something different about her, though he couldn't have said what. He wondered what her fiancé had been like, the one killed at Dunkirk.

'Eat as much as you wish, I'm not particularly hungry,' he told her.

'You must be after that walk.'

'No, not really.' That was a fib; he wanted to ensure she ate her fill. And anything left he'd have her take home with her.

Holly polished off the pâté and started on the sandwiches, trying not to be bad mannered by wolfing them down. When her glass was half empty Peter topped it up again.

'Tell me about Edinburgh,' she said.

Peter lay back, supporting himself on an elbow. He was enjoying watching her eat and delighted the hotel had provided such an excellent meal.

'Like your Jersey, Edinburgh is a beautiful place, though in a totally different way. It has very imposing and interesting architecture, some very old, medieval in parts, while there's a large Georgian section which they call New Town.

'The castle dominates the city, towering over Princes Street, the main thoroughfare. And then there's Rose Street . . .' He smiled in memory. 'That runs parallel to Princes Street and is famous for its pubs. I spent many enjoyable nights in Rose Street doing what you call a pub crawl. The people are very kind, very friendly, very hospitable.'

She couldn't resist asking, 'And the women?'

He glanced at her, wondering why she'd asked that. 'Do you mean in general or in my own particular experience?'

Holly blushed. 'Both.'

'I had a few girlfriends when I was there, but nothing serious. I was far too busy studying to cope with that.'

Holly attacked another sandwich, while Peter reflected, sipping his wine.

'As I said, very friendly. Especially when they find out you're a foreigner. I have a great admiration for the people of Edinburgh and the Scots as a race. Hard working, industrious, invariably polite. I would like to return there one day.'

'They might not be so welcoming if the Nazis succeed in invading,' Holly stated quietly, and immediately wished she hadn't.

'True,' he nodded, a pained expression coming across his face.

'The awful thing is,' he went on, equally quietly, 'many of the chaps I knew there must be fighting in this war. I find that extremely sad.'

'Yes,' she agreed.

'And how many of them will be killed, cut off in their prime? That's an even sadder thought.'

'Are you a Nazi?' she asked.

'No.'

She believed that. After all, why should he lie?

'Between you and me, Holly? And I mean that. I'm telling you this in strictest confidence.'

'Between you and me, I swear.'

'I loathe the Nazis and all they stand for.'

'So why are you in the army? Were you conscripted?'

'I joined before that could happen, better that way. I might not agree with the war but I am a German loyal to the Fatherland, no matter who's currently our leader. But above all, I'm a doctor and they're always badly needed in any war.'

Holly dished herself out some salad and a generous portion of ripe camembert. 'Where did you practise in Germany?'

'A place called Geislingen which isn't far from Stuttgart. I worked there with my father who's also a doctor. We're what you call GPs.'

Holly nodded.

'It was he who suggested I study at Edinburgh. We have many fine medical schools in Germany of course, but my father always wanted me to go to Edinburgh, which he is convinced is the best medical school in the world. And perhaps it is, it's certainly one of the best.'

'I see,' she murmured.

'It's because of my father I'm returning to Germany next week.'

She stopped eating to stare at him.

'My father is seriously ill, which is why I've been granted compassionate leave,' he explained.

'I am sorry, Peter. You will be back though?'

He shrugged. 'Who knows? I could easily be posted elsewhere. In fact the chances are fairly high that I will.'

She was going to miss him, she realised. Not just for the scotch and coffee, but for himself. She'd come to think highly of Peter Schmidt.

'When next week?'

'Monday. I'm flying to Berlin and taking the train from there.'

Suddenly she wasn't enjoying the food as much as she had, though she continued to eat.

'I only hope they don't send me to the Russian Front; it's dreadful there apparently.'

'I hope so too.'

He glanced at her, and smiled. 'Thank you, Holly.'

'Is your mother alive?'

'Oh yes. Very much so. She worries about her two sons a great deal, my brother more than me. Being in the Luftwaffe, he's in far more danger than myself. Or at least has been up until now.'

'You mean if you're posted to the Russian Front?'

Peter nodded. 'The casualty rate there is extremely high, for all concerned.'

'So we hear on the wireless.'

'A real hell on earth, according to reports.'

'It's a pity you have to go back.'

'I have to, Holly, it is my duty. Besides, I would never forgive myself if my father died and I'd neglected the chance to see him before that happened. It may be I'll be too late, of course, and it may be he'll recover. Whatever, I must return home.'

Holly knew that if she'd been in the same position she'd also have gone home for Dan, no matter the consequences.

'Tell me about your childhood,' she requested.

Which Peter did. A happy story about a loving and caring family.

The two-storey cottage was in a secluded area, out of sight of any other dwelling. There was a garden at the front and what appeared to be a walled garden at the rear. The front garden was in a sorry state from lack of attention.

'I'll bet it's empty,' Holly stated.

'It certainly looks deserted.'

'Probably the owners were amongst those evacuated before your lot arrived.' There were many such houses on the island, simply left when their owners fled.

'It's a pretty little place, isn't it,' Peter said.

'Hmmh.' Then, 'I wonder if it's been looted?'

It was an appalling and shameful fact that the majority of those houses abandoned had been systematically looted by those who'd stayed behind, often by neighbours and so-called friends, and often before those leaving the Island were even aboard ship.

'Shall we look inside and see?' Peter suggested.

Holly was undecided, it just didn't seem right somehow. It had been someone's home, after all. 'I wonder if that's a vegetable garden at the rear?' she said. 'If so I wouldn't mind helping myself to whatever's there.'

'Good idea,' Peter enthused.

The front door wasn't locked and opened straight away when he turned the handle. They found themselves in a white-painted hall with a sitting room leading off to the left, kitchen to the right.

'What a charming room,' Peter smiled when they entered the sitting room. It too was painted white with a number of black beams criss-crossing the ceiling. The fireplace was large and constructed of brick.

'Doesn't appear to have been looted,' Holly declared, glancing around.

There were two magnificent brass standard lamps, the larger of the two curving into the shape of a dragon from which a multicoloured Tiffany shade dangled. On one of the walls was an ornate wooden pendulum clock, now stopped.

'I wonder who lived here?' Holly murmured.

'Perhaps they still do, and we're intruding? They might be out to work or something.'

Holly shook her head. 'Smell the air; it's stale. No one's been here in a long time. No, it's abandoned all right.'

Peter thought how pleasant it would be to live in this cottage.

The kitchen, which they went into next, was well appointed, dominated by an inglenook fireplace which Peter thought delightful. There was a large dog basket in the centre of the fireplace with stacks of logs on either side. In the sink were several dirty plates now green with mould.

Holly pointed to those. 'That confirms it. Whoever lived here is long gone.'

'Shall we go upstairs?'

Holly hesitated. 'Do you think we should?'

He shrugged. 'I don't see why not. Anyway, I'm curious.'

There were three bedrooms, one a child's. In the main bedroom discarded clothes were strewn everywhere, on the bed, on the floor, on top of a chest of drawers, one drawer of which had been pulled right out and left like that.

'They must have left in a hurry,' Holly commented.

Peter went to the window and glanced out. 'You were right about the rear being a vegetable garden. There should be plenty down there for you to take home.'

Holly discovered an opened envelope addressed to a Mr and Mrs Vardon, Half Hidden.

'The cottage is called Half Hidden,' she told Peter.

He laughed softly. 'I would have thought Whole Hidden would have been more appropriate.'

Holly smiled in agreement. He was quite right, that's exactly what the cottage was.

They returned downstairs, through the back door into the vegetable garden, where Holly exclaimed in delight at what she saw.

'I'll see if I can find a bag or something,' Peter said, appearing again several minutes later carrying two substantial-sized leather shopping bags.

Soon the bags were bulging with a variety of vegetables and fruit.

They were about to leave Half Hidden when Holly had another thought. The kitchen cupboards were a treasure trove of canned goods of all sorts.

'What a find!' she breathed. 'This'll keep Dad and me going for ages.'

Peter frowned, the problem being to get it all back to St Helier. Then he had a suggestion which Holly approved of. They'd take a few cans now and hide the remainder, returning for them another day. Hiding them in case someone else ransacked the place in the meantime. They hid the cans in the vegetable garden, concealing them beneath a pile of rotting material.

'What a day,' Holly beamed to Peter as they continued on towards town, he carrying the shopping bags, she the wicker basket.

On the outskirts of St Helier they swopped.

'Are you sure you can manage those by yourself?' Peter asked anxiously, knowing how heavy they were.

'Don't you worry about me, I'll be all right.' She paused. 'Thank you, Peter, I had a wonderful time.'

'Me too. I could take those to your door if you wish?'

She quickly shook her head. 'No, no, I'll be fine, I assure you.'

He touched her lightly on the arm. 'See you at the hospital tomorrow.'

'See you then, Peter.'

' 'Bye now.'

' 'Bye.'

He watched her struggling off down the road, he as pleased as she was by their finds at Half Hidden.

He whistled happily all the way back to the Grand.

*

'What's for tea?' Dan inquired, rubbing his hands. He stopped rubbing and gawped when she told him.

'You're joking!'

'Nope.'

'But . . . how?'

His face broke into a huge smile when she told him. 'And you say there's more?'

'That's right.'

'Well, I'll be . . .' He broke off and shook his head in delighted amazement.

Tea was vegetable soup, after which there was tinned beef stew, spuds and carrots. That followed by the remainder of the camembert from the picnic.

'A feast,' Dan declared at the end of it all. 'A veritable feast!' The remaining cans were secreted under the floorboards in case of another unexpected call by the Germans checking on hoarding.

'I've a surprise for you,' Holly declared to Elspeth whom she'd dropped by to visit.

'Oh?'

She decided to tease her friend a little. 'What could I give you that you'd appreciate most?'

Elspeth frowned. 'I've no idea.'

'Come on, have a guess!'

Elspeth glanced at Terry sitting by the fireplace. 'Don't look to me for an answer,' he grinned.

'A fortnight in the Bahamas?'

Holly laughed. 'Be serious.'

'Some new French knickers? Mine are becoming decidedly the worse for wear and as you know you can't buy any in the shops.'

'Not knickers, French or otherwise,' Holly replied.

'The news that I'm pregnant?' That still hadn't occurred though both Elspeth and Terry desperately wanted a child.

'Here, steady on!' Terry exclaimed, colouring a little. He fiddled with his glasses in embarrassment.

'One last try,' Holly said to Elspeth.

Elspeth's face crinkled in thought. 'Is the surprise in there?' she queried, indicating the shopping bag Holly had placed on the table.

Holly nodded.

'Hmmh,' Elspeth murmured. 'Well, it can't be anything from the black market as I know you and your father refuse to use it.'

'True,' Holly confirmed.

'Oh, I give in. I'm hopeless at this sort of thing.'

A smiling Holly picked up the bag and handed it to her friend.

Elspeth screeched when she opened the bag and saw its contents. 'Holly! This is brilliant. But where did you get it all from?'

Elspeth took the bag over to Terry. 'Look!'

'Good grief!' he exclaimed.

Holly then explained about Half Hidden, leaving out Peter's participation, merely saying she'd come across the cottage while out for a long walk.

'And as my best friend I thought it only right to share my good fortune with you.'

Elspeth laid the bag back on the table and hugged Holly. 'You're a diamond, Holly, a real diamond. We can't thank you enough for this.'

Holly thought of the trip she and Dan had made out to Half Hidden to recover what had been hidden in the vegetable garden. It was during the walk home she'd had the idea of sharing with Elspeth and Terry, Dan agreeing when she'd put it to him.

'I've got some tea in, proper tea, that is. Will you have a cup?' Elspeth asked.

'Please.'

Elspeth embraced Holly a second time. 'Thanks.'

'You're welcome.'

Dan snapped off the wireless, upset by the news broadcast. The Nazi noose was tightening round Stalingrad where intense fighting was taking place. It seemed to be only a matter of time before Stalingrad fell, after which speculation was that Moscow was next on the list.

Holly thought of Peter off to Germany that Monday, and his fear that he might be sent to the Russian Front at the end of his leave. She hoped and prayed he wasn't.

'It's just not going well for the Allies,' Dan declared, shaking his head. 'If only the Americans would come into the war.'

'Do you think they will?'

'I'm sure Roosevelt wants to, but would the American people willingly follow him? That's another thing entirely.'

It would be wonderful if the Americans came in on the side of the Allies, Holly reflected. What a blow that would be to the Nazis, and what a major boost for Britain.

'We're not doing well in the Western Desert either, according to reports,' Holly stated.

'No,' Dan agreed. He made a fist and smashed it into the palm of his other hand. 'Damn Hitler and his cronies to everlasting hell!' He sighed, and flopped into a chair. 'I've been thinking about those logs at Half Hidden. We could certainly use those here when winter comes, for sure as eggs are eggs there's going to be precious little coal or wood to be had.' They'd discovered that there were not only the logs in the kitchen but more in a shed outside.

'It's getting them here,' Dan mused.

'Perhaps you'll think of something.'

'Perhaps. But it's a poser.'

It was a problem he never did solve.

'Nurse Morgan, wait!'

A startled Holly stopped outside the hospital, on the way home at the end of her shift. She turned to see Peter running towards her. What was this all about? She glanced nervously around, noting several other members of staff were within hearing range.

'You forgot your parcel,' Peter smiled, thrusting it into her hands.

This was news to her. What parcel? She hadn't had a parcel to leave anywhere.

He wagged a finger at her. 'Silly girl. You might have had it stolen.'

'Thank you, Dr Schmidt,' a bewildered Holly replied.

He then startled her further by clicking his heels and giving her a bob of the head. Having done that, he turned on his heel and strode back into the hospital.

*

Of course I should have known, she thought, on opening the parcel and the box it contained. Inside the box were two bottles of scotch and a large bag of coffee. It was a parting gift from Peter, the farce outside the hospital his way of getting it to her.

She smiled, thinking him a lovely, thoughtful man. She was going to miss Peter Schmidt.

Chapter 8

'What are you doing on your week off?' Elspeth asked Holly. As luck would have it they were both having the same week off together.

'Having lots of late lie-ins for a start.'

Elspeth laughed. 'Me too. Lazy as can be.'

'Besides that, I'm going on holiday.'

Elspeth stared at her friend. 'Holiday! Where?'

'Well, on the island obviously. Do you remember that cottage where I got the food from, Half Hidden? I've decided to go there. I could use a break away from St Helier and that place is just lying empty.'

'What about your father?'

Holly shrugged. 'He's quite capable of looking after himself for a while. So that isn't a problem.'

'Hmmh,' Elspeth murmured, face crinkling in thought.

'There's everything there I need, sheets and so on. All I have to do is move in and make myself at home. Providing it hasn't been looted in the meanwhile that is, in which case I'll simply come back again.'

'Won't you be scared there by yourself?'

'Elspeth! I'm a big girl now. Being by myself doesn't worry me in the slightest.'

'And it's a lovely cottage, you said?'

'Beautiful. Pe—' She broke off, having been about to mention Peter's name.

'Yes?'

'Nothing,' Holly said, shaking her head.

They walked a little way in silence. 'How would you feel about me coming with you?' Elspeth asked eventually.

'Would Terry agree to that?'

'Terry will agree all right if he knows what's good for him,' Elspeth laughed in reply.

It seemed Elspeth wore the trousers in that relationship, Holly thought. Not that it surprised her really, knowing Elspeth as she did. 'Will he be able to cope?

'I don't see why not. Anyway, his mother can pop in and check he's OK. She'll enjoy that.'

'Then that's what we'll do.'

Elspeth giggled. 'I can't wait to see Terry's face when I tell him I'm buggering off for a week.' She winked at Holly. 'But I'll make it up to him before I go and when I get home again. That'll put the smile back on his cheeky face.'

They began making arrangements.

There wasn't any gas or electricity at the cottage but the girls had found two storm lanterns and a large metal container of oil to refill them. They'd also discovered a number of candles so there wasn't going to be any problem about light.

Elspeth rubbed her stomach appreciatively. 'I'll say one thing about this place, it's certainly lucky where food is concerned. That supper was yummy.'

On arriving at Half Hidden they'd come across a chicken pecking away in the front garden. God alone knew where it had come from, they certainly didn't. There had certainly been no sign of it or any other chickens during Holly's previous visits.

Elspeth had immediately pounced on the fowl, wringing its neck there and then. Later they'd plucked it and roasted it over a log fire in the inglenook, supplementing the meat with some late vegetables they'd turned up out back.

'Hmmh,' Holly murmured in agreement, thinking how wonderfully full and relaxed she felt. This was the ticket.

'And more tomorrow. And after that, and another root round in that vegetable garden, we can make soup with the carcass.'

Holly yawned and stretched, starting to feel drowsy. They'd remade the bed in the main bedroom where they intended sleeping together.

'And I got my French knickers, even if they weren't new,' Elspeth laughed. Replacing clothes had become a major problem on the island so both girls had gone through Mrs Vardon's wardrobe, clearing up in the process, looking for anything they could appropriate. That was the word Holly had used, rather than stealing, in justifying their action. As Elspeth had pointed out, if they didn't take whatever there was then someone else might happen along who would.

'And me a winter coat,' Holly said. The coat was slightly too large for her, Mrs Vardon having been a bigger size, but that hardly mattered in the circumstances. The coat would keep her nice and warm, which was what was required. Her own winter coat had needed replacing before the Occupation and after that had occurred there was no chance.

'Holly?'

'Hmmh?'

'Can I say something, best friends and all that?'

Holly nodded.

'Don't you think it's time you started getting out and about a bit more. You're either at work or at home from what I can make out.'

'I go for walks, bike rides,' Holly protested.

'You know what I mean.'

Holly sighed. 'It's too soon yet, Elspeth.'

'You can't grieve for ever, Holly. You're a young woman, you must begin living properly again.'

Holly found herself irritated, but tried not to show it. She didn't reply.

'There's that dance at the hospital in a fortnight's time. Terry and I are going, why don't you come with us?'

Holly shook her head.

'You've always been an obstinate female, Holly Morgan, do you know that?'

'I don't want to go to any dance.'

'Tony will be there.'

Holly stared blankly at her friend. 'Tony who?'

'You met him at our wedding, remember?'

'Oh yes!'

'He fancied you.'

'Well, I didn't fancy him.'

'He's great company, Terry says.'

'I don't need company, thank you very much. At least, not the male variety. My father suffices for that.'

'You need to be taken out of yourself,' Elspeth persisted.

Holly had an idea which made her smile. 'Anyway, how do you know I haven't been meeting someone?' She was thinking of Peter Schmidt.

Elspeth's face lit up. 'Are you?'

'Maybe I have been. That's for me to know and you to wonder about.'

'Why, you sly cow!'

'I didn't say I was, mind you, only that I might have been.'

'*Might have been*. Does that mean it's over?'

Holly shrugged. 'Perhaps.'

'But why all the secrecy?'

'There could be reasons.'

Elspeth sat up straight in sudden alarm. 'He wasn't a bloody German, was he?'

Damn! Holly inwardly swore, feeling her face colour slightly. 'Of course not!' she retorted sharply. 'What do you take me for, a Jerrybag?'

'I should hope not. Then why the secrecy? Is he married, is that it?'

'I wouldn't go out with a married man. I'm not like that.'

'Hmmh,' Elspeth snorted.

Holly rose. 'Anyway, it's bed for me. I'm dog tired.'

'Not before you tell me who you've been seeing.' Her tone changed to a pleading one. 'Please? I tell you everything about me after all.'

'There's no one,' Holly stated firmly. 'I was only teasing to get you off my back.'

Elspeth wasn't certain whether or not she believed that. But Holly remained adamant it had only been a tease.

Later, in bed, Holly thought of Peter Schmidt. A single walk was hardly going out with a person. A walk she'd only agreed to because he'd been so kind to her and Dan.

'Holly,' Elspeth whispered urgently. 'There's someone downstairs. I can hear them moving about.' It was their third night at Half Hidden.

'Eh?'

Elspeth repeated herself and this time Holly came wide awake. Elspeth was right, there was someone downstairs.

'Who do you think it is?' Elspeth further whispered.

'It could be looters or Germans. It certainly isn't the owners back to reclaim their property.'

Elspeth shivered with fright, praying that it was looters and not Germans. Who knew what the latter might do? Rape was always a possibility. And worse, rape and then their throats slit afterwards.

'Shall we light the candle?' she queried.

'No. Just lie still and they might go away.'

Elspeth didn't think there was much hope of that, but what was the alternative.

Holly bit her lip. This was terrible. The same thoughts that had gone through Elspeth's mind were also going through hers. She considered escape via the window, but that was a considerable drop and she couldn't remember what lay beneath. She'd have a look, she thought, and was about to get out when there was the sound of footsteps on the stairs.

Elspeth clutched her in alarm. 'They're coming up,' she whispered.

Christ! Holly thought.

The door swung open to reveal a shape behind torchlight whose beam now played over them.

'Who is it?' Holly queried nervously.

'No need to be scared, miss. We're British commandos.'

Both Holly and Elspeth sagged with relief.

'We're lost, miss, and stopped here hoping to be given directions. We don't mean you any harm.'

Holly took a deep breath. 'How many of you are there?'

'Four, miss. One with a badly twisted ankle.'

'And you're lost?'

'We became separated from the major and captain; they've got the compasses and maps. It's a right old cock-up. Anyone else in the house, miss?'

'No, just the pair of us.'

The commando nodded.

'Tell you what,' Holly said. 'You go back downstairs and we'll join you in a moment.'

'Right, miss.' And with that the commando closed the door again.

'There aren't any maps in the house that I'm aware of,' Elspeth declared, scrambling from the bed and reaching for her dressing gown.

'Nor me,' said Holly, doing the same.

They found the four commandos in the sitting room, three standing, one seated. The one seated was rubbing his ankle. The commandos had already lit both storm lanterns.

'Where are you headed for?' Holly demanded.

The commando, who'd come to their bedroom, whom she recognised by his voice, told her.

'Well, you're going roughly in the right direction.'

'Let me see that ankle,' Elspeth said, kneeling beside the seated commando. 'I'm a nurse. We both are.'

'Bleeding nuisance,' the man in the chair said, meaning his ankle.

'How did it happen?'

'Tripped over something in the dark. It's pitch black out there.'

'What are you doing on the Island anyway?' Holly queried.

The first commando pulled a face. 'Can't say, miss. Secret. Besides, what you don't know can't hurt you.'

'I understand.'

'You got a map, miss?'

Holly shook her head.

'Then if you can explain the way to us we'll be off again.'

Elspeth sat back on her haunches. 'This foot's badly swollen. If I take the boot off you'll never get it back on.'

The man in the chair grunted. 'I'll manage the way it is. Just have to.'

'There is a walking stick in the kitchen. That should be some help,' Holly suggested.

'I'll get it,' Elspeth said, and left the room.

'Those directions, miss?' the first one asked again.

Holly's mind was racing. 'It's pitch black out there?'

'As the Earl of Hell's waistcoat, miss. There's a blanket of low-lying cloud which made this an ideal night for our operation. The night turned out just as forecast.'

The directions were complicated. If the night had been otherwise they could probably have followed them, but as it was she could just imagine them getting lost again, stumbling around in the dark. While this was going through her mind she noticed a patch of blood on the first commando's leg.

'Are you hurt also?' she queried, pointing to the patch.

'No, miss, that isn't mine. There was a fight, you see, sodding Jerries everywhere. That was how we came to be separated from the major and captain. We're only hoping they're all right.'

'There was no time to regroup,' one of the two who'd so far remained silent explained. He grinned. 'I reckon we downed a good dozen of them, maybe more.'

Holly made a decision. 'I'll take you to where you want to go.'

'Miss!' the first commando exclaimed.

'You can't, Holly. The curfew,' Elspeth, who'd returned with the walking stick, objected.

'Bugger the curfew.'

'It would be risky, miss. The alarm will have been raised by now. Bound to be lots of patrols out.'

'I'll take my chance,' Holly stated firmly. 'Now wait here while I get dressed, then we'll be off.'

'I don't like it, miss,' the first declared.

'Neither do I particularly. But I sincerely doubt you'll find the way on your own.'

'This is very good of you, miss,' the man in the chair smiled.

A worried Elspeth chewed a nail, wondering if she too should volunteer.

Holly shook her head when Elspeth offered to accompany them. 'There's no need for both of us to stick our necks out. One is sufficient. Now,' she swung on her heel, 'I won't be long.'

Elspeth hurried after her friend.

A grim-faced Holly began quickly to dress, thinking she'd wear the appropriated winter coat because it was dark coloured. Then she paused as it struck her whom the first commando reminded her of. She'd thought there was something familiar about him, now the penny had dropped. Facially he bore a resemblance to Martin. Not a tremendous similarity, but enough.

'You will take care, won't you?' Elspeth queried anxiously.

Holly nodded. 'Of course.'

Elspeth wrung her hands.

'If anything . . . *does* happen, explain to Dad, will you?'

'Oh, Holly!' Elspeth wailed.

'None of that now. I'll be fine, I'm certain of it.'

When Holly had finished dressing she went back downstairs, put on her coat and rejoined the commandos. 'Right then,' she said briskly.

The seated commando hauled himself upright to lean heavily on his stick.

The commandos slipped from the cottage, Elspeth giving Holly a warm embrace before she too left.

'Follow me,' Holly instructed, praying that she wasn't going to lose her way. The commandos hadn't been exaggerating when they'd said it was pitch black outside.

Their progress was slow on account of the man with the twisted ankle. He had his Sten gun slung over a shoulder while the others carried theirs at the ready.

'Did the other girl call you Holly?' the first commando asked in a whisper.

'Yes.'

'Pretty name.'

'Thank you.'

'Mine's Bill.'

'How are you getting off the Island, Bill?'

'We came ashore in two boats which are hidden. They'll take us out to a sub that's waiting for us.'

'What about the major and captain? If they've arrived there first will they go without you?'

'No, they'll hang on till nearly dawn. To wait any longer would jeopardise the submarine.'

'And you'll do the same, wait for them if they're not there?'

'That's right, Holly.'

They came to a stile which they crossed, then made their way along the side of a high hedge. Holly was purposefully keeping off the roads on the assumption that's where the majority of German patrols would be. Doing this made their journey more difficult, but safer.

They skirted a farmhouse, giving it a wide berth because of dogs, at Bill's suggestion. Then a shallow stream had to be waded through.

'How are you doing, Ted?' Bill asked the man with the twisted ankle when they reached the other side and halted for a quick breather.

'OK. I'll survive.'

'If it gets really bad we'll take it in turns to piggy-back you.'

'That won't be necessary. I'll get there under my own steam.'

'Good chap.'

Holly was frowning in concentration, getting her bearings. This wasn't an area she knew well but she had an excellent sense of direction and knew the way they should be heading.

'Isn't that cove fenced off with barbed wire?' she queried when they'd resumed walking.

'We cut our way through. Didn't take long with the special gear we brought along.'

They emerged into a narrow lane which Holly decided to take a chance on using. Bill briefly flashed his torch to glance at his watch.

'How are we doing?' she inquired.

'That depends on how far we've left to go.'

'Another mile at least. Maybe a mile and a half.'

Bill grunted. 'We'll be all right. What about you getting back?'

'If I don't make it by dawn I might hide until after curfew. I'm not sure, I'll just have to play it by ear.'

'I wish there was some way of us knowing that you got home safely, but of course there isn't.'

'That isn't my home.' She then explained about her and Elspeth having a holiday break in the abandoned Half Hidden.

'Lucky for us you decided to take that holiday break,' Bill chuckled.

Suddenly Bill stopped dead and whipped a hand over Holly's mouth. The other three halted behind them.

Holly heard it then, the low murmur of voices. They have to belong to Germans, she thought. There again, it could be the major and captain.

Bill went down into a squat, pulling Holly with him. He motioned her to stay there, and Ted to do the same. He then gestured for the other two to follow him. The three moved off like ghosts to be swiftly swallowed up in the darkness.

A few minutes later there was the sound of a scuffle, then silence.

'That's put paid to them,' Bill announced to Holly in a whisper when the three returned as silently as they'd left.

Holly shivered. 'What did you do to them?'

He tapped the black-handled knife strapped to his thigh. 'I doubt they even had time to be surprised.'

'How many . . . were there?' Holly queried, and swallowed.

'Two, having a crafty smoke.'

Two men dead, just like that, Holly thought, and swallowed again.

'Let's move on,' Bill instructed, and they continued on their way.

Holly glanced sideways at Bill, wondering how many men he'd killed altogether. It certainly didn't seem to have perturbed him.

'Were you at Dunkirk?' she asked quietly.

'Yeah.'

'It was horrendous there, I understand.'

'Fairly. Why do you ask?'

'I had a fiancé called Martin, another Islander. He died at Dunkirk.'

There was a few moments' pause, then Bill said, with genuine sympathy in his voice, 'I'm sorry.'

'I was thinking back at the cottage that you look a bit like him.'

'Really?'

'There's a resemblance.'

Bill didn't reply to that.

Off in the distance headlights appeared, slicing through the darkness. 'Probably another patrol,' Bill whispered.

Suddenly the cloud blanket broke and the moon shone through, which was useful for Holly as it allowed her to verify where they were. She changed direction slightly, veering to their left.

The moon was swallowed up again, which pleased Bill and the other commandos.

'Not far now,' Holly whispered sometime later. By her reckoning they were almost there.

They emerged on to open scrubland which led directly down to the cove. This they snaked across till they arrived at the large rolls of barbed wire.

Bill did a visual check of their surroundings before flicking on his torch and proceeding along the length of wire until they came to the section he and the others had earlier cut their way through.

'This is it,' Bill stated to Holly.

'I'm coming down to see you off.'

'There's no need for that,' he protested.

'I want to, Bill. I've come this far and now want to see you safely away.'

He glanced at his watch. 'You really should start right back.'

'I'm coming down and that's that,' she insisted.

He sighed. 'Suit yourself.'

He smiled when she replied, 'I usually do.'

The cut wire was heaved aside and the five of them slipped through. 'We'll leave it like that for you,' Bill declared to Holly as they proceeded further down the beach.

Two shadowy figures detached themselves from a cluster of rocks. 'Tomkins?'

'Here, Major.'

So, Holly thought in delight. The major and captain, for that's who his companion must be, had made it after all. The only casualty of the sortie was Ted with his twisted ankle.

'Who's this?' the major demanded with a frown on joining them. Bill explained about Holly.

'Jolly good show, miss,' the major declared, shaking Holly by the hand. 'Without maps and compasses I feared this lot would never find their way back in time.'

'We wouldn't have without Holly,' Bill stated.

The major ordered the boats brought out of concealment, after which he and the captain had a swift confab. The captain went to the water's edge where he flashed a signal from his torch. There was a single brief flash in reply.

'God save the navy,' the major smiled to Holly.

She walked with the major to where the captain was overseeing the launching of the boats.

'I can't thank you enough, miss,' the major said to Holly when that was completed.

'Let's just say I'm pleased I was able to do my bit.'

'You've certainly done that.'

Ted and the two others came up to Holly and profusely thanked her, Bill lingering a little behind. Then it was his turn.

'Thank you, Holly, for everything,' he said, shaking her hand.

She pecked him on the cheek. 'You look after yourself, Bill Tomkins.'

He touched the spot she'd kissed, remembering what she'd told him about her dead fiancé. He understood the reason for the kiss.

'Now be careful on the way back.'

'I will.'

'Goodbye then, Holly.'

'Goodbye, Bill. And good luck.'

The party clambered into the boats, pushing them further out into the water as they did. Paddles dipped, and they glided away.

When they were gone, Holly turned and returned to the wire.

'Thank God you're safe!' Elspeth exclaimed as Holly sauntered into the cottage. 'Where have you been; it's almost noon? Did they get off OK?'

Holly laughed. 'They got away OK. The major and captain were there waiting for them.'

'And what about you?'

'I was halfway back when it started to get light. I thought it best in the circumstances to hide out until after curfew, which I did in a ditch.' She laughed again. 'You won't believe it, but I nodded right off and only woke up a short while ago.'

Elspeth glanced at Holly's coat which bore evidence of her hours in the ditch. 'I've been up since you left, worrying myself sick about you. I was beginning to think the worst had happened.'

Holly's face clouded. 'They killed two Germans on the way. Knifed them.'

Elspeth paled. 'Did you see it happen?'

'No, nor did I see the bodies.'

'How ghastly,' Elspeth breathed.

'It was. Bill said they probably didn't even have time to be surprised.'

'Bill?'

'The one who came into our bedroom. His name is Bill Tomkins and I thought he looked rather like Martin. Didn't you?'

Elspeth shook her head. 'That never struck me.'

'Well, it did me.' She paused, then added. 'He was nice. I liked him.

'I wonder what their mission was?' Holly mused, hanging up her coat.

That was something she and Elspeth never did find out.

Chapter 9

With a lump in her throat Holly stared at Martin's engagement ring nestling in its box. Then she gazed up at the silver-framed photograph of them together. Taking the ring from the box she brought it to her lips and closed her eyes.

Letting out a heartfelt sigh she opened her eyes again. Elspeth was right, she told herself. This just wouldn't do. And with that she made a decision.

She returned the ring to its box and snapped the lid shut. Rising from her bed on which she'd been sitting she crossed to her chest of drawers, knelt and opened the bottom drawer.

She put the box at the very back, underneath the clothes there. And shut the drawer again.

Now what could she wear?

Holly didn't tell Elspeth she intended going to the hospital dance in case she changed her mind at the last moment. Now she was there and the hall abuzz with conversation, the band having taken a break. She spotted Elspeth with Terry, and waved.

They immediately came over. 'Holly!' Elspeth exclaimed. 'This is a surprise.'

'I thought, why miss all the fun. So here I am.'

'It's good to see you,' Terry declared. 'I must say, you look fabulous. A real bobbydazzler.'

Holly laughed. 'Flattery will get you everywhere. It's just an old rag that I've re-made.' The dress in question was blue with white polka dots. There was white lace round the v-shaped collar which Holly had added herself. She'd toyed with the idea of adding lace to the cuffs but in the end had decided against that. The lace was taken from an old pair of curtains that she'd cannibalised.

She was about to say this was just like the old days, but stopped herself in time. Of course it wasn't. Martin would have been there in the old days.

I must put him firmly out of my mind for now, she chided herself. She hadn't come to mope but enjoy herself.

'Pity there's no bar,' Terry complained. 'There isn't even beer available.' By now the Island, for the Islanders that was, and apart from private stocks, was almost completely dry. The Germans, who'd taken over the breweries, weren't going without, however.

'The horrors of war,' Elspeth teased him, winking at Holly.

'Darned tooting.'

'Why don't you ask Holly up for the next dance,' Elspeth suggested to him, noting that the band had returned and were taking up their instruments again.

'May I have the pleasure, Miss Morgan?' Terry requested, making Holly smile when he gave her a mock bow.

'I'd be delighted, Mr Le Var.'

What a change in Terry, Holly thought as he took her by the arm and led her on to the floor. Where was the shy young man they'd originally met? Elspeth and marriage had wrought wonders with him.

Holly spotted many faces she knew. There was Meggy Hill with her new young man whom she'd been raving about earlier in the day. And there was Helen Mason with someone Holly didn't recognise.

They had two dances together, then returned to Elspeth who was deep in conversation with a man whose back was to them. When he turned round, Holly saw that it was Tony, Terry's cousin.

'Hello,' he smiled. 'Remember me?'

'Of course.'

'Tony.'

'We met at Elspeth and Terry's reception.'

'It's been a while. I thought I might have bumped into you in town sometime, but never have.'

'How's the potato business?'

'Boring,' he replied, pulling a face. 'Farming is.'

'Have you ever considered doing anything else?'

'Not really,' he shrugged. 'It's what my family do and have done time out of mind.'

He has an easy manner about him, Holly thought. Quite a personable chap.

'Come on you,' Elspeth said, grabbing Terry. 'It's my turn now for the light fantastic.'

'Would you care to dance?' Tony asked Holly.

'Certainly.'

'I was sorry to hear about your fiancé,' Tony said when she was in his arms. 'Terry explained about him after their honeymoon.'

Holly didn't reply.

'It must have been a terrible blow for you.'

'It was,' she replied softly.

'Do you mind talking about it? Or would you rather I dropped the subject?'

'I don't mind. Though I'd rather not.'

'I understand.'

They danced for a little in silence, then he asked her about her job. The ward she was on, the type of cases dealt with there.

They applauded at the end of the number.

'Will you stay up?' he queried.

She didn't see why not, and so accepted, which clearly pleased him.

'The trouble with the curfew is you have to leave everything so early,' Tony said some time later. They'd danced quite a bit together though Holly had been up with other men.

'There's a while yet,' she replied.

'Not if I'm going to walk you home and then get to Elspeth and Terry's before the witching hour.'

Walk her home? She wasn't at all sure about that.

'Can I?'

'I don't think so, Tony.'

His face fell. 'What if I say pretty please?'

Where was the harm, after all?

'Well?'

'All right then.'

He was delighted. 'Smashing! We'll collect our coats at the end of this number.'

Elspeth grinned like the proverbial Cheshire cat when they told her and Terry they were off.

They stopped outside Holly's front door. 'Thank you,' she said, extending a hand.

'I was rather hoping for a kiss?'

She dropped her head to stare at the pavement. 'I'm not ready for that yet, Tony. I'm sorry.'

He bit back his disappointment. He'd really taken a shine to Holly Morgan. 'Can I see you again?'

'I don't know,' she mumbled.

'I'd like to very much. And I do appreciate . . . your situation about Martin. That was his name, wasn't it?'

'Yes.'

'I'll tell you what, I'm coming into St Helier next Saturday anyway. I'll be at the junction of King Street and Queen Street at two o'clock. If you turn up, great. If you don't . . . well, you don't. Shall we leave it like that?'

Holly nodded.

'Goodnight then.'

'Goodnight.'

Ten past two, his watch said. She wasn't coming. 'Blast!' he muttered. He'd been so desperately hoping she would.

And then, suddenly, she was hurrying towards him.

'Sorry I'm late,' she apologised. 'I got held up.' The latter was a lie. A dozen times she'd changed her mind during the course of the morning. Deciding, yes she would go. Then a short while later, no she wouldn't. And then yes again. Halfway to their rendezvous she'd stopped, filled with indecision. It was because of

Emma Blair

that stop, and a little aimless wander, that she was late.

Tony beamed at her. 'That doesn't matter. You're here, which is all that counts.'

'Have you done whatever it was you had to do?'

'Oh yes.' He remembered what was in his pocket which he now produced and handed to her. 'A present.'

Holly looked at the small paper bag, wondering what it contained. Whatever, it was hard. 'For me?'

'It's nothing much. Just a little something.'

She opened the bag and glanced inside, her face lighting up at what she saw.

Tony placed a finger over his lips. 'Don't say what it is out loud.'

The present was soap, a large blue bar of it. Soap was another commodity almost impossible to get on the island, the shops having long since run out of it.

'How?' she queried.

He winked. 'I have my ways and means. You'd be surprised what we farmers can lay our hands on.'

She was intrigued.

'Potatoes,' he whispered.

She understood then. It was barter. 'But I thought the Germans accounted for everything produced?' she further queried in a low voice.

Tony laughed. 'They try, and very hard too. But, eh . . . we have our methods of outwitting their so-called famed efficiency. Farmers are naturally devious. It's a trait we're born with.'

'I can't thank you enough, Tony. Really.'

'Don't mention it.'

It was awful washing with only water, Holly reflected. There were some substitutes around, but nothing that really worked. This was a real treat.

She tucked the soap away safely in her coat pocket, the same coat she'd appropriated from Half Hidden and which had been brushed clean after her night in the ditch.

'I was thinking,' said Tony. 'Normally I'd suggest lunch, or a drink in a pub, but both are out. There is a concert in the park, however, that we could go to.'

110

Holly had heard of these concerts given by the Germans but had never been to one. 'Sounds fine.'

'Good. They've already started so we'll get along.'

As they walked side by side he wanted to take her hand but doubted that would be appreciated. He was going to have to take things slowly with Holly.

'I suppose I'm lucky you're not working today,' he said. 'That never crossed my mind the other night.'

'I'm working every other weekend at the moment. Early on Saturdays, late on Sundays.'

He nodded.

'Elspeth's on today. We're working alternate weekends. What about you?'

'It varies according to the seasons. Harvest time is murder, then you can be going twenty hours a day.'

She murmured in sympathy.

'But it's not too bad right now.'

She had a sudden thought. 'How did you get into St Helier?' For St Mary's was right at the other side of the island.

'I drove.'

'Drove? Where did you get the petrol from?'

'Farmers get a special ration from the Germans. They have to give it to us for deliveries et cetera. We're only supposed to use it for business purposes, but that's something else that can be circumvented. The trick is to make it *look* as though you're on official business.'

'Devious again, eh?' she laughed.

'Exactly.'

They chatted away together until they reached the park where various knots of people had formed, listening to the band. It wasn't a particularly popular attraction, Holly thought. The crowd was smaller than she would have anticipated.

'No seats, I'm afraid,' Tony smiled. 'I'm afraid we'll have to stand.'

'That's all right.'

Again he wanted to take her hand, but didn't.

The music was all of German origin, with the accent heavily on martial tunes which made it rather tedious after a while. Tony suggested a walk and a stop in a café. The ersatz coffee, as always, proved to be revolting.

'I would ask you to the pictures,' he said. 'But as you know they're only showing German propaganda films nowadays and I doubt you'd want to see any of those.'

Holly laughed softly. 'They're pretty dreadful by all account.'

'Therefore, I was thinking, would you like to come out to our house for Sunday lunch?'

She stared at him in astonishment. 'You don't want me sharing your rations. They're small enough as it is.'

Now he laughed. 'You're forgetting, Holly, we're farmers. Understand?'

The penny dropped. 'You mean devious again?'

'Precisely.'

Her mouth watered at the prospect of some decent food for a change.

'You can also meet my family,' he went on. 'I think you'll like them.'

'When do you have in mind?'

'A fortnight tomorrow?'

She nodded. 'OK.'

'I'll pick you up at a quarter to twelve. That all right?'

'Marvellous.'

He whispered conspiratorially, 'It'll have to be in a lorry, I'm afraid. You won't mind that, will you?'

'Not in the least.'

'Then it's a date.'

She winced inwardly at the use of the word date. Getting together was one thing, but a date!

When they parted they shook hands and this time Tony didn't mention a kiss. Nor did he even attempt a peck on the cheek.

'I'm going to hide mine. Bugger the sods!' Dan declared hotly.

'And where would you hide it. Tell me that?' Holly queried. They were referring to their wireless set, the Germans having decreed that all those in private hands had to be handed in.

'I don't know. I'll think of somewhere safe. And if they come pounding on the door I'll simply say I never possessed one.'

Holly sighed. 'Dad, you're a professional man. They'd know you were lying. Someone in your position, you're a teacher after all, is bound to have a wireless. They'd ransack the place looking for it, and haul the pair of us off whether they found it or not. You're not talking sense.'

Dan fumed, reluctantly admitting to himself that Holly was right. It was another case of complying so as not to put her life in danger.

'I'm only surprised they've allowed us to keep our wirelesses for so long,' Holly added.

'It's because the bastards thought they'd have invaded the mainland long before now,' Dan said tightly. 'Except they haven't, which has put a right old spoke in their wheel.'

Dan crossed to their set and caressed it. 'It's going to be galling not knowing what's going on. At least we had that up until now.'

'And the other programmes, they'll be a great loss as well.'

'Blast the Jerries!' Dan muttered.

'You'd better hand it in tomorrow after school.'

Dan flicked the knob that turned on the wireless. 'At least we have one last night.'

'There's always your record collection. Don't forget that,' Holly pointed out, hoping that might take a little of the sting out of the situation.

Dan flung himself into a chair.

'I managed to pick up a jar of jam,' Holly stated.

His face brightened. '*Real* jam?'

She shook her head. 'Something new. Carrot jam.'

'Carrot . . .!'

'It's the latest thing.'

'Bloody hell! What next?'

The war news that evening was good. The United States, which had entered the war the previous December, had routed the Japs at the Battle of Midway.

'This is my mother and father,' Tony declared.

Mr Le Noa was an older version of his son while Mrs Le Noa was short and dumpy with an open smiling face. She wiped her hands on the pinny she was wearing before shaking with Holly.

'How do you do,' Holly said. Mrs Le Noa's keen eyes were quickly appraising her, taking everything in. A fact not lost on Holly.

'I'm fine. And yourself?'

'Fine as well.'

Mr Le Noa's hands were unmistakably those of a farmer, hard and callused. 'Welcome,' he said.

'And these are my sisters, Rosemary, Bunny and Hope.'

Holly shook hands with each in turn. All three girls favoured their mother in build and openness of face. They looked well fed, Holly couldn't help thinking, eyes sliding sideways to where a number of saucepans were bubbling merrily away on a large cooker.

'Something smells delicious,' Holly commented.

'We're having roast pork,' Mrs Le Noa informed her.

Roast pork! Holly's stomach tightened at the thought. 'Sounds wonderful,' she croaked.

'One of the benefits of being a farmer,' Mr Le Noa stated, giving Holly a conspiratorial wink.

'Now, Frank, where are your manners? Offer the girl a drink.'

Mr Le Noa rubbed his hands together. 'We usually have a sherry before Sunday lunch. Or if that doesn't appeal there's cider.'

'A sherry would be lovely,' Holly answered. How long was it since she'd had alcohol? She couldn't remember.

'We don't bother with the parlour most times. We're kitchen people,' Mrs Le Noa explained, crossing to the cooker.

It was a large kitchen, as farm kitchens invariably are, with a warm, cosy feel about it. Holly felt right at home.

'I'll have cider, Dad,' Bunny said.

'And me,' added Rosemary.

'Tony tells us you're a nurse,' Mrs Le Noa said.

Holly nodded. 'That's right.'

Mr Le Noa was busy with the sherry bottle. 'Quite a turn-up for the book him bringing you here like this. Never done that before. Bring a girl to meet us, I mean,' Mr Le Noa said bluntly.

Tony coloured. 'Dad!'

'Well, you haven't, and that's the truth of it.'

Tony looked at Holly and raised his eyebrows, his expression pained.

Holly didn't know what to make of Mr Le Noa's statement. But it alarmed her. Discomforted her too.

'There you are,' said Mr Le Noa, handing Holly a brimming glass. He then swiftly attended to the others.

'Death to all Jerries!' he declared, raising his glass in a toast. 'Particularly that bugger Hitler.'

'Amen,' agreed Mrs Le Noa.

Holly gasped at the size of the joint Mrs Le Noa produced from the oven. It was big enough to feed an army! She could hardly take her eyes off it as it was transferred to a platter and brought to the table.

'There's a story behind that pig,' Mr Le Noa said, sharpening a carving knife on a long steel.

'Oh?'

He laughed. 'You won't believe it. It's had us all in stitches for the last couple of days.'

'You sit down while I dish up. Rosemary, you help,' Mrs Le Noa instructed Holly and her eldest daughter.

Holly sat, Tony having taken her now empty glass from her.

Mr Le Noa attacked the joint, cutting thick slices. As he was doing this, Mrs Le Noa was draining the vegetables while Rosemary made gravy.

'The pig was slaughtered at my neighbours' house,' Mr Le Noa went on, chuckling. 'Which is strictly illegal of course. The Jerries insist on supervising all slaughtering in St Helier. Anyway, the beast had been slaughtered, the evidence cleared away, when a Jerry patrol was sighted making its way to the farmhouse. The neighbour knew what that meant as it happens regularly, a spot check on what's going on. And they're thorough, believe me. There wasn't time to hide the carcass, so what to do?'

Holly was fascinated.

'The Jerries pitched up and the first thing they do is go through the farmhouse itself. Finally they get to a bedroom where the curtains are drawn and the lady of the house is grieving beside a bed with the bedclothes pulled up over a body. "My old mother's died," she tells the Jerries, who are apologetic at intruding in such a moment of grief. The spot check was abandoned after that and off they go after words of sympathy and condolence with the farmer.'

Mr Le Noa's face cracked into a huge smile. 'There was a body under those bedclothes all right, only it wasn't the lady's mother but this here pig!

'Terrific, eh?' Tony said to Holly, who nodded. It most certainly was.

'They laughed and laughed when the Jerries had gone, and so did the rest of us when we heard the tale.'

'Ingenious,' Holly declared.

'It was that. A bit of quick thinking and no mistake.'

Mr Le Noa began placing slices of pork on the top one of a pile of plates.

'Pass that to Holly,' he instructed, handing it to Bunny.

Holly stared at the thick slices of succulent pork as if mesmerised. There was also a large chunk of crackling. It took all her willpower not to get stuck in there and then.

To go with the pork were boiled potatoes, roast potatoes, cabbage, parsnips, beans and boiled onions.

When Mrs Le Noa and Rosemary had joined them at the table Mr Le Noa paused to say a short prayer of thanks.

'Right, set to!' he boomed.

'Hmmh,' Holly murmured in appreciation when she bit into the pork. It was absolutely divine.

Mrs Le Noa eyed her in sympathy, well aware of what conditions were like in St Helier. She'd ensure the girl got something to take back with her.

'More meat?' Mr Le Noa asked Holly a little while later.

She shook her head. 'I'm stuffed, thank you.'

'But you haven't eaten all that much!' he protested.

'I'm not used to a lot of food any more. My stomach must have shrunk.'

'There's sweet for afters,' Mrs Le Noa informed Holly. 'Stewed apples from our own orchard.'

Holly held up a hand. 'I couldn't, Mrs Le Noa. Honestly, I'd explode.'

When the meal was concluded Holly offered to help with the washing up, but the offer was immediately refused.

'Would you like me to show you round the farm?' Tony asked.

'That would be nice.'

'Come on then.'

'That was truly wonderful,' she said when they were outside.

'You'll feel the better for a decent meal.'

Holly couldn't have agreed more.

The farm's main crop was potatoes, but they also grew other things which, under normal circumstances, they varied from year to year.

Tony took her to see their cows, only six of those, the pigs and chickens. They also kept a small number of sheep.

'That's about it,' Tony declared when they'd done the rounds, leaning against a wooden fence to stare pensively out over the fields.

Holly frowned. 'Is something wrong? Your mood's completely changed.'

'Sorry. I was just thinking.'

'About what?'

He sighed. 'I don't know if you've heard, but there's a rumour going the rounds that all men of enlistment age are to be deported to Germany.'

Holly was aghast. 'I hadn't heard.'

'That would mean both Dad and I would be carted off.'

'Does your mum know about this?'

He shook his head. 'Dad does, but we've managed to keep it from her so far.'

Holly thought of her own father. He too would be included if this was true.

'You know how many rumours go about,' she said. 'Half of them, more than that, never amount to anything.'

'That's what I'm counting on. But in the meantime it's a helluva worry.'

She touched him lightly on the shoulder, the concern she felt showing plainly on her face. 'We'd best get back.'

As they returned to the house she made up her mind not to tell Dan about this. It was probably all nonsense anyway.

*

'You had what!' an incredulous Dan exclaimed.

'Roast pork and all, and I mean *all*, the trimmings. You should have seen the joint. It was ginormous.'

Dan slowly exhaled. 'Lucky old you.'

'I ate so much I couldn't face the sweet.'

'Imagine turning down food,' he said in wonderment. For the people of St Helier that was strictly a pre-Occupation luxury.

'This is for you,' she declared, handing him a carefully wrapped paper package.

'Me?'

'Compliments of Mrs Le Noa, who was ever so nice. They all were.'

Dan undid the paper to discover four slices of cold pork. 'Blinking Ada,' he breathed.

'Not only that, there's a bag of potatoes in the hall. Tony put it there when he saw me in.'

'A *whole* bag?'

Holly nodded.

'Do you know how much that's worth? About a hundred quid on the black market.'

'That's right. Wasn't it kind of them?'

'I'll say.'

'So how about I do you mash and reheated pork?'

His eyes gleamed. 'Oh yes, please.'

He roared when she recounted the story of the pig.

Chapter 10

Meggy Hill closed the door of the nurses' room, leant against it, and burst into tears.

'What's wrong?' Sally Pallot demanded.

'We're . . . We're . . .' Meggy broke off with a choke.

Holly went to her and put an arm round her shoulders. 'Has someone upset you? One of the doctors?'

Meggy, face awash, shook her head.

'Come and sit down.'

Helen Mason handed her a handkerchief. 'Use that. It's clean.'

Meggy dabbed at her face. 'It's official. I'm being deported to Germany. My whole family are.'

'What!' Holly exclaimed while the others looked on in shock.

'Official,' Meggy sobbed. 'Everyone who's non-Island born is to register prior to deportation. And of course I was born in Manchester, as were my parents.'

'Bloody hell,' Helen Mason breathed. Meggy was the only one in the room not from Jersey.

Holly thought of Tony and the rumour that had so worried him, and her, concerning her father. A rumour that had so far proved groundless. Now this.

'Are you sure it's official?' she queried.

Meggy nodded. 'Posters went up earlier this morning apparently.

Davina Evans saw them with her own eyes and it was she who told me. It also affects Davina, who's from Wales somewhere.'

'Deported to Germany,' Heather Aubin murmured, and shuddered.

Meggy started to shake. 'Davina says they'll probably put us in a concentration camp.'

She looked at Holly with terrified eyes. 'None of us will ever return alive. I just know it.'

'You don't know that at all,' Holly replied, more conviction in her voice than she actually felt.

'A camp perhaps,' Sally said. 'But not a concentration camp. They wouldn't do that.'

'The Germans are capable of anything,' Meggy hissed. 'Remember what we heard about the Jews.'

'That's different, they hate the Jews,' Holly pointed out.

'They don't exactly love us,' Meggy countered.

'But why are they doing this now?' Helen wondered.

Meggy shook her head. 'Davina didn't know.'

She buried her face in her hands, still unable to believe that this was actually happening.

'Maybe they'll change their minds?' Heather Aubin declared hopefully.

Fat chance, Holly thought. If it was official then it would be carried through.

Dan knocked on the door and waited. He was about to knock again when the door was opened by an aged cleric.

'My name's Dan Morgan, I'm a schoolteacher. I have a problem I was told you could help me with.'

The cleric nodded. 'Come in, Mr Morgan, and we'll have a chat.'

The cleric glanced up and down the street before closing the door again.

Twenty minutes later a jubilant Dan left with what he'd come for.

Men, women and children, guarded by German soldiers, lined the quayside, the process of embarkation already under way. The men were grim faced, the women wore apprehensive expressions and many of the children were crying.

The people of St Helier and surrounding area had come in their hundreds in protest. They now began to sing, songs they'd heard on the wireless sung by Vera Lynn.

An Oberstleutnant (lieutenant colonel) yelled at those in the forefront to stop, threatening them with his gun which he produced from a hip holster. Those threatened were undeterred and the singing swelled in volume.

Holly was amongst the throng, she and a few others having been given time off to say goodbye to Meggy. They'd spotted Meggy and her family waiting to embark but hadn't been able to have a word. They had been able to wave, though, and Meggy had waved back.

A scuffle broke out involving some youths and soldiers, the youths being quickly overpowered and dragged to a German truck into which they were unceremoniously bundled.

Most of the deportees were now aboard, including the Hills. And still the defiant singing continued unabated. Shouts of anger went up when there was another scuffle, and again some youths were dragged to the same German truck to be thrown in with those already under arrest.

My God, Holly thought when she saw the soldiers fix bayonets. If the crowd wasn't careful there could be wholesale slaughter here. She was glad she was in her nurse's uniform. That might be to her advantage in the event of real trouble.

'I don't like the look of this at all,' Heather Aubin whispered to Holly.

There was no escape for the time being, Holly thought. It would be next to impossible to force their way back through the throng behind them. Besides, if others were brave enough to stay, then so would she.

Now the gangplank was being disengaged and the hawsers thrown into the water. The ship got under way as the hawsers were winched aboard. A great roar of rage went up from the onlookers and a forest of fists were shaken.

The singing ceased and the crowd fell silent as the ship slowly steamed away.

'Poor Meggy,' Holly whispered.

'Poor all of them,' Heather added.

The assembly stood firm, watching the ship's departure. No one moved off.

Then someone on the ship began to sing 'There'll Always Be An England', others quickly joining in.

The onlookers continued to wait in silence as the words of the song came hauntingly across the water.

It was the most poignant thing Holly had ever heard.

'So how are you getting on with Tony?' Elspeth asked. Holly had dropped by for a natter while Terry was out.

Holly shrugged. 'OK.'

'Just OK?'

'Well, you know how it is.'

'I don't, that's why I'm asking, silly.'

Holly thought for a few moments before saying, 'I just wonder if I'm not short-changing him somewhat.'

'How do you mean?'

'He's not the man for me, Elspeth. I know that.'

'You can't,' Elspeth protested. 'It's much too soon.'

'No, it's not. These things are either right, or they aren't. I like Tony a lot. He's a smashing bloke, and they don't come kinder. But he's not the man for me.'

'It's Martin's memory . . .'

'No, it isn't,' Holly interjected. 'That was there to begin with, I grant you. But . . . I suppose it's chemistry. You either have it or you don't.'

'He has it for you. He's said as much to Terry.'

'Chemistry works both ways.'

Elspeth nodded. 'I'd hoped . . . but there we are.'

They left it at that.

'The Germans have been routed near Stalingrad,' Dan informed Holly.

She stared at him. 'How do you know?'

He tapped his nose.

'Dad!'

'I have my sources,' he declared mysteriously.

'Do you know someone with a wireless?'

He shrugged and didn't reply.

'What else have you heard?'

'The French have scuttled their fleet in Toulon harbour.'

'No!'

'It's true. Sad, but true nonetheless.'

'You do know someone with a wireless,' she accused.

'I'm not saying.'

'Hmmh,' she muttered. 'That confirms it.' She hesitated, then said, 'Do be careful whom you pass on information to, Dad. You could easily be informed on, and then what?'

'I'll be careful, don't you worry. I'm not stupid, Holly. Far from it.'

He chuckled. It was wonderful hearing the news again, learning what was happening outside the island.

Holly would have a fit if she found out that the wireless belonged to him and was in his jacket pocket that very moment.

Fit, she'd have a heart attack!

'I wonder how Meggy's getting on?' Sally Pallot said.

'And where they were taken to. Whether it was a concentration camp or not,' Heather added.

'Let's just hope it wasn't,' Viv Radmore said.

It had been a while after the deportations before the Islanders had learned what had caused them. The order had come direct from Hitler apparently after he'd learned that Britain was asking for German citizens in Iran to be expelled because they had been acting as Nazi agents. The deportations were his revenge.

Holly shook her head, thinking of Meggy and all those others who'd steamed off into the unknown. Would they ever see any of them again? God alone knew.

'Pat Le Clerq's resigned. Some of the girls on her ward were talking about it earlier,' Helen Mason said.

'I'm not surprised,' declared Sally. 'They were giving her hell for being a Jerrybag.'

'Bitch!' Viv hissed, referring to Pat.

'They say she's gone off with her Jerry officer,' Helen went on.

'Really?' That was Holly.

'So they say.'

'Well, she won't be going without, that's for sure,' Holly commented.

'Imagine living with the enemy. It's obscene,' Viv said.

'Pat always swore she was in love with him, so there is that,' Helen said.

'And that he loves her,' Sally added.

'He's still the enemy, a bloody German officer. And she wouldn't have fallen in love with him if she hadn't gone out with him in the first place,' Helen said.

'Hell mend her,' Viv spat.

At which point Sister Moignard stuck her head round the door and that was the end of that conversation.

'Stop seeing one another!' Tony exclaimed, dismay written all over his face.

'I'm sorry.'

'But we get on so well together, Holly.'

She thought of the last time they'd been together when she'd finally allowed him to kiss her. It was that kiss which had made up her mind. It had been pleasant enough, certainly not unpleasant. But that was all it had been. There had been no electricity, no zing, no special something as there always had with Martin.

'You're fun and a good companion, Tony. And I hope we'll remain friends. It would upset me if we didn't.'

This had rocked him, the last thing he'd expected. He'd firmly believed there was a future to their relationship.

'Is it Martin?' he queried.

'No, it's us.'

He shook his head. 'I just don't understand.'

'I can't be more than friends with you, Tony. It simply isn't there.'

He reached out and placed his palm against her cheek. She'd come to mean so much to him in such a short time. He'd convinced himself if he only took things slowly then it would all, in time, work out between them. She was the girl he wanted eventually to marry, there was no doubt about that. And now here she was breaking it off between them. He was devastated.

'It is for me, Holly.'

That's what he'd told Terry, she remembered. The chemistry thing, there on his side but not hers.

'Can't we give it a little longer?' he pleaded.

She shook her head.

'Please, Holly?'

Tall, dark, handsome and probably in love with her. What more did she want? Perhaps she was being foolish. Love might only come once in her life, in fact she was certain of it. There would never be another Martin. Couldn't be.

She sighed, and gently removed his hand. 'I'm sorry if I've hurt you. But I'd only hurt you more deeply if I allowed this to continue.'

He knew then it was over between them. That was clear on her face. 'Was it something I did?'

'No,' she smiled. 'You couldn't have been nicer. It just wasn't to be, that's all.'

'On your part, you mean.' There was bitterness in his voice when he said that.

She nodded.

'Oh, Holly!'

'How are things at the farm?' she inquired.

'I don't want to talk about the bloody farm!' he replied hotly. 'I want to talk about us.'

'Don't drag this out, Tony.'

'But I must. I have to! I . . .' He trailed off, and took a deep breath.

'Buggeration!' he swore.

She could see the pain in his eyes. 'I'd better go.'

He grabbed her by the arm. 'Not yet, Holly.'

'There's no point in discussing this further. We'd only go round in circles.'

'I don't agree.'

'There's nothing you can say or do will make me change my mind. That's made up.'

He released her, biting back words he knew he'd regret uttering. It was as if a big black hole had opened up and he'd fallen in.

'Goodbye, Tony. And thanks for everything.'

'Goodbye, Holly. If you should ever change your mind, let me know.'

'You're sweet.'

She pecked him on the cheek before turning and walking away.

Holly stopped to stare at the lines of marching men. Without exception they were skeletal and dressed in tattered rags. Even at that distance she could smell the appalling stink of them.

Who are they? she wondered. And what are they doing in St Helier?

One of them stumbled and fell, to be kicked to his feet again by a German guard.

'Bastard,' Holly muttered.

The lines of wretched humanity continued on up the street.

Dan breezed into the staff room. 'Where's Miss Dupré?' he queried. 'I want a word with her.'

Mr Fortesque swallowed hard before answering. 'She's been arrested.'

Dan was stunned. 'Arrested?'

'For owning an illegal wireless set.'

That stunned him even further, his own being in his jacket pocket. 'What happened?'

'The Germans raided her house and found the wireless concealed up a chimney. The thing is, they knew where to look. Went straight to the damned thing.'

'She must have been informed on, then.'

'Must have been,' Mr Fortesque agreed. 'As you know, she isn't the easiest of characters and has probably made enemies. Enemies who found out about the wireless and where it was.'

Dan ran a hand through his hair. 'When does she go before the court?'

'This morning some time. It'll be prison for certain. The only question is how long a sentence. Nor will they make that lighter because she's a woman. Gender won't be taken into account.'

I've been careful up until now, Dan thought. From here on in he'd be doubly so.

'They're Russians, Lithuanians, all sorts,' Viv Radmore informed Holly. 'Prisoners of war.'

'But why are they here?'

Viv shrugged. 'No one knows yet. Perhaps it's something to do with the huge amounts of concrete the Germans have been landing.'

'Could be,' Holly mused. 'You should have seen the state of them. Most of them looked half dead.'

'Speak to you later,' Viv said, and bustled off while Holly went in search of the bed pan she needed for a patient.

'A year in prison in France,' Dan said to Holly. 'Some hell-hole, no doubt.'

'That's a long time,' Holly sympathised.

'God knows what the conditions will be like.'

'She knew the risk she was running, Dad. She should never have had that wireless set.'

Dan's hand went involuntarily to his pocket. Perhaps he should get rid of his own, ditch it somewhere.

No, he decided. Miss Dupré's set had been the genuine article while his was a crystal job only matchbox size. He was safe enough as long as he watched his step.

'Fortifications,' Heather Aubin declared. 'That's what those prisoners of war are here to build.'

'How did you find that out?' Holly queried.

'From the grapevine. Apparently huge amounts of concrete are arriving now on a daily basis. So whatever the Jerries have planned, it's big.'

Both girls reflected on the possibilities.

'There's someone here to see you,' Dan announced, ushering a sheepish-looking Tony into the room.

An astonished Holly stared at her unexpected guest.

'I was just passing, or was close by anyway, and knowing it to be your weekend off I thought I'd drop by on the off-chance.'

'Excuse me,' said Dan, leaving them to it.

'It's nice to see you,' she smiled.

He nervously shuffled his feet. 'I've brought you a present.' Crossing to her he handed her a paper bag.

A present! That meant it was highly unlikely he'd called in on the off-chance, as he put it. He'd planned the visit.

'Eggs!' she exclaimed in delight.

'A dozen. I had them in the lorry.'

Another clumsy lie, she thought. 'Thank you very much, Tony. You know how much they're appreciated.' Eggs were selling on the black market for eight shillings each.

'So how are you?' he asked, a false smile on his face.

'Not too bad. And you?'

He didn't want to say how awful he'd been since she'd broken it off between them. The fitful nights, the anguished thoughts. He knew it was over and yet he'd still come. Perhaps he was hoping for a miracle. Women did change their minds after all, he'd argued with himself a thousand times. But in his heart of hearts he knew Holly wouldn't. And still he'd come. Madness, if not downright stupidity. At least seeing her again was something.

'Fine,' he declared.

'Good.'

'Mum and Dad often ask after you. You made a huge impression with them.'

'I liked them too. As you said I would.'

She gestured at the empty fireplace. 'I'm sorry it's cold in here but we've nothing to burn.'

'That's an advantage of being on a farm and in the countryside. There's always wood available.'

'Lucky old you.'

'Yes.'

She carefully placed the eggs aside, then turned again to him.

'You said you hoped we'd remain friends,' he mumbled.

'And so I do.'

'You're looking terrific, Hol.'

She smoothed down the sides of her dress. 'Still losing weight, I'm afraid. But then everyone in St Helier is, apart from the Germans, that is.'

'You still look terrific.'

There was an awkward silence between them. 'What have you been up to then?' she asked.

'Nothing really. Work on the farm and that's about it. How about you?'

'Work at the hospital and that's about it as well.'

They both laughed and the tension between them eased. 'I hope you don't mind me calling in?' he queried.

'Not at all. I've been thinking about you.' She shouldn't have said that she realised when she saw his face light up. It gave him false hope. 'Wondering how you were, I mean.'

'I've been thinking about you too.'

She didn't reply to that. Instead she said, 'Would you like some beet tea?'

He shook his head.

'I can't offer you the real thing, I'm afraid.'

'That's OK. I understand.'

'Dad will be over the moon when he learns about the eggs. We'll have one each for tea.'

'They're from our chickens. Good layers those birds.'

'There's nothing nicer than a fresh egg,' she smiled. 'It'll be a real treat.'

He cleared his throat and steeled himself. 'Holly, I . . .'

She knew immediately what was coming. 'No, Tony,' she interjected softly.

He nodded. 'I didn't expect anything else but I had to try. It's just . . .' He stared down at the floor. 'I miss you so much.'

Oh God! she thought.

'So much,' he repeated.

'I think you'd better go, Tony.'

'There's no chance then?' he queried in desperation.

'None.'

I was a fool to come, he told himself. A complete idiot. He'd have given anything to kiss her again, hold her in his arms. It seemed inconceivable he'd do neither again.

'Take care, Hol,' he said in a strangulated voice. 'I'll see myself out.'

Normally she would have insisted on accompanying him, or any guest, to the door. On this occasion she didn't, thinking it best she remained where she was.

She sighed when he was gone, feeling dreadful and somehow guilty. It was he who'd pursued her, she reminded herself, not the other way round. And she'd never promised him anything, never reneged in any way.

'Well?' Dan asked, reappearing a few moments later.

She shook her head.

Pity, he thought. That was a nice lad. They made a handsome couple together.

He too exclaimed in delight when Holly showed him the eggs.

'Well, Gill, here I am again,' Dan smiled down at the grave, visualising his dead wife. There was no one else about so he could talk aloud to her.

'Things are getting really bad on the island, Gill. They've cut our rations again. People are beginning to really suffer. That young man Tony I've told you about called in the other day bringing us a dozen eggs from his farm. They were welcome, I can tell you. It's ages since Holly and I have had an egg.

'She won't go back with him, I'm sorry to say. I had thought they might be a match but Holly had other ideas. And you know what she's like – once her mind's made up, that's that. They don't come more stubborn than our Holly.

'It was sad really. They made a fine pair together. Good-looking lad too, and well off. That farm will be his when his parents go, which won't be for some while yet as they're about my age. But inherit he will when the time comes.'

Dan paused to finger his pipe. He never smoked it any more as there wasn't any tobacco available, but he still liked to carry it around with him.

'I'm beginning to worry that she's a right chip off the old block,

Gill. Me, I mean. I could never conceive of marrying again after you and I'm wondering if it's the same for her with Martin. It's been over two years now since Dunkirk and Tony's the only chap she's been out with. I couldn't bear the thought of her ending up a dry old spinster wedded to the memory of a long-lost love. That would be tragic, and yet . . .'

He broke off and shrugged. 'We'll just have to wait and see, I suppose. Keep on hoping that another knight in shining armour will come riding over the hill. A knight who'll capture her heart as Martin did.'

Dan sucked in a deep breath. Then, as always, he went on to recount the minutiae of his life since he'd last visited his wife's grave.

Chapter 11

Holly glanced up at the darkening sky. Rain was definitely on the way.

She'd decided to spend the weekend at Half Hidden, something she'd done on several occasions since her stay there with Elspeth and had come to think of the cottage as her own little private retreat. She found it peaceful, serene almost, and had never failed to thoroughly enjoy herself. As usual she'd brought her rations with her, which she hoped to be able to supplement from the vegetable garden.

She smiled when the cottage came into view, the smile fading when she spotted a car parked out front. Now who on earth could that be?

It wasn't the owners', that was for certain. They were on the mainland. A farmer perhaps? Only a farmer would have petrol to run a car. A farmer and . . .

She stopped dead in her tracks and bit her lip. If the car belonged to a German or Germans it was best she keep away. To intrude would only be inviting trouble.

At which point there was a great rumble of thunder and the heavens opened. Lightning zig-zagged across the sky as a deluge fell. Within moments she was soaked.

I'll have to go on, she thought. It would be foolish walking back to St Helier in this downpour; it'd be asking for pneumonia.

A figure, huddled against the rain, dashed round the side of the cottage. A farmer, she thought with relief, for he'd been wearing civilian clothes. That was all right then, she'd be safe.

She started to run, breathless when she arrived at the front door, on which she quickly rapped. The door opened and a man stared out at her.

Her jaw dropped in astonishment when she realised who it was. 'Peter!'

'Holly!' Peter Schmidt was equally astonished. 'Come in.'

'What are you doing here?' she demanded when inside.

'Later. We'd better get you out of those wet things. You're drenched.'

She laid her rations on a chair, after which he helped her out of her coat. Outside the lightning flashed and thunder continued to rumble and crack.

'I can't believe it,' she said. 'You of all people!'

He laughed. 'And *you* of all people.' He shook his head, bemused.

Holly fingered her sodden blouse, acutely aware of how it was clinging to her and outlining her breasts. 'That's some downpour,' she declared.

'A real storm by the looks and sounds of it.'

'There are some clothes upstairs. I'll go and change into those.'

He nodded his approval. 'And I'll light a fire, there's plenty of wood available. Bring your wet things down and we'll dry them in front of the hearth.'

She still couldn't believe Peter was at the cottage. Talk about surprises!

'Off you go then,' he said and, giving her a flashing smile, vanished into the sitting room.

Holly located a towel in the bathroom, deciding to strip off and, for the moment anyway, put on a warm woollen dressing gown that must have belonged to Mr Vardon, the cottage's owner.

When she was naked she towelled her hair, then dried the rest of herself. She was shivering by the time she slipped on the dressing gown.

She found a skirt and jumper but had to put on wet knickers as she and Elspeth had appropriated those when they'd been there before.

Peter had the fire going and great tongues of flame were shooting up the chimney. He took Holly's wet things and arranged them over chairs that he'd brought from the kitchen and placed by the hearth.

'Now,' declared Peter, picking up two glasses containing clear liquid from the mantelpiece, 'drink this. Schnapps from my hip flask,' he informed her. 'It'll warm you.'

She had a sip, gasped as the schnapps burned her throat, but took another one anyway. She jumped when there was a boom of thunder so loud it might have been a cannon going off.

'Do storms frighten you?' Peter asked, lighting a cigarette.

'Not normally. It's just . . . I don't know. It does seem a particularly ferocious one.'

'Let's just hope we don't get hit by lightning. I'd hate for either of us to end up as toast.'

She laughed. 'Quite.'

He looks older, she thought. More careworn. And his face had thinned a little. She realised she was very pleased to see him.

'When did you get back?' she asked him, sitting on a pouffe adjacent to the fire, making sure her legs were together and skirt well pulled down.

He had a swallow of schnapps. 'The day before yesterday. I take up my duties again at the hospital on Monday. As I had some time off, I thought I'd take a friend's car for a spin and ended up here.' That wasn't totally true; it had been his intention to come to Half Hidden before leaving St Helier. But he didn't want to tell Holly that.

'And your father, how's he?'

'Well on the road to recovery, I'm happy to say.'

Holly was delighted to hear that. 'And they didn't send you to the Russian Front after all?'

'No, happily as well. When my leave was over they posted me to Berlin, where I worked in a hospital. Then, suddenly out of the blue, I was sent back here.' He shook his head. 'I honestly never thought I'd be back, but fortune was kind.'

'It's good to see you, Peter,' she said softly.

'And to see you, Holly.'

She glanced away to stare at the fire. 'What about your brother?'

'Shot down.'

'Oh, Peter!' She gazed at him in concern.

'That's the bad news. The good news is he's a prisoner of war in Britain. So he's now safely out of it.'

'That's not so bad then.'

'No,' Peter agreed.

'Was he wounded at all?'

Peter shook his head. 'Not a scratch apparently. He was extremely lucky. He could easily have been badly burned, and you and I both know what that can be like.'

Holly had a sudden thought. Was it forward of her to ask? she wondered. And decided she would go ahead anyway. 'Did you see Marlene when you were in Berlin?'

Peter glanced sharply at her. 'Yes, I did.'

'Oh!' Holly wondered why that should upset her.

'But we didn't speak. I was walking along the street when I spotted her on the opposite pavement. I considered going across and saying hello. Then thought the better of it. I simply didn't want to renew our acquaintance.'

'How did she look?'

'Well enough. As far as I could make out at that distance.' He drained his glass. 'More schnapps?'

'No, thank you, this is enough for me.'

'Do you mind if I have some?'

She laughed gently. 'Of course not. Go right ahead.'

What elegant hands he has, she noticed as he refilled his glass from a silver hip flask. Then she wondered who'd given him the flask. His parents? Marlene?

'Now why are *you* here?' he queried.

Holly flinched when there was another loud boom of thunder which seemed to be centred directly over the cottage. She explained about using Half Hidden as a retreat, mentioning her visit with Elspeth, though leaving out the bit about the commandos.

'It does rather lend itself to that,' he said when she'd finished.

'It's normally so tranquil here. Though not today.'

'I'm billeted at the Grand again,' he informed her. 'I thought it was full when I left but now it's positively jam-packed. I'm even having to share a room.'

She made a sympathetic face.

He glanced around. 'You know, it's just struck me that I could move in here. I could easily get myself a car and have the services reconnected. And there's a telephone, which would be necessary.'

There goes my retreat, Holly thought ruefully.

'What do you think?' he queried.

'It can't be very nice at the Grand the way it is.'

'I would need permission, of course, but that's easily obtained. The telephone would be the important thing so that I could be on call.'

He focused on her, his blue eyes boring into hers. 'There again, I would be denying you. I can't do that.'

'Of course you can, Peter, I only come here once in a while after all. It would be a shame for you to miss out because of that.'

'Even so.'

'No, I insist. If you want to move in, then you must. It'll give you the privacy you clearly need.'

'You're very kind, Holly,' he smiled.

'Besides, *I* haven't any say in the matter. The cottage isn't mine.'

He went to the fire and threw on some more wood, then rearranged her drying, steaming clothes. 'It'll be morning before you can put these back on again. In the meantime, are you hungry? I know I am.'

She nodded. 'I brought food with me. My rations.'

'There's no need for that. I have a packet of sandwiches in the car and a flask of coffee, courtesy of the Grand. We can share those.'

'Real coffee?'

'As real as real.' He rose. 'I'll go and get them.'

'Wait,' she said. 'There's a raincoat and hat in the kitchen, hanging behind the door. You'd better put those on to save you getting drenched as I was.'

'Right,' he declared and strode off.

When he returned he found Holly had brought plates and cups and saucers into the sitting room.

'Picnic time again,' he laughed. 'It seems to be a thing with us.'

She divided the sandwiches equally between them, waiting to hand him his plate while he poured the coffee.

'How's your father?' he asked, settling back into his chair.

'OK.'

'Still drinking scotch whisky?'

'You must be joking! Chance would be a fine thing.'

'I must see what I can do, then.'

'Would you!' Holly exclaimed. 'He'd be grateful. He really misses his tipple.'

The sandwiches are gorgeous, she thought, munching appreciatively. Half were of a meat paste unknown to her, but delicious. The other half were cheese. And the bread had butter on it!

'How's the coffee?' he queried with a smile.

'Hmmh.'

'I shall get you some of that as well.'

'Oh, Peter!' she breathed. 'Thank you.'

It fascinated him how her hair was fluffing as it dried. He found it extraordinarily appealing. There was a sensuousness about her that he'd never really appreciated before.

'I thought of you when I was in Germany,' he declared.

'Oh?'

'We were friends after all. Weren't we?'

'Of a sort.'

'Well, I considered us to be.'

That embarrassed her for some reason. She dropped her gaze to stare at her plate. 'These sandwiches are very good,' she mumbled.

'I take it the rationing for you Islanders is still bad?'

'Worse than when you left. It's been cut several times since then.'

'I'm sorry to hear that.'

'Not as much as we are, I can tell you.'

He made up his mind to see what he could do other than scotch and coffee. A word in the hotel kitchens perhaps, and there were other sources open to him. It shouldn't be too difficult.

'Berlin was quite changed,' he commented, making conversation. 'Totally different from when I was there last. It was very sad.'

'Changed in what way?'

'Before it was a gay, happy place. Full of lights. But that's all changed since the British began their bombing. No gaiety any more, no happiness. And no sparkling night-time lights. Sad, as I said.'

'You can hardly blame the RAF for bombing after what the Luftwaffe did to London and other British cities,' she stated.

'Very true, I agree. We started the war, that can't be denied. And now . . .' He broke off and shrugged. 'As Newton once remarked, for every action there is a reaction.'

'It'll be over one day, Peter. Everything has to end.'

He gave her a wry smile. 'Doctors know that only too well. We encounter it every day in our profession, and yours.'

'I'm sorry about Berlin,' she said. 'Just as I'm sorry about London, Manchester, Coventry and all the rest of it.'

Peter finished his sandwiches, laid his plate aside and lit another cigarette. 'I must be going shortly.'

'Must you?'

He glanced at the window and the streaming rain. 'Though I must say I don't . . .' He groped for a word, unusual for him with his excellent English vocabulary. 'Relish, is that it?'

She nodded.

'I don't relish the prospect, lassie.' Then, in a cod Scottish accent, 'Don't relish it at all.'

Holly laughed.

'More coffee, hen?'

She laughed again. 'Please.'

He rose, refilled her cup and then his own. 'Now tell me about everything that's been going on while I've been away.'

'Are you sure you don't mind me moving in here?' he asked later, standing at the door, ready to leave. He was wearing the borrowed raincoat and hat.

'If that's what you want to do, then you should go ahead.'

'I'll think about it, then.'

'Just let me know if you do.'

He nodded. 'I understand. Well, goodnight, Holly Morgan.'

'Goodnight, Peter. Take care driving back.'

'I will.'

There was an awkward moment between them before he opened the door to be faced with driving rain. She hurriedly closed the door against it as he dived for his car.

She heard the car start up as she returned to the sitting room, thinking she'd best fill the storm lanterns as it was rapidly getting darker and darker even though it was still the afternoon.

She was aware of the engine being turned repeatedly, but the car didn't move off. Something wrong? she wondered.

A few minutes later Peter was back. 'The damn thing's stuck,' he proclaimed. 'The ground's so wet and soft the wheels won't grip. It's started to dig itself in.'

She stared at him in dismay. Of course, they should have thought of that. 'So what are you going to do?'

'Walk I suppose, and return for the car tomorrow.'

'You can't walk in this weather,' she protested. 'That would be daft.'

He sighed. 'I could hang on and see if the rain stops. Perhaps I'd be able to do something then.'

'The ground will still be wet and soft, Peter.'

'Even though, I—'

She cut him short. 'You'll just have to stay the night and hope to rescue the car in the morning.'

He frowned. 'Stay the night?'

'What other sensible option is there?'

'But you, I mean . . .' He broke off in confusion.

'I'll be in the main bedroom, you can have the spare. No different from a hotel really, except we'll be sharing the bathroom. And you have to do that in some hotels anyway.'

'But it wouldn't be proper, Holly.'

She decided to tease him. 'Why, you wouldn't take advantage of me, surely?'

He went bright red. 'Of course not. I'm surprised you could even suggest such a thing.'

'I'm only joking, Peter,' she said softly. 'I completely trust you. You're a gentleman if ever there was.'

'I'll take this raincoat off,' he said, and went into the kitchen.

What else could I have done? Holly reasoned with herself. She certainly couldn't have allowed him to trudge back to St Helier. That would have been a complete nonsense. And, even if he was a German, she did trust him. There would be no attempted hanky-panky from Peter Schmidt.

'It's a pity the coffee's finished,' he declared on rejoining her. 'But I didn't come equipped for an overnight stay.'

Holly had an idea. 'Do you play cards?'

'A little.'

'There's a deck in that bureau. We could do that for a while.'

He smiled at her. 'No gambling, I hope? I'm against that.'

Now he was teasing her, she realised. She pouted. 'Spoilsport! I'd fully intended rooking you.'

'Rooking?' he queried with a frown.

'Slang for taking all your money off you.'

He dug in his trouser pocket and produced a handful of change. 'Much good that would have done you.'

She laughed when she saw they were German coins.

She lay in the darkness wondering if Peter was asleep yet. He'd bid her a formal goodnight on the landing before going into the spare room and firmly shutting his door behind him.

She'd closed her door too, of course, before undressing and slipping into bed. He'd taken one of the storm lanterns with him, as had she. Hers was now extinguished.

What a turn-up for the book Peter Schmidt being at Half Hidden, she thought. And what a pleasant evening they'd had. After a few card games, which had been limited by there only being two of them, they'd talked and talked, he about Germany and his student life in Edinburgh.

We do get on well together, she thought. He was so easy to be with. It was as if they'd been friends all their lives.

She shifted in her bed, listening to the rain hammering against the window panes. At least the thunder and lightning had stopped, which was a relief. That thunder! She couldn't recall ever having heard the like.

She pitied the poor sailors, of whatever nationality, out at sea on a night like this. It must be dreadfully dangerous for them.

What was that? Peter was moving around. For a brief moment she panicked. Had she misjudged him, after all? A few minutes later she smiled at the sound of the toilet flushing. So that was it. She should have guessed. Then silence settled over the cottage once more.

Later, she drifted off to dream, for the first time in a long while, of Martin.

They were in the caravan the night before he left, making love as they had. The peculiar thing was his face was hazy, not clear at all. And his voice was indistinct and came from a long way off.

Holly woke to find a bright shaft of sunlight slanting through the curtains. When she threw them back she discovered it to be a glorious day outside. She hurriedly washed and dressed. She wondered if Peter was already up.

He was already out at the car, which was where she joined him.

'Well?' she queried.

He was squatting, studying the rear wheels which had sunk into the ground.

'Should be able to get it out with a bit of perseverance,' he declared.

'What will you do? Put things under the wheels?'

He nodded. 'The ground's still very wet but not as bad as last night.'

'Did you sleep well?'

He glanced up at her. 'Extremely. You?'

'I had a rather strange dream.'

'Oh?'

She wasn't about to tell him it had been of her and Martin making love. 'Just strange, that's all,' she prevaricated.

When he realised she wasn't going to be more forthcoming he stood up. 'I'll look about, see what I can find.'

'You'll have breakfast first.'

'I'm not going to eat your rations,' he protested. 'That wouldn't be fair.'

'You'll do what the nurse orders. It isn't much, but at least it's something. A piece of bread, that's all.'

'There's some sacking out back,' she informed him as they ate standing up in the kitchen. A few mouthfuls each, and the bread she'd allocated for breakfast was gone.

'Ideal.'

'And a few panels of wood beside it. I think they may have been used for fencing. Or were intended for that purpose.'

His face broke into a smile. 'Ideal again.'

'I'll help you,' she declared, rewrapping the remainder of her rations.

'Might be somewhat messy.'

'That doesn't bother me. I'm not one of those females who balks at getting her hands dirty. Anyway, a little bit of dirt never hurt anybody.'

He nodded his approval.

Holly sighed, thinking of the coffee they'd had the previous day. How welcome a cup of that would have been right then. Even cold, she'd have been grateful for it.

She showed him where the sacking and panels were, and together they carried them out to the car.

They arranged the sacking, then jammed the panels hard against the wheels.

'Right, let's see if that'll work,' Peter said.

'I'll push,' Holly volunteered.

Peter started the car, and as he applied the accelerator Holly pushed with all her might.

The wheels spun, sending mud flying in all directions, but the car didn't move forward.

Peter, hanging out of the open car door, swore in German. He stopped the engine and got out. He studied the rear wheels, frowning in concentration.

Holly had another idea. 'I know where there's a spade. We could perhaps make it easier for the wheels by digging them out a bit. I vaguely remember reading a story where they did that in a similar situation.'

'It's worth a try.'

'I'll get the spade.'

When she returned, she found Peter smoking a cigarette. 'It's a beautiful day,' he commented.

'Quite a contrast to last night,' she said, leaning on the spade, waiting for him to finish his cigarette.

He laughed. 'It most certainly is.'

She sucked in a deep lungful of air, air that was fresh and clean and full of countryside smells. She found herself to be delightfully happy.

'I've decided I will move in, if that's still all right with you?' he said.

'Of course.'

He glanced at the cottage, and smiled. 'I hope you won't be a stranger when I'm here. It would upset me if you were.'

She wasn't sure about that. 'I don't know,' she murmured. Visit Peter here on his own, was that really on?

'Then I won't move in.'

'That's blackmail!' she protested.

'Precisely.'

She didn't wish to deprive him of his privacy, or the opportunity of living in such tranquil surroundings. 'We'll see then,' she demurred.

He knew he'd have to settle for that. 'Can you drive a car?'

She shook her head.

No matter, he thought. They'd get round. 'Out here it's easy to forget there's a war on,' he mused.

True, she thought.

'I hate the whole damn thing,' he said fiercely. 'Such a waste of so many lives. And for what? I've never really understood that.'

'One man's ambition and vanity?'

'You mean the Führer?'

She nodded.

He stared at his cigarette, had a final puff and threw the stub away. 'Shall we?'

They removed the panels and sacking, after which Peter set to with the spade. While he was doing this, Holly recalled there were some old newspapers in the cottage. When she suggested fetching them he instantly agreed.

He paused as she walked away, admiring the sway of her hips, the whole movement of her. She's some woman, he thought. In other circumstances . . .

They put the paper first into the twin excavations Peter had made, then the sacking followed by the panels.

'If this doesn't work it'll have to be a tow,' Peter declared when they were finished.

'Can you arrange that?'

'Oh yes. But I don't want to. This may sound silly but it would somehow desecrate this place having outsiders, particularly military ones, tramping all over it.'

Holly fully understood and thought the more highly of him for sharing those sentiments.

'Now,' he said. 'You're going to drive while I push this time, which I should have done in the first instance.'

'But I told you, I don't . . .'

'I'll show you what to do, Holly,' he interjected. 'It's easy. At least for what's required.'

He settled her in the driving seat and then began to explain how it all worked.

'That's the clutch which you depress, when you've done that you move the gear shift into first which is . . .'

A thrill ran through her when his hand closed over hers. A tingle of electricity as flesh touched flesh. The insides of her thighs quivered.

If he felt anything similar he didn't show, it she thought after a quick glance at his face.

'So,' he declared a few minutes later. 'Let's try again.'

He went to the rear of the car, rubbed his hands and leant against the boot.

'Now, Holly!' he called out.

She slowly let out the clutch and pressed on the accelerator. For a few moments the rear wheels spun as before, then suddenly they caught and the car lurched forward.

'Keep going!' Peter shouted as they headed for a nearby dirt road.

When they reached that, he dashed forward and helped her stop the car.

'Success,' he grinned.

'Success,' she agreed.

Peter gulped in a couple of deep breaths, then produced a cigarette packet and lit up. He next said something in German.

'What does that mean?'

He shook his head. 'Doesn't matter.'

'I think it best we don't mention you stayed over last night,' she said.

'You won't tell your father?'

She shook her head.

'And I won't say anything to anyone either.' His eyes lit up with laughter. 'We have your reputation to think of after all, Holly Morgan.'

'Indeed.'

Later, when he was gone, she found herself missing him. Half Hidden seemed empty without Peter Schmidt.

Chapter 12

'Are you awake?' Terry queried in the darkness, sensing that Elspeth still was. He couldn't sleep either, the gnawing hunger in his belly stopping him from dropping off.

'Yes,' came the whispered reply.

He reached under the bedclothes and touched her arm. 'Are you all right?' There had been something in her tone.

'I feel . . . such a failure, Terry.'

He rolled on to his side. 'Why, darling?'

'Not being able to get pregnant. I should have been long before now.'

'It'll happen in its own time, Els. You mustn't worry.'

'But I *do* worry. What if the doctor's wrong and I can't have any? That would break my heart, and yours. I know how much you want a child.'

He cupped a breast and gently squeezed. 'It wouldn't be the end of the world, Els. There are worse things in life to contend with than that.'

'I ache to have a baby, Terry. I positively ache.'

He kissed her lightly on the cheek. 'I'm sure it will happen one of these days, pet. We have to be patient.'

'I was watching a mother feeding her newborn in the hospital

146

last week. I nearly cried with jealousy and frustration. There was one awful moment when I could have hit her for having what I can't.' Elspeth started to sob. 'Oh, Terry!'

'There, there,' he murmured, trying to comfort her.

'Imagine feeling like that! Wanting to hit someone for having a baby when I don't.'

He pulled her to him and held her tight. Then he began stroking her hair. 'I love you so much, Els.'

'And I love you, Terry. But maybe you should have married someone else.'

'Don't say that!' he retorted sharply. 'Don't ever say that. I married the right woman for me. There's no question about that.'

Tears welled in her eyes. 'My period started today. I think that's what's brought this on. I keep hoping, praying, I'll miss. And every month it's regular as clockwork.'

He had been considering making love to her, but now couldn't. That was something Elspeth never allowed in the circumstances.

'Maybe you should go and see the doctor again, have another chat,' Terry suggested.

'I've had chats with him and what good do they do? Nothing at all. As far as he's concerned, and the specialist, everything's as it should be.'

'There you are then.' He continued stroking her hair.

'And I'm so hungry!' she suddenly wailed.

'You're not alone there, Els, everyone in St Helier is. Me included.'

'I keep thinking if only I could eat properly that would help. But there's no chance of that.'

Terry had a few pounds tucked away that Elspeth knew nothing about. Money he'd been saving for a rainy day. Well, time to spend it, he decided.

He knew someone in the black market whom he'd contact in the morning. Tomorrow night they'd have a proper meal which hopefully would cheer her up a bit.

He continued stroking her hair.

*

Four women had surrounded a fifth whom they were thumping and scratching. One was pulling her hair. The woman being assaulted was screaming at the top of her lungs.

'Jerrybag!' one of the attackers yelled. 'Fucking rotten Jerrybag.'

With a shock of recognition Holly realised the fifth woman was Pat Le Clerq.

A fist landed and blood spurted from Pat's nose.

Dear God, Holly thought, I should try and put a stop to this before real damage is done to Pat.

'Jerrybag! Jerrybag!' another of the attackers taunted.

Holly remained rooted to the spot. What would happen to her if she intervened? She didn't want to be branded the friend of a Jerrybag. The consequences of that were daunting, even if there was no truth in it.

Pat wasn't a chum, she reminded herself. Only an ex-colleague whom she knew slightly. And she had brought this upon herself by being precisely what they were calling her: a hated Jerrybag.

Pat suddenly managed to break free and ran off down the street with her attackers following in pursuit.

Holly dropped her head, ashamed of her cowardice. But she knew her decision had been the right one. Pat had made her own bed and now had to lie in it.

God help her.

'Holly,' Peter whispered.

She turned to face him, not having heard his approach. She quickly glanced about to see if they were being watched.

'Can you come to Half Hidden this Saturday?'

'Why?'

'I've got a surprise for you.'

A surprise? She wondered what it was. 'I . . .'

'Thank you, nurse,' he said brusquely, and walked away.

Holly smiled at the Sister who'd turned the corner a few feet away as she passed her.

*

'Come in,' Peter said, on opening the door to her knock. 'How are you?'

'Fine. Yourself?'

'Enjoying living here. It's smashing.'

'I saw your car on the road.'

He grinned. 'That's where it stays parked. I don't want a repeat of what happened with the other one.'

'No,' she agreed. 'I suppose you had it requisitioned.'

He shrugged. 'That's the procedure for us. I fill out a form and an Islander loses his vehicle. A vehicle he wouldn't be driving anyway as he wouldn't have any petrol.'

'That doesn't alter matters,' she replied drily. 'Requisitioning is only a euphemism for stealing.'

'You're right of course, I can't deny it.'

'Hmmh!' she snorted.

He studied her. 'We're not going to fall out over that, I hope?'

'Not really. I suppose if you hadn't requisitioned it some other German officer would only have done so in time.'

'Exactly.'

They went into the sitting room where a cheery fire was blazing. 'I hope you appreciate how lucky you are having wood,' she commented.

'I do. And when what's already cut is finished I'll chop down a tree and replenish my store.'

'But it's forbidden to chop down trees!' she exclaimed.

'Only if you're an Islander,' he pointed out. 'I'm a German, remember. I can do as I wish.'

True, she thought. 'How convenient for you.'

He ignored the sarcasm in her voice. 'Very. Now how about a cup of coffee before I give you lunch?'

'Lunch?'

'Made with my own fair hands especially for you.'

'Especially?' she queried sceptically.

He nodded. 'I eat most of my meals at the Grand, where they're only too happy to accommodate me. But because you were coming, or at least I hoped you were, I decided to cook myself.'

'Something nice, I hope?'

'Come and see for yourself.'

They went through to the kitchen where her nose was immediately assailed by the smell of cooking meat. Her tummy rumbled. 'Excuse me,' she apologised.

'Tell me what you think.'

He removed a dish from the oven and took the lid off. 'Rabbit casserole,' he declared.

'Yummy.'

'I caught it myself. There are quite a few rabbits round here so I put out a couple of snares and there we are.'

'You are resourceful,' she smiled.

'All good doctors have to be and I flatter myself that I'm a good one.'

He replaced the lid on the dish and popped it back into the oven. 'Not quite ready yet so you'll have to wait a bit.'

She didn't care how long she waited as long as there was casserole at the end of it. 'Is this the surprise?'

'No. But coffee first.'

He crossed to a bubbling percolator and poured out two cups. 'Milk and sugar?'

'You really are well provided for,' she said.

'I take it that means yes on both counts?'

'Please.'

He added sugar and milk to both cups and handed her one. 'Try that.'

'Hmmh,' she sighed in pleasure having tasted the cup's contents. 'Absolutely delicious.'

Her expression delighted him. It was like . . . He cleared his throat in embarrassment realising what it did remind him of. Another time, another lady, different circumstances.

'I'd love to give you some apple strudel to go with that, but I'm afraid it's off today,' he joked.

'I like apple strudel.'

'Do you? It's always been one of my favourites. My mother makes marvellous strudel.'

She could see the fondness in his face when he spoke about his mother, and it saddened her she'd never known her own. Well, that wasn't quite true. It was simply that she'd been so young when her mother died she couldn't remember her.

'So what is this surprise?' she prompted.

He smiled at her.

'Well?'

'Maybe I'll make you wait a little longer,' he teased.

She had another sip of coffee. 'Suit yourself, Peter. If that gives you pleasure.'

'Pleasure? That isn't a word I'd have used.'

'What then?'

He pulled out a packet of cigarettes and lit up while he considered that. 'I'm not sure.'

She raised an eyebrow.

'A little bit of fun, that's all, Holly Morgan,' he said at last.

'Why do you sometimes call me by my surname as well as my Christian name?'

He shrugged.

'Is it a German habit?'

'Does it annoy you?'

'No, I just find it strange.'

'Again, I'm not sure.'

'Holly Morgan,' she repeated. No one else ever called her that, except when being introduced. At least not since childhood and school.

Peter laid down his coffee and went to a cupboard from where he produced a canvas bag. 'Your surprise,' he said, handing it to her.

She gasped when she opened it. Inside were two bottles of Cream of the Barley scotch, two large tins of coffee, black German bread, butter, a long German sausage and a packet of lard! There was also something wrapped in newspaper.

'Another rabbit,' Peter enlightened her when she asked what that was.

'And!' he said, wagging a finger at her. 'There will be no mention of payment, please. This is a gift from me to you for having taken over your retreat. It's the least I can do.'

'Oh, Peter,' she whispered, 'this is fabulous.'

'The rabbit isn't skinned so you'll have to do that yourself.'

On impulse she pecked him on the cheek. 'Thank you.'

He stared at her for a moment, a quizzical look in his eyes, then turned away. 'I may not be able to get any more whisky for your father; my source says his supplies are drying up and can't be restocked.' He laughed. 'For some reason the Scots have stopped exporting to here and the continent.'

'I wonder why?' Holly said, tongue firmly in cheek.

'Yes, I wonder.'

This time they both laughed.

'But I still have access to brandy and schnapps if your father won't mind those.'

'He certainly enjoys brandy though he prefers scotch. But beggars can't be choosers; he'll be thankful for whatever you can lay your hands on.'

'Food is becoming a bit of a problem for us too you know. I've noticed since returning that the portions served up at the Grand are smaller than they used to be.'

Holly didn't show the satisfaction it gave her to hear that. Why should the Germans be able to stuff themselves while the Islanders starved! It wouldn't do them any harm to have to tighten their belts a little.

'It struck me that I might work on the vegetable garden out back,' Peter declared.

'But you'll need seeds for that?'

'I'm pretty certain I can get some. I thought you might help me and we could share what we grow?'

That meant coming out to Half Hidden on a regular basis, Holly thought. Which she decided, there and then, she would do. It was too good an opportunity to pass up.

'I don't know much about gardening,' she confessed. 'I'm a real townie, born and bred.'

'I can teach you. My father has always kept a vegetable garden and although I was never all that interested I've picked up enough over the years to know what's what.'

Their own regular supply of fresh vegetables, Holly thought with

glee. Worth more to her and Dan in the circumstances than a handful of diamonds.

'I only hope you can get those seeds,' she said.

'So do I.' Secretly, he was looking forward to Holly visiting regularly as he thoroughly enjoyed her company. It would be fun
having her around at weekends. If he was honest with himself the
idea of the garden was a device to see her more often, but he certainly wasn't going to tell her that.

For a while they talked about a case at the hospital which was
bothering him. Holly was flattered to be taken into his confidence
and have her advice asked. She enjoyed discussing medical matters,
as did he. A common bond between them.

When he served up the casserole they scoffed the lot, washing it
down with a bottle of Medoc he'd brought.

'Close your eyes and hold out your hand,' Holly instructed Dan
who'd just arrived home.

He regarded her with suspicion. 'What for?'

'I've got something for you.'

'Such as?'

'Close your eyes and find out.'

'Hmmh,' he mused. 'What are you up to, young lady?'

'You'll enjoy it, I promise.'

'I know your promises! You're not going to play a trick on me.
I'm too long in the tooth to be caught out by your pranks. And
you're too old to be playing them. Shame on you.'

Holly sighed. 'Just close your eyes and hold out your hand, Dad.
You're spoiling it.'

'No frogs or toads I hope?' He hated those, as she well knew.

'Dad, you're being ridiculous!'

He did as he was bid, resisting the temptation to cheat by peek-
ing.

Holly pulled the glass from behind her back and placed it on his
upturned palm. 'Don't drop it,' she said.

He exclaimed when he saw what the glass contained. 'Scotch
whisky!'

'There are two bottles for you, compliments of my friend Dr

Schmidt.' She'd previously told him that Peter was back at the hospital.

He tasted the scotch, and smiled. 'Nectar.'

'Not only scotch but . . .' She went on to inform him of the other items Peter had given them.

'So he's moved into Half Hidden,' Dan mused. Holly had neglected, on purpose, previously to mention that he was going to.

'He's well ensconced, and thoroughly enjoying it there.'

Dan sipped more whisky. How he'd missed his tipple! Two bottles would last him quite a while as long as he went easy on it, which he would.

Holly now explained that these bottles might be the last Peter could get, but there was the alternative of brandy and schnapps. At least for the time being.

'And what's more, Peter believes he can get some seeds and plans to grow vegetables. He wants me to help him and we'll share whatever we grow together.'

'Peter?' Dan repeated softly. 'You're on Christian name terms then?'

Holly flushed. 'There's no harm in that when there's no one else around.'

'He's a *German*, Holly.'

'I'm well aware of that, Dad.'

'And you wish to consort with him?'

'I do nothing of the sort,' she snapped angrily in reply. 'The relationship is purely a friendly one.'

Dan fervently hoped so.

'You would welcome a regular supply of vegetables, I take it?' she said caustically.

'Of course.'

'And brandy?'

'Naturally.'

'Well, then.'

Dan didn't like this development one iota but knew better than to try and forbid Holly to take up the offer. He had another sip of whisky.

'What if the pair of you are seen?'

'You've been to Half Hidden, Dad. That's highly unlikely. It's off the beaten track.'

'Even so.'

'Peter's always in civilian clothes and speaks perfect English. Who's to know he's a German?'

'You mentioned he's acquired a car.' Dan raised an eyebrow.

'That can somehow be explained if necessary.'

'Hmmh,' Dan murmured.

'Anyway, I've said yes and that's that.'

'I just hope you know what you're doing,' Dan said, and finished his whisky.

Holly hoped she did too as she set about their tea, which was to be sausage, black bread and coffee.

Peter and Half Hidden weren't mentioned again that evening.

'What's that!' Helen Mason exclaimed in alarm to Holly at the sound of an explosion.

'We're being bombed,' Holly said, both girls rushing to the nearest window and peering out.

'I can't see any planes, can you?' Helen declared.

'What is it? What's going on?' the patient in the nearest bed queried, eyes wide with fright.

'What are the bleeding RAF up to?' the patient in the adjacent bed cried out.

There was another explosion, louder than the first.

'Dear God,' Helen breathed.

Holly opened the window, stuck her head out and scanned the sky. There was still no sign of any planes.

Sister Moignard came hurrying on to the ward from the sluice room, her face creased with concern. 'What's going on?' she too queried.

Helen shrugged. 'We don't know.'

Sister took a worried look round the ward, wondering what to do. If they were under attack the patients should be evacuated. But were they?

'Still no planes visible,' Holly said over her shoulder.

'Oh!' Helen exclaimed when there was a third explosion.

Matron, Sister thought. She'd best consult Matron. She hurried from the ward as quickly as she'd come into it.

Down in the street below a group of pedestrians were staring sky-wards and talking animatedly amongst themselves.

'Can you see anything?' Holly called down.

'Not a blinking thing,' shouted one of the pedestrians in reply, while a few others shook their heads.

Holly closed the window again and, turning to Helen, shrugged.

Later that day they learned that the explosions had been caused by the Germans who were blasting on the outskirts of town. Why they were blasting wasn't yet known.

Terry was on his way home from work, tired after a hard day and looking forward to being with Elspeth. Suddenly he was shoved aside.

He was about to yell out angrily when he saw that the man who'd pushed him was one of the POWs the Germans had imported, now labouring on the many defence installations the Germans were constructing.

The man, a virtual skeleton, glanced behind him, eyes starting in terror. More people were sent scattering as he continued running.

A command rang out in German ordering the escaping prisoner, for that's what he was, to stop.

The man then made the fatal mistake of trying to dash across the street, which gave his pursuers a relatively clear line of fire.

There was a single shot and the man threw his hands in the air. He slumped to the ground where he lay in an ever widening pool of blood.

Suddenly there were Germans everywhere, many carrying rifles. They quickly surrounded the body.

An officer barked out an order, at the conclusion of which he viciously kicked the dead man.

A thoroughly sickened Terry averted his gaze. Nor did he glance at the corpse when he passed by on the pavement.

Holly paused to wipe sweat from her brow. She and Peter were making a start on the garden by clearing away the debris which they were then burning.

'Hard work, eh?' Peter grinned at her.

'I'll say.'

'But worth it in the end.'

He thought of the bag of seed potatoes he'd managed to acquire which he'd plant in the spring. He'd also be planting runner beans, onions, cabbage and broccoli.

Holly gathered up an armful of debris and took it over to the bonfire, where she chucked it on top.

Peter watched her, thinking again what an attractive woman she was. She'd make someone a fine wife one day. Lucky chap.

'I tell you what,' he said when she returned to where they were working. 'How about a break and some coffee?'

'Sounds lovely.'

He threw down the rake he'd been using. 'Right, let's go in.'

Holly paused for a moment to stretch.

'Tired?'

'A bit.'

'Me too. I'm not used to physical work. Well, not this sort anyway.'

They went inside where Holly filled the percolator. While she was doing this Peter sat and lit up a cigarette.

'I had to tell my father about our arrangement,' she said with her back to him.

'And?'

'He wasn't best pleased.'

Peter studied her through a cloud of smoke. 'I see.'

'You are a German, after all. One of the enemy.'

'I can't deny that.'

'He was worried about us being seen together.'

Peter didn't reply to that, having a sinking feeling she was about to say she wouldn't be coming again. 'And what did you say?'

'We desperately need the vegetables, Peter, it's as simple as that.'

Relief flooded through him, she wasn't going to back out after all.

'It's not as if there was any involvement,' she went on. 'What we have is purely a sort of business arrangement.'

'I agree.'

'But you know what people are like, they can so easily get hold of the wrong end of the stick.' She thought of the scene she'd witnessed when Pat Le Clerq had been assaulted, and shuddered.

'Then we mustn't let them. We'll have to be extremely careful while you're here. And you must be that coming and going.'

'Dad says folk will know you're a German because of the car.'

Peter frowned; he hadn't thought of that. It was a point. 'Leave it to me, I'll come up with some plausible explanation,' he said.

'It'll have to be good. There are few Islanders running cars nowadays.'

He then smiled. Of course, he wouldn't even have to lie. 'But doctors do. They're still being given a weekly petrol ration. And I'm a doctor.'

She matched his smile, and nodded.

'Problem solved then. Should anyone inquire, that's why I'm able to run a car.'

He flicked away a lock of blond hair from his forehead, wanting to say how pretty she looked standing there. But of course he didn't; that would have been most inappropriate in the circumstances.

'Holly!'

She stopped and turned to find Tony, a beaming smile on his face, striding towards her. She'd just come off duty.

'What are you doing in town during the week?' she asked.

'Business.'

She nodded.

'How are you?'

'Getting by. And you?'

'The same.'

She shivered under her nurse's cloak, for it was cold. 'I can't wait for the good weather to come round again,' she said.

'It does seem to have been a long winter. Longer than usual.'

'Yes,' she agreed, thinking this awkward.

'Are you off home?'

'That's right.'

'I'll walk you, then.'

She groaned inwardly, not wanting that at all. 'I've got someone to see first who lives close by,' she lied. 'A friend.'

He couldn't help himself. 'Man?'

Oh dear, she thought. 'No, colleague. Female.'

'Ah!'

She glanced at her watch. 'I'd better get on.'

His disappointment was obvious. 'Me too, I suppose. We could have had a coffee together.'

'Another time perhaps.'

'Yes, perhaps.'

'Elspeth tells me you're seeing someone else,' Holly declared brightly.

His face fell. 'That's right.'

'Elspeth mentioned that her name is Ann.'

'We only met recently,' Tony admitted grudgingly.

'I'm sure she's nice.'

'Very.'

'I'm pleased for you.'

He nodded wretchedly. He'd been keen on Ann up until then. But now he'd seen Holly again he knew he'd only been kidding himself. Ann meant nothing to him, and never would.

'Well, goodbye,' she smiled.

'Goodbye.'

As she walked away he knew that his next meeting with Ann would be the last. It simply wasn't the same being with another woman.

Not the same at all.

Normally all the food trays at the hospital were accounted for, strictly so, but an hour previously a patient had suddenly and quite unexpectedly died, which meant Elspeth had a meal going spare.

She stared at it, knowing she should return it to the kitchens, deeply tempted to eat it herself.

What if she did and was found out? There would be hell to pay from Sister. She might even be sacked. In peacetime it wouldn't have mattered so much, but under the present rationing restrictions it would be a serious offence.

She mentally caved in. It was just too tempting. And who was to say a member of the kitchen staff wouldn't eat it anyway?

She carried the tray to a nearby linen store, glanced around to ensure she was unobserved, and slipped inside.

Racked with guilt, she wolfed the meal down.

'How's the gardening going?' Dan inquired casually.

'OK. There's not much we can do just now, but we'll really get going in the spring.'

Dan grunted. 'And yet you're still traipsing out there every free Saturday?'

'I said there isn't much to do, that doesn't mean there still isn't something,' she replied defensively.

'How old is this Dr Schmidt?'

'I've no idea.'

'Young, though?'

'Ish.'

'Good-looking chap?'

'Some might think so. It's never crossed my mind.' The latter was a lie. It certainly had.

'Married?'

'Dad!' she exclaimed. 'What is this, the Spanish Inquisition?'

'Just curious, that's all.'

'I'm not interested in him that way. I certainly have no intention of becoming a Jerrybag if that's what you're getting at.'

'Pleased to hear it.'

'Now leave off will you, please?'

Dan changed the subject by informing her of the latest war news that he'd heard earlier on his clandestine wireless.

Chapter 13

Peter wondered what was wrong with Klumpp, because the man was decidedly agitated. There were six of them round the table in the bar of the Grand relaxing over beers.

Dieter Hercher delivered the punchline of a particularly filthy joke and roared with laughter, as did others in the company. Peter noted that Klumpp didn't laugh, while he allowed himself a simple smile. Though no prude he wasn't particularly keen on filthy jokes, and certainly not ones as coarse and vulgar as that Dieter had just told.

Hauptmann Klipstein drained his glass. 'Who'd like another?'

Peter noted that Klumpp was suddenly eyeing him anxiously. Now why was that?

He announced that he must be getting along, thinking he had things to do back at Half Hidden including some medical reading he had to catch up on. For a moment it crossed his mind how wonderful it would have been to go home and find Holly waiting for him. A thought he quickly dismissed. It was Thursday, he'd see her soon enough when she came that weekend. He experienced a warm tingle of anticipation.

He was in the lobby when Klumpp came hurrying up. 'Peter, can I have a word?'

'Of course. What is it?'

161

'Not here,' Klumpp said quietly. 'My room would be better. We can be private there.'

Peter frowned. 'If you like.'

Klumpp didn't say anything further until they were in his room and the door locked.

'You're lucky not to have to share,' Peter said, glancing around. For there was only a single bed. 'I had to when I was last here, which was the main reason I moved out.'

'I need your help, Peter,' Klumpp beseeched.

'In what way?'

Klumpp swallowed hard. 'I've got VD.'

So that was it. 'Are you sure?'

Klumpp recounted symptoms which convinced Peter that the poor chap was right.

'Will you treat me, please?' he pleaded.

'You know that's strictly forbidden.'

'And you know what'll happen to me if I report my condition to the Medical Officer. It'll be straight to the Russian Front.'

Peter's expression was grim, that was only too true. Officer or private soldier, it didn't matter. If they were found to be infected they were despatched there forthwith where their chances of survival were slim.

'I couldn't even if I wanted to, Hans,' Peter said softly. 'We have only a very small amount of sulphonamides at the hospital which are strictly supervised. It's impossible for me to get access without explaining my reasons. And if I told them, it would be the Russian Front for me as well.'

Klumpp crossed to the bed, where he sat holding his head in despair. 'It was just one of those things,' he croaked. 'I met a local girl and the opportunity unexpectedly arose . . .' He glanced up at Peter, face contorted. 'She seemed such a clean and healthy female, the last you'd have thought, so I took a chance.'

Fool, Peter thought, though he wasn't entirely unsympathetic. When aroused, many men threw caution to the winds. As a tutor once said to him, when the penis is up the brain is out.

'I won't report it,' Klumpp said.

'They'll get you at your next medical, you know that.'

'But until then I can stay on here. The Russian Front . . .' He broke off and shuddered.

Peter was thinking furiously. 'There may be a way,' he mused.

Klumpp stared at him, hope in his eyes. 'How?'

'If you could get yourself some leave and return to Germany, you might possibly be treated there.'

Klumpp considered that. It was over eighteen months since he'd had leave. He might just be able to swing it.

'And there's the black market,' Peter went on. 'I doubt they'd be able to come up with sulphonamides, but it's worth a try. If they do, it'll cost you an arm and a leg.'

'Sod the price,' Klumpp replied. 'I'd pay anything. Anything at all.'

Peter went over and patted Klumpp on the shoulder. 'That's the best I can do. I'm sorry. Do you have a contact in the black market?'

'No, but Wolf Sohn does. I'll speak to him.'

'I wouldn't tell Wolf what it is you're after. You don't wish this to get around. Ask him for the name of his contact and take it from there.'

Klumpp nodded. 'Good advice, Peter. Thank you. I'll try the black market first and if that fails I'll apply for leave.'

'I got mine on compassionate grounds. You might forge a letter which you could show, if required, to the Oberst.'

What Peter didn't say to Klumpp was that should he succeed in getting leave he might still be sent to the Russian Front on its conclusion.

That was a risk Klumpp was going to have to take.

Holly laughed; Peter could be extremely funny at times when the mood took him. The stories he came out with, many of them medical, were outrageous. It was said that Germans didn't have much of a sense of humour but he certainly did.

Peter ran a hand through his hair and stared skywards. 'I do believe spring is definitely on the way. There's a change in the weather, can you feel it?'

She nodded.

He thought of Klumpp who'd departed several weeks previously and wondered how he was getting on and if they'd ever see him again. It was a pity the black market had failed to come up with sulphonamides though, according to Klumpp, they'd done their damndest to accommodate him.

'I must go to the toilet,' Holly declared.

'Well, it won't be newspaper like the last time you were here. I managed to get a dozen rolls of real toilet tissue. A bit hard perhaps, but real tissue nonetheless.'

'That's good,' she enthused.

'You can take a couple home with you if you wish.'

She smiled at him. 'You spoil my father and me, Peter.'

He shrugged, and didn't reply. He enjoyed spoiling Holly Morgan. It gave him great pleasure.

When she'd finished in the toilet she washed her hands, and it was while she was doing this she wondered what changes, if any, he'd made to the main bedroom. Curious, she decided to have a look.

It was more masculine, there could be no doubt about that. Nor was he particularly neat and tidy, which surprised her.

There was a framed picture of a couple whom she took to be his mother and father, and another of a young man who, because of the resemblance, was undoubtedly his brother. There was a silver-backed hairbrush and matching comb, several sets of expensive-looking cuff-links, an enamelled mug with Berlin inscribed on it, a . . .

And then she saw what was hanging behind the door and it wiped the smile from her face. A tremor went through her. His Wehrmacht uniform.

She realised then she'd never seen him in his uniform; he never wore it at the hospital or Half Hidden. The uniform of the enemy, those who'd killed Martin.

For the first time ever it really struck home who and what the man out in the garden was and it made her feel sick.

I must have been mad becoming friendly with such a person, she thought. Laughing, joking, sharing a meal with a member of the Occupying Forces, the scourge of the continent, murdering beasts who'd killed millions to date and would no doubt kill millions more before the war ended.

And Peter, no matter that he spoke perfect English and was kindness itself, was one of them, a hated Hun.

I have to get out of here, she thought, not stay a moment longer. Out of the room, the house, away. And never come back. What was she trying to do, sell her soul for a handful of vegetables?

She stumbled from the bedroom.

'Leave? So soon?' a bewildered Peter said.

She nodded.

'But why?'

'I just have to, that's all.'

'I have some lunch in. You'll like it.'

'No, Peter. Thank you very much.'

She moved away when he tried to catch her by the arm, revolted at the thought of him touching her.

'Goodbye.'

His bewilderment increased. What on earth had got into her? She'd been fine when she'd gone inside, and now this. 'Have I said something? Done something?'

'No,' she whispered.

'Then why?'

'Enjoy your lunch,' she said, and wheeled away, heading for St Helier.

Peter stared after her, slowly shaking his head.

It was almost a week before Peter was able to get Holly on her own. 'Will you please tell me what happened the other day?' he pleaded.

She regarded him coldly. 'Nothing happened.'

That irritated him. Why was she lying? 'Of course it did. One moment you were right as rain, the next you'd completely changed.'

She glanced around, making sure they weren't being observed.

'I think you owe me an explanation, Holly. We are friends, after all.'

'Not any longer. The friendship's finished.'

'But why?'

She bit her lip. 'Because you're a German, Peter, that's why.'

'But you've always known that,' he protested.

'Known, but not really taken on board. I had a sneak look round your bedroom on Saturday because I was curious to see what you might have done to it. And there was your uniform behind the door. Seeing that uniform was like having a bucket of cold water chucked over me. You're one of "them" and nothing will alter the fact.'

'I see,' he murmured.

'I'm sorry, but that's how it is.'

'So you won't be coming back?'

She shook her head.

'That's a great pity.'

'And I'd appreciate it if you didn't speak to me again except on hospital business.'

'Isn't that taking things a bit far?'

'Not in my book.'

And with that she strode off.

I'm going to miss her visits and friendship, he thought sadly. He'd come to think an awful lot of Holly Morgan.

An awful lot indeed.

'There's something different about you recently,' Dan commented to Holly.

'Is there?'

'I can't quite put my finger on it but there is. A sort of . . .' He groped for a word. 'Wistfulness.'

'It's your imagination, Dad.'

'No, it isn't.'

'Well, it is as far as I'm concerned,' she retorted defiantly.

'Now that I come to think of it,' Dan mused, 'you've been that way ever since you stopped going to Half Hidden.'

She turned away so he couldn't see her face. 'That really is nonsense.'

'Hmmh,' he murmured.

'You were the one worried about me consorting with the enemy, after all.'

'That's not what I'm talking about. What I'm saying is that you've been different since you ended your friendship with that man.'

I do miss Peter, she thought. She couldn't deny it, but wasn't going to let on to her father. Missed him even more than she cared to admit even to herself. It infuriated her that she'd allowed her feelings to show.

'Well?' Dan queried.

'It's tripe tonight. And don't complain. I was lucky to get it.'

Dan made a face. He loathed tripe. It made him gag getting it down. But of course there was no likelihood of his refusing to eat it. Food was food, even if it was disgusting.

'Do you see him at the hospital?'

'Who?' she queried, pretending she didn't know to whom Dan was referring.

'Dr Schmidt.'

She shrugged. 'From time to time.'

'Does he try and speak to you?'

'I asked him not to and so he hasn't.'

'Pity. Mind, he was a very useful contact.'

'Oh, I see!' she snapped scornfully. 'You didn't like me consorting with him as you put it, but would be happy to go on taking his brandy or whatever.'

Dan looked shamefaced. 'Double standards, eh?'

'Exactly.'

He sighed. Now it was his turn to be wistful thinking of the scotch, brandy and coffee the German had been able to supply them with.

'Ugh!' he exclaimed, wrinkling his nose when Holly produced strips of tripe from a rolled-up newspaper. He'd rather have eaten horse, anything, rather than tripe.

'I'm going to catch my death before long,' Dan complained, taking off his sodden shoes, both of which had large holes in the soles. Shoes were a major problem on the island, as new ones were impossible to buy and there was no leather to repair the old ones.

He removed the soggy cardboard that he'd used to cover the

holes. What good was cardboard when it rained! None at all. Useless.

'If only I could lay my hands on a decent piece of thick leather,' he wished.

'You're not the only one with that problem,' Holly declared. 'Half the Island is walking around with holes in their shoes.'

'That isn't a consolation, I can assure you.'

He took off his equally sodden socks and hung them in front of the empty grate. 'It'll take these days to dry without a fire,' he further grumbled.

It was then Holly had an idea. She knew where there were men's shoes to be had. The only trouble was getting them.

It was Holly's half-day and she'd checked the doctors' duty roster to confirm that Peter was at the hospital that day. She intended going out to the cottage and taking some of the shoes left behind by Mr Vardon. Even if they weren't the right size, Dan would be able to cannabalise the soles in some way.

She stopped to gaze at Half Hidden, then at the track where Peter parked his car. There was no sign of it, which was what she'd expected. This shouldn't take long, she thought, making for the cottage door.

Peter had got in the habit of leaving a spare key under a flower pot, partly for her use and also in case he locked himself out or left his own key behind at the hospital. The spare key was still there.

She opened the door and closed it again behind her, heading for the stairs.

She was halfway up when she heard a groan that stopped her in her tracks. There it was again, another groan. Somebody was upstairs.

Well, it couldn't be Peter, she thought. So who? Her face flamed when she realised it might be a woman.

What to do? Turn around and leave straight away was the obvious answer.

'Ooh!'

That groan was the loudest yet. A groan that certainly wasn't one of pleasure but pain. She worried at a nail in indecision.

Her nose twitched when a smell assailed it. A combination odour that she recognised only too well from the hospital. That of excrement mixed with vomit.

This is none of my business, she told herself. Then another waft hit her, stronger and more virulent than before.

Part of her insisted she get out of there, she was trespassing, after all. (So was Peter by living there, but that was beside the point.) Another part, her feminine instinct, told her she should investigate. That and her training as a nurse. Someone was definitely ill and she should offer help if required.

Another groan which, like the others, she couldn't tell if it had been made by a man or woman.

Taking a deep breath she continued on up the stairs, the smell becoming worse as she went.

The source was the main bedroom, Peter's. The bedroom door was partially ajar. She poked her head round.

Peter lay in bed, covered in a tangle of bedclothes. His face was white as milk, his hair plastered to his forehead. His eyes were closed.

Holly went to him. What a state, she thought. There was vomit on the bedclothes and pillows, more on the carpet and yet more on the wall nearest to where he was lying. She knew only too well what was under the bedclothes.

'Peter?'

His eyelids fluttered.

'Peter?' she said more urgently.

His eyes flickered open to stare blankly at her. Then recognition slowly dawned. 'Holly!' he croaked.

A hand on his forehead informed her he had a high temperature. His forehead was slick with sweat.

'Water. Water.'

She went to the bathroom where she filled a tumbler at the tap. On returning to his bedside she helped him to drink, which he did greedily.

'Take your time, Peter. You'll just vomit again if you gulp it down like that.'

He sank back on his pillows. 'How . . . why . . .'

'I'll explain that later,' she said. 'You've got d and v.' That meant diarrhoea and vomiting.

'Flu, I think. Came down with it . . .' He paused to think. 'Day before yesterday, but I'm not certain. Time's been a blur.'

There had been some severe cases of flu going round and it seemed he'd also succumbed. How awful for him to have been on his own like this.

'First thing to do is get you and the bed cleaned up,' she stated brusquely.

A hand groped for, and found, hers. 'No, Holly, you can't do that.'

'I'm a nurse, Peter. I'm used to it.'

'Not that, I . . .' He trailed off in embarrassment.

She smiled, realising what the trouble was. 'I've given hundreds of bed baths to men, Peter, and seen just as many willies. It's nothing new, I can assure you.'

'I know, but . . .' He trailed off a second time.

'And you certainly can't remain as you are. You'll have to be sorted.'

He sighed, 'So . . . humiliating.'

'I hope you remember that when you get back to work. That's often how patients feel.'

He groaned again. 'My head. It's spinning. Did try to get to the toilet but couldn't make it. Couldn't even get out of bed.'

'Do you think you'll be ill again?'

'Nothing left to come up, I shouldn't think.'

'I'll get you something to use anyway just in case.'

He closed his eyes and muttered in German.

'Where's the car?' she asked, remembering it hadn't been outside. She wouldn't have come in if it had been there.

'Being repaired. It broke down.'

That explained it. 'Right,' she said. 'Back in a jiffy.'

She went down to the kitchen where she looked out a large mixing bowl that would be just the job, placing that by his bedside within easy reach.

The next thing she did was to make up and light the fire in the sitting room. She needed hot water which the back boiler would provide.

After that she rooted out fresh linen and spare blankets, taking those through to the bedroom and placing them on top of the chest of drawers.

When she turned to speak to Peter she found he'd drifted back to sleep.

When the hot water was ready she woke Peter, then began stripping the bed.

'I'm so ashamed,' he whispered when the awful mess he was in was revealed.

'There's nothing to be ashamed about, it could happen to any of us. And you as a doctor should appreciate that.'

She removed his dirty pyjama bottoms, rolled them up and dumped them in the bath. Then his top, which joined the bottoms.

Holly assisted him, he shivering, to his feet and wrapped a large towel round him. He groaned as he sank into the wicker chair she'd placed by the side of the bed.

She wet the flannel she'd brought in the basin of hot water and proceeded to wash him all over, rinsing the flannel again and again. Twice she went through to the bathroom to change the water.

That done to her satisfaction she dried him, using another towel. He continued to shiver and occasionally groan. When she'd completed that she helped him into fresh pyjamas and a dressing gown.

'Feel better?' she asked breezily.

He tried to nod which only produced another groan. 'Thank you, yes,' he croaked.

She sat him down again in the wicker chair. 'You'll have to remain there for a few minutes while I re-make the bed,' she declared.

He watched her do that, thinking how gentle she'd been while washing and drying him. She was a damn fine nurse, but then he'd already known that. Now that had been confirmed from first-hand experience.

'In you go,' she said when the bed was ready.

He sighed as he slid between the fresh sheets. 'Lovely,' he muttered.

'Is there any food in the house?'

'A little. Not much.'

'Could you eat something?'

'I'm not sure.'

'Hmmh,' she murmured. 'It's best you try. Have you any tea?'

'In the caddy.'

'I'll make a pot. That'll do you good as well.'

'Aspirins in the kitchen drawer nearest the door, Holly. Give me two.'

That was a bonus, she thought. Aspirins were another thing normally impossible to come by for the public, but Peter had access to such items.

She returned a couple of minutes later with the aspirins and a tumbler refilled with water. He had trouble swallowing, but finally managed to get the tablets down.

'Good,' she said.

She went back to the kitchen where she found a small piece of meat and a few vegetables, enough to make a light broth. He was too weak to feed himself so she did that for him, sitting on the side of the bed and spooning the broth into his mouth. Again he had trouble swallowing.

'Enough, can't take any more,' he croaked when the bowl was half empty.

Holly decided not to press him on that. What he'd had was sufficient for the moment.

'How's the head?' she inquired.

'Going round and round. Like I was drunk.'

She laughed, but it was a sympathetic laugh.

'Why . . . did you come?'

She explained about the shoes and that she'd intended pinching some of Mr Vardon's. That brought the ghost of a smile to his face.

'Take whatever you need,' he said.

She felt his forehead and it seemed to her his temperature had gone down a bit. A forehead now moist, not slick as it had been when she'd arrived.

'I have to contact the hospital and explain,' he said. 'They'll be wondering about me.'

He coughed, a rattly sound. 'The phone has rung several times, them probably trying to get in touch, but I couldn't answer it.'

'Do you want me to do it for you?'

'Can you?'

Holly thought about that. 'I'll pretend I'm a neighbour, which should do the trick. I certainly don't want them knowing it's me on the line.'

'No,' he agreed.

When she spoke to the hospital she deepened her voice and broadened her accent. The woman who answered, a name Holly didn't recognise, thanked her for her trouble.

What to do about this lot? Holly wondered, staring down at the sheets and blankets in the bath. At least there were some soapflakes available left behind by the Vardons.

She rinsed the sheets under the tap, then took them out to the rear where there was a wash-house. She filled the copper and deposited the sheets inside.

The blankets were another matter as they couldn't go in the copper. She rinsed the larger patches of vomit away then pummelled the blankets in lukewarm water, having added vinegar as a disinfectant.

That completed, she carried the blankets, one at a time because of their weight, out to the rear where she spread them on a section of grass. The line would never have taken the strain.

I've earned a cup of tea, she told herself when all that was finally finished. More than earned a cup, thankful there was one to be had.

Peter smiled weakly when she handed him his, and while they drank, she sitting in the wicker chair, she explained what she'd done about the bedclothes.

'I can't thank you enough, Holly,' he said.

'You're looking a lot better already.'

'Thanks to you and the aspirins. How many are left?'

'Eight. I'll bring them up to you later.'

He closed his eyes, then opened them. 'I've been dreaming a lot.'

'Oh?'

'Nothing much that made sense. All very confused. Delirium, no doubt.'

She glanced at the bedroom fireplace. 'I'll make you a fire in here. Heat the room up.'

He gave her another weak smile. 'You're being extremely kind, Holly Morgan. I appreciate it.'

There was something in his tone that made her smile also. 'You mean I'm being kind despite the fact that you're a German?'

'One of the enemy.'

'Well, I could hardly leave you the way you were, German or not.'

'Does that mean we're friends again?' he asked softly.

She finished her tea.

'I'll make a start on that fire.'

Chapter 14

'Once we began discussing the matter we both soon realised that he couldn't remain at Half Hidden on his own. For a start there was very little food in the cottage, which he was far too ill to deal with anyway.

'I did consider trying to get out to him every evening, but that's impossible with the shifts I've got coming up. Nor could I take time off work; flu can last for weeks. And the only food I could have taken him would be part of my rations, which he would never have accepted in a month of Sundays.

'So in the end we agreed the only sensible thing to do was to ring the hospital again and have them sort it out.'

'Hmmh,' Dan murmured.

'I got Peter into his dressing gown and downstairs where he contacted a German colleague who said that an ambulance would be on its way within the hour. I helped him back into bed, rescued the sheets from the copper, pegged them out, said goodbye and left.'

'He was lucky you turned up. I've heard that several people have died of this flu,' Dan commented.

'It's a particularly virulent strain, apparently.'

'Dr Gallichan the headmaster is down with it as well. He's very poorly from all accounts.'

'I didn't know.'

'He's been off for two days now. I thought I'd mentioned.'

Holly recalled Peter as she'd found him. Without attention and food who knew what the outcome would have been. She gave a slight shudder, imagining him lying dead in that mess.

'These shoes are terrific,' Dan said. Holly had brought him two pairs, a pair of stout black brogues and an ordinary walking pair. No matter they were several sizes too large for him, a little bit of newspaper would soon take care of that. He couldn't have been more pleased, as it meant he'd have dry feet again when it rained.

'So have they taken him into hospital?' Dan queried.

'I've no idea, but would imagine so. He is a doctor and one of their own, after all. They'll want to give him the best of attention.'

'Fortunate chap.'

If he was in the hospital Holly wondered if it would be possible to see him. She doubted it would. He'd be bound to be put into a German ward where there would be no excuse for her to visit. Nor could she request to see him, that would soon have rumours flying around.

Dan decided to wear the walking shoes first, smiling with delight at the prospect.

'Terry . . . Terry,' Elspeth moaned. She too had fallen victim to flu and been admitted to Holly's ward.

A worried Holly wiped her friend's forehead. There were now over two dozen cases in the hospital while many others were being treated by their GPs at home. The outbreak was rapidly becoming an epidemic.

Sally Pallot, working on an adjacent ward, came up to the bedside. 'How is she?'

'Still delirious.'

Sally made a sympathetic face. 'I only hope I don't get it.'

Holly fervently hoped she didn't either.

'Terry,' Elspeth mumbled again.

'How is Terry?' Sally asked.

'How do you think? Worried sick.'

'There's been another death from it this morning on ward six,' Sally informed Holly.

'Oh?'

'A young boy apparently. I heard he was Candia Ruellen's cousin.' Candia was another nurse both of them had worked with in the past.

Elspeth's lids flew open to reveal fevered eyes. She stared blankly at the ceiling, seeing nothing.

'I wish there was more we could do,' Holly commented. For the fact was there was very little that could be done other than keeping the patient warm and well attended to.

'I said a prayer for her last night and I'll say another tonight,' Sally smiled thinly.

Holly again wiped Elspeth's forehead.

'Well?' Terry demanded anxiously.

'She's as well as can be expected,' Holly replied.

'Has she come round yet?'

'I'm afraid not.'

Terry clutched her arm. 'She will be OK, won't she? I mean . . .' He swallowed hard.

'We're doing everything possible, Terry. We can't do any more.'

He closed his eyes. 'Please, God, please,' he whispered.

Later that day, quite by chance, Holly learned that Peter had been discharged.

Peter, still weak but otherwise recovered, entered the bar at the Grand to be confronted by a beaming Hans Klumpp. He didn't have to ask, it was obvious that Klumpp had been treated successfully in Germany.

Klumpp nodded, then said, 'I owe you a very large drink. Brandy?'

'If I had a large brandy right now I'd probably keel over,' Peter replied. 'I've had flu. But a beer would be nice.'

'Coming straight up,' Klumpp declared.

'And you clearly have been posted back here.'

'That's right.'

Lucky on both counts, Peter thought.

He was warmly welcomed by his friends at their table when he joined them, all of them having visited him at one stage or another during the latter part of his stay in hospital.

Holly hung up the phone with a frown. Peter hadn't answered her call. What did that mean? Was he simply out, in town perhaps? Or was he staying elsewhere for the time being?

She decided to leave it a couple of days and ring again. She just wanted to check on how he was.

Terry squeezed Elspeth's hand. Thankfully she was now well on the road to recovery. 'I can't wait to have you home again,' he stated.

'And I can't wait to be there.'

'It's dreadful without you. I feel like the proverbial fish out of water without you around.'

She smiled. 'It's nice to know I'm missed.'

'You're certainly that. Missed and more.'

He leant closer to her. 'I love you, Elspeth. With all my heart and soul.'

'And I love you the same way, Terry. You know that.'

He gently squeezed her hand again. 'Holly says only another few days and possibly, possibly mind you, they'll let you go.'

'She's been an absolute brick throughout all this. Looked after me as if I was her own flesh and blood.'

'She's a great girl,' Terry nodded.

'The others have been smashing as well, fussing over me like a load of mother hens.'

'I'm sure you'd have done the same for them. One for all and all for one, eh?'

'Of course.'

'I'll have another word with Holly before I leave. Thank her yet again for everything.'

Sister Moignard, watching from across the ward, sighed. Talk about lovebirds! Love was something she herself had never known, being married to her profession like many of the Sisters and older nurses.

'Now then,' she said sternly, turning to the nurse in attendance. 'This is what you do.'

'*Ja?*'

He's home at last, Holly thought. This was the fourth time she'd rung Half Hidden.

'Peter, it's me, Holly.'

'Hello!' he exclaimed. 'This is a pleasure.'

'I thought I'd ring and find out how you were. I would have come and seen you at the hospital but that just wasn't on.'

'No,' he agreed. 'I fully understand.' He groped for his cigarettes, excited at hearing her voice and to think she'd bothered to ring.

'I discharged myself in the end, as they needed the bed. I stayed at the Grand for a bit, mainly sleeping and reading while I built up my strength again.'

'I thought that might be the case.'

'They looked after me extremely well. Now I'm home again and starting work next week.'

She smiled. 'You sound in the pink.'

'Hardly that. I still feel a little weak, flu really does take it out of you.'

'Then perhaps you should delay returning to the hospital.'

He laughed. 'Work will do me good. I'm looking forward to it.'

'Well, you must know what you're doing, you're the doctor.'

He lit a cigarette. 'Exactly. But how have you been?'

'OK. Somewhat concerned about one of my friends who came down with flu as well. But she's now also been discharged.'

He said tenderly, 'I can't thank you enough, Holly, for what you did. You probably saved my life.'

She didn't reply to that.

'Are you still there?' he asked after a few seconds.

'Yes.'

'I said . . .'

'I heard what you said,' she interrupted.

'It's true.'

'I'd better go,' she said.

'No, wait. I'd like to see you again.'

'You will, at the hospital.'

'I meant here at Half Hidden. I'll try and get the same weekends off as I had before, the same ones as you.'

Again she didn't reply.

'Holly?'

'I'll think about it,' she heard herself say.

'Good. How were the shoes?'

'Wonderful. Dad was thrilled.'

'I'm pleased.'

'Now I really must get on. Goodbye, Peter.'

'Goodbye, Holly. Thank you for ringing.'

She hung up, took a deep breath, stared at the phone, and slowly exhaled.

Now why had she said she'd think about it when she should have said no? She had absolutely no intention of going back to Half Hidden for the same reasons she'd given him originally.

He was a German, one of the enemy.

He was also Peter. And whether she liked to admit it or not, her friend.

Dan came awake with a start, having been dozing in the chair. Now who could that be rapping on the door?

When he opened it he was confronted by two Germans. Checking for hoarding again, he thought.

He couldn't have been more wrong.

Holly entered the cell to find her father sitting on the bed it contained, the cell's only piece of furniture. His expression was one of dismay combined with extreme apprehension.

'You bloody fool!' she spat, and burst into tears.

He immediately went to her and tried to put an arm round her shoulders but she angrily shrugged it off.

'You bloody fool,' she repeated. She was tempted to hit him, slap him across the face, but didn't.

'I'm sorry, Holly.'

'No wonder you had all the up-to-date news. You had a wireless!'

Dan hung his head.

'I can't think of anything more stupid. You knew what they'd do to you if they caught you, and now they have.'

'An informer,' Dan whispered.

'You must have been shooting your mouth off, sharing the news with others.'

'I thought I was being so terribly careful.'

She barked out a scornful laugh, meanwhile wiping away her tears. 'It looks like it, doesn't it?'

'I can't think who would have informed. They're my closest friends.'

'Well, one of them did.'

Dan ran a hand through his hair, a hand that was trembling. 'They tore the place apart until they found the earphones. I didn't think they would, they were so well hidden. But the bastards did. Then they discovered the wireless itself when I was ordered to turn out my pockets.' He shook his head. 'They've obviously become well acquainted with these tiny crystal sets. Mine was so small I carried it about with me in my jacket.'

Holly stared at him incredulously. 'You carried it about with you?'

'Seemed the safest bet.'

'But you needed earphones as well?'

Dan nodded. 'I'm sorry about the mess at home.'

Holly thought of the sight that had greeted her return from work, standing staring at it in disbelief when a neighbour had knocked to tell her that Dan had been arrested. She had witnessed him being driven away by the Germans.

'That can be fixed,' she replied tightly.

'There's something else,' Dan said quietly, a tremor in his voice. 'They interrogated me about you.'

'Me!' she exclaimed.

'They wanted to know if you knew about the set.'

Sudden fear filled her. In her concern for Dan she hadn't thought about herself. 'What did you say?'

'I swore blind that you had no knowledge whatsoever of the set.'

'And did they believe you?'

'I think so.'

'Only *think* so!'

'It's not unusual for one member of a family to have a secret wireless that the other members are totally unaware of,' Dan gabbled. 'They appreciate that.'

'When's your trial?' she asked.

'Tomorrow morning sometime. Will you come?'

'I'll try to.'

Dan hung his head a second time. 'I really am sorry, Holly. I . . .'

'Will you stop apologising!' she snapped. 'You've done nothing else but.'

She'd stopped crying and wished she had a handkerchief, but had come out without one.

'Those earphones were so well hidden,' Dan murmured, shaking his head.

Further recriminations were useless, she thought. The deed was done and now had to be paid for.

'Good luck for tomorrow,' she said. He was her father, after all, whom she dearly loved, no matter how stupid he'd been.

'I'm . . .' He broke off, having been about to apologise again.

She kissed him on the cheek. 'Take care.'

'And you, my darling.'

Now he was crying.

He turned away from her as she banged on the door as instructed when she wished to leave.

The man at the desk studied her through unblinking, reptilian eyes as she walked past, half expecting to be ordered to halt at any moment.

Two other men appeared, halting to stare at her. One of them smiled, and it seemed to her the smile said, 'I know something you don't.'

Then she was outside on the pavement, walking away from the medieval jail as fast as her legs would take her without actually breaking into a run.

They'd let her go, but did that mean they believed Dan? From what she'd heard the Geheime Feldpolizei, the secret military police, were entirely capable of playing cat and mouse with her. Letting her go now, picking her up later when she thought she was safe and in the clear.

'*Ja?*'

He was home; she'd been praying he would be. He was the only one she'd been able to think of who might be able to help. 'Peter, it's Holly.'

'Oh hello! This is a surprise.'

'I must speak to you, it's urgent.'

'All right, go ahead.'

'No, no, in person. Can we meet?' Rumour had it that telephone conversations were sometimes eavesdropped on by the authorities.

'You mean now?'

'If that's possible.'

Peter frowned on the other end of the phone. 'Where do you suggest?'

'I could come to Half Hidden.'

He glanced at his watch, thinking she'd never get to Half Hidden and back again on foot before curfew. He could drive her back, of course, but that was tricky. Urgent, she'd said, and her voice was shaking. Something had happened. Best he go to her. 'Why don't I jump in my car? What's your address?'

'You mean come to my house?'

'Unless you prefer somewhere public?'

She thought furiously. He was right. She told him the street and number, which he jotted down.

'You will dress properly?' she said.

He knew she meant wear civvies and not his uniform. 'Of course, Holly. And I'll, eh . . . park in an appropriate place.'

'See you shortly, then.'

'I'm on my way.'

She was trying to tidy up, dithering about, her mind not on the job at all, when he arrived.

'You were quick,' she said, ushering him through.

'You said urgent, and I . . .' He trailed off when he saw the state of the room. 'What happened?' he asked softly.

Words tumbling from her mouth, voice still shaking, she explained.

'And you knew nothing about this wireless set?'

She shook her head. 'On my life, Peter, I swear.'

'Hmmh,' he murmured, thinking.

'I just don't know whether they believed Dad or not. You know what they're like, the games they play. And what if it's the Gestapo who turn up for me?'

He shook his head. 'There are no Gestapo on the island.'

'People say they go around dressed as you are, as civilians.'

'I assure you, Holly, there are no Gestapo on Jersey. That's a fact.'

Holly swallowed hard. 'I'm worried sick, Peter, not only about myself but Dad.'

'There's nothing I can do for him,' Peter stated matter of factly. 'He was caught red-handed and that's that. But you're something else again.'

He glanced round and swore in German. Dan Morgan may have been guilty, but there was no need to reduce his home, Holly's home, to this. And what if Dan had been innocent? Thugs, he thought. That's all some of these people were, thugs. At times they and their ilk made him ashamed of his own race.

'Can you help?' she queried.

'I personally don't have any connections within the Geheime Feldpolizei, but as chance would have it I know someone who has.'

And that someone was Hans Klumpp who owed him a favour. Klumpp's connection was a high-ranking officer whom he'd known before the war.

'I'll see what I can do,' Peter declared.

Tears welled in her eyes. 'Thank you.'

He smiled at her, thinking that Klumpp should be at the Grand, probably in the bar. He left Holly a few minutes later and she resumed trying to tidy up.

He'd promised her that, one way or the other, he'd be back.

'Are you certain she's innocent?' Klumpp queried.

'She swears it and I believe her.'

Klumpp grinned. 'I never knew you had a girlfriend, Peter.'

'She's not a girlfriend in that sense of the word. Just a friend, a colleague.'

Klumpp's expression said he clearly disbelieved that. 'Be careful with these island girls, Peter. I speak from bitter experience as you well know.'

'I told you she's just a friend, nothing more. But a *good* friend.'

'All right, don't get annoyed,' Klumpp chuckled.

'So will you help?'

'Of course.' He patted Peter on the shoulder. 'I owe you, don't forget. I'll get right on to it. Now give me her details.'

Holly crawled into bed but doubted she'd get any sleep that night. Peter had returned as he'd promised, saying that his brother officer had the matter in hand. He'd done his best to reassure her before leaving again.

She thought of Dan in his lonely cell, wondering how he was. Tomorrow they'd know the worst.

She sighed in the darkness, her mind whirling. What if Peter's brother officer failed, what if . . . Sticking a finger into her mouth she chewed on it.

She was proved right about not sleeping a single wink through-out a very long night.

Holly slumped on the wooden bench where she'd been instructed to sit. Two years! To be served in a prison in France. Double the sentence Miss Dupré had been given.

An ashen-faced Dan turned to stare at her. Their eyes met, but only for a few brief seconds before he was hustled away, back to the cells.

'Oh, Dad!' Holly whispered.

Holly returned home and sat in one of the chairs by the fire. She'd tried to see Dan again but permission had been refused, as would all further requests, she'd been informed. She'd also been told he was to be taken to France on the first available ship.

Although she'd been given the day off by Sister Moignard she wondered if it wasn't best she return to work. That would occupy her mind, stop her worrying for a while. There again, she was hardly in any fit state to look after patients.

Two years in some hellhole in France, she thought in despair. She prayed with all her heart Dan would come through it all right.

There had been some dreadful stories.

Dan finally stopped pacing his cell and perched dejectedly on the edge of his bed. He was in a state of shock at the severity of his sentence. He found it unbelievable.

The reason that had been given in court was that too many Islanders were flouting the law about banned wireless sets; a sterner example had to be made. And he was the first of that sterner example.

'Just my rotten bloody luck,' he muttered. 'Just my rotten bloody luck.'

What would become of Holly in the meantime? All alone in the house, by herself. No company to come home to.

I shouldn't worry too much about her, he thought. She was a resilient, capable girl, she'd get by. If the Germans allowed her to, that was, that was his real concern.

Had they believed him? He prayed God they had. The awful thing was, even if they had, they were quite capable of arresting her out of sheer bloodymindedness, insisting that she had known about the set.

He shook all over. If they did arrest her . . . How could he live with that? The fact she too had been sent to prison, all because of his stupidity, would eat at him night and day. He'd be consumed with guilt.

Damn! He'd been so convinced he wouldn't be caught. Totally and utterly convinced. And the few friends he'd confided in were ones he'd trusted completely. Only one of those so-called friends had betrayed him by informing. Why, though? That was what he couldn't understand, was completely beyond him, why? He wondered if he'd ever find out the answer to that.

*

Holly glanced at the clock on the mantelpiece when there was a knock on the outside door, then remembered the clock was broken. Broken when the house had been so brutally torn apart.

'I've got news,' Peter declared when she answered the knock.

She quickly ushered him inside.

'No one saw me, so relax,' he said. 'The street's deserted.'

'News?'

'You're in the clear, Holly. It's been fixed.'

'Oh!' she exhaled, immense relief bursting within her. 'Are you sure about that?'

'Positive. I don't know whether they intended arresting you or not, but they certainly won't be now.'

This time it was tears of joy that came into her eyes. 'That's wonderful. I can't . . . I can't . . .'

Somehow she was in his arms, she laughing, he laughing, hugging each other. And then suddenly his lips were on hers.

She froze for a moment, a voice at the back of her mind reminding her he was a German, the enemy.

The voice vanished and there was only the dizzy sweetness of his mouth, the warm smell of him in her nostrils.

It was bliss.

Chapter 15

Holly studied Peter, who was standing in the vegetable garden gazing up at the sky. Her feelings were mixed, but she'd felt she'd had to come to Half Hidden that Saturday, her first free one since the night they'd kissed. A kiss she hadn't been able to put out of her mind and which she could even now taste. A kiss that had haunted her.

'A penny for them!' she called out.

He turned and smiled. 'Hello, Holly.'

'I thought I'd drop by and see how you were getting on.' That was true, but there was more to it than that.

'Fine.'

'What were you looking at?' she asked as she approached him.

He shrugged. 'Nothing really. Day-dreaming, I suppose.'

'About what?'

He stared her directly in the eye. 'You.'

She flushed. 'Really?'

'Really.'

She glanced away in confusion. 'It's almost time to start sowing and planting.'

'Have you changed your mind about helping me?'

'I don't know . . .' She swallowed. 'I want to thank you again for what you did.'

'It was my pleasure, Holly Morgan.'

She wanted to touch him, for him to touch her. She wanted . . . 'It always sounds so strange when you call me by both my Christian and surname.'

'They're both nice names.'

He pulled out a packet of cigarettes and lit up. 'I'm thinking of stopping,' he said, waggling the cigarette at her.

'Oh?'

'I'm developing a cough. Besides, they're becoming harder and harder to come by.'

'The Islanders can't get any at all.'

'Look on the bright side, that's good for their health.'

She laughed, finding that funny. 'I suppose so.'

'Filthy habit really. I started in Edinburgh when I was there. The Scots are heavy smokers, everyone I knew there seemed to be one. And their diet!' He rolled his eyes upwards. 'No wonder they have so many heart problems.'

'What's wrong with their diet?'

'Too many fry-ups and baking. Combine that with heavy smoking and a large alcohol intake and you have a recipe for disaster.'

'I thought Germans were traditionally big drinkers as well?'

'They are,' he confirmed. 'Though mostly beer, which isn't quite so bad for you as spirits. The Scots love their whisky.'

As had Dan, Holly thought sadly, who was probably incarcerated in France by now. That brought a lump to her throat.

'What's wrong?' Peter queried, noting her expression.

'I was just thinking about Dad.'

Peter cursed himself for mentioning scotch whisky; he should have been more tactful.

'It was his own fault, but still . . .' She trailed off and made a face.

'Two years isn't for ever,' Peter said softly.

'No.'

But he knew only too well what the conditions in these prisons and camps were like. Her father was in for a very tough time indeed.

'At least I was spared,' Holly said.

He couldn't bear the thought of her being imprisoned. The

images that flashed through his mind made him feel sick.

Holly made a decision. 'I'll come back and help you.'

He brightened immediately. 'That's wonderful!'

'It'll be enjoyable.' Being with him more than anything else.

'Holly?'

She gazed at him, noticing how uncomfortable he now appeared.

'About the other night when we . . .' He cleared his throat. 'I hope you don't think I took advantage of the situation?'

She shook her head.

'Good.'

'I could have stopped it at any time,' she said in a low voice.

'But you didn't?'

'No,' she whispered.

He placed his hand on her arm. 'What does it mean, Holly?'

'I honestly don't know.'

'Neither do I. What I do know is I find you terribly attractive and enjoy being with you. Wouldn't you agree we have a good rapport between us?'

She nodded.

'And yet . . . The fact remains I'm a German and you're a Channel Islander. If only things were different.'

If only they were, she thought.

'I appreciate how you feel about Jerrybags.'

She didn't reply to that. Instead she was thinking how wonderful it was to have him touching her, even if it was only his hand on her arm.

'I'll tell you what,' he said suddenly, changing the subject. 'It's a beautiful day, so why don't we go for a walk and then we can come back here and I'll feed you. I have several freshly caught plaice in the house which were landed this morning.'

Her mouth watered at the prospect. But she wasn't at all sure about the walk. 'What if we're seen, Peter?'

'We'll keep off the main roads. There are lots of little-used paths round here, I've discovered. And if we do meet anyone, a simple hello, goodday should suffice. We have been for a walk together before, remember, and that was OK.'

'All right then.'

He smiled at her. 'Shall we?'

The plaice, when she eventually cooked them after a splendid, invigorating walk during which they chatted more or less non-stop, were delicious.

'Have you heard anything about your dad?' Viv Radmore asked Holly.

'No. Nothing.'

Viv pulled a sympathetic face.

'I presume he's now in France, though I've no idea where.'

'He'll be all right,' Viv said, trying to cheer Holly up. 'You'll see.'

Holly fervently hoped so. If only they could correspond, that would be something. But that wasn't allowed. Neither on her part nor on his.

Holly sat staring out over the Channel. It was a gorgeous spring day, the third year of the Occupation. It seemed like thirty.

What am I going to do about Peter Schmidt? she wondered. She'd been back to Half Hidden twice since the night they'd kissed, but so far he hadn't made any further move in that direction. She knew if a move was to be made it had to come from her, though that hadn't been admitted between them.

Could she become involved with a German, become a Jerrybag? She shuddered at the thought.

And yet the chemistry between them couldn't be denied. There were occasions when it positively zinged. How different from when she'd been with Tony Le Var, there it had been all one-sided on Tony's part. But with Peter the zing went in both directions.

She thought of Martin, now, strangely, only a distant memory. He belonged to the past, this was here and now. As for the future? Nobody knew what that would be in wartime when everything was so uncertain. A future there would be, but what would it be?

The question to be faced was the here and now, and Peter.

Klumpp lurched up to Peter standing at the bar in the Grand. 'How's your little friend then?' he queried in a lewd whisper, winking as he spoke.

The man was drunk, Peter thought. That was obvious. 'She's OK.'

'Aha! So you admit she is your girlfriend?' Klumpp held on to the bar to steady himself.

Peter regarded him coldly. 'I do nothing of the sort. She is not my girlfriend, I told you that.'

'So you say.' Klumpp hiccuped and called for another brandy.

'Don't you think you've had enough?' Peter said quietly.

'Never enough where brandy is concerned.'

'Much more and you'll pass out.'

Klumpp shook his head. 'Won't. I never do that. Never happened in my entire life.'

The brandy was delivered. 'You?' Klumpp asked Peter.

'No, thanks.'

'Come on.' He nudged Peter's arm. 'Have one with me. I'm still in your debt. If it wasn't for you I'd be . . . Well you know where. Dead or alive that's where I'd be.'

Peter had an idea. 'Instead of brandy, you could get me a bit of information. I'd appreciate that far more.'

'Which is?' Klumpp inquired conspiratorially, leaning closer to Peter.

Peter told him.

Klumpp tapped his nose. 'Good as done, dear friend and saviour. Good as done.'

A few moments later Peter made his excuses and left, hoping that Klumpp would remember their conversation.

As it transpired Klumpp didn't pass out, at least not until he almost reached his bed.

'Where did you get real coffee from?' a wide-eyed Elspeth queried.

'I have my sources,' Holly replied evasively. It had of course come from Peter.

'Oh! The black market, eh?'

Holly neither confirmed or denied that.

'I thought your father was completely against the black market?'

'He was.'

'But not you?'

Holly shrugged.

'Are you seeing someone?'

The question, straight out of the blue, startled Holly. 'Why do you say that?'

'Because I'm your best pal and have been for years. I know you. That twinkle in the eye. The new bounce in your step. Well?' she demanded eagerly.

Holly shook her head.

Elspeth sank disappointedly back in her chair. 'I would have sworn you were.'

'Well, you're wrong.'

Elspeth studied Holly. 'You wouldn't fib, would you?'

'Why would I do that?'

'No idea, you just might.'

Holly snorted.

'Tony still asks after you. He'd come back in a second if you crooked your little finger.'

'Tony's not for me, Elspeth. I thought I'd made that plain to him.'

'Oh, you have, but he lives in hope. The poor bugger is quite smitten.'

Holly considered offering Elspeth sugar for her coffee, then decided against it. That would only cause more comment. She paused for a moment to think fondly of Peter, wishing he was there. Not with Elspeth, of course, just the pair of them. She wondered what he was doing. Was he at the Grand or Half Hidden? And if the latter, what was he up to?

'Holly?'

She came out of her reverie. 'Sorry. Did you say something?'

Elspeth gave her an odd look, then went on to complain that, even though she and Terry were trying like billy-o – that made Holly smile – she still wasn't pregnant.

'Nurse, can you please assist me with this patient?' The patient in question, who was anesthetised, was lying on a trolley in the corridor waiting to be taken into theatre.

Holly hurried to Peter's side. What was this all about?

Peter made a small gesture beckoning her close. He then pretended to examine the patient.

'I've discovered where your father is,' he whispered. 'The Cherche-Midi prison in Paris.'

Elation leapt in Holly.

'Right, thank you, nurse,' Peter declared in his normal voice, and strode away.

It wasn't much, but something. She was extremely grateful to Peter for having gone to the trouble of finding out Dan's whereabouts.

'What's a *Futzenlecker?*'

Peter stared at Holly in astonishment. They'd spent all afternoon in the vegetable garden and were now relaxing by listening to the BBC Home Service. The ban on wireless sets didn't apply to Peter, he being a German.

'I beg your pardon?'

'A *Futzenlecker.*'

His lips curled upwards in a smile. 'Where on earth did you hear that?'

'At the hospital. Two German walking patients were having an argument and one called the other that, repeating it several times. The latter was absolutely furious, which is why it stuck in my mind. Is it rude?'

Peter nodded.

'So come on, what does it mean?'

She blushed bright red when Peter told her. How embarrassing!

'Well, you asked,' he said.

'I never knew . . . men did that to women.'

'No?'

'It's . . . disgusting.'

'A lot of people, male and female, would disagree. It can be very pleasurable.'

Holly couldn't believe that. 'Are you speaking from personal experience?' she queried hesitantly.

He raised an eyebrow.

'You are, then.'

Peter puffed on his cigarette.' I think you've led an extremely sheltered life, Holly Morgan.'

'I wouldn't say that!' she retorted hotly. 'Just because I don't know about nauseating practices like that doesn't mean my life has been sheltered.'

He regarded her with amusement. How beautiful she looked, how very alive.

Holly couldn't stop herself. 'I suppose you did that with Marlene?' She blushed again and glanced away.

Jealousy? he wondered. Now that was interesting. 'I don't think that's a question you should ask or I answer,' he reproached her. 'How would you feel if I asked similar things of Martin?'

She didn't reply.

'There then.'

'It's hardly the same,' she said in a small voice.

'No?'

It was, and she knew it.

'Why are you curious anyway?' he prompted.

She shrugged.

He ground out his cigarette. 'What duties are you on next week?' he queried, changing the subject.

When it was time for her to go, he walked her to the door. 'Thank you for your help today,' he smiled. 'And I'm sorry about that little awkwardness earlier.'

'I was just . . . thrown, that's all. Embarrassed.'

'I appreciate that.'

'And I had no right to ask what I did. It was not only bad manners but in bad taste.'

'I'll tell you anything you wish to know about me, Holly, with the exception of delving into my sex life. All I have to say is that I've had one.'

Holly gazed at the floor. 'I have too,' she mumbled.

He'd often wondered about that.

She looked up at him. 'Only with Martin and only on the one occasion. The night before he left.'

'There are many girls who have done the same, Holly. It's perfectly understandable in the circumstances.'

'I'm glad I did,' she whispered. 'It would have been terribly sad otherwise.'

'I agree.'

'You don't think less of me then?' He gave a soft laugh. 'Not in the least. You were in love, he was going off to war. What happened was quite natural.'

She nodded.

'And do you think any less of me?'

'You're a man, that's different.'

'An argument I've never quite subscribed to. But then I have fairly liberal ideas about certain things – which in this case I suppose I can sum up with your English saying, what's good for the goose is good for the gander.'

On impulse she kissed him on the cheek. 'You're a lovely man, Peter.'

'And you're a lovely woman.' He touched the spot she'd kissed. 'Thank you. I won't wash that cheek for a week.'

She laughed. 'Don't be daft!'

'I'm not. I mean it.'

She sobered again. 'Do you?'

'You know I do.'

She stared deep into his eyes, he into hers. She knew what he wanted, and that he wouldn't make a move, waiting for her. It had to be her decision. She respected him for that.

She melted into his arms, and raised her face.

He sighed as his lips dropped to meet hers.

Where does it go from here? Holly wondered, walking home. One thing was certain, the barriers were down.

She'd truly believed she'd never love again after Martin. But if it wasn't love, what did she feel for Peter Schmidt? She couldn't answer that.

And feel she did, feelings that had been steadily growing for a long while now. There had been no blinding flash, nothing like that. It was more like standing on quicksand and slowly, slowly sinking without realising. And then, when you did, it was too late and you were in it up to your neck.

She smiled at the analogy. Up to her neck indeed! What else would you call being involved with a German during wartime? Dan would have had apoplexy!

Of course she could deny her love, their love, for she was now certain he felt the same about her. But she knew, against all her better instincts, judgement and beliefs, she wouldn't do that. Having lost Martin she couldn't bear to lose Peter as well. That would have been too much. She'd been given a second chance and would be foolish in the extreme not to grasp it with both hands, difficult and dangerous though it might prove to be.

One thing was certain, she must do her utmost to ensure that her relationship with Peter remained a secret.

Dan sank on to his bed holding a bowl of thin soup and a small piece of black bread, his main meal of the day. His hands were trembling from exhaustion.

For a man unused to physical labour, ten hours a day in the stone-yard was a nightmare. Every morning they were roused at six, given a cup of water and small piece of bread, then led out to the yard where a mountain of stones awaited him and the other prisoners. They were issued with sledgehammers and ordered to start work, smashing the stones into chips which were used for road repairs.

Nor were the prisoners allowed to speak to one another, the entire shift having to be completed in silence. The penalty for even a whisper was three whole days and nights without food while having to work as normal.

Thankfully his hands had at long last hardened so that he no longer suffered from the awful blisters he had in the first weeks of his imprisonment.

The worst thing of all was the uncertainty about Holly. Had the Germans really believed him or not? If only he could find out, but of course that was impossible.

It was torture to think she might be in a female prison somewhere having to do the female equivalent, whatever that was, of the stone-yard all because of him. Every single day he prayed she was safe and at home in St Helier.

He gazed about his cell, ten feet by six, the walls, ceiling and floor of grey stone. The only natural light came from a tiny window high up.

Mercifully the weather had improved, which meant it wasn't as cold as it had been. He dreaded to speculate what it must be like in the cell during the depths of winter. Prisoners must die at that time, he thought, that had to be the case.

If only he had something to read: he'd have given anything for a book, that would have been a relief. Or a newspaper, anything.

He stilled to hear a long-drawn-out anguished howl reverberate along the corridor outside. Was it torture or had someone snapped and gone out of their mind? It could be either.

There was the sound of a shot, followed by silence. It had been the latter, he concluded.

Dan bent to his meal, drinking every last precious drop of soup, licking the inside of the bowl afterwards, eating every last crumb.

'What's wrong with Klumpp?' Peter asked Wolf Sohn, joining him at the bar. Klumpp was sitting in a corner by himself staring fixedly ahead, a twisted grimace on his face.

'He's been posted. To the Russian Front.'

Peter slowly exhaled. In recent months the Russian Front had degenerated into a complete bloodbath. The casualty rate had been extremely high before, now it was horrendous. Almost beyond belief.

'When did he hear?'

'A couple of hours ago. He flies out on Thursday.' That was two days away.

Peter digested this news. Although he didn't like Klumpp he wouldn't have wished that posting on his worst enemy.

'How's he taking it?'

'He's already drunk most of a bottle of brandy. The words shell-shocked spring to mind.'

Peter ordered a beer.

'He's not the only one to be posted there,' Wolf said.

'Who else?'

'Dieter Hercher and others.' He reeled off a list of names, all officers known to Peter.

'Thank Christ I'm not amongst them,' Wolf muttered into his beer, wondering grimly if the day would soon dawn when he too would be ordered there.

Peter picked up his beer and wandered over to Klumpp. 'I've just heard the news. Bad luck.'

Klumpp blinked, blinked again and, having trouble doing this, focused on Peter.

'I thought I'd got away with that,' he croaked.

Peter nodded.

'After returning to Germany then being sent back here again, I thought I'd got away with that.'

'Yes,' Peter sympathised.

Klumpp straightened his shoulders. 'But I will do my duty by the Fatherland and my *Führer. Heil* Hitler!'

The man was in shock, Peter thought. No doubt about it. He watched as Klumpp refilled his glass with brandy and then threw the drink down his throat.

'Have one with me,' Klumpp said, giving Peter a grisly smile. 'It may be a while before we can have one together again.'

The last thing Peter wanted was brandy, but how could he refuse? 'Of course, Hans.'

There were several spare glasses on the table. Klumpp poured a generous tot into the nearest and handed it to Peter.

What to toast? Peter couldn't think of a thing that was appropriate. Instead he saluted Klumpp with the drink, then sipped.

Klumpp acknowledged that with a nod.

'I think this may be the first time,' Klumpp said in a quiet voice.

Peter was puzzled. 'For what?'

'Passing out.'

Peter later learned that was exactly what happened and Klumpp had to be carried to his room, from which he didn't re-emerge until departure time that Thursday.

He said goodbye to no one. Just left.

'I had a conversation the other day with a doctor who told me that many women on the island who couldn't conceive before the war now have,' Elspeth declared to Holly.

'Really? Why's that?'

'He didn't know. He couldn't come up with a single medical reason why that should happen. All he could offer was the speculation that it had something to do with weight loss.'

'I suppose that's feasible,' Holly mused.

'Imagine, all these women who'd previously thought themselves barren now pregnant. At least that's one good thing to come out of this war.'

Holly smiled at her friend. 'Don't you think you should worry less about getting pregnant? You've become quite obsessive about it.'

'That's what Terry says.'

'I'm sure he's right.'

Elspeth gazed at the floor. 'I'm becoming a bore on the subject, aren't I?'

'Not at all,' Holly protested. That a lie.

Elspeth pulled at her uniform which was hanging from her. 'Well, if weight loss is the key, then I more than qualify.'

They both laughed, laughter that turned to screams when a rat ran into the nurses' room. It was not the first rat to have been sighted in the hospital of late, a plague of them having developed throughout the city.

Holly and Elspeth fled, banging the door shut behind them.

Chapter 16

'Peter!' Holly exclaimed, then hurriedly glanced up and down the street to see if his arrival had been observed. It didn't appear to have been.

'Come in. What's wrong?'

He followed her through. 'Nothing's wrong. I had some things for you and thought I'd deliver them personally.'

She didn't like him coming to the house, it was dangerous. But he was here now.

'These are for you,' he declared, handing her a brown paper parcel. 'Mainly food, but there are a couple of little gifts from me to you.'

She exclaimed again when she undid the parcel. There was margarine, sugar, coffee, tea, lard, a packet of raisins, several tins of meat, a loaf of black bread, rashers of bacon, half a dozen eggs and a small joint of lamb.

'Perfume,' she murmured in delight. 'How did you manage to get hold of this?'

'I have my ways and means.'

She removed the bottle from its box, took the top off the bottle and sniffed. 'Hmmh.'

'Will it suit?'

'Very much so. And it's French!'

He grinned. 'Only the best for you, Holly.'

That made her blush. She replaced the top, laid the bottle down and picked up a soft, tissue-wrapped object. When she opened the tissue a lacy, white negligée was revealed.

'I hope it fits.'

She held the negligée against herself. 'It'll fit all right. It's wonderful, Peter! I can't thank you enough.'

'It pleases me you're pleased.'

She kissed him on the lips. 'You're a darling.'

He crossed the room and sat on one of the chairs by the fireplace.

'Would you like some coffee?' she asked.

'That would be nice.'

'Coming up.'

Peter closed his eyes and sighed.

'Something wrong?'

He opened his eyes again to regard her sadly. 'I lost another patient today. The third this week. Three patients I wouldn't have lost if I'd had the proper medications to treat them with.'

'I know, that side of things at the hospital is getting bad.'

'There's nothing we can do about it either. We put in and put in for medicines and if any do arrive, it's always far less than we asked for.'

'Have you any idea why that should be?'

'It's simply that the war isn't going the way we would wish, Holly. The Russian Front in particular is a huge drain on resources, men as well as materials.'

He sighed again. 'The big worry for me is that I might be posted there.'

'Is that possible?' she queried in alarm.

'Oh, yes. A number of my fellow officers were sent there only last week. And there's bound to be more following.'

'But you're a doctor, Peter. Surely they wouldn't send you? You're needed here.'

'Doctors are very much in demand on the Russian Front, Holly. The casualty figures are staggeringly high. Our army is being mauled by the Russians. At least it's now spring, the winter out there killed off just as many as the Russians themselves.'

Holly filled the kettle and put it on. It would be dreadful if Peter was sent to Russia. Not only would she lose him but his life would be in terrible danger.

'The chap who helped you out with the Geheime Feldpolizei has gone. Flew out Thursday.'

Holly opened the bag of coffee that Peter had brought and spooned some into the percolator. 'So we won't be able to find out anything further about my father?'

'I'm afraid not. But at least you know where he is.'

She smiled at him in gratitude.

'How are things with you at the hospital?' he inquired.

'Fine, apart from the rats. Another one appeared on the ward today, that's the fifth.'

'Rats,' he said, shaking his head. 'The whole town is becoming infested with them. I'm glad I live at Half Hidden.'

'I haven't had any in the house so far. I'm keeping my fingers crossed it stays like that.'

'And with the rats will come all kinds of diseases. We can bank on that.'

She nodded her agreement. 'Well, I'll be out of it for a little while anyway. I've got next week off.'

'Oh?'

'Give me the chance to get lots of lovely lie-ins.'

He grinned. 'I enjoy a lie-in myself. Particularly on a Sunday morning. Those are the best.'

'Followed by a slap-up breakfast. Bacon, eggs, sausages, mush-rooms and fried bread. Yummy!'

'You British and your breakfasts,' he laughed. 'They're positively unhealthy.'

'That's a matter of opinion. A good breakfast sets you up for the day, Dad always said.'

'I don't know how you can face such a concoction at that time of the morning. It makes me ill just thinking about it.'

'Far better than rotten old bread and jam. Though I have to admit, since rationing there are many times I'd have been more than happy to settle for that.'

Peter lit a cigarette.

'I thought you were going to give up?'

'I will, sometime. I may have to come to that. As I told you, cigarettes are getting harder and harder to get hold of. There may come the time when the supply dries up altogether.'

Holly picked up the negligée and stared at it. 'This really is gorgeous,' she declared.

He smiled, imagining it on her. Marlene had had some stunning negligées. There was one . . . He swallowed and put the vision from his mind.

'I was thinking,' he said slowly. 'If you've got a week off why not spend it at Half Hidden?'

She frowned. 'With you? I mean, the pair of us alone together?'

'You won't come to any harm, Holly, I swear it. My word of honour. You'll be in the spare bedroom and I'll stay firmly in mine. Just as it was that night of the storm. No . . . what's the expression? . . . hanky-panky.'

She knew she could trust him, but all the same. 'I'm not sure,' she demurred.

He had no intention of pushing it. 'You don't have to decide right now. Just turn up if you wish to. I'll be at work during the day, of course.'

'What about food?'

'I'll lay in enough for two. Don't worry about that.'

A week at Half Hidden would be just the ticket, she thought. It would be very relaxing. And it would be lovely having Peter there in the evenings to talk to. A week there would do her the world of good. It would help take her mind off her father's plight for a while.

'As you say, I'll consider it.'

'Good,' he beamed.

Holly turned her attention to the coffee which had started to perk.

The matter wasn't mentioned again.

'What are you doing during your week off?' Elspeth inquired casually.

Holly shrugged.

'I wish I had a week off. I could certainly use it.'

'When's your next one?'

'Not for ages yet.'

Holly smiled her sympathy.

'Tell you what, why don't I come round and visit Tuesday night? We could have a good old gossip.'

Alarm flared in Holly. 'No, I don't think so,' she murmured.

'Are you busy then?'

Holly nodded.

'Well, what about Wednesday night?'

Holly exhaled slowly. Damn! She couldn't explain to Elspeth but would have to give her friend some excuse. 'I'm thinking of going away,' she said.

'Oh! Where to?'

'A relative in St John,' she lied.

Elspeth frowned. 'I've never heard you mention a relative there.'

'On my mother's side. A sweet old thing. I thought I'd go and see how she was.'

'I thought you said you didn't know what you were doing?'

'I've just made up my mind while we were talking. I was only considering it, you see, and now I've made up my mind.' Did that sound plausible? She hoped so.

'Are you going for the entire week?'

'I'm not certain. It depends on how things are there. I might stay a few days, there again I might stay on. It all depends.'

God, Holly thought. This was awful. Lie upon lie, and to her best friend! But what else could she do?

'Well, I won't bother then,' Elspeth declared, still frowning.

'I'll tell you what, if I return before the week's up I'll call round on you. How's that?'

'Fine.'

'That's settled.'

Why don't I believe Holly? Elspeth wondered. For she didn't. Holly was up to something, but what? It was intriguing.

Holly arrived at Half Hidden only to find Peter absent. This was strange, as it was his weekend off. Oh well, she thought, he'll be back eventually from wherever he's gone.

She set about cleaning and tidying, something she'd never done for him before.

It made her feel quite the little housewife.

Peter's face lit up when he entered the sitting room. 'You came, after all!'

'And to prove it I'm here,' she replied drily.

He went to her and pecked her on the lips. 'Sorry I wasn't at home but I had a call from the hospital. An emergency with one of my patients.'

So that was where he'd been. 'And?'

'I think I've sorted it out. He should live. With a bit of luck.'

'You don't sound too sure?'

His face darkened. 'It's what we were talking about last week, lack of medicines.' He shrugged. 'I did the best I could in the circumstances.' He glanced around. 'Something's different?'

She explained what she'd done. 'You really are quite a messy sod,' she admonished.

He looked sheepish. 'Sorry.'

'You need someone to look after you full time.'

A crafty glint came into his eyes. 'Are you applying for the job?'

'No, I am not.'

'Too bad, you'd be perfect.'

'Hmmh,' she snorted, enjoying the banter.

He ran a finger along the mantelpiece. 'Things were getting rather dirty. I was thinking that only the other day.'

'But didn't do anything about it.'

'I would have done, in time.'

'Typical male,' she teased. 'I suppose you think housework is beneath you, the great doctor.'

How relaxed she felt in his company, she thought. They might have been an old married couple.

He took off his jacket and threw it over a chair.

'Why don't you just hang it up?' she said.

He nodded, tongue firmly in cheek. 'So this is what I've invited into my home, a nagging woman. A shrew. Is this the true Holly Morgan, I ask myself?'

She laughed. 'Maybe it is and maybe it isn't. That's for me to know and you to wonder about.'

He picked up the offending article, held it at arm's length, and walked from the room. He returned without it. 'Happy now, Miss Shrew?'

'Of course.'

'Because you got your way?'

'Naturally.'

He wagged a finger at her. 'Typical female.'

'Would you do anything I asked you to?' she queried softly.

He stared at her, having noted the new tone in her voice. A sultry, sexy tone. 'That depends.'

'On what?'

'On what you ask.'

She crooked a finger, moving it back and forth, beckoning him. 'Come here, Dr Schmidt.'

'Ah! So it's Dr Schmidt now.'

He looks gorgeous, she thought. Good enough to eat. She smiled as he slowly approached.

'Why don't you kiss me,' she asked huskily, amazed by her boldness. She wanted his arms round her, his mouth on hers. To taste the sweetness of him.

But Peter hadn't finished teasing. He pecked her lightly on the lips. 'How's that?'

'Not good enough.'

'No?'

She curled a hand round his neck. 'I want the real thing. A proper kiss.'

'You mean like this?'

She shivered when his hand accidentally brushed over her breast.

Dan paused to stare despairingly at the pile of stones confronting him. His chest was heaving from exertion, his back breaking. And there were hours yet to go before the long shift was over.

He sobbed, filled with self-pity, wishing with all his heart and soul that he'd never acquired that damned crystal set. If only he could turn the clock back, if only he'd never heard of that bloody cleric.

The breath whoofed out of him as a rifle butt smashed into his ribs, sending him crashing to the ground. A guard shouted at him in German, indicating with his rifle that he was to get on with it.

Despite the agony in his side Dan hastily scrambled to his feet and swung his sledge.

The guard grunted in satisfaction and strode away.

Holly turned out her bedside light and snuggled beneath the bed-clothes. It was the third night of her stay at Half Hidden and so far, as she'd known he would, Peter had kept his word. There had been lots of kisses, cuddling and touching, but that was as far as it had gone. She was having a heavenly time.

She came awake to the sound of scratching. Now what's that? she wondered groggily.

She glanced down the bed, snapping wide awake when she saw a pair of beady eyes staring back at her.

She shrieked at the top of her voice.

Peter instantly tumbled out of bed and grabbed his pistol from its holster. He flew into her room and flicked on the overhead light, coming up short at the sight of a large brown rat glaring balefully at Holly who was still shrieking hysterically.

The rat turned its attention to Peter, then, suddenly, leapt, scampering for the open door.

Peter's pistol banged, banged, and banged again. The rat, hit in the body, exploded into a gory, bloody mess.

Peter strode to the bed and enfolded Holly in his arms. 'Calm down, calm down, it's dead.'

Shaking like a leaf, Holly buried her face in his shoulder. 'I . . . I . . .' She gulped, trying to get the words out.

Peter's eyes flicked round the room, looking to see if there were any more rats present. And how had the damn thing got into the bedroom in the first place? Holly's door had been shut.

She stared up at him through tear-stained eyes. 'It was horrible, horrible,' she stammered.

'It's over, Holly. Over.'

'Are you sure it's dead?'

He glanced at the mess close to the door. 'Quite sure. See, look.' He pointed to the bloody remains.

She followed his finger, and shuddered. She loathed rats, hated them. They terrified her. 'Are there any more?'

'Doesn't seem to be. But I'd best check.'

'No!' she exclaimed when he started to release her. 'Hold me for a few moments more.'

He stroked her back, which was still shaking like the rest of her. 'I thought we had intruders,' he said lightly. Then, trying to make her smile, 'And we did have one, though not the sort I imagined.'

She tried to wipe the wet from her cheeks. 'I heard scratching and then saw . . . two eyes staring at me from the bottom of the bed. It was ghastly.'

He moved his hand up to stroke her hair. 'Lucky I was here and you weren't on your own as you've been before,' he murmured.

She shuddered again, not knowing what she'd have done if that had been the case. She had visions of the rat attacking her, sinking its teeth into . . . 'Oh Peter,' she sobbed.

The rat must have come into the cottage earlier, he thought, and got into the room before Holly went to bed. That was the only explanation for its presence when the door was shut. Which meant, if that rat hadn't been alone, there might be others elsewhere in the cottage. He'd comb the place from top to bottom in the morning.

'Right,' he declared, pulling himself from her, she reluctantly letting him go.

He looked everywhere in the room, stamping his feet and making noises that might startle another out of hiding. He finally concluded the rat had been on its own.

'Thank God for that,' she whispered.

He returned to sit beside her. 'Would you like a glass of water?'

She shook her head.

'Or a brandy?'

'No, thank you.'

'Then you'd best try and get back to sleep and I'll do the same.'

She clutched his arm. 'Don't leave me, Peter. Please. I don't want to be on my own.'

He frowned. 'You mean for the rest of the night?'

She nodded.

He could think of nothing he'd like more. 'If that's what you want.'

'I do, Peter. Thank you.'

'Do you want to sleep with the light on?'

She thought about that. 'It's not necessary if you're with me.'

He turned off the overhead light and got in under the bed-clothes. 'You're still shaking,' he said.

'I know.'

'Shall I hold you?'

Her answer was to wrap her arms round him and lay her cheek on his chest.

After a while, still entwined, they both fell asleep.

Peter stared at the breast exposed where Holly's nightdress had fallen aside.

His hand moved, then hesitated. It would be taking advantage, after all. Then desire overcame his scruples.

Holly's eyes blinked open as he continued to caress. He stopped, but didn't remove his hand.

She smiled lazily. 'Go on.'

He needed no further urging and soon both breasts were free, his mouth going from one to the other.

We shouldn't, Holly thought. But somehow it felt so right. In fact it couldn't have felt more right. She moaned when his hand slipped beneath her nightie.

'Well?' he asked when it was over.

'That was . . . just wonderful.'

'No regrets?'

Had she? She didn't think so. 'None,' she replied emphatically. She stroked his cheek. 'Except next time you should wear something. I don't want to get pregnant. That would be a disaster.'

'I wasn't prepared. I swear I hadn't planned . . .'

She silenced him by placing a finger across his lips. 'I know that, silly. I hadn't planned to either.'

'I've wanted to do that for so long, Holly. You've no idea.'

'I think I have,' she smiled. 'I've had the same thoughts myself.'

'Bless that rat,' he said. 'Without it who knows how long it might have taken. Or if it ever would have happened?'

'It was only a matter of time, Peter. We were both aware of that.'

'I wasn't, knowing how you feel about Jerrybags. I was aware, of course, that you felt strongly about me, as I do about you, but wasn't at all certain you'd allow this to happen.'

A Jerrybag, she thought with distaste. For that's what she now was. One of those despised creatures like Pat Le Clerq. 'No one must find out about us,' she said.

'Well, I won't say anything. You can be sure of that.'

'Nor will I.' Not even to Elspeth, she told herself. Elspeth would be horrified.

'Perhaps it wasn't inevitable,' she mused. 'I certainly hadn't consciously decided to go to bed with you.'

'But subconsciously you had?'

'It's all very confusing. Anyway, it's happened now and that's all there is to it.'

He drew her to him, holding her close. 'This isn't a casual fling for me, Holly. I want you to know that.'

A thrill ran through her. 'What exactly are you saying?'

'That I love you,' he whispered.

She sighed, his words reverberating like sweet music round and round inside her head. He loved her!

'And I love you, Peter. I've known that for some time.'

He smiled, overjoyed that his love was reciprocated. 'Oh, Holly.'

'I wish . . .' She trailed off.

'What?'

She turned her head away. 'I'm embarrassed.'

'Don't be. There's nothing you can't tell or confide in me.'

Why shouldn't I be honest? she thought. Admit what she was thinking. They were lovers now, after all. 'That you had been prepared. Then we could do it again.'

He laughed. 'The same thought occurred to me a moment ago.'

'But we mustn't, Peter.'

'No,' he agreed. Then, 'Tell you what, why don't I take a run into the hospital later and pick up some gummis.'

'Gummis?'

'German slang word for condoms.'

She flushed slightly. 'That's a brilliant idea.'

'And I'll get lots and lots and lots.'

That caused her to laugh. 'Greedy.'

'Where you're concerned, most certainly.' She closed her eyes as his lips met hers. It didn't matter any more that he was a German and she a Channel Islander. All that mattered was that they had each other. That they loved each other.

Well, that was it, she was well and truly committed now, Holly thought, on her way home after her week at Half Hidden. And what a week it had turned out to be, one she'd remember for the rest of her life.

Her insides tingled at the memory of their lovemaking. And what a lover Peter was! His previous experience had shown itself in the way he'd on almost every occasion slowly roused her to fever pitch before letting himself climax. Quite different from her time with Martin, who'd been a virgin the same as herself.

She shook her head in wonderment, remembering the sensations that had coursed through her. She'd never realised, dreamt, that a woman could feel like that, or that she was capable of acting with such abandonment.

And Peter had certainly been right about one thing. That particular practice was neither disgusting or nauseating, once you got used to the idea.

It was mind shattering.

'Elspeth, this is Juan. He's an escaped prisoner of war.'

She stared at her husband in astonishment, then at the filthy, ragged creature accompanying him.

Juan bobbed his head. 'So pleased to meet you, Mrs Le Var,' he declared in heavily accented English.

'You've brought an escaped prisoner of war here!' Elspeth exploded. 'Are you out of your head?'

Terry nervously shifted his feet. 'I didn't know what else to do. I found Juan hiding in the basement at work where he'd been for two days. He wants to get to the mainland and I'm going to try and help him.'

Elspeth was outraged. 'Do you know what will happen to us if they find out about this?'

'They won't.'

'But if they do?' she persisted.

'I couldn't just leave him there,' Terry said wretchedly. 'Could you?'

'Damn tooting I could! The risk is enormous.'

'I go. I no cause upset between man and wife,' Juan declared, and turned to the door.

He was almost through it when Elspeth called out, 'No, wait!' She glared at Terry. 'Idiot!'

Terry's face broke into a huge smile. 'You can stay,' he told Juan.

Shortly after that, at Elspeth's insistence, the Spaniard was in the bath.

And after that, using a steel comb, she tackled the lice in his hair.

Chapter 17

'What about food?' Elspeth demanded of Terry, while Juan was getting dressed in some old clothes of Terry's through in the spare room. 'How are we going to feed a third mouth on the rations we get?'

Terry's expression became grim. 'I hadn't thought of that.'

'Well, you'd better.' As if to emphasise the point her stomach rumbled.

'I'll come up with something,' Terry muttered apologetically. 'The question of food just never crossed my mind. The big problem was getting him here without the Germans lifting him.'

'And *you*,' she stated. 'You were together, don't forget.'

'We came all sorts of devious ways, back alleys and the like. My heart was in my mouth from start to finish.'

'I'm not surprised. How did he escape anyway?'

'I haven't asked him that.'

'I'd heard there were some Spanish amongst the POWs,' she said.

'Moroccans too apparently. A right mish-mash, all imported to build those bloody fortifications. Every time you look there seems to be another one being started. If it keeps up like this, the whole blinking Island will be under concrete before long.'

'Well, I'd better get the supper on the table, what there is of it that is, before the gas is cut off.' Gas rationing had recently been introduced.

Elspeth was busy at the stove when Juan reappeared. 'How I look?' he queried.

Elspeth and Terry both smiled. Juan was taller than Terry, subsequently the turn-ups of the trousers he was wearing were up above his ankles.

'You'll pass,' Terry told him.

'Don't worry about the trousers being a rotten fit. With the clothes shortage there are all kinds of weird and wonderful sights walking the streets,' Elspeth informed the Spaniard.

'I can no thank you enough, Mr and Mrs Le Var. You both ver kind.'

'Let's get one thing settled straight off,' Elspeth said. 'You don't leave the house. Not under any circumstances. Understand?'

Juan nodded.

'And keep away from the windows. Everyone knows everyone else round here. A stranger glimpsed at a window might be commented on and it's amazing how things get around. Especially if that stranger was glimpsed on more than one occasion.'

Juan nodded. 'I no go near window. I stay well away.'

He stared at the food Elspeth was cooking, ravenous hunger obvious in his large brown, soulful eyes.

'Don't worry, you'll get your share,' Elspeth said.

'Food ver bad where we kept. How you say? Potato peelings. We get many of that.'

'Potato peelings!' Terry exclaimed.

'No cooked.'

'Dear God,' Terry muttered in sympathy.

'Las week we catch seagull. Guard think it ver funny to watch us eat. He laugh and laugh.'

'A seagull! Elspeth was appalled. 'You mean you ate it raw?'

'Raw, yes. We pull apart and eat. No ver nice but like feast to us.'

'How revolting,' Terry said.

Juan shrugged.

'So how did you escape?' a curious Elspeth asked.

'We work by sea and I find tunnel, all covered up. Guards get lazy and when no looking I go in tunnel. I crawl long way and lucky get out other end. Ver . . .' He mimed claustrophobic.

'Whereabouts in Spain are you from?' Terry inquired.

'Valencia.'

'Are you married?'

Juan beamed. 'Wife name Maria. Two childs. Juan same as me, and Conchita. Girl ver pretty, like wife.'

'And you want to go to England,' Elspeth stated.

'Easier than Spain. I be free there.'

Terry crossed to the mantelpiece and leant against it, his expression both sombre and thoughtful. 'The trick is getting there,' he said to no one in particular.

'Any ideas?' Elspeth queried.

'Has to be by boat, that's for certain. I have heard rumours . . . but who knows if they're true or not. All I can do is make inquiries and see if I can come up with something. There is someone I know who may be able to help.'

'Who's that?'

He named a fisherman he was acquainted with.

'That's a possibility,' Elspeth mused.

'In fact I'll go and see if I can find him after we've eaten. No time like the present.'

'If you sit down I'll dish up,' Elspeth declared. 'Only swede rissoles I'm afraid, but better than potato peelings or raw seagull,' she said to Juan.

There were four rissoles which meant one and a third each. That was to be washed down with beet tea. Juan scoffed down his portion in seconds.

'A Spaniard, eh?' Jack Levine mused.

'That's right. Escaped prisoner of war.'

'And he's at your place now.'

'Large as life. Nice chap, for a foreigner.'

'You're sticking your neck out, aren't you?'

Terry shrugged. 'You should have seen the poor sod, cowering with fright in that basement. How long would he have lasted if I hadn't taken him in?'

'Not long,' Jack agreed.

'Can you help?'

Jack sniffed. 'This is strictly between you and me, OK?'

'Strictly. You have my word.'

'Four people have got off the Island to my certain knowledge. Although whether or not they made England I can't say. So, theoretically it can be done.'

'By boat presumably?'

Jack nodded. 'No other way. The Jerries are hardly going to be obliging enough to give anyone a lift in one of their planes.'

Both men laughed.

'Hardly,' Terry agreed.

'And it's a bit far to swim, so a boat is the only method.'

'Fishing boat?'

Jack shook his head. 'That's been tried. One of the fleet made a run for it last year in a sudden fog that had blown up. But the patrol boat caught up with them and when it got within range it blew them right out of the water.' Jack's face hardened. 'A couple of them survived the explosion apparently only to be machine gunned.'

'Bastards,' Terry hissed.

'That's too good a word for the Jerries.' Jack's large, powerful hands knotted and unknotted. 'I know what I'd like to do to those aboard the patrol vessel. George Cummins, the skipper, and his crew were mates of mine.'

'Machine gunned,' Terry repeated, shaking his head. That was awful. More so after they'd survived being blown up.

'George was a bachelor, thank the Lord,' Jack went on. 'As were the others. I suppose that's why they took the chance. They were a young crew.'

'So what about the Spaniard?' Terry asked.

'Leave it to me, squire. For George's sake, if nothing else, I'll do what I can.' He grinned evilly. 'A little bit of revenge, eh?'

They shook hands on it.

'I got the story out of Juan as to how he became a prisoner of the Germans,' Elspeth said to Terry later that night in bed. They'd both undressed in the dark. The electricity had been cut off as that also was now rationed, and they'd run out of candles.

'Go on.'

'He was on the losing side in the Spanish Civil War, part of a force of many thousands who were nearly trapped by Franco near Andorra.

'They crossed the border and were met by French soldiers who escorted them to some moorland, I think that's what Juan was trying to say, where they were given to understand that they'd be interned.

'A few tents were allocated them, most had to sleep rough, then they were surrounded by barbed wire and patrolled by guards.

'They were kept there for a long time, then typhoid broke out thanks to the poor sanitary facilities. Men started to die and their numbers consequently dwindled. They were kept there for eighteen months under the most appalling conditions.

'With the fall of France the Germans appeared and they were "liberated". The survivors were formed into four groups, the group Juan was in eventually ending up here on Jersey.

'And that's it.'

'He must have been through hell,' Terry commented quietly.

'Certainly sounds like it. There was a lot he couldn't tell me because he simply doesn't have the English.'

Elspeth reached for Terry. 'Let's hope Jack Levine comes up with the goods.'

'He'll do his damndest, you can count on that.'

'Terry?'

He knew that tone of voice and what it meant. It was a tone she used most nights.

'What are you looking so happy about?' Elspeth demanded of Holly. They were at work.

'Am I?'

'Like a cat who's discovered a large tub of cream.'

Holly had been thinking about Peter and their lovemaking at Half Hidden. She was going there again that Saturday and couldn't wait, positively itching to be with him again.

'I'm just happy, that's all,' she prevaricated.

'There must be a reason?'

'Nope,' Holly lied.

'I think you're fibbing, Holly Morgan!'

A shiver ran through Holly to be called by both names the way Peter sometimes did. 'I'm nothing of the sort.'

'Look me straight in the eye and repeat that.'

Holly laughed. 'You're being ridiculous.'

'You're up to something, Holly, and I intend finding out what it is.'

'Why should I be up to something?' she protested.

'Because you just are. All the signs are there.'

'You're imagining things.'

'We'll see.'

Elspeth suddenly put her arms round Holly. 'Whatever it is I'm pleased for you. Though why it should be a secret I can't imagine.'

'Perhaps it's because summer's here. I'm always happy in summer.'

'My arse,' Elspeth said, and walked away.

Was it that obvious she was in love? Holly wondered. Had others noticed beside Elspeth? If they had they hadn't commented.

In love, she thought dreamily. Oh yes, she was certainly that. Ever since going to bed with Peter she'd felt she was bubbling inside with champagne.

'It can be done,' Jack Levine said to Terry. 'The bad news is it's going to cost.'

'Cost?' Terry frowned.

'The price of the boat. The owner will be losing it after all. You can't expect him just to give it away. That would be ridiculous.'

Terry thought about that. 'What sort of money are we talking?'

Jack named a figure. 'That's the overall cost. The good news is you'll only be paying half because there's someone else going along who'll be paying the other half.'

'What sort of boat?'

'A rowing boat. And don't worry, I'll personally ensure she's in good nick.'

'Who's this other person?' Terry asked.

'I can't tell you that. All I can say is he's a farmer's son who didn't want to go off and fight originally, but has since changed his mind. There was some sort of ugly incident involving the Germans that changed it for him.'

'Hmmh,' Terry mused. 'He's trustworthy I take it?'

Jack spread his large hands. 'As far as I know.'

'And when do you need the money?'

'You can get that amount?'

Terry made a face. 'I can try. Though how at the moment is beyond me.'

'If you can't raise it the other chap will go on his own. They're a fairly well-off family.'

'I don't suppose he'd consider taking Juan for nothing?'

Jack barked out a laugh. 'They're farmers, Terry. Since when did farmers ever give anything away for nothing? Never to my knowledge. They're a tight-fisted bunch and no mistake. If the Spaniard goes he'll have to pay his whack.'

'And when would they leave?'

'Possibly next month.'

'Next month!' Terry exclaimed, thinking of the food situation. 'Can't it be sooner?'

'These things take time to organise. Not least getting the boat to the departure point. That's going to be tricky. They can hardly just row on out the harbour, can they?'

Terry smiled at the ludicrousness of that. The harbour was always crawling with Germans, day and night.

'OK, I'll do my best to raise the cash.'

'Another thing, is the Spaniard strong enough to make the journey? That's a fair old haul after all.'

'He's undernourished like all of us, but used to hard work. I'm sure he'll cope.'

'Be in touch then.'

'I will. And, Jack, thanks.'

Jack ran thick fingers through his black, bushy beard. 'My pleasure, squire. My pleasure.'

*

'My engagement ring!' Elspeth exclaimed.

'Your engagement ring, wedding ring and mine,' Terry elaborated. 'I simply can't think of any other way to raise the cash.'

Elspeth swallowed hard. This was too much. With her right hand she fingered both rings.

'I'm sorry,' Terry apologised.

She shook her head. 'I won't do it. They mean so much to me. Desperately hungry as we've been it's never crossed my mind to sell off those.'

A soulful-eyed Juan was watching them, clearly disturbed by the conversation. Not all of which he fully understood, though he'd got the gist.

'Elspeth,' Terry said patiently. 'There's a man's life at stake here. I can always get you other rings after the war. They can be replaced. If Juan was to be recaptured and shot, he can't.'

And Terry, she thought. He could be shot as well for what he'd done. Or sent off to prison like Holly's dad.

Juan crossed to them, laying a palm on Elspeth's left hand. 'No, you no do this. Mus' be other way.'

'There isn't,' Terry said. 'Or if there is I can't come up with it.'

Elspeth stared at Juan. I am being selfish, she told herself. Terry was right. What were a couple of rings, no matter the sentimental value, against a human life? There was Juan's family to consider as well, Maria and the two children. If Juan was to die they'd be losing a husband and father.

She sighed. 'Wait here.' And with that she left the room.

When she returned she was carrying a cameo brooch and pearl earrings that had belonged to her maternal grandmother and which she rarely wore, which was probably why Terry had forgotten about them.

'If the engagement and wedding rings aren't enough then sell these as well. In fact you'd better sell them anyway to pay for the extra food we're going to need till Juan leaves.'

Terry gave her a soft, loving smile. 'I knew you'd understand once you'd thought it through. You're an angel.'

'Hardly that,' she smiled back.

Elspeth removed her engagement and wedding ring, gazed wistfully at them for several seconds, then silently handed them over.

'You so kind. I no forget this,' Juan murmured, voice clogged with emotion.

'All part and parcel of the war effort,' Elspeth declared briskly in an effort to hide her own emotions, and turned away.

'Now who's for some of that bloody awful beet tea?'

'That was wonderful,' Holly sighed, aglow with sexual satisfaction.

'It just gets better and better between us,' Peter smiled. He kissed her lightly on the lips, then reached for his cigarettes. She watched as he lit up.

'What are you going to do after the war, Peter?'

'Good question,' he mused. 'I know what I'd like to do.'

'What's that?'

'Go back to Geislingen and take up where I left off. But that might not be possible.'

She frowned. 'Why?'

'Can't you guess?'

She couldn't. 'No.'

'*You*, Holly,' he said softly.

She caught her breath as that sunk in. 'Explain.'

'I could hardly take you back with me, could I? The good folk of Geislingen, and believe me I know them, would hardly take kindly to an English girl in their midst. Particularly if what I believe is going to happen, does.'

'Are you talking marriage, Peter?'

'What else? Now that I've found you I'm never going to let you go. I'd marry you now if marriage on the Island between our races wasn't forbidden.'

'Oh, Peter,' she breathed. 'Come here.'

She stared into his eyes, then kissed him deeply. 'I never want to lose you either,' she stated when the kiss was over.

'Nor can I stay here for the same reason. The people of Jersey, like many others, are going to hate Germans for a long time to come.'

'It's a bit of a problem, isn't it?'

'Just a bit.'

She frowned. 'You say when the Germans are gone, at least that's what you're insinuating. Does that mean you believe you're going to lose the war?'

'I think that's almost a certainty now. It's treason for me to say that, of course, but I can't see any other outcome. The war was lost when the Führer took on the Russians and then lost at Stalingrad. Hitler should have learned from Napoleon's mistake, but stupidly didn't. His enormous ego overrode what should have been his better judgement.

'And then there's the Americans. How could we possibly fight them, the Russians *and* the British Empire all at once? Sheer madness! As for the war in the east, the Battle of Midway was a turning point there. I don't think there can be any doubt about that. The Japanese may appear to be doing well in the Southwest Pacific but that won't last now they've lost control of the ocean. For them too, and the struggle may continue for some while, years even, it's only a matter of time.'

Holly digested that. 'And what about here, Jersey and the other Channel Islands?'

His expression became ultra serious. 'Hitler is obsessed with them, hence the massive fortifications and huge amounts of military personnel based here, because they're British territory. When the British return to retake them, which, if the scenario I've painted is correct, they will one day, then there's going to be extremely heavy fighting with massive losses on both sides, and that includes the Islanders themselves. It's going to be a bloodbath.'

'That's a daunting thought,' she said grimly.

'Exactly. My advice to you is, when it starts, head off into the middle of the Island somewhere. You should be safer there.'

'Aren't you forgetting something?'

'What?'

'I'm a nurse,' she smiled. 'I'll be needed at the hospital.'

He nodded. 'Of course.'

'Which means we'll both be in the thick of it.'

'That makes the time we have together now, Holly, all that more important. A future isn't guaranteed for either of us.'

They fell silent for a few moments, each reflecting on what had just passed between them.

'Scary, isn't it?' she said eventually.

'There are thirty thousand troops on Jersey alone,' he declared. 'Yes, the prospect is certainly scary.'

He flicked the tip of his cigarette into an ashtray. 'This is something I shouldn't be telling you but there's a vast tunnel being excavated out at Meadowbank. The original intention was for it to be an artillery barracks with workshops, a plan that's recently been revised. The tunnel is to be extended and turned into a military hospital where the patients will be safe from bombardment. So the powers that be see matters as I do and believe that the British will eventually return.'

Holly, despite her German lover, and the danger to both of them, prayed for that day. Though she dreaded to think what it was going to cost, in lives and otherwise, her beloved Jersey.

'Wait a minute though,' she said slowly. 'If there's going to be a German military hospital inside a tunnel, then surely you'll be there and relatively safe?'

He shrugged. 'Who knows what'll happen? It might not even be finished in time. Or I might not be assigned there.'

Peter reached across and stroked a nipple. 'You're beautiful, *mein Liebling.*'

It was rare for Peter to use German to her. 'You're rather beautiful yourself.'

When his cigarette was finished he stubbed it out and crawled back into bed.

'Hello, Holly,' Elspeth smiled nervously, thinking, blast!

'I thought I'd drop by.'

She couldn't turn Holly away at the door, that would be most odd. 'Come in. Come in.'

Elspeth's eyes flicked to the stairs as they passed them. Juan was upstairs where he'd been instructed to be as quiet as a mouse.

'Terry not home?'

'No, he's out.' He was in fact with Jack Levine discussing plans for Juan's escape.

'So,' said Elspeth, rubbing her hands together. 'How are you?'

Holly was frowning. 'Where are your rings? You're never without them.'

Trust Holly to be so eagle-eyed! 'I took them off for safe keeping. I've lost so much weight they'd started to slip off my finger.'

'Oh!' That made sense.

'I've nothing to offer you except acorn coffee or beet tea.'

Holly made a face. 'Neither, thanks.'

'Then take a pew.'

'Are you all right?' Holly queried, thinking Elspeth's manner and behaviour strange. She was like a cat on a hot tin roof.

Upstairs, a worried Juan was listening at his bedroom door. Holly was the first visitor the Le Vars had had since his arrival. He'd go and lie on the bed, he decided.

Holly was about to speak when a floorboard squeaked. 'I thought you were alone?' she queried. 'Sounds as if there's someone upstairs.'

Elspeth couldn't even blame the cat. Holly knew they didn't have one.

'Sounded like a floorboard to me,' Holly went on. 'Happens in my house all the time when someone's moving about.'

Juan was standing stock still, his face covered in sudden cold sweat.

Oh hell, Elspeth thought. If she couldn't confide in Holly who could she confide in? She went to the door and called out, 'Juan! Come on down here.'

'Juan?'

'A Spaniard.'

'A Span— Jesus Christ, Elspeth, what are you and Terry up to?'

'You mustn't say anything, Holly, it could cost us our lives and his if you do.'

'Of course I won't say anything. What do you take me for, a bloody fool?'

'He's an escaped POW whom we're trying to help get to the mainland,' Elspeth explained.

Juan entered the room, fear etched on his face. He was still sweating.

He was full of apologies to Elspeth. 'The . . . floor . . . no do that before. I sorry.'

'The fault is mine. I should have warned you about that floorboard. It hasn't squeaked in ages.'

'I sorry,' he repeated, voice dripping remorse.

Elspeth turned again to Holly. 'That's where my rings went, to pay for a boat.'

'I see,' Holly murmured.

Elspeth went on to explain how Terry had found Juan hiding in the basement at work and his decision to help the Spaniard.

'You and he are taking a big chance,' Holly commented.

'Don't I know it. Anyway, you're one to talk after what you did. Remember the commandos?'

Holly smiled. 'True enough.'

'This is no more dangerous than that. At least I hope not.'

'Except my little adventure was over and done with in the same night. How long till . . . ?'

'We don't know that yet. Probably next month. There are all sorts of arrangements to be made.'

'Well, I wish you all the luck in the world.'

'Thanks.'

Holly stayed for half an hour, then left, again wishing Elspeth good luck.

Later, when he got home, Terry and Juan fixed the offending floorboard. Something, Terry berated himself, he should have done a long time ago.

Thank God it had been Holly who'd called and no one else.

Chapter 18

T erry was returning from a meeting with Jack Levine during which it had been agreed that Jack would call at the house the following Sunday to start instructing Juan about some of the things he'd have to know if he was to successfully make England.

Suddenly there was the distant rattle of gunfire. Terry came up short and stared out over the Channel, where he spotted four small ships being attacked by aircraft.

The RAF in action, he thought in satisfaction, shading his eyes with a hand.

The ships were returning fire, puffs of smoke discernible from their decks.

A Spitfire swooped, guns blazing, raking one of the vessels from prow to stern. There was an explosion, a large ball of black and orange sprouting upwards.

'Got you,' Terry muttered with a smile.

The ship listed, and began to sink. Terry could make out tiny figures leaping from its deck into the water.

The other three ships were milling in confusion as the flight of Spitfires continued to attack.

Another vessel was hit and began to burn. It heeled over and again tiny figures could be seen abandoning ship.

The Spits are having a field day, Terry thought with grim satisfaction. Two down, two to go.

The remaining craft went off in different directions, both zigzagging like crazy.

'Come on, you beauties,' Terry whispered, meaning the Spits.

A third ship was strafed and strafed again, taking a terrible pounding. The magazine must have been hit, or something explosive, for it simply blew apart, reminding Terry of what had happened to George Cummins and his crew. If there hadn't been others in the near vicinity he would have shouted Hooray!

Suddenly the Spits broke off the attack and went winging away in the direction of England, leaving the fourth vessel still frantically zig-zagging.

Out of ammunition, Terry guessed.

The fourth ship came round, returning to pick up survivors. The debris that had been the other three floated serenely on the water.

Terry couldn't wait to get home and tell Elspeth what he'd witnessed.

'The date's been set, Saturday the twenty-fourth,' Jack Levine informed the Le Vars and Juan.

'From where?' Terry asked.

'Bertram's beach, which is one of the few that haven't yet been mined.' To Juan he said, 'You'll leave just after eleven o'clock when the patrol boat has gone by.' He smiled. 'Regular as clockwork those boats, you could set your watch by them.'

'Bertram's beach,' Terry mused.

'Do you know it?'

'Oh, yes. Quite well really. I used to go there fairly frequently as a kid. It's a very safe bathing area.'

'How are you getting the rowing boat there?' Elspeth inquired.

'By furniture van earlier in the evening.' He chuckled. 'We've been syphoning off German vehicles so we'll have plenty of petrol. Also we have the necessary documentation if stopped, so there's no problem there.'

'What about sea mines in that section?' Terry queried.

'None that we're aware of. But if there are . . .' Jack shrugged.

'That's a risk they'll have to take. No one said this will be easy.'

'Do you understand so far?' Elspeth asked Juan.

'*Sí. Sí.*'

'The good news is I've managed to get a twelve-foot sailing dinghy with an outboard motor which will give them a far better chance of making a successful crossing.'

Terry frowned. 'That must have cost more than a rowing boat?'

'I twisted a few arms and managed to get the dinghy for the same price. That and . . . well a little contribution of my own. Not money, something else.' He winked conspiratorially.

'Thank you, thank you,' Juan gushed, and vigorously shook Jack's hand.

'I've even, and you'll like this, arranged to have regular weather forecasts for the period leading up to the launch and beyond from a friendly German in the Met. Office. That way we'll know what sort of weather we're sending them off into. Obviously if the forecast isn't favourable we'll cancel until it is.'

'You're amazing, Jack.'

Levine picked up his ancient, battered briefcase and snapped it open, producing a pile of charts and other paraphernalia which he threw on to the table.

'Now, squire,' he said to Juan. 'It's back to school for you. You've got a lot to learn in a relatively short time.'

Terry and Elspeth left them to it.

'Guess what?' an excited Elspeth said to Holly.

'What?'

Elspeth lowered her voice. 'I've missed a period and I *never* do that. I'm regular as can be, almost to the hour.'

Holly, who'd been expecting to hear about Juan, was delighted. 'That's wonderful. I'm so pleased for you.'

Elspeth beamed.

Holly decided to sound a cautionary note. 'Just . . . well, don't get your hopes up too high in case it isn't what you think.'

'I'll try, but . . .' She shivered. 'I'm so absolutely certain. I'm positive I'm pregnant.'

'What does Terry say?'

'He's over the moon, what else?'

Holly laughed. 'I can imagine. Keep me informed, will you?'

'You can bet on it.'

'And how's . . . the other thing?'

'Coming on. Everything's going ahead smoothly.'

Elspeth didn't elaborate on that, nor did Holly expect her to.

Peter was working feverishly, trying to save his patient, but in his heart of hearts he knew it was a hopeless task.

'He's gone,' the theatre sister said a few minutes later.

Peter straightened and swore volubly. The lack of medicines, drugs and general medical supplies was going from bad to worse. This was yet another unnecessary death.

'Take him down to the mortuary,' he instructed through clenched teeth, starting to strip off his gloves.

'Do they think I'm a miracle worker? Is that what they believe?' he hissed at Sister.

She regarded him sympathetically. 'You did your best in the circumstances, Doctor. No one can ask for more than that.'

'But it wasn't my best, that's the whole point. I could have saved him under normal conditions.'

'The conditions aren't normal, Doctor. We all have to accept that.'

Peter sighed. 'I suppose so. It just makes me so damned angry, that's all.'

He stared at the body of the deceased, a nineteen-year-old. It made him feel wretched and useless.

Part of Dan's mind knew he was hallucinating, but it didn't matter. All that did was Gill was there.

She smiled at him, and he smiled back.

'Hello, darling,' he whispered.

The voice was faint, yet crystal clear at the same time. 'What a pickle to get yourself into, Dan.'

'Yes,' he agreed.

She shimmered closer, his eyes glued to her face. A face exactly as he remembered it.

'You needed me so I came.'

He was dimly aware that he was crying. 'Oh, Gill!'

He desperately wanted to take her into his arms, but knew that was impossible.

She faded a little, like a light being turned down. Then the light was turned up again.

'It's so good to see you. I can't tell you how much.'

'And to see you, Dan.'

'I visited you every week, you know.'

'I know.'

'I used to speak to you.'

She smiled again.

'Bring you up to date on all the news.'

'I looked forward to it.'

'You heard then?'

'Oh yes.'

'I somehow knew you did.'

He blinked, his vision blurred by tears.

'I'll be waiting for you when it's time, Dan. Then we'll be together again.'

His heart leapt within him. 'Promise?'

'I promise.'

'When, Gill?'

'Soon, Dan. Soon. But not yet.'

A great sense of peace washed over him. Together again with Gill. The pair of them, as it had been in the old days.

'I never stopped loving you, Gill. There was never anyone else after you'd gone. There couldn't have been. You were always the only one for me.'

'And you for me, Dan. It would have been the same if you'd gone and I'd stayed.'

It seemed to him that her lips brushed his, and there was the smell of her perfume in his nostrils.

'Gill,' he muttered.

And then there was sleep again. The untroubled sleep of the young and innocent.

A sleep of profound peace.

*

Sally Pallot glanced up as Holly entered the nurses' room. Her expression was grim. The expressions of the others present were equally so.

'What's up?' Holly demanded.

'Have you heard the latest?'

'Which is?'

'Your dad was lucky after all,' Viv Radmore said.

'Why's that?'

'He only got a prison sentence for possessing an illegal wireless. The Jerries have now announced that from here on in they'll shoot anyone with one.'

'Dear God,' Holly whispered.

'That's not all,' Sally went on. 'There's been a naval engagement in the Bay of St Malo in which a British cruiser and destroyer were sunk. Bodies have been washed ashore.'

'Twenty-nine to date,' Heather Aubin added.

Holly crossed to an empty chair and sat. She'd been feeling quite cheery up until then, but not any more.

She thought of Dan languishing in Cherche-Midi. Viv was right, in the event he had been lucky.

'When will it all end?' Sally whispered, shaking her head.

Naturally, no one could answer that.

The man was a deserter, Peter reminded himself. He fully deserved what was about to happen.

There had been many executions, for varying offences, of late, Islanders and Germans alike. Peter was thankful that this was the first he'd had to attend in his capacity as doctor. His job would be to verify that the executed man was well and truly dead.

The soldier was clearly terrified. He was having trouble standing and therefore had to be supported by two others. Close by was a young girl, the man's lover, who'd been dragged there to witness his death. A quite unnecessary, cruel ruling in Peter's opinion. The girl was sobbing into a large handkerchief, her face puffed and swollen. Peter pitied her with all his heart.

What has happened to the famed German discipline? he wondered. This soldier had deserted, one of a number, while brawling and theft had become endemic. Why, an officer had even been shot while trying to stop a fight, his killer later executed at this very spot where the deserter would shortly meet his fate.

It must be because the war was going so badly for them, Peter reasoned. The troops knew this and it was why their morale was so badly affected.

He watched, showing no emotion whatever, as the soldier was pushed against a wall and a black scarf tied round his eyes. When he was released the soldier's legs gave way and he slumped to the ground where he jerked as though already shot.

The officer in charge looked at him with total contempt. The officer didn't bother having the soldier heaved back up on his feet, deciding the man could die where he was.

The officer lifted his arm and six rifles were raised and pointed.

Peter swallowed hard. The girl screamed.

The officer's arm descended and the rifles cracked in unison.

Peter strode forward to do his duty, the girl's continued screaming ringing in his ears.

Afterwards they let the girl go, her punishment over.

That evening Peter went to a night spot called the Bel Ami that was patronised in the main by his fellow officers, some of these with their Jerrybag girlfriends. If Holly had been present she would have recognised Pat Le Clerq among the latter, Pat having a whale of a time. Peter's intention was to get blind drunk.

'How did the execution go?' Hermann Goetz, another doctor, asked when Peter joined him and a few others at their table.

'How do you think?'

Hermann smiled thinly. 'Not the most pleasant of duties I must admit. The last one I attended was a woman who shat herself when they pushed her up against the wall. It ran down her legs, a disgusting sight.'

'I can imagine.'

'That happens from time to time apparently. Can't say I'm surprised.'

'Mine couldn't stand up and got it sitting down. He took two bullets full in the face so there was no chance of his still being alive. Why the hell don't they tie them to something?'

Goetz shrugged. 'No idea.'

Peter threw a large glass of slivovitz down his throat, and immediately poured a refill. He was thinking of Holly, aching for her. He wondered if he should take the risk of calling in at her house later, and decided against it. He was in full uniform, that had been required for the execution.

Music struck up and some can-can dancers recently imported from Paris came bounding on to the stage. Peter viewed them dyspepsically, thinking they all looked like low-class tarts.

'Good eh?' Goetz beamed.

The second glass of slivovitz followed the first.

'Peter, wake up.'

'What is it?'

'Ssshhh. There's someone downstairs,' Holly whispered, the pair of them in bed together.

'Rats?'

'I don't think so. I heard glass being broken.'

Peter sat up and listened.

She was right, and they were speaking German. 'You stay here,' he whispered, and got out of bed. Naked, he shrugged into a dressing gown, then took his pistol from its holster.

'Be careful, Peter.'

'Don't worry. I will be.'

He picked up a torch he'd recently acquired batteries for, and silently left the room.

'What . . .!' a figure exclaimed in German when the torch snapped on.

There were three of them, all in the uniform of the Wehrmacht. One of them started towards Peter.

'Stay where you are!' Peter rapped out authoritatively.

The man who'd been moving stopped and gaped, startled at being addressed in flawless German.

'He's got a gun,' another said.

As far as Peter could make out they were unarmed. 'What the hell do you think you're up to?' he demanded.

'Who are you?'

Peter gave his rank and surname. On hearing these the three soldiers clicked to attention.

Peter played the torchlight over them, memorising their faces. He didn't bother flicking the nearby electric switch, knowing the electricity to be off for the night.

'We're sorry, sir. We had no idea an officer was quartered here.'

'Officers,' Peter lied, playing safe. 'There are six of us.' He studied them. 'So what are you doing, thieving, I presume?'

There was no reply.

Peter grunted. 'Names?'

The three hesitantly divulged them.

Peter nodded. 'Now get out and don't ever come back. If you do . . .' He waggled his pistol at them. 'You won't live long enough to regret it. Understand?'

'Yes, sir!' the three replied in unison.

'Use the front door.'

He moved aside as the three filed past, watching as they unbolted the door. When they'd gone he reshot the bolt.

He found a broken window in the kitchen where they'd entered. He closed the window again, wondering if he was going to be able to have the broken pane replaced. Glass was something else that was difficult to come by.

'Well?' Holly queried when he rejoined her in the bedroom.

'Thieves. I sent them packing.'

Her eyes were wide. 'How many?'

'Three of them, German soldiers. They got a fright when they found out I was an officer.'

He replaced the pistol in its holster. 'They knew they were lucky I didn't report them, all I had to do was pick up the telephone. They would have been court-martialled if I had.'

'Why didn't you?'

He smiled at her. 'I didn't want the military police crawling all over here with you present. Anyway, they might have jumped me if they'd known I was the only man in the house. I bluffed them that there were six of us, officers I mean. A bluff they'd have seen through before long if I'd remained downstairs on my own.'

'I was so scared for you, Peter,' she said softly.

He sat on the bed and put his arms round her. He'd been scared for Holly. If those men had jumped him, probably killing him, there was no knowing what they'd have done to her. Rape no doubt, and then . . . He shivered.

'Are you cold?'

'A little,' he lied, not wishing to tell her what had been going through his mind.

'Then get back under the clothes and cuddle up. My hero,' she whispered when he'd done that.

Hero, him! That was too absurd for words. But nonetheless – and he smiled – it was nice to be thought of like that.

Particularly by the woman he loved.

Elspeth hummed as she darned, using wool she'd unravelled from an old cardy. It wasn't the same colour as Terry's socks, but that couldn't be helped. Wool was wool, regardless.

Boy or girl? she wondered for the umpteenth time. Not that she cared as long as the baby was healthy. There again, Terry would probably prefer a boy, a son and heir.

What shall I call him? Elspeth mused. Terence after his father? Big Terry and little Terry. She laughed aloud at that thought.

She paused to rub her tummy, imagining the baby growing inside. Still only a speck, minute, but that would soon change with the passing weeks and months.

She wondered who he'd take after. Terry himself, her, the pair of them? Her colour hair, Terry's nose? Would he eventually need glasses like his dad? She hoped not. Glasses were all right on adults but difficult things for children. She knew what went on in schools, four-eyes, that sort of nonsense.

She'd have Holly attend the birth, she decided, that would be a great help and easily arranged as she intended having the baby at the hospital. She'd already chosen the doctor she wanted to deliver her. Mr Garlick was *the* man for that.

She could have it at home of course with her GP and a midwife in attendance. But no, she preferred the hospital. That was safer in case, and pray God it didn't, something went wrong.

She finished off the sock she'd been darning, placed it on the floor and picked up another.

Baby clothes would be a problem, but surely she'd be able to scrounge what she needed. Nappies too, that was another thing.

She paused to smile broadly. It was just dandy being pregnant. She couldn't have been happier.

'Nigel Hart, this is Juan Garcia.' Nigel was to be Juan's companion in the dinghy.

A smiling Nigel extended his hand. 'How do you do.'

'I do OK. And you?'

Nigel was a powerfully built chap in his early twenties. He had reddish hair and a snub nose, his face covered with freckles.

'I thought it time you two met,' Jack Levine said, having decided it was best they did so before the night they set off together.

'Spanish, eh?' Nigel grinned.

'*Si.*'

'Well, I don't have any trouble with that.'

'You strong,' Juan commented, patting one of Nigel's biceps.

'Comes from humping potatoes around most of my life.'

Juan nodded. 'I skinny. No eat well long time. The Germans . . .' He shook his head. 'Ver bad to me.'

'I've seen how they treat prisoners of war,' Nigel declared softly. 'I wouldn't treat an animal like that.'

'You go England to fight?'

'That's right.'

'We get there together, heh?'

'I hope so. I sincerely do.'

'You can't say you haven't been warned how dangerous the crossing will be,' Jack said. 'There are all sorts of things could do for you on the way over.'

'I appreciate that,' Nigel replied.

Juan nodded his head. 'Me appreciate too.'

Elspeth and Terry had been watching this meeting and now Elspeth stepped forward. 'How about some beet tea or acorn coffee? I've nothing else in, I'm afraid.'

'Not for me, thanks,' Nigel replied.

'Nor me,' Jack added.

'I wish I had the proper stuff, but you know how it is.'

Everyone in the room did.

'Juan's married,' Jack informed Nigel.

'Really!'

'Two kids,' Juan stated proudly.

'You must miss them all.'

Juan's expression became one of extreme sadness. 'I do, Nigeel. I do ver much. I think of them all time.'

'Well, I'm a free agent in that department so I've no one to worry about, except my parents that is.'

'In England I safe, see family after war. That's why I escape. I might be shot but . . .' He made a gesture with his hands. 'I die if I remain prisoner, that for sure.'

Nigel turned to Elspeth. 'Don't worry about provisions for the crossing. I'll provide those.'

That was a relief to her. 'Thank you.'

Nigel stayed for a little while longer, continuing to chat and get to know Juan whom he wouldn't meet again until Bertram's beach.

'He fine man,' Juan said to the Le Vars when Nigel and Jack had gone.

'He certainly seemed to like you,' Terry commented.

'And I like him. We get on good.'

'Six days to go then,' Terry smiled.

'Six days,' Juan repeated.

Elspeth crossed her fingers that all would go well for Juan and Nigel. They all knew it would be a dangerous journey.

Jack and Nigel had arrived first and already loaded the provisions, including containers of water, that Nigel had promised to bring. The patrol boat had just gone by when Terry and Juan turned up.

'Sorry for cutting it fine,' Terry apologised. 'It took us longer than I expected.'

'Doesn't matter, you're here now,' Jack replied.

'How do you feel?' Nigel asked Juan.

'I sheet scared. You?'

Nigel was grinning. 'The same.'

'Right, let's launch,' Jack declared briskly, moving to the dinghy which was under an overhang of rock.

The dinghy slid effortlessly over the sand to the water's edge where it was quickly afloat.

Juan grasped Terry's hand. 'Thank you, my friend. I no forget you and Mrs Le Var. I come see you after the war. I promise.'

'We'll hold you to that.'

The other goodbyes were said, then Nigel and Juan clambered aboard. They'd been advised to row for at least a couple of hours before starting up the outboard whose tank had been filled to the brim with stolen German petrol. There were several large canisters on board to refill the tank. They also had a sail to use, the pair of them having been instructed in its handling by Jack. Unfortunately the instructions had all been in theory, there had been no means of providing practical ones.

'God speed,' Terry whispered, a lump in his throat.

Nigel had taken the oars which now dipped into the water. Terry and Jack watched until the dinghy had faded from view. It was moonless with only a few stars showing, that particular night being chosen for that reason.

'Well, that's that,' Jack said.

'Yes.'

'Everything's been done that could have been, the rest is up to them and fortune.'

Jack sighed. 'Right, there's a house not far away where we're expected. We'll spend the night there and return to St Helier in the morning.'

They left Bertram's beach, each with a heavy heart, worrying about Nigel and Juan.

Nigel and Juan did make it safely to England, as the Le Vars found out after the war when Nigel returned home and called on them.

In 1949 Juan kept his promise. Face wreathed in smiles, he pitched up on the Le Vars' doorstep with Maria and the children in tow. It was a wonderful reunion.

*

When Terry arrived back home he found Elspeth sitting by the fire staring blankly into space.

'Elspeth?'

She sort of shook herself, then turned to gaze at him. Her face was drawn and haggard and it was clear she'd been crying. 'Did they get off all right?'

'Yes. Everything was fine.'

'Good.'

He went to her and squatted. 'What's wrong, darling?'

She gave him a thin, pained smile. 'I miscarried in the night. Cramps in my stomach woke me and then it just happened. Right there in our bed.'

'Oh, Elspeth,' he whispered.

Then she was in his arms, her whole body shaking. 'I couldn't believe it,' she choked. 'I just couldn't believe it.'

'There'll be other babies. You'll see,' he crooned, trying to console her.

But all Elspeth could think about was the one she'd lost. Little Terry who was to be named after his dad.

The foetus had been far too small to tell its gender. But she knew it had been a boy.

She just knew.

Chapter 19

Holly gazed up at a duck-egg-blue sky, thinking what a glorious day it was. Peter lay beside her, the pair of them in a small clearing in a wood. She turned and smiled at him when he reached out and took her hand.

'What are you thinking?' he asked.

'How wonderful this is.'

'It is that,' he agreed.

'I wish this summer would go on and on for ever,' she said softly.

'Nothing does that, Holly.'

'I know. But in the case of this summer I wish it would.'

'Unfortunately autumn's not far off. Who knows what that will bring.'

'You mean the war?'

'I mean the British. We've been expecting a counter-assault for some time now. It might happen this autumn.'

A thrill ran through Holly to hear that.

'There again,' he mused, 'it could come next year, or even the year after that. Who knows? But come it will eventually, that's certain.'

He released her hand and sat up. 'I have something for you.'

'Oh?'

'I've been waiting for the right moment to give it to you, and I think that moment's now.'

He fished in his jacket pocket to produce a small ball of tissue paper which he solemnly passed over.

The breath caught in her throat, and her eyes widened, when she unwrapped the paper. 'What's this?' she croaked.

'What does it look like?'

'A wedding ring?'

'Exactly.'

She stared at him in astonishment. 'But you know we can't get married, Peter, that it's forbidden.'

'Maybe officially, but unofficially we can do as we please.' He took the ring from her and slipped it on to the third finger of her left hand. 'Do you, Holly Morgan, take Peter Schmidt as your husband?'

Tears of joy and happiness sprang into her eyes. For a brief moment she thought of Martin and the ring he'd given her, then she banished him and it from her mind. 'I do.'

'Now you ask me.'

'Do you, Peter Schmidt, take this woman, Holly Morgan, as your wife?'

'I do.'

He beamed at her. 'That's it. As far as I'm concerned we're now just as married as if there had been a ceremony in a church conducted by a clergyman.'

He kissed her on the lips. 'And that's the seal that binds us.'

How did she feel? Ecstatic was the word that came to mind. 'I do love you, Peter,' she declared.

'I should hope so! You've just married me after all. I'm a great believer in loving the person you marry.'

She twisted the gold ring that was a little large for her, not that she cared a fig about that. 'I won't be able to wear it except when I'm at Half Hidden,' she said.

'I appreciate that.'

'But it will always be on my person no matter where I am or what I'm doing.'

'We'll do it properly after the war, when all this madness is over,' he said.

'But where will we live? We can't stay on in Jersey or go to Germany.'

Peter shrugged. 'We'll cross that bridge when we come to it, as you English say. I'll think of something.'

'You know what?'

'What?'

'I feel as though I truly am married. That you and I are now man and wife.'

'In my eyes we are too, I assure you. This is no silly piece of play-acting, Holly. I mean it for real.'

She put a palm on his cheek, loving him with all her heart. 'If there's one good thing came out of this war it's that it enabled you and me to meet.'

'I agree,' he declared softly.

They stared silently at each other for a few seconds, then he said, 'I wish I had a bottle of champagne to open. But, as I don't, we'll just have to think of another way to celebrate.'

She laughed as he reached for her blouse and began unbuttoning it. He'd come prepared, intending this to happen.

Afterwards he nibbled her ear, then whispered into it, 'Thank you, Mrs Schmidt.'

Holly spotted Elspeth talking to Sally Pallot, and immediately turned down a corridor in order to avoid her best friend. She felt guilty as hell for being so happy while Elspeth was quite the opposite.

'Are you avoiding me?'

Blast! Holly thought.

'Well?'

'What makes you think that?' she prevaricated.

Elspeth, a frown on her wan, haggard, face studied her friend. 'I don't know. It's just the impression I get.'

'Well, I'm not,' Holly lied.

Elspeth sighed. 'Sorry, it must have been my imagination. Ever since . . . Well we'd better not talk about that.'

'How are you anyway?'

'Not too clever. I feel so drained all the time. And I'm having trouble sleeping. I just toss and turn all night long.'

Holly wished she could do something to help, but what? 'It'll take you a while to get over what's happened. To come to terms with it.'

Elspeth shook her head. 'I'll never get over it, Holly. I know that. It'll haunt me till my dying day.'

On impulse, even though they were at work and in uniform, Holly threw her arms round Elspeth and hugged her tight. Elspeth sniffed.

'Thanks, pal,' Elspeth mumbled.

'I'll come over one night this week, how about that?'

'Sounds great.'

Holly found that she too was sniffing as she walked away.

Dan groaned as he came awake to the usual morning ritual of his cell door being unlocked then smashed back against the wall. God, another day. Another long back-breaking shift in the stone-yard.

How long had he been there now? He didn't know for certain, having to guess by the changing seasons. And how long was left of his sentence? That was the real question.

Dan shivered, knowing he was ill, as he'd been for the past few days. There was no point whatever in mentioning his illness to the guards who'd just have clouted him for his 'complaints' as they would have called it. Anyway, there weren't any medical facilities for the prisoners. No doctor, medicines, anything. If you were ill you simply had to put up with it.

He felt his forehead which was slick with cold sweat. And his throat was sore, a new symptom. Whatever was wrong with him was getting worse not better.

He groaned again as he swung his feet out of bed. When he stood up he swayed on the spot.

He'd never felt so tired in all his life.

Holly had been bored sitting home alone with nothing to do so had decided to play some of Dan's big band records to cheer herself up. She now rewound the gramophone and put on a Glenn Miller number.

She hummed in accompaniment as she began to dance, holding her arms as though she had a partner.

She smiled, imagining that partner to be Peter, her husband of ten days.

Her husband! How elated that one word made her. Pausing for a moment she fumbled in her skirt pocket, pulled out his ring and slipped it on.

'I love you, my darling,' she whispered.

And I love you, she imagined him reply.

In her mind's eye they were together after the war, he a practising GP again, she the wife at home, cooking his dinner, awaiting his return.

What would their house be like? Wouldn't it be wonderful if it was similar to Half Hidden. A comfortable cottage with a vegetable garden out back. And a proper garden too where their children could play.

How many would they have? One, two, three? She was filled with a warm anticipation at the thought.

Peter and she sharing the same bed night after night, not just every other weekend. He always there for her to reach out and hold, to snuggle up against. To have when he wanted her.

The pair of them growing older together, loving each other as much as they now did. A love that would never diminish but rather deepen and expand with the passage of time and shared experience.

Now he was back in her arms, smiling at her, she at him. It was a moonlit night; they were alone as they danced, his eyes gazing deeply into hers, hers into his. He laughing, she also, happiness enveloping them like a feathery cloud.

She sighed with pleasure as the record finished, and stopped dancing.

'Silly sod,' she muttered, meaning herself. If anyone had walked into the room they'd have thought her mad cavorting around like this.

She rewound the gramophone, put on another record and started to dance again.

Peter there in her arms. Peter . . .

Dan was finished, and knew it. He hadn't a particle of energy left in his body thanks to the combination of the stone-yard and his illness, whatever the latter was.

His sole regret was that he'd never see or speak to Holly again. He'd have given anything to say goodbye to her. But that couldn't be.

He dropped his sledgehammer and sank to his knees. I'm coming, Gill, he thought. I'm coming.

The nearest guard, a pot-bellied man with an acne-pitted face, strutted over and screamed at him in German. Slowly, wearily, Dan shook his head.

He knew what would happen next, he'd seen it happen many times before. Now it was his turn.

He wasn't afraid of death any more, but rather welcomed it. For in death he'd be reunited with Gill who was waiting for him. He believed that totally and utterly.

The guard screamed a second time and again Dan slowly shook his head. The guard was grinning as he raised his rifle.

Dan closed his eyes on this world, ready for the next.

He mumbled. 'Our Father, who art in . . .'

'You did what?' Peter laughed.

'Danced for hours pretending you were there with me. It was lovely.'

'There's a name for people who do things like that,' he teased.

'I know. I thought that at the time.' She stirred the vegetable stew she was making. For afters there was apple tart, Peter having been able to get some flour. The apples, as were the vegetables, were their own.

'Some day I'll take you dancing,' he said. 'We'll get all dressed up and waltz the night away. Then I'll take you home and . . .' He winked salaciously at her.

'Oh yes please,' she enthused.

'You're shameless,' he further teased.

'Only where you're concerned.'

He crooked a finger at her, and waggled it. 'Come here, wife.'

'Can't. I'm busy.'

He put on a stern voice. 'Come here, I say. Or else.'

'Or else what?'

'You'll be punished.'

'Brute!' she teased back. 'What sort of punishment?'

'A smacked bum.'

'You wouldn't dare!'

'No?' He rose and placed a finger across his upper lip, then proceeded to goose step round the kitchen. In a mock German accent he declared, 'I am a Nazi, don't forget. *Sieg Heil! Sieg Heil!*'

He was pretending to be Adolf Hitler, she thought, bursting out laughing. It was very funny.

The laughter ceased abruptly when there was the sound of a car outside. He frowned in puzzlement.

'Are you expecting anyone?' she queried, suddenly afraid.

'No.'

'Then who could it be?'

'You stay here,' he said, and left the kitchen, closing the door firmly behind him.

Four German officers were standing on the doorstep, friends and acquaintances of his.

'Ah, Peter, we decided to visit you in your hideaway,' Joachim Zormeier declared, slapping leather gloves against his leg.

'We've brought a bottle,' Erwin Von Roon added, waving lead-sealed calvados in the air.

'Can we come in?' Ernst Klinger asked.

Peter's thoughts were racing. How did he get out of this one? 'I'm of course delighted to see you all,' he beamed. 'You're most welcome.'

The four made as though to enter the cottage.

Peter held up a hand. In a quiet, conspiratorial voice he said, 'Unfortunately you've caught me at rather a delicate moment. I'm, eh . . .' He cleared his throat. 'Entertaining just now.' He made piston movements with his right arm.

The four immediately caught on and roared with laughter. 'You sly old dog, Peter. Who is she?'

'The wife of eh . . .' He whispered the next bit. 'A local. She can only stay for a short while and has only just arrived. We were about to get into bed.'

'Then we will leave you to it,' Erwin Von Roon declared. 'Don't want to spoil your fun.

'Is she pretty?' Ernst Klinger, a notorious ladies' man, demanded eagerly.

Peter rolled his eyes heavenwards. 'Gorgeous. With huge . . .' He mimed very large breasts.

'Lucky you,' Klinger breathed.

'Come another time, but not at weekends.' Peter gestured inside and the four got the message.

'As Erwin said, we'll leave you to it then,' Hans Beck smiled, turning to the car.

Peter waved them away, then returned to the kitchen where he found a wide-eyed Holly sitting chewing a nail. He quickly recounted what had happened.

'Wasn't it dangerous saying you had someone here?'

He shrugged. 'I couldn't think of anything else that would have explained me not inviting them in.'

'How did they know where you live?'

'I've no idea. I must have mentioned it sometime. I never dreamt anyone would call, though.'

She went to him and put her arms round him. 'That gave me quite a turn.'

'The main thing is they didn't see you or learn your name. These things can get around. Especially as one of them was Hans Beck, a colleague of mine at the hospital.'

Holly had a thought. 'Something I've never asked you, but have any of your neighbours ever called in?'

'Only once. A chap wanting to know who I was. They were curious because of my car. I told him I was a doctor whose own house in St Helier had been requisitioned by the Germans and so I moved out here. I also explained that as a doctor I'm allowed a petrol ration, one of the few exceptions. He left quite satisfied and I haven't heard from him or any of the other neighbours since.'

Holly released Peter, who lit a cigarette. He was more rattled by what had happened than he was letting on. If it ever got out that Holly was a Jerrybag, her life would be hell.

Peter was bushed. It had been a long arduous day and all he wanted now were a couple of beers before returning home and going straight to bed. As he entered the bar of the Grand he was imme-diately struck by the atmosphere, which was sombre as opposed to the usual one of men thoroughly enjoying themselves.

He joined a gloomy Wolf Sohn standing hunched over a drink. 'What's up?' he asked. 'Why all the long faces?'

'You haven't heard?'

Peter shook his head.

'The Italians have surrendered unconditionally to the Allies. That clown Badoglio has done the dirty on us.' Marshal Pietro Badoglio had become Prime Minister on the fall of Mussolini.

'Well, well,' Peter mused.

'Yellow Eyetie bastards.'

This was news indeed, Peter thought. Why only the previous day Berlin radio had reported solid resistance by the Italian and German troops to the British invasion of southern Italy.

'I've also heard, unofficially that is, that the Italian garrison on Corsica have overpowered our forces on the island.'

Peter called for beers as Wolf had nearly finished his. No wonder there was such a sombre atmosphere in the bar.

Wolf went on. 'Eisenhower has apparently made a declaration that all Italians who help eject the German aggressor from Italian soil, as I'm told he put it, will have the assistance and support of the Allies. Which means we could now be fighting our so-called former friends as well.'

Another blow for Hitler, Peter reflected. The Führer would be raging.

'Something else,' Wolf said, lowering his voice. 'Word has it that we're now sending youngsters of only fifteen to the front line.'

Peter was aghast. 'Fifteen! That can't be so.'

'I tell you, it's the truth.'

'Why that's . . .' He bit his tongue, having been about to say it was criminal.

Wolf gave Peter a jaundiced look. 'What's it all coming to, Peter? What's it all coming to when we're doing things like that?'

Peter shook his head.

Wolf gulped down what remained in his glass, then saw off half the beer Peter had bought him. Having done that he ordered two large brandies. 'I need it because I feel sick,' he said quietly to Peter.

Peter felt the same. Fifteen years old and facing the Russians amongst others. Sending babies up against battle-hardened veterans. It didn't bear thinking about.

'Let's get drunk,' Wolf proposed.

'I can't, Wolf. I've had a long hard day and there's another ahead of me tomorrow. I'm sorry.'

Wolf nodded that he understood. 'I'll find someone else to get drunk with.'

He glanced round the room. 'Which shouldn't be hard.'

'I just had to come,' a weary Peter said to Holly. 'Don't worry, I was very careful.'

She led him through to the kitchen. 'You look dreadful.'

'I feel even worse. I did something today that . . .' He broke off and shuddered.

'Sit down before you fall down.'

He slumped into a chair. 'I got to thinking about you and, well, simply had to see you.'

Her heart swelled to hear that. She went to him and smoothed his brow.

'That's lovely,' he smiled.

'So what did you do that was so awful?'

'An amputation. Gangrene had set in so the leg had to come off.'

'You've done those before, surely?' she frowned.

'Oh yes. But never when the patient was fully conscious and screaming the place down.' He sighed. 'We've completely run out of anaesthetic at the hospital.'

'Dear God,' she breathed.

'I lost the patient. He died about half an hour afterwards.'

'Poor Peter,' she sympathised.

'Poor bloody patient. The agony and stark terror in his eyes was unbelievable. I felt like a butcher.'

'I have a little slivovitz in,' she said. 'The remains of some you gave me a while ago. Would that help?'

'Please.'

She crossed to the sideboard where she tipped slivovitz into a glass.

'I could never have been a surgeon in the old days. What I did today was barbaric,' he declared as she handed him the glass.

'They didn't have any choice in the matter, don't forget. And you might have saved the man who died. Who'd have died anyway from gangrene.'

'No anaesthetic,' he murmured, and shook his head. 'Nor do we know when, or even if, we'll get any more.'

He drained the glass in one long swallow. 'That's better,' he sighed.

'Is there anything else I can get you?'

He gave her a thin smile. 'Nothing. Just stay with me, that's all.'

'Of course.'

He gently pulled her down on to his lap and laid his head on her shoulder. 'Hello, wife,' he murmured.

'Hello, husband.'

'It's so good to be with you. You bring me peace.'

She stroked his hair.

'I've got another couple of operations to do tomorrow. Urgent cases that can't wait. I don't know how I'll manage to get through them.'

'You'll cope.'

'I only hope so.' He paused, then went on softly, 'It's not only me but the theatre staff as well. One of the nurses fainted and another vomited all over the place.'

'It must have been horrendous for them.'

'All highly qualified and experienced theatre personnel as well. But they, like me, had never conducted a major operation without anaesthetic before. The lassie who fainted had hysterics when she came round. What with her shrieking and the patient's screaming . . .' He broke off and closed his eyes.

'I'm so tired,' he mumbled.

She kissed him on the forehead. 'Are you going to stay the night?'

'Can I?'

'Where's the car?'

'Don't worry. It's parked where no one will connect it with here.'

'You'll have to leave early in the morning. Apart from the fact you're who you are, I also have my reputation to consider.'

'I'll leave early,' he agreed.

'You stay there and I'll make down the bed.'

'OK.'

When she returned from the bedroom she found him fast asleep in the chair. Not having the heart to wake him she fetched Dan's quilt and covered him with it.

She had just completed that when the electricity was cut off. There were no set times for this any more, it varied from day to day and evening to evening.

Holly took herself off to bed leaving Peter gently snoring in the chair.

'Peter, wake up!'

He grunted, and changed position.

Holly smiled as she shook him again. 'Wake up.'

He opened his eyes, gazed blankly at her for a moment, then recognition dawned.

'How do you feel now?'

He yawned and stretched. 'A lot better than I did last night.'

'You dropped off as I was making down the bed. You were in such a deep sleep I couldn't bring myself to wake you, so left you where you were.'

He pulled the quilt aside and stood up.

'Stiff?'

'Not in the least.' He ran a hand over his bristly chin. 'Do you have a razor in the house?'

'Dad's, you can use that. It'll have to be cold water I'm afraid, I can't put a kettle on as the gas is still off. I've checked.'

She took him to the bathroom and showed him where things were. 'There's no proper toothpaste I'm afraid,' she apologised. 'We haven't had any for yonks. What we use now is ground up cuttle-fish.' She made a face. 'It doesn't taste very pleasant but it works.'

She then left him to it, returning to the kitchen where she laid out a meagre breakfast for the pair of them, a slice of dry bread and cup of water each.

'That's better,' Peter declared on rejoining her.

'What time are you in theatre?' she asked as they munched their bread.

His face clouded. 'It's a morning list. One shouldn't be all that bad, the other . . .' He broke off, shaking his head.

'As I said last night, you'll cope.'

'I'd better be off,' he said when they'd finished their bread and water.

'It's well before the end of curfew.'

He smiled. 'That makes it all the easier as there won't be anyone around except us Germans.'

'Good luck,' she said at the door before opening it, meaning with the operations.

'Did you mind me dropping by?'

'I'm never happy about it. But in the circumstances I understand.'

'It seems an awful long time till you're next at Half Hidden,' he said.

'I know.'

'But it'll come round. It always does. And then we can be together, alone, for two whole glorious days.'

She kissed him lightly on the lips. 'Now go.'

He smiled, drinking her in for several seconds, and then, after quickly checking that the street was clear, left.

Holly leant against the door and sighed. It was lovely seeing her man off to work. Even if it was such a furtive affair.

She hugged herself as she returned to the kitchen. Some day, if God was good, she'd be doing that every working morning.

Chapter 20

'What's in the box?'

Terry smiled mysteriously. 'A surprise.'

'For me?'

'Of course.'

Elspeth was delighted. This was a surprise in itself. She went to take the cardboard box from him but he snatched it away. 'You've got to try and guess what's in it first.'

Elspeth regarded the box thoughtfully. Trust Terry to make a game of it. 'I've no idea,' she declared eventually.

'Come on!' he urged.

'A hat?'

Terry shook his head.

'Something to eat?'

He laughed. 'Not that either.'

She then heard a sound that could only have come from inside the box. 'Something alive.'

'Correct. But what?'

A flash of irritation crossed her face. This was becoming silly. She was about to say rabbit, then changed her mind. A rabbit could be eaten. And most certainly would have been. So it wasn't that.

'Give up?'

She nodded.

He handed her the box. 'A present from me to you. I hope you like him.'

Elspeth exclaimed when she opened the box and a small frightened kitten was revealed. 'He's gorgeous!' She scooped the black and white bundle out and cuddled it.

'You'll have to name him. He hasn't got one yet,' Terry declared.

'He looks like a Tiddles to me.'

'Then Tiddles it is.'

Elspeth stroked the kitten who immediately began to purr. 'Where did you get him from?'

'Someone at work. Tiddles was the pick of the litter. I chose him myself.'

'How will we feed him though? Our milk ration is tiny.'

'You'll just have to wean him straight off. He's due to be weaned anyway.'

The kitten was a device on Terry's part to try and cheer up Elspeth who'd been moping dreadfully since her miscarriage. It was hardly a baby, but the best substitute he could come up with.

'I'll make him a bed straight away,' Elspeth said, furiously thinking about what she could use for that purpose.

'He isn't toilet trained, I'm afraid. You'll have to teach him that.'

'Of course mummy will,' she crooned, scratching the kitten under the chin. Tiddles' reaction was to purr even louder.

It was working, Terry thought jubilantly. The change in Elspeth was amazing. She was positively glowing.

He gave himself a mental pat on the back.

'A kitten,' Holly repeated.

'That's right. I've called him Tiddles. Wasn't it sweet of Terry to give me that as a present?'

'Very.' The astute Holly, who'd noted the difference in Elspeth, correctly guessed at Terry's motives behind the gift. Clever old him, she thought.

She listened with amusement as Elspeth prattled on about Tiddles. It was Tiddles this, Tiddles that.

Holly suspected she was going to get very tired of hearing about Tiddles before very long.

St Helier stank, Holly reflected that evening as she made her way home. And no wonder. When was the last time the populace had washed with soap? Or washed their clothes with soap for that matter?

She was lucky, so far Peter had been able to get her the odd bar which she eked out till the last tiny bit. Nor was she quite as thin and emaciated as others, again thanks to Peter and the food he was able to acquire. Not forgetting their vegetable garden of course. That was another boon.

A woman clacked by, the soles of her shoes carved wood. Uncomfortable to wear as the shoes didn't bend as with leather soles, but far better than walking around barefoot. The clacking of wood on cobbles and pavement was being heard more and more.

Again Holly was fortunate having access to Mrs Vardon's shoes at Half Hidden. But those wouldn't last for ever and then the day would come when she too would have to resort to wooden soles.

Some of the sights were laughable really, if they weren't so pathetic. Only a few minutes previously she'd seen a man wearing a suit that was enormous on him. Whether it was his own suit and he'd lost an incredible amount of weight, or someone else's he'd appropriated, she couldn't say. It might have been either.

She was in quite a jolly mood when she arrived home. That is, until she opened the letter awaiting her, delivered after she'd gone to work that morning.

'Surely there must be something that can be done? Some anaesthetic that can be found somewhere?' Peter pleaded. He'd just come from the theatre where he'd carried out an operation that had almost totally unnerved him.

The German Medical Officer regarded Peter sympathetically. 'I'm doing my best, Dr Schmidt, believe me. I've sent off form after form, request after request, to no avail. I don't like this any better than you.'

'It's positively medieval. Today I . . .' Peter broke off and ran a hand over his forehead. He couldn't bring himself to describe what had happened earlier in the theatre. It was just too awful for words.

'All I can do is keep on trying,' the MO stated.

'We don't even have any pain-killers left. Nothing.'

'I know,' the MO nodded.

Peter gave a heartfelt sigh. This wasn't getting him anywhere. There was no point at going on at the MO, it wasn't his fault.

'There is one thing. I wonder,' the MO mused.

'What?'

The MO crossed to the window and stared out. It was a grey day, heavily overcast. Peter waited patiently while he thought.

'It's somewhat irregular,' the MO said slowly. 'But then so is the entire situation.'

He swung on Peter. 'I could personally go to France and see what I can get there. Failing that, I could travel on to Germany itself.'

Hope surged in Peter. 'That's a wonderful idea, sir.'

'I shouldn't really leave the island, but . . . needs must.'

'When will you go, sir?'

The MO considered that. 'I'll have some arrangements to make first, say a couple of days from now. Depending on the transport, that is.'

'I hope you're successful, sir. I pray to God you are.'

The MO fervently hoped so too.

Holly was stunned.

She stared again at the letter from the authorities informing her that Dan was dead. That was it. No explanation of how he'd died or in what circumstances. And certainly no word of condolence. The simple bald statement that he was dead.

'Nurse Le Var, can I speak to you,' Sister Moignard requested.

'Of course, Sister.'

'Do you know anything about Nurse Morgan?'

'No, Sister. How do you mean?'

'She hasn't reported in for duty for the past three days, nor informed us why, which is most unlike her.'

'I thought I hadn't seen her about,' Elspeth commented. 'But I presumed I just hadn't bumped into her, or that she was on nights.'

'I'm worried that she might be ill and unable to cope, living on her own as she now does.'

'I'll call in on her after my shift,' Elspeth proposed. 'I'll find out what's what.'

Sister smiled. 'Excellent, nurse. I'll look forward to hearing from you tomorrow.'

Something must be wrong with Holly, Elspeth thought as she continued on her way. As Sister rightly said, it was completely out of character for Holly to stay off and not get in touch.

Elspeth knocked yet again. Why wasn't Holly answering? Did that mean she wasn't there, or in bed unable to answer the door? A door she'd already tried and found to be locked.

'Who is it?'

That startled Elspeth for a moment. Why ask who it was, why not just open the damn door as she did normally.

'It's Elspeth. Can I come in?'

There was a pause, then the door slowly opened to reveal a dishevelled, sunken-eyed Holly.

Elspeth bustled inside while Holly shut the door again.

'Are you ill?' a concerned Elspeth queried.

Holly didn't answer, instead she brushed past her friend and headed for the kitchen where she slumped into a chair.

'He's dead,' she croaked. 'The bastards killed him.'

'Who's dead?'

'Dad. My father.'

Elspeth's hand involuntarily flew to her mouth. She was appalled. 'No,' she breathed.

Holly nodded.

'How?'

Holly gestured towards the sideboard. 'There's a letter.' She laughed bitterly. 'Of sorts that is.'

Elspeth quickly crossed to the sideboard and read the letter. 'I'm sorry,' she said gently to Holly.

In her mind's eye Holly was seeing Dan in court that day he'd been sentenced. And other images of him throughout the years. Her lovely sweet father who'd single-handedly brought her up after her mother's death. Now he was gone. She'd never see him ever again. The pain she felt was almost unendurable.

'It doesn't say how he died,' Elspeth frowned.

'Does it matter? However, they killed him. Whether it was natural causes or whatever, they murdered him.'

Elspeth went to Holly and put an arm round her. 'Is there anything I can do?'

'No,' Holly whispered.

'Have you eaten?'

'I couldn't. I'd throw up if I tried.'

Tears welled in Holly's eyes. 'The worst thing is . . .' She hesitated, having been about to mention Peter.

'What is?' Elspeth prompted.

'I can't say,' Holly whispered.

'Surely nothing you can't tell me?'

Holly's expression was tortured as she stared at her friend. She had a desperate need to speak about Peter, tell someone. And she could trust Elspeth with her life if needs be.

'This is strictly between us. Understand?'

Elspeth nodded.

'Swear it.'

'I swear.'

Holly took a deep breath and wiped tears from her eyes. 'I feel so dirty, unclean. Just thinking about it makes me want to vomit.' She suddenly grabbed Elspeth's wrist, squeezing so hard it made Elspeth wince.

'I've been sleeping with one of them, one of his murderers.'

She was raving, Elspeth thought. 'Sleeping with whom?'

'A German.'

Dear God, Elspeth thought. Holly a Jerrybag! She'd long suspected something was in the wind, but this! 'Who?'

'Peter, Dr Schmidt at the hospital. He's staying at Half

Hidden, which is where we've been meeting.'

'Oh, Holly,' Elspeth said softly.

'A German, Elspeth, do you understand? One of those who murdered my father.' Her voice rose almost to a shriek, eyes starting in her head. 'May they all roast eternally in hell!'

Elspeth didn't know what to say. What could she say?

'We even went through a stupid mock marriage ceremony in which he gave me a ring. And all the time his fellow countrymen were putting Dad through God knows what.'

Holly shook. 'How can I live with myself after what I've done? How can I possibly?'

'Do you love him?'

'I thought I did.'

'And does he love you?'

'So he says. And no doubt does.'

'There are such things as good, decent Germans, Holly. Surely he's one of those?'

'Good!' Holly barked out a laugh. 'Oh, sure, he's good and decent all right, but that doesn't change matters. He's still a German, a Nazi, a bloody Hun. And to think I let him touch me, kiss me, get inside me. Dad must be spinning in his grave.'

She stared at Elspeth, and in a cracked voice said, 'I'm so ashamed. So very ashamed.'

Elspeth was rapidly becoming more and more alarmed for her friend, whose state of mind seemed quite unhinged. 'You won't do anything stupid, will you?'

'How do you mean?'

Elspeth swallowed. 'You know, *stupid.*'

'Kill myself?'

Elspeth nodded.

'I have thought of it. After the full realisation of what I'd done dawned on me it did cross my mind.'

'You mustn't, Holly.'

'Don't worry. I won't. That would be letting Dad down even more and I've let him down far enough as it is. No, I'll just have to somehow come to terms with what I've done. Living will be a worse punishment, I assure you.'

Elspeth breathed a sigh of relief. 'So what are you going to do about him?'

'Do? Nothing.'

'And what about this ring he gave you? Aren't you going to return it?'

Holly laughed again. 'I can't. I went out into the street and dropped it down the nearest drain. It's gone.'

'What if he contacts you? He's bound to try.'

'He'll get a flea in his ear if he does. I never want to see him ever again. He can jump off a cliff for all I care.'

Elspeth didn't believe she really meant that. Holly was dreadfully upset, which was entirely understandable, but she wasn't a vindictive person. She was speaking figuratively.

'It was Sister Moignard who asked me to call in,' Elspeth explained. 'She was worried that you hadn't been in touch.'

Holly shrugged. 'I meant to, but just never got round to it. The only time I've been out of the house since that letter arrived was to go to the drain.'

'I'll tell her what's happened and I'm sure she'll say to take as much time off as you want.'

'Thanks, Els.'

'And you must try to eat something. You'll make yourself ill if you don't.'

Holly didn't answer that.

'Is there any food in the house?'

'Some bread, though it's probably hard by now.'

'I'll dip it in water to soften it. Is it in the bin?'

'Not for the moment, please. I really couldn't get it down.'

Elspeth took off her cloak, went to the hall and hung it up. She then returned to the kitchen. 'I'll sit with you for a while. Terry will just have to wait for his tea.'

'How's Tiddles?'

This complete change of tack slightly threw Elspeth. 'Fine, thank you.'

'It's funny but I've been thinking about him. I don't know why I should be thinking about your cat at a time like this, but I have.' She blinked rapidly. 'Dad liked cats you know. We never had one ourselves but he liked them. I'm sure he would have made a big fuss over your Tiddles.'

Mr Morgan dead, it was just beginning to sink in for Elspeth. She wondered how he'd died, something they'd probably never find out. There was no use inquiring; as Holly no doubt appreciated, the Germans wouldn't be forthcoming. They were notoriously tight-lipped about official matters. And if they had killed him they were hardly likely to admit it.

'What about a cup of something?' Elspeth asked.

'There's tea.'

'Shall I make a pot of that?'

Tea Peter had given her, Holly thought bitterly. But it would be ridiculous throwing that away as well when it was in such short sup-ply. 'Please.'

But the gas had been cut off again so they had to do without.

Elspeth stayed with Holly for several hours before returning home and telling Terry the dreadful news.

Peter was talking to a German colleague when he spotted Holly coming towards him. When she saw him she stopped short. A brief look passed between them, then she wheeled and strode away.

A look that rocked Peter to the very core because it had been one of sheer hatred.

What have I done to deserve that? He had no idea.

Peter went again to the window and stared out. Holly should have arrived hours ago. Where was she?

Perhaps she was having to work? It was possible her shifts had been changed, that happened on occasion. But he would have thought she would have found a way to tell him if they had. There was always the telephone after all.

And what was the meaning of that look she'd given him. It had been bothering him acutely ever since. Something was amiss, that was certain. But what?

He sighed, and turned away from the window. He picked up a book and sat, abandoning it a few minutes later when he found he couldn't concentrate.

After a while he started preparing lunch, which he ate alone. He didn't give up hope that she'd appear until he finally went to bed that night.

A night he'd expected to spend with her.

'Holly certainly has had rotten luck,' Sally Pallot commented to the others. 'First her fiancé, then her dad.'

'I met her dad several times, he was a nice man,' Helen Mason commented.

'She looked awful when she came back to work,' Viv Radmore said. 'But what else would you expect.'

'Bloody Krauts,' Sally spat.

'Pat Le Clerq's got a bun in the oven I hear,' Heather Aubin declared.

'Really!' Sally's eyes widened at this titbit.

'Five months gone apparently.'

They stopped talking when Holly entered the nurses' room, Holly still as sunken-eyed as when Elspeth had called in on her to find out what was wrong.

'Sodding Jerrybags,' Helen Mason hissed.

'When the war's over I hope they shoot every last one of them,' Sally further spat.

Holly blenched to hear that.

'What do you think, Holly?' Viv asked.

'Bit extreme, isn't it?'

'Not as far as I'm concerned,' Sally went on. 'I'd shave the hair off their heads, tar and feather them, parade them before the whole town, then shoot them.'

Holly quailed inside imagining that happening to her. Thank the Lord her secret was safe with Elspeth.

She sat and wearily ran a hand over her face. She felt so tired of late, tiredness that never left her no matter how much sleep she got. Mind you, she wasn't sleeping all that well. Sleeping yes, but not the deep refreshing kind.

'If Pat has a boy I wonder if she'll call him Adolf,' Sally said nastily, and laughed.

'Or Herman,' Viv added, laughing also.

'There are quite a few of these little German bastards around nowadays,' Heather stated.

'It's hardly their fault they're born to mixed parentage,' Holly commented quietly. 'No one should hold it against them.'

Heather sobered. 'You're right of course. It's their mothers I blame, traitors all.'

Holly dropped her gaze so they couldn't see her expression, and a few minutes later left the room saying she had to attend to something she'd forgotten about.

The others continued discussing the hated and reviled Jerrybags.

'Nurse Morgan, can I have a word?'

Holly halted as Peter came running up to her. She'd just left the hospital having completed her shift.

Her eyes were cold as ice, her face devoid of expression, her lips a thin slash as she stared at him.

He dropped his voice. 'You never came at the weekend.'

'Your lot killed him.'

Peter frowned. 'Who?'

'My father. Your lot killed him. Stay away from me from now on. I never want to speak to you again.'

And with that she swung on her heel and strode off leaving a stunned Peter staring after her.

Peter paced up and down the sitting-room floor at Half Hidden. He couldn't just leave things as they were, he thought. He just couldn't.

Holly clearly blamed him for her father's death, not personally, but because he was a German, which was quite unfair from his point of view. It was a terrible thing to happen, of course, he totally sympathised with her. But to throw away their love like this! That was madness.

And love her he most certainly did, with all his heart. Just as she loved him, he had no doubt about that.

If anyone was really to blame it was her father himself. He'd known the regulations about illegal wireless sets and what would happen to him if caught in possession of one. The man had gambled and lost.

Peter swore. If only he could talk to her, reason with her, make her see sense, then their relationship might still be salvaged. But how? She wouldn't be returning to Half Hidden, that was obvious, and speaking to her at length at the hospital was out of the question. Which left her house. Dare he call there?

She was right up to a point about Germans killing her father. The conditions in the prison must have been harsh in the extreme and it was more than likely that her father had succumbed to them. Conditions that would never have been allowed in peacetime.

But there again, Dan Morgan would never have ended up in prison if he'd obeyed the rules. He hadn't been thrown in prison for no reason. *The man had possessed an illegal wireless set, damn it!*

His thoughts were interrupted at that juncture by the phone ringing.

It was the hospital. He was needed.

Later that night found Peter sitting in his car agonising about whether or not to call on Holly at home. Maybe he should leave it for a while, a couple of weeks say. Perhaps she'd cool down a bit, be more open to reason.

No, he doubted that. It wouldn't make any difference whether he went now or in a couple of weeks, she'd be the same.

He'd go, he decided. Grasp the bull by the horns, as the English said.

He got out of the car and locked the door. As he made his way to her house he realised he was extremely nervous.

The instant Holly saw who it was she tried to slam the door in Peter's face, but he stopped that by whipping his foot over the jamb.

'I must speak to you, please?' he pleaded.

'Go away,' she snapped.

'Holly, it can't end like this.'

'I said go away. I've absolutely nothing to say to you.'

'Please let me come in.'

'No.'

'You're being very unfair.'

'Am I?' Her voice dripped sarcasm.

'At least let me say my piece.'

'Remove your foot,' she ordered.

'Please?'

She regarded him coldly. 'If you feel anything at all for me then go. I told you I never wanted to speak to you again and meant it.'

'It was your dad's own fault, Holly. He should never have . . .'

'Shut up!' she barked, cutting him off. How dare he blame Dan. How dare this German blame her father when it was his lot who'd murdered him.

'At least let me say how sorry I am. Truly.'

'Fine. Now bugger off.'

'How did you find out?' he asked, desperately trying to prolong the conversation.

'Do you want people to see you here, a sodding German? Is that what you wish?'

'No, of course not.'

'Then go to hell away. And don't ever come back again. Do you hear?'

'Holly, I . . .'

She strained at the door, making him grimace with pain. The words he'd been about to utter died in his throat.

He slowly nodded, admitting defeat. She eased the door and he pulled his foot free. A second later the door banged shut.

What a mess, he thought as, shoulders hunched, he returned to his car.

What a bloody awful mess.

Chapter 21

Holly had got into the habit of taking her lunchtime break in the park facing the hospital. And it was there she was joined one day by Elspeth.

'So how are you?' Elspeth inquired.

Holly's reply was a shrug.

'You're looking very thoughtful.'

'And you're looking well, if thinner than ever. But then who isn't.'

Elspeth glanced at several off-duty German soldiers strolling by. Both were smoking, both had happy smiling faces. Neither appeared old enough to yet shave.

'I saw him today,' Holly said quietly. 'But he didn't see me. I made sure of that.'

'You mean Peter?'

Holly gave her friend a tight smile. 'Who else?'

'And he hasn't attempted to speak to you again since that night he came to your house?'

Holly shook her head.

'Then he got the message.'

'Oh he did that all right. Loud and clear.'

Elspeth gently patted Holly's arm. 'Any regrets, Hol?'

There was a long pause, then Holly replied, 'I just can't get him out of my mind. He's somehow always there.' She sighed. 'It's strange, I'd never have believed you could hate and love someone at the same time. It's most odd.'

'But you don't hate him, Holly. His race yes, but not the man himself.'

'How can you differentiate between the two?'

'The man is the man, Holly.'

'He's a German first though. And they killed my father, who was one of the sweetest people on God's earth. Do you know Peter actually said my father's death was his own fault?'

Elspeth bit her lip. There was a lot in that, not that Holly would ever agree. But then, when was anything ever black and white. In her experience things were always many shades of grey.

'I miss Half Hidden,' Holly said. 'I enjoyed it there. Particularly the vegetable garden. We had some fun with that.'

'You'll never forgive him then?'

'Never,' Holly declared vehemently.

It seemed to Elspeth that Holly had made a rod for her own back. She understood only too well the difficulties and dangers of being a Jerrybag, but this had nothing to do with that.

'Tony still asks after you,' Elspeth stated.

Holly stared blankly at her friend. 'Tony?'

'Terry's cousin. Remember you used to go out with him.'

'Oh yes! *Him.*' She laughed. 'That seems an eternity ago. I'd quite forgotten about Tony.'

'Well, he still asks after you. You might have forgotten about him but he certainly hasn't forgotten you.'

Holly shook her head, but didn't comment further on the subject of Tony.

'Perhaps I should ask Terry to get you a cat.'

'Eh?'

Elspeth smiled. 'A cat, a kitten. Tiddles helped me enormously after my miscarriage.'

'My dad liked cats.'

'You told me that once.'

'How is Tiddles?'

'Full of mischief. It's as if he's always been with us. He's taken to sleeping on our bed, down at the bottom. Terry isn't best pleased about that but I rather enjoy it. He's great company when Terry isn't there.'

'Maybe I will get one,' Holly mused. It would be nice having a cat round the house. It could be very lonely all by herself in the evenings.

Elspeth glanced down at her breast watch. 'Almost time to go back in.'

'On with the grind, eh?'

'I'm afraid so.'

Holly pulled her cloak more tightly about her for it was a chilly day.

A company of Germans appeared on the street separating the park and hospital, their boots stamping in unison as they marched by.

'The war can't last for ever,' Elspeth said quietly, watching their progress. 'And then we can all get back to normal.'

Holly smiled cynically. The war must surely end one day, but get back to normal?

That, for her anyway, would be impossible. Not after all that had happened. Her life, and that of many others, had been changed irrevocably.

Peter was drunk, a rare occurrence for him. Normally he kept his alcohol intake well under control because of his job if nothing else, but he had two days off and that afternoon had gone to the Grand where he'd got to brooding about Holly. And in the depths of depression glassful after glassful had slid down his throat.

He blinked at the table in front of him, seeing double. Time to go home, he told himself.

'Are you all right?' Wolf Sohn inquired anxiously, having come across to where Peter was sitting.

Peter nodded.

'Unusual to see you hitting it so heavily.'

Peter gave him a lopsided grin. 'Enjoying myself, that's all,' he slurred. Which was a lie.

'Do you want to use my room to sleep it off a bit?'

Peter considered that. 'No, I'm OK. Thanks though.'

'Shall I join you?'

'Just leaving, I'm afraid.'

'Right then.' Wolf patted him on the shoulder. 'You take care now.'

Peter waggled a finger at Wolf indicating he would. He watched two Wolfs move to another table.

He burped, not liking the taste that came into his mouth. He then lurched to his feet, did his best to compose himself, and headed for the door trying not to weave as he walked.

'What's wrong with Peter?' Hauptmann Klipstein asked Wolf.

Wolf stared after Peter. 'I don't know, but he hasn't been himself of late. I think something's worrying him.'

'It's the first time I've ever seen him drunk.'

'Me too.'

Klipstein sighed. 'It's probably this damned war. It's getting to a lot of us.'

They left it at that and Peter was soon forgotten as they began discussing the latest war news, little of which was in their favour.

Outside Peter stopped and sucked in a deep breath of night air. A mistake that instantly made him feel even more drunk and sent him reeling.

'Shit,' he muttered.

He staggered to his car parked in the hotel driveway and fumbled for his keys, cursing again when he dropped them.

'Bloody woman,' he muttered, squatting down and groping in the darkness, the hotel completely blacked out. 'Bloody stupid woman.' He was referring to Holly.

Somehow he lost his balance and the next moment crashed to the driveway where he landed with a jarring thump on his bottom. He swore again, this time viciously. Perhaps I should have taken up Wolf's offer after all, he thought.

'Can I help you, sir?' a nervous sentry asked, having been observing Peter and deciding to step over.

'Lost my keys,' Peter hiccupped.

Pissed as a rat, the sentry thought. He could have done with a few glasses of schnapps himself for it was bitter cold.

The sentry produced a torch. 'Here we are, sir,' he said, picking up the keys. He debated whether or not to assist Peter who was struggling to his feet, and decided not to. You never knew with officers, especially drunk ones, a kindly act could land you in trouble.

'Thank you,' Peter mumbled, accepting the keys. He had difficulty getting the relevant key in the lock but at last managed it.

The sentry saluted him, then returned to his post thinking to himself that the last thing Peter should be doing was driving. He wondered idly if Peter would even get out of the driveway.

Peter slumped over the wheel and closed his eyes. Holly . . . Holly . . . Holly . . . the vision that kept dancing in his mind was tormenting him. It was like living in a waking hell since she'd broken it off. He was obsessed with her.

'Home,' he murmured. 'You must get home and into bed.' Thank God he could sleep in tomorrow. He was going to have an enormous hangover.

He succeeded in inserting the ignition key on his fourth attempt. He swallowed hard, peering intently ahead, as he eased the car past the vehicle in front.

The sentry shook his head in amazement when Peter navigated the length of the driveway without bumping into anything. He continued watching as Peter slowly drove off.

I could use another drink, Peter thought, although he knew that was the last thing he needed. His head was whirling and he was still seeing double. With a bit of luck he wouldn't encounter any other traffic en route back to Half Hidden.

He breathed a sigh of relief when St Helier was behind him. At least that was out of the way.

There was a full moon, glinting off the Channel. It would have been murder, in his present condition, if he hadn't had that to help light his way.

There she was again, dancing in his mind. The sound of her laughter loud in his ears. Jesus, she was beautiful. The tumbling brown hair, those bewitching hazel eyes. The figure he so adored and would have given anything to possess again.

He saw her asleep, lying beside him at Half Hidden. Her chest gently rising and falling with her breathing. The delightful way she had, when asleep, of reaching out and touching him as if reassuring herself that he was still there.

Making love to her, how passionate she could be, abandoned on occasion. Matching his own fire and ardour with her own. Stroking him, caressing him, urging him on.

All now lost because her damned father couldn't obey the rules and had ended up dead as a result. How could she blame him for that? It was ridiculous. Simply illogical. But she did because he was a German.

He ground his teeth in fury, his hands on the wheel tightening till the knuckles were white. Breath hissed from his nostrils.

Holly in the vegetable garden, a smudge of dirt on her face that he wiped away. Sunlight glistening in her hair giving a halo effect. She might have been an angel descended, a goddess from another world. His angel, his goddess.

'Oh Christ!' he sobbed, despair thick within him.

And then, suddenly, a lapse in his concentration, partially due to the alcohol, partly to his emotions, the car sliding out of control, upending as it entered a ditch.

He yelled out as the car slewed and went over. He was aware of his head banging against glass which shattered.

Then blackness.

He came to, having only been unconscious for several seconds. His head was throbbing and he could feel blood on his cheek. I have to get out of here, he told himself. The car could go up in flames. He mustn't be trapped.

He squirmed across the seats and, thank God, the door opposite opened when he turned the handle. He pushed the door fully open and crawled out, dropping to the ground to land in shallow muddy water.

He staggered away from the car which was still running. When he judged himself a safe distance from the car he slumped against the side of the ditch, and promptly threw up. The hot vomit tasted vile and disgusting in his mouth.

When he was finished he wiped his mouth with his sleeve, and stared at the car, waiting for it to explode. He found himself to be shaking all over.

The engine shuddered to a halt, though he couldn't think why it should do so. He was only relieved that it had.

There is nothing I can do here, he thought. The car would have to stay where it was. In the morning he'd arrange for it to be towed away.

That had been a near thing, he told himself as he climbed out of the ditch and resumed his journey on foot, a lot more sober than he'd been before the crash. Too damned near for his liking.

A little further down the road he halted and threw up again.

He was on the operating table held down by four burly porters. They were trying to calm him but he was having none of it. His eyes widened in terror when he saw the surgeon approach wielding a scalpel.

The surgeon grinned and told him not to be such a baby. This would hardly hurt at all.

He shrieked and shrieked as the scalpel descended.

He was screaming when he came awake and quickly sat up. God, that had been awful. He couldn't remember having such a realistic nightmare.

He ran a hand over his forehead, discovering it to be covered in cold sweat. He reached for the cigarettes and lighter on the bedside table and lit up. When he tried the lamp there was no response, the electricity was off.

He felt like death. He'd been only too right about having an appalling hangover. He had the mother and father of one.

He groaned, remembering the accident he'd had the night before. He could easily have been killed. And what if the car had gone up with him still inside? That didn't bear thinking about. That in itself was a nightmare.

He thought of the Medical Officer who hadn't yet returned from France. What was keeping the man? Perhaps he'd had to travel on to Germany after all. Maybe something had happened and he wasn't even coming back.

Peter prayed that he was, and with anaesthetic. His nerves were shot from operating without the damned stuff. The last one had been a burst appendix which the patient had thankfully survived.

He could still hear the man shrieking just as he'd been doing in the nightmare.

After a while and several more cigarettes he got up and used the telephone to sort out the business of his car.

'I'm really worried about Holly,' Elspeth said to Terry one evening.

'She just hasn't been the same since the death of her father,' he agreed.

There was a lot more to it than that, Elspeth thought. She dearly wanted to confide in her husband but couldn't because of the promise she'd made Holly.

'Perhaps if she had some time off work that might help,' Terry suggested.

'I don't know if she's due any leave. I could ask her.'

'What she should really do is find herself a chap. There's been no one since Martin, has there? Only Tony, and she didn't reciprocate his feelings.'

Elspeth shook her head, thinking that was the trouble. There had been, a blinking German whom she'd fallen in love with, and he her.

'I wish I could think of someone she might take to,' Terry mused.

'I doubt she'd be interested.'

'Oh? Surely if it was the right person?'

The right person was Dr Peter Schmidt, but she couldn't tell Terry that.

Tiddles padded into the room, mewed, and jumped on to Terry's lap where he quickly snuggled down.

'How are you then, beauty?' Terry crooned, stroking Tiddles' neck. The response was a contented purring.

'Can you get another kitten?' Elspeth asked.

Terry stared at her. 'Isn't one enough?'

'Not for us, for Holly. She could use the companionship.'

'Good idea, it might buck her up a bit,' Terry enthused. He pursed his lips. 'I could ask around. There are bound to be some kittens available somewhere.'

Elspeth was about to reply when the electricity was cut off, plunging them into darkness. 'Damn,' she muttered. This was happening more and more of late, and for longer periods of time.

After a while, with nothing else to do, they simply went to bed.

In the morning Elspeth reminded Terry about the kitten and he assured her he wouldn't forget. He'd ask around.

Holly scratched her head, wondering what was making it so itchy. She washed it regularly but without soap it wasn't the same. A few minutes later she was scratching again.

Then it struck her what might be the cause. There had been an outbreak of it in the town, particularly amongst the children. There was only one way to find out.

To her disgust it so proved. A good combing of her hair confirmed she had nits. And without black soap or anything else that could be applied . . . 'Bugger!' she swore.

With a heavy heart, for she'd always considered her hair one of her best features, she set to with scissors.

'Heavens! What's happened to you?' Elspeth exclaimed.

Holly gave her friend a rueful smile, extremely conscious of her shorn head. 'Nits. There was nothing else I could do.'

Elspeth giggled. 'You look so . . . different.'

'I know,' Holly sighed. 'I feel bald.' In fact she'd cut her hair to an overall length of about an inch.

Elspeth touched her own hair. 'I hope I don't catch them. Terry would go bananas if I had to do that.'

'You wouldn't have much choice in the present circumstances. It's either that or suffer the bloody things.'

Elspeth studied Holly from first one angle, then another. 'It's not that bad once you get used to it.'

'I doubt I ever will.'

'It gives you a certain . . .' Elspeth giggled again. 'Boyish charm.'

'Oh, thank you very much,' Holly replied sarcastically.

'Can I rub it?'

'Get lost.'

'It must feel funny.'

'It does, I assure you.'

'Wait till the other girls see you. They'll have a fit.'

'They won't be laughing if they catch the little buggers. Crying more like.'

'Which reminds me. Terry's got a kitten for you.'

'A kitten!'

'You said you wouldn't mind one, remember?'

Holly nodded. 'I'd forgotten about it.'

'Well, I hadn't. I spoke to Terry on the matter and he's found one for you.'

'What colour or colours?'

'He says the pick of the litter is a little grey. A female, is that OK?'

'Lovely.'

'She won't be ready for a fortnight yet and then you'll have to wean her straight off as we did Tiddles.'

'I understand.'

'Good,' Elspeth beamed.

Holly felt immensely cheered. It didn't even bother her when she entered the nurses' room and those there fell about laughing before offering their commiserations.

She was the first to offer her own commiseration when three days later Sally Pallot turned up with the longest face imaginable and her hair shorn.

Peter's mouth dropped open in surprise when Holly, staring fixedly straight ahead, walked past.

Good God, he thought. What on earth had she done to her hair?

Later, he guessed the reason why.

The face was vaguely familiar but Holly couldn't place it. The man was standing on the pavement idly glancing through that day's paper. Then the penny dropped.

Speak or not? She couldn't decide. Then thought she would. She was more than curious as to why he was in St Helier dressed in civilian clothes.

'Hello, Bill.'

Startled, he looked up from his paper.

'Remember me?' She touched her hair. 'I've changed a bit since the last time we met.'

'I know you,' he said.

She dropped her voice. 'Night time, a walk to the beach.'

'Holly,' he breathed.

She glanced around. There was a group of German soldiers about twenty yards away, and a couple more beyond that.

'What are you doing here?' she asked.

He folded his paper, slipped it into his jacket pocket, and took her by the arm. 'Let's walk,' he instructed.

They strolled a little way in silence, he tense and nervous though trying not to show it.

'Are you here alone?' she queried.

'No, there are several of us. We're on a mission.'

'Ah!' That explained why a British commando was in the middle of St Helier wearing what he was. 'Spying?'

'Sshhh!' he whispered. Then, 'Is there somewhere we can go and talk without being overheard?'

'How much time have you got?'

He eyed her speculatively, clearly turning something over in his mind. 'That depends.'

'Why don't you come home with me? It's safe there.'

'OK.'

They made small talk until they arrived at the house and were inside. 'I can only offer you beet tea or acorn coffee I'm afraid,' Holly stated.

'Not for me, thanks.'

'Then sit down and tell me what this is all about.'

Bill Tomkins sat, stared at Holly, then slowly smiled. 'Now there's a coincidence. You and your oppo from that night are the only ones I know on the entire Island and I go and run into you.'

'I couldn't place you right away, probably because of the clothes. How are you?'

'Oh, fine.'

'And what sort of mission are you on?'

He hesitated replying to her question. Again that speculative look came into his eyes.

'Don't tell me if you feel you can't, Bill. It's only that I might be able to help in some way.'

He sighed. 'It's simple really. We're here to find out what we can about the state of things. How many Germans are on the Island, the extent of their fortifications and how well they're built, manned and armed. What the morale is of both the Germans and Islanders. That sort of thing.'

She smiled. 'Prior to invasion, eh?'

He shrugged, and didn't answer.

'There are about thirty thousand German troops here,' she declared.

'How do you know that, Holly?'

'Never mind, I just do. The fortifications are extensive, as has no doubt been seen from the air and they're well constructed, believe me. There must have been millions of tons of concrete poured in their building. Unfortunately I can't tell you how they're armed, but substantially from what I've heard. Big guns, some ex-naval.'

He regarded her shrewdly. 'Are you sure about all that?'

'Most definitely.'

'And the German morale?'

'Not brilliant. I know at least one German officer who believes that it's only a matter of time before the Allies win the war. And only a matter of time before they land here and on the continent.'

Bill pulled out a packet of cigarettes. 'Do you?'

She shook her head. 'And I wouldn't be seen smoking those outside. Locals haven't been able to buy either cigarettes or tobacco for years.'

He nodded. 'Thanks for the tip.'

'As for the Islanders' morale, it's pretty fair considering all that we've been through. Day to day survival is pretty hard, we lack just about everything you can think of. And the rationing is grim. But despite all that their collective spirit hasn't been broken.'

'That was what we expected,' Bill replied slowly. 'You appreciate we know very little about what's been going on here since you were occupied. There have only been a few who've managed to escape.'

Holly recalled Elspeth's 'guest'. 'Do you happen to know if a Spaniard called Juan Garcia and an Islander made it across?'

Bill shook his head. 'I'm afraid not.'

Pity, Holly thought. She'd have loved to be able to tell Elspeth and Terry that they had. 'When did you arrive?' she asked.

'Last night. We're here for two days then off again.'

'And what about accommodation?'

'We'll find a place to hide out. Wherever available that we think is safe.'

She mentioned the curfew which he already knew about. 'I've an idea,' she said. 'Why don't you all stay here with me? The only thing is you'd have to be careful leaving in the mornings. I know this sounds daft but I have my reputation to consider, also there's been a lot of informing which means you'd have to leave individually rather than together. If that was spotted someone might think it odd and report the matter.'

'It's a very kind offer, Holly, but no. You see there are things we might be able to accomplish at night that we couldn't during the day. Besides, I don't want to get you into any trouble. If we're caught we'll be shot as spies, that's certain. If you were discovered to be involved you'd undoubtedly be shot as well and I certainly don't want to be responsible for that.'

'I understand.'

'Here,' he said, delving into a pocket. Crossing to her he handed her a large bar of chocolate. 'You might like that.'

Her eyes opened wide. 'Oh thank you, Bill. This is wonderful. Are you sure you don't need it yourself?'

'I can do without. I'm not madly keen on chocolate anyway.'

'This is a real treat,' she beamed.

He sat down again. 'Now what else can you tell me?'

When he'd pumped her for all the information she could give he declared he must go. At the door he said, 'This is the second time you've helped me, Holly. I can't thank you enough.'

'I'm only pleased I've been able to.'

As previously, she kissed him on the cheek. 'You take care, Bill.'

'And you, Holly.'

He does rather resemble Martin, she thought after he'd gone. What a nice man he was. She prayed he and his companions were going to be all right.

*

Peter was jubilant, the Medical Officer had finally returned bringing anaesthetic with him. Not a huge amount, but enough to keep them going for some months.

The 'torture chamber' as the theatre had commonly become known, could stop being called that for a while.

A week had now passed since Holly had run into Bill Tomkins and there had been no reports of spies being caught, which could only mean he and his companions had completed their mission and got safely away.

She would have been devastated if it had been otherwise.

Chapter 22

Holly tapped on Sister Moignard's office door, she and Heather Aubin having been told to report to her.

'Come in!' Sister called out.

Holly and Heather entered to find Sister busy at her desk. 'Be with you in a moment,' Sister said, frowning at a sheet of paper before her. She wrote something on the paper then laid her pen aside. Looking up, she smiled.

'I've got news for you both, you're being transferred to another ward,' she declared.

Heather glanced briefly at Holly, then back again at Sister.

'The German nurses are being withdrawn from the Island, which means we'll have to staff those wards again. You already have experience there, Nurse Morgan, so you're an obvious choice.'

Holly's heart had sunk at this pronouncement for it meant her coming into direct contact with Peter, having to work with him, the last thing she wanted.

'I don't know why the German nurses are being withdrawn,' Sister went on. 'I'm not privy to that information. I can only presume they're badly needed elsewhere.' She said that with a certain smug satisfaction for it was generally known that the war wasn't going at all well for Germany.

'When do we start?' Heather asked.

'Next Monday. It's all rather rushed I'm afraid, but there we are.'

Holly bit her lip. It would be extremely bad form to say she didn't wish to be transferred – not without a good reason. And she could hardly tell Sister that her ex-German lover was a doctor on those wards. Damn and blast! she thought.

'Any further questions?'

Both girls shook their heads.

'That'll be all for now then. Thank you.'

Heather and Holly turned for the door, Holly's mind racing, trying to come up with something valid that she could offer as an excuse. But she drew a blank.

'Well,' said Heather once they were outside again in the corridor. 'How about that then?'

'How about it,' Holly muttered.

'It'll make a change if nothing else.'

Oh, stop prattling, you silly cow, Holly thought. Perhaps she could still come up with something and see Sister later. But what?

'Why so glum?' Heather demanded.

'Am I?'

'That's how you look.'

Holly shrugged that off.

Heather glanced round to make sure they couldn't be overheard. In a whisper she said, 'Perhaps we can knock a few of the buggers off. Our contribution to the war effort.' And having said that she giggled. Thinking of her father and Martin, Holly was tempted to do just that.

'Well, Jemima, tomorrow's the day,' Holly murmured to her kitten, an adorable creature who was pale grey with large blue eyes.

Jemima gave a soft mew in reply.

Holly hadn't been able to think of a single thing that would have persuaded Sister to keep her on the ward. If she'd said that she had an aversion to dealing with Germans, which she could hardly do in the circumstances having tended them before, Sister would only have replied that a patient was a patient no matter his or her nationality.

It would be just my luck for Peter to do the first ward round, she thought. It was going to be agony being close to him, remembering what it had been like between them. That, despite everything, she still loved him.

'Ouch!' she exclaimed when Jemima clawed her thigh.

Jemima glanced up contritely and, as though understanding Holly wasn't pleased, sheathed her claws again. She could give quite a dig despite being only a kitten.

Holly took the offending paw in her hand. 'You're not to do that, young lady, understand?'

Jemima mewed.

'Good.'

Holly lay back in the chair and closed her eyes. She was dreading the morning's shift, quite dreading it. Perhaps she could ring in ill? Except that would only be prolonging the inevitable.

She wondered what he thought of her hair, for she'd passed him several times since taking the scissors to it. He couldn't possibly find it attractive, though Elspeth had said it gave her a sort of boyish charm.

There were quite a few shorn heads round the hospital now so it wasn't exactly an uncommon sight. Nits, she thought with disgust. Horrible things. At least having got rid of hers they'd stayed away, for which she was extremely thankful. And her hair had started to grow again though God alone knew how long it would take to get back to what it had been.

Peter Schmidt, she reflected. How different things would have been if it had been Peter Smith, he British and not a hated German. If only . . .

Sister Porthcarron was a tiny brunette with a reputation for being a stickler. Holly judged her to be in her mid fifties.

Sister gazed round the group of nurses assembled in her office, eyes glinting. It was the beginning of their first shift on the ward.

'Despite everything we heard about German efficiency et cetera the ward is in an absolutely disgusting state, there's filth everywhere.'

She snorted. 'I will not tolerate a ward in such a condition, therefore our first job is to get it cleaned. Luckily I've managed to procure some disinfectant and a little floor wax to help matters. And there's bags of hot water available which means there's no excuse for the ward not to be sparkling by the time doctor does his rounds. And I mean *sparkling!*'

She drew in a deep breath. 'Any questions?'

There weren't any.

'Right, let's set to.'

Staff instructed Holly and Heather to work as a pair, telling them to get buckets of water and mops to which they were to add an appropriate amount, bearing in mind the supply was limited, of disinfectant.

'She's a right firebreather and no mistake,' Heather whispered to Holly as they were filling their buckets, referring to Sister.

'Got a wonderful reputation though. I've heard that even the most senior doctors hold her in awe.'

Heather giggled. 'And her so tiny. She can't even be five feet.'

'Napoleon wasn't very tall either,' Holly replied, and they both laughed.

'Something funny?' Sister's voice snapped behind them.

Holly and Heather whirled. 'No, Sister.'

'Then why are you laughing? Only idiots laugh at nothing. Are you both idiots?'

'No, Sister,' Heather said softly.

'Then don't let me hear you laugh again. Being on a ward, either as a nurse or patient, isn't a laughing matter.'

'Yes, Sister,' they replied in unison.

Sister snorted, she did a lot of that as they were to find out, and strode from the room.

'Phew!' breathed Heather.

'I don't know about you, but she scares the pants off *me*,' Holly whispered.

Heather couldn't have agreed more.

The word spread like wildfire: doctor was about to appear on his rounds. Staff Nurse Le Vesconte glanced quickly round the ward, giving it a final check. She hurried over to straighten a sheet that had somehow become slightly rumpled. She'd have had a flea in her ear if Sister had seen that.

Holly sighed with relief when Dr Gerber and Sister Porthcarron swept into the ward, Sister dwarfed by the German. It wasn't Peter, she'd temporarily been spared that.

In fact Peter didn't appear on the ward all that day.

But he did the next, halfway through the afternoon. He ambled in, coming up short when he spotted Holly with a patient. He'd known of course that the German nurses were being replaced by their local counterparts, but for some reason it had never crossed his mind that Holly would be one of those replacements.

Part of him was delighted, though he realised it could make things difficult. He spoke briefly to Staff when she hurried to his side, and together they crossed to examine a patient due in theatre the following day.

Holly, aware of Peter's presence, continued with her task of rebandaging a suppurating wound that was getting worse rather than better. A wound that would have swiftly healed had they been able to apply the proper medication of which there wasn't any. When she'd finished she straightened and smiled at the soldier, an eighteen-year-old youth.

'Nurse, can you please assist here,' Peter called over to her, Staff having been called away.

Holly glared at him, his response being to raise an eyebrow.

Sod, she thought, marching over.

'You seem to be the only one free at the moment,' he said mildly by way of explanation. A quick glance from her round the ward confirmed that to be so.

'Now,' said Peter, and told her what he wanted her to do. While she went about that he chatted to the patient in German.

'Congratulations,' smiled Terry.

Elspeth blinked. 'For what?'

'Do you realise it's a whole month, I repeat that, a whole month, since you last mentioned getting pregnant.'

Elspeth smiled in return. 'Is it really?'

'I'm proud of you, Els. I really am.'

She reflected on that. 'I suppose I've just . . . come to terms with the situation.'

'As I've been asking you to do all along.'

She went to him and sat on his lap. 'Have I told you recently that I love you?'

'No.'

She jiggled his glasses. 'Well, I do.'

'And I love you, Els. Baby or no. You must always remember that.'

She kissed him lightly on the lips. 'Perhaps it isn't a good idea having a baby during wartime anyway. It's hardly the best of time to bring a baby up in.'

'I agree.'

'Still . . .' She trailed off wistfully. 'It would be nice.'

He fondled her gently, her breathing rapidly changing in a way he knew only too well. 'Know what I would like right now?' he murmured huskily after a while.

'What?'

'A cup of acorn coffee.'

It took a moment for that to sink in, Elspeth having thought he was about to suggest something else.

'Beast!' she hissed, jumping from his lap.

He laughed. 'Serves you right, you randy cow.'

'I am neither randy nor a cow!' she protested hotly.

'Well, forget the cow part but you're certainly the other.'

'Huh!' she sniffed. 'You should be so lucky, Terence Le Var. I know plenty of men who'd give their eye teeth to be married to a red-blooded woman such as myself.'

'Who's complaining? I'm merely stating fact.'

'Huh!' she sniffed again, stalking over to fill the kettle, hoping the gas was still on.

Neither ever realised it, but that was the night it happened and little Holly was conceived.

It was the first time since Dan's death that Holly had been able to bring herself to visit her mother's grave. She laid a bunch of wild flowers that she'd gathered by the headstone.

'I hope you like those, Mum. They were the best I could manage,' she whispered, a huge lump in her throat.

Holly sighed. 'I hope it's true and that you're now together again, happy as you once were. Dad always believed that and I know it brought him great comfort. If he was at all conscious I'm sure you were in his mind at –' she broke off and choked – 'the moment of passing.'

A few seconds ticked by, then she continued. 'I'll come more often from here on , I promise you.

'If you're listening, Dad, I have a kitten now. A little grey one called Jemima. You always said you liked cats, and you'd certainly like this one. She's a good companion in the evenings now that you're gone. I talk to her all the time, which is a bit silly I suppose, but it beats talking to yourself.

'She really is a sweet little thing who'll never grow into a big cat on the small amount I'm able to feed her. Still, she's surviving and thriving and that's the main thing.

'Please forgive me for having a relationship with a German, Dad, one of those who killed you. I shouldn't have, I know. It somehow just happened.

'It wasn't a casual fling, Dad, I want you to appreciate that. He's a wonderful man who unfortunately is one of "them". I love him, Dad, and he loves me, but how could I continue on with him after what happened? It was impossible.

'We're working together now which is tricky, though I have to say he's been nothing but pleasant. I think he's accepted the situation as I have done.

'We even went through a sort of mock wedding ceremony, that's how strong our feelings were for one another. And we planned to get married after the war, though Heaven knows where we would have lived.

'It's not easy seeing him on an almost daily basis, and I'm sure it's the same for him.

'It's Peter Schmidt, Dad, remember the doctor who used to get you whisky? Trained at Edinburgh would you believe, I can't recall if I ever mentioned that to you. It's quite funny really, he comes out with these Scottishisms occasionally, calling me lassie, things like that. And him a German.

'He's staying out at Half Hidden, remember there? A lovely house.

I . . .' She trailed off, and swallowed hard. Tears weren't far away, but she was determined not to succumb.

Holly bowed her head. 'Goodbye for now, Mum, goodbye, Dad. Please forgive me.'

And with that she turned and slowly walked away.

'Nurse, can you assist me in the sluice room, please,' Peter requested of Holly. He'd been waiting days for an opportunity to talk to her alone and now, with Sister off the ward, and Staff busy at the other end, it had occurred. He led the way into the sluice room and swiftly closed the door behind them.

'Let me out,' Holly said sharply, realising what had happened, and trying to brush past him.

'This has got to stop,' he declared.

'Let me out!'

'For your own good, Holly, it's got to stop. Every time I go near you you bristle and send off all sorts of signals. I'm only surprised others haven't noticed before now. And maybe they have.'

She stepped back several paces. 'Signals?'

'Your animosity is clear. Only yesterday you were looking at me as though you wished you had an axe to stick in my head.'

Her shoulders slumped. 'I didn't realise I was being so obvious.'

'You couldn't be more so, and that's the truth.'

'I'm, eh . . . sorry.'

'It's not me I'm concerned about, it's you. People aren't daft, you know. And it only needs someone to put two and two together and then you're in the shit.'

'They'd never do that, surely?' she protested.

'Why take the risk? You know even better than I what it's like to be branded a Jerrybag. Is that what you want?'

'No, of course not,' she whispered.

'Then buck up your ideas. At least pretend indifference, that shouldn't be beyond you.'

'No.'

He suddenly smiled. 'I like your hair by the way. It's very sexy.'

She glared at him. 'I don't need to hear that sort of thing from you, thank you very much.'

'I'm only remarking, no offence meant. Though I hardly think it offensive to be called sexy. Nits wasn't it?'

She nodded.

'I guessed as much.'

He paused, then said softly, 'So how are you?'

Holly shrugged.

'That bad, eh?'

'I wasn't implying that!' she snapped back.

'Well, if you feel anything like I do you must be completely wretched.'

She was damned if she was going to admit that to him.

'I miss you terribly,' he stated quietly.

'I have to go.' She nearly added 'Peter', but stopped herself in time, thinking that too intimate.

'Of course.' He moved aside. 'And remember to try and act as if I'm just another colleague and not an ex-lover whom you'd like to take that axe to.'

Despite herself she smiled. 'I'll remember.'

They left the sluice room together, he immediately walking off in the opposite direction to her.

Later, when he returned to the ward, her attitude towards him was completely changed. His point had been taken.

I'm not going to tell anyone I'm pregnant again, Elspeth thought. Not even Terry, at least for the time being. It would be her secret until the pregnancy was well and truly established. When she began to show, she decided. That's when she'd let on.

'What are you so happy about?' Terry demanded, the pair of them getting ready for work.

She crossed and kissed him on the lips.

He frowned. 'What's that for?'

'Do I need a reason to kiss my husband?'

'Not really I suppose.'

'Well then.'

He regarded her with amusement. Women, he mused. What peculiar creatures they were. Just when you thought you knew one she went and surprised you. Still, he wouldn't have it any other way.

'What's for supper tonight?' he queried.

'Steak, mushrooms, fried onions and chips.'

'Eh!'

She laughed. 'Only joking. It's bread and tomatoes.'

His face fell, tomatoes yet again! He was sick of the sight of the damn things. Still, better them than nothing at all.

'I thought there was mention of a little fish?'

'Tiddles got that.'

'Did he now!'

Elspeth went to Terry and hugged him. 'He too has to eat you know. Surely you wouldn't begrudge the poor thing?'

Thinking of the fish made Terry's mouth water. 'I bloody well do.'

'Tough,' she said, and continued brushing her hair which, to her relief, had so far remained free of the dreaded nits.

Holly was rolling newly washed bandages with Emmeline Holt who'd also been assigned that duty, when she began to feel light-headed. Frowning, she stopped what she was doing and sucked in a deep breath.

Emmeline glanced at her. 'You OK? You've gone pale.'

Holly brushed a hand over her forehead and managed a weak smile. 'I'm fine, I . . .'

The next thing Holly knew she was lying on the floor and Sister, Staff, Emmeline and others were clustered round her.

'Don't move, girl, just stay where you are,' Sister ordered, concern written all over her face.

'What . . . happened?'

'You fainted,' Sister informed her. 'Doctor's on his way.'

Fainted? Good gracious.

'Lucky for you Nurse Holt managed to break your fall otherwise you could have hurt yourself,' Sister went on.

'How do you feel now?' Staff queried anxiously.

Holly considered that. 'Muzzy. Head all muzzy.'

Staff glanced at Sister, then back at Holly. Heather appeared in the room with a blanket which they draped over her.

'Feel so . . . stupid,' Holly murmured.

'Are you having a period?' Sister inquired.

'No.'

'Well, it's not that then.'

'Feel sick,' Holly croaked.

Emmeline grabbed a nearby bowl and laid it by Holly's head. 'I'll help you,' she declared, squatting. 'If you have to use that.'

Holly groaned inwardly when Peter bustled in. Trust the doctor called to be him.

He hastily knelt beside her, nodding his approval that her uniform had been loosened at the neck. He began to examine her, asking a series of questions as he proceeded.

'All right everyone,' Sister said to the other nurses present. 'The drama's over. Back to work. Doctor and I will attend to Nurse Morgan.'

Finally Peter straightened. 'There's nothing wrong with her except malnutrition,' he declared to Sister. 'She's thin as a rake. Skeletal almost.'

It was on the tip of Sister's tongue to say, and whose fault is that? But of course she didn't. Instead she replied, 'I'm afraid there are many in St Helier like that, Doctor.'

The implication wasn't lost on him. He and his kind were to blame. 'I want you to send down to the kitchens for a meal, Sister, and after that Nurse Morgan is to go home for the rest of the day.'

'She's a member of staff, Doctor, I can't possibly give her a meal. It's strictly forbidden.'

'For the moment she's my patient, Sister,' Peter countered. 'And as such is entitled to a meal. That's a direct order, understand?'

Sister sighed. That let her off the hook, though she didn't like it as it set a precedent. And precedents, as she well knew from experience, could be dangerous things. She might have nurses dropping all over the place just to get food.

'If you insist,' she replied.

'I do.'

When Sister had left the room Peter helped Holly up into a sitting position. 'Oh, my bonnie, my wee bonnie,' he whispered which brought the ghost of a smile to her face. His Scottish expressions never failed to amuse her.

'Are you sure about the meal, Peter? Sister wasn't best pleased.'

'I'm sure, all right. And I don't give a damn whether Sister's pleased or not. She'll do as I say.'

'*Sieg Heil!*' Holly joked quietly, which made him smile.

Sister returned. 'The meal's been sent for, Doctor. Don't you think we should try and move Nurse Morgan into the nurses' room. She'll be more comfortable there.'

'Good idea, Sister.'

Between them, he taking one arm, Sister the other, they assisted Holly to her feet where she swayed unsteadily. She thought she was going to faint again, but it passed.

'When she's ready to go home can someone go with her?' Peter asked Sister as they slowly progressed to the nurses' room.

'Of course.'

'Can it be Nurse Aubin, please?' Holly requested in a weak voice. 'She's a friend.'

'That'll be arranged,' Sister assured her.

Peter wished he could take Holly himself in his car, but that was out the question as it would undoubtedly cause comment that he, a German doctor, had personally escorted a local nurse home. Tongues would wag.

Holly slumped into a chair. 'A glass of water, please,' Peter said, and Sister hurried off to get one.

'Rest when you get home,' Peter told Holly. 'Preferably in bed.'

She nodded.

He studied her, thinking how much weight she'd lost since they'd split up. Her ribs had never stuck out as they now did when they'd been together, thanks to the extras he and the vegetable garden had provided. He had to do something about this.

'You'd better get back to your duties,' Holly croaked. 'I'll be OK.'

'Are you certain?'

She stared into his anxious face, he allowing his concern to show with Sister absent. 'Yes.'

Sister reappeared with the water which Holly sipped.

'Ensure she eats every last scrap that comes up from the kitchens,' Peter said to Sister.

'I will, Doctor.'

Half Hidden

He grunted, wanting desperately to stay. 'I'll be on my way then.'

'Thank you, Doctor,' said Sister.

'Thank you,' Holly echoed.

'It's amazing how well he speaks English,' Sister commented after Peter had gone. 'Not even the trace of an accent.'

Holly closed her eyes, the smell of Peter still strong in her nostrils.

When the meal arrived it comprised carrot soup, a piece of fatty, gristly meat and a small dollop of mashed potato.

Holly gobbled down the lot, fat, gristle and all.

Peter pushed his way in the moment the door was opened, not wanting it slammed in his face again.

'Are you alone?' he whispered.

'Yes.'

'Good.'

He took himself through to the kitchen where he placed a leather bag on the table. 'That's for you,' he declared. 'And I don't want any nonsense about refusing because it comes from me.'

Jemima mewed up at him.

'Who's this little chap?' he queried, squatting and stroking the kitten.

'It's a she, Jemima. I acquired her recently.'

Jemima purred and arched her back against Peter's hand. 'She's cute. And very friendly.'

Holly smiled at the kitten. 'I got her for company. It was Elspeth's idea.'

Peter glanced up at her. 'And you're giving her part of your rations, right?'

'I have to feed her. She doesn't eat much.'

'Perhaps enough to make the difference between you fainting and not fainting.'

'I doubt that.'

Peter decided not to pursue the subject. 'You haven't looked in the bag yet.'

Holly exclaimed when she opened it. 'Where did you get all this from?'

293

'I have my sources.' He didn't tell her the bag's contents had cost him, as the English said, an arm and a leg. Even black-market food was becoming very hard to come by and extremely pricey, far more than previously, when available.

'A whole chicken,' Holly breathed, extracting the bird.

'You'll have to pluck it, I'm afraid.'

'That doesn't matter.'

He watched with satisfaction as other goodies were produced and laid on the table. A tin of ham, two of sardines, a loaf of bread, butter, coffee, sugar, tea, lard, a tin of biscuits, macaroni, fish paste, sago, German sausage, flour, powdered egg and lastly three cans of peaches.

'This is wonderful, Peter,' she declared, eyes bright with excitement.

'I can't have you fainting again, can I?'

She glanced away, her conscience pricking her. How could she accept this from a German? But common sense, not to mention hunger, prevailed. You shouldn't look a gift horse in the mouth, she reminded herself. And certainly not when you were starving.

'Thank you,' she said, husky with emotion.

'You're welcome. Anything for you, Holly,' he replied quietly.

'As you've gone to all this trouble the least I can do is offer you a cup of that coffee,' she said.

'That would be nice. Do you mind if I smoke?'

'Not at all. You still haven't given up then?'

His lighter flicked. 'I keep meaning to try and somehow just never get round to it. And the last few months have hardly been the best time to attempt that sort of thing.'

She realised he meant since they'd parted. 'No, I can understand that.'

He sat while she filled the kettle and placed it on the stove. For a brief moment she wondered if the gas would be on; luckily it was. He studied her as she went about doing this.

'Holly, I want to repeat how sorry I am about your father. If only we could turn the clock back.'

She lowered her head, and didn't reply.

'I appreciate how much you must hate us, but we aren't all tarred with the same brush, you must realise that. I've never wanted to hurt anyone in my entire life. A life I've dedicated to saving and helping people, not hurting and destroying them.'

She felt her resistance crumbling, her love for this man welling within her.

'Can't we still be friends?'

Again she didn't reply.

'I was hoping very much that we could.'

She still didn't answer.

'Please, Holly? I've been in a terrible state since we broke up. Absolutely terrible. It's like nothing I've ever gone through before.'

She crossed to the cupboard and began laying out cups and saucers, noting as she did that her hands were trembling.

'Is there anything I can possibly do to make amends? Just name it, Holly.'

While at school she'd studied Shakespeare's *Macbeth*, and a line from that play now came into her mind. 'What's done is done and cannot be undone,' she said.

He sighed. 'But it wasn't I who did it. I had nothing whatsoever to do with your father's death.'

'You're a German,' she stated.

'There's absolutely nothing I can do to alter that.'

'No,' she agreed.

She wasn't going to change her mind, he thought in despair. She'd told him several times in the past that she could be extremely stubborn. Well, here was confirmation that was so.

'How's Half Hidden?' she asked, changing the subject.

They chatted amicably enough during the rest of his stay though there was an underlying strain of tension throughout.

'Thank you again, Peter, for bringing what you did. It was kind of you,' she said as he was leaving.

'Shall I see you again?'

'You do most days at the hospital.'

'That's not what I mean, Holly.'

She hesitated, then said firmly, 'Goodbye, Peter.'

He sighed. 'Goodbye, Holly.'

When he was gone she leant against the door for a good five minutes before returning to the kitchen where she prepared the best meal she'd had in a long time.

Jemima's treat was a whole sardine.

Chapter 23

Peter and Wolf Sohn were in the lounge of the Grand, sitting by the window overlooking the promenade. They'd come there for its peacefulness and to take coffee. They were watching a long line of newly arrived POWs marching past. If you could call it marching, that was. The POWs were in a pitiful state.

'And still the construction goes on,' Wolf commented, shaking his head.

'I doubt half of that lot will survive the summer. Look at them, more dead than alive.'

Wolf shrugged. 'It doesn't really matter. Russians are sub-human anyway.'

That angered Peter. 'There's nothing sub about them, they're as human as you and I,' he castigated his friend.

Wolf regarded him with astonishment. 'You don't mean that, surely?'

'I do.'

'That's hardly the Party line, Peter. Russians, Jews, nothing but vermin. Their deaths are of no account.'

Peter sipped his coffee while he tried to control his temper. Party line or not, how could an intelligent man like Wolf come out with such a statement. Not only come out with it but apparently believe it. However, he wasn't going to press the point further. That could be dangerous. He'd already said enough.

'I wonder if they treat their prisoners the way we treat them,' he mused instead.

Wolf frowned. 'How do you mean?'

'We use them as slave labour. Perhaps they use our boys the same way.'

Wolf was shocked. 'They wouldn't dare!'

'Why not? Particularly if they're sub-human as claimed.'

'Dear God,' Wolf breathed. That thought had never entered his head.

'There again, I've heard the Russians don't take prisoners, which may or may not be true. Who knows?'

'I've heard that too, though I didn't believe it.'

'Sub-human, Wolf,' Peter said mildly.

One of the marchers fell and a soldier immediately rushed up to him. Seconds later a bayonet flashed.

Sub-human, Peter thought grimly with disgust. And it wasn't the fallen prisoner he was thinking about.

Elspeth was helping Staff lift a patient when a sudden pain lanced through her stomach. Clutching herself as a second pain hit her she staggered to the chair by the patient's bed and collapsed on to it.

Staff stared at her in consternation. 'Nurse Le Var?'

Elspeth groaned and bent over as another pain stabbed her insides. 'Please, God, no,' she muttered.

Staff quickly sorted out the bemused patient then hurried over to Elspeth. 'What's wrong?' she asked quietly.

Elspeth stared up at her through tortured eyes, convinced she was miscarrying again. 'I'm . . . pregnant,' she gasped.

Staff realised the implications of that. 'Is something . . . happening?'

'I'm not sure.'

Little fool, Staff thought. She should have informed Sister of her condition. Now this.

'Please let it be all right, God, please,' Elspeth silently prayed.

'Can you stand?'

Staff helped Elspeth to her feet. 'Let's get you to the examination room.'

Elspeth teetered down the ward, waiting for the wetness that would tell her she'd lost the baby. But the wetness didn't occur, and by the time she'd reached the examination room the pains had passed.

'What's all this about?' Sister demanded, appearing in the doorway.

Staff told her.

'Get one of the obstetricians,' Sister snapped to Staff who strode briskly from the room.

'You should have said,' Sister admonished Elspeth, assisting her on to the table.

Elspeth explained about her first miscarriage and how she hadn't wanted to tell anyone, including her husband, until she was certain the pregnancy was well on its way.

Sister understood, but didn't approve, not with the sort of work expected of nurses. The girl had been extremely foolish in her opinion.

The obstetrician arrived and began examining Elspeth. 'You're lucky,' he eventually pronounced. 'But that was a warning. From now on you must take it easy.'

Elspeth, who'd just breathed a sigh of relief, nodded.

'Light duties only in future,' the obstetrician informed Sister.

'Yes, sir.'

'Thank you,' Elspeth said to him.

'When are you due?' he queried.

She told him.

'Quite a while to go then. I suggest a full month's leave prior to birth. Can that be arranged, Sister?'

'Certainly, sir.'

'Any further trouble and you consult one of us or your GP immediately,' he said to Elspeth.

'I will, sir. I promise.'

'Good.'

He smiled at Sister. 'I'll deliver her myself when the time comes. You can arrange that also.'

'Yes, sir.'

He wagged a finger at Elspeth. 'Remember what I said, young lady, you must take it easy.' Elspeth closed her eyes and thanked God for listening.

As it was her Saturday off and a gorgeous day Holly had decided to go for a walk. Perhaps subconsciously she'd already planned her destination but she was almost there before she realised she was heading for Half Hidden.

She stopped and chewed a nail. Continue on or change direction? If she was honest with herself she'd admit she was dying to see the cottage again, just to look at it if nothing else.

Who am I kidding? she thought. It was Peter she wanted to see and talk to. The man she loved and couldn't keep out of her mind. Even if he was a German.

She stopped again when the cottage came in sight. He might not be home, she told herself, even though she knew from the duty roster that his weekends off still coincided with hers. He might well be in St Helier doing whatever, maybe in the company of friends.

She was in a turmoil of indecision as she approached his door, part of her telling herself this just wasn't right, another part urging her on. She'd sworn to herself that it was all over between them, that their relationship was finished. And yet here she was despite herself. She swallowed hard as she raised her hand.

Peter answered her knock. 'Holly!'

'I was just passing and thought . . .' She trailed off and smiled.

'Come in.'

She hesitated, knowing once she went inside she'd be lost. 'I'm not sure, I . . .'

'Please?' he interjected, his tone a pleading one.

'Just for a few minutes then,' she said.

Peter couldn't conceal his delight. This was the last thing he'd expected. 'Any more fainting fits?' he asked as he closed the door, half teasing, half in earnest.

She shook her head.

'How's the food supply?'

'What you brought is finished, I'm afraid.'

'Then I'll have to get you some more.'

'No, Peter, you mustn't,' she said firmly.

'And why not?'

'You just mustn't, that's all. You've been too kind already.'

'Worried it puts you under some sort of obligation? Well, it doesn't, I assure you.' He held up a hand. 'Anyway, we're not going to argue about that now.'

He led her through to the sitting room. 'This calls for a celebration. I have a bottle of wine in, I'll open it.'

'No, no, please.'

'I insist, Holly. And that's all there is to it.'

She gazed round the room while he was gone. How many happy hours they'd spent here together. Talking, listening to the wireless, laughing.

'Here we are,' he declared breezily on his return, waving a bottle and two glasses in the air.

She smiled, thinking at that moment he looked like a little boy who'd had an unexpected treat. 'As I said, I was just passing,' she lied.

He shot her a sideways glance, but didn't challenge her statement. For now it was simply enough that she was there.

'It's not the best,' he commented, handing her a filled glass. 'But you have to be thankful for what you can get nowadays.' He held up his own glass in a toast. 'Cheers!'

'Cheers.'

'Sit down, and tell me all your news.'

He sat facing, his eyes eagerly devouring her.

'There isn't any. I go to work, go home, go to work. That's more or less it.'

'How's Jemima?'

He's remembered the kitten's name, she thought. That pleased her. 'Fine.'

'And still getting part of your rations I presume?'

She shrugged.

'God, it's good to have you here, Holly,' he said softly. 'I've missed you so much. Have you missed me?'

She dropped her gaze. 'Of course.'

He nodded, pleased to hear that. 'You gave me a terrible fright that day you fainted. I thought . . . well I don't know what I thought. It was such a relief to find out there was nothing wrong with you other than lack of food.'

He wanted to take her in his arms, crush her to him. He wanted her so badly it hurt. 'Speaking of food, I'm having stew for lunch. Mainly vegetables but there is some meat in it. Will you stay and share it with me?'

She thought of what she had at home, and was tempted. 'It sounds nice.'

'That's settled then. Come and talk to me while I lay the table.'

She followed him into the well-remembered kitchen, the smell of cooking heavy in the air. 'How have you been keeping?' she asked, and immediately wished she hadn't, knowing what his reply would be.

He halted and stared at her. 'Miserable,' he said simply.

'I'm sorry to hear that.'

'It's a kind of ache that never goes away.'

'It will in time, Peter,' she replied unconvincingly. It was an ache she knew only too well, the same ache that had been twisting her insides since she'd broken it off.

'Will it?'

She crossed to the window and looked out. 'Isn't that a different car?'

'I wrecked the last one.'

She whirled on him in concern. 'Were you hurt?' He shook his head. 'How did it happen?'

'I was drunk and ran it off the road.'

Drunk? That was unlike him. And then she guessed the reason he'd been that way.

'It was easy to get another vehicle. I just put in the necessary re-quisition order and it appeared.' He shrugged. 'Whoever lost it couldn't have driven it anyway.'

'German logic, eh?'

'Fact.'

She watched him as he laid out knives and forks, then plates. He extracted half a loaf of bread and began cutting slices.

'Do you want me to help you?'

'If you wish.'

He looked at the stew in the oven while she did that. 'Soon be ready,' he declared. 'Hungry?'

She laughed wryly. 'What do you think?'

'Silly question really. Of course you are.'

They gazed into one another's eyes, causing Holly to shudder.

'Are you all right?'

'Yes,' she whispered.

And then suddenly what he'd wanted was reality. Holly was in his arms, pressing tight against him. There was a brief moment when Holly knew she could still have pulled away, then his mouth was on hers, his tongue probing, and the moment was gone for ever.

Peter took her right there on the kitchen floor, and their union was bliss for both of them. She forgot he was a German, forgot about her father, all that mattered was that she loved him and he her.

'My darling, my darling,' he crooned over and over again.

'Yes, oh yes,' she breathed in reply, the volcano inside her rapidly boiling to eruption.

He smiled when she opened her mouth and screamed in ecstasy. Then it was his turn.

When it was over he lay beside her and cradled her head with his arm. 'No regrets, I hope?'

'None.'

'Welcome home, wife.'

I am home, she thought. For home was with Peter with whom she belonged. They were made for each other.

'Guess what?' she said.

'What?'

'I'm even more hungry now.'

He laughed. 'Me too.'

'Can we go to bed afterwards? It's a bit hard down here.'

'Bed it is when I've fed you.'

He helped her to her feet. 'Promise you'll never leave me again, Holly? I don't think I could survive a second break.'

'I promise,' she whispered.

He sighed. 'I feel whole again.'

She felt the same. Whole, complete, utterly at peace. It was wonderful.

He picked up her knickers and, eyes twinkling, handed them to her. 'Yours, I believe.'

Holly blushed. 'Cheeky!'

For modesty's sake, which he found highly amusing, she turned her back to him while she put them back on and readjusted herself.

She'd been right, she reflected. Once inside Half Hidden and she'd been lost.

She couldn't have been happier.

Holly gazed at Peter's sleeping form. Reaching over she gently stroked his hair.

He muttered something unintelligible and shifted position.

'Peter, I have to go.'

He sniffed, then opened his eyes, smiling dreamily when he saw her. 'Not again, I simply couldn't,' he mumbled.

She kissed him lightly on the cheek. 'I said I have to go.'

'But why? I want you to stay the night,' he queried, sitting up.

'I can't, darling. I've got to get home to Jemima.'

He groaned, he'd forgotten about the kitten. Damn!

'I wish I could stay the night but it's impossible. I'm sorry.'

'You look gorgeous,' he declared.

'You don't look so bad yourself.'

She kissed him again on the cheek, then brushed her lips over his. 'And sexy with it.'

Holly squirmed away when he reached for her. Then laughed when he lunged at her which she managed to avoid. Hopping out of bed she reached for her underthings.

'That was an afternoon I'll never forget,' he said as she began dressing.

'I doubt I will either.'

'When are you coming back?'

'How does tomorrow sound?'

He pulled a face. 'So long? How will I possibly get through the rest of the day?'

'You'll just have to somehow,' she teased in reply.

He watched her hook up her bra. He hadn't been exaggerating when he'd said she was gorgeous. She was truly so. And *his* again.

'Aren't you going to get dressed?' she queried.

'Not until you've finished. I want to watch.'

'*Voyeur*,' she further teased.

'Most certainly where you're concerned.'

He gave a low wolf whistle as she slipped on her skirt. 'Wow!'

Holly couldn't resist waggling her bottom at him which he applauded. 'More! More!' he demanded.

Turning to him, her previous modesty forgotten, she jiggled her breasts, thinking this enormous fun.

It was then Peter realised he'd been wrong; he could.

When he announced this to Holly, and showed her the evidence, she snatched up the remainder of her clothes and, laughing, fled the room.

Enough was enough. For the time being anyway.

'Pregnant!'

'That's right.'

'Elspeth, that's wonderful,' Holly beamed.

'I knew you'd be pleased for me.'

The two girls, who'd bumped into one another coming off shift, continued on down the street, Elspeth relating the scare she'd had on the ward and what the obstetrician had said.

The German doctors' common room had formerly belonged to their British counterparts, the latter having been evicted from the premises directly after the Occupation. The British doctors now had to make do with a pokey little windowless room on another floor.

Peter was tired, it had been a long and busy day. And worryingly the supply of anaesthetic was running low again. The thought of returning to operating without anaesthetic was a nightmare.

He found his fellow colleagues in a grim mood. 'I tell you the Allies will be thrown back into the sea,' Helmut Gerber was declaring. 'Rommel will see to that.'

'What's happened?' Peter asked.

'Haven't you heard?'

Peter shook his head.

'The Allies have gone ashore in Normandy.'

Peter sucked in a breath. This was news indeed. Then he frowned. 'Surely not? They would have invaded us first.'

'That's what we all thought,' Hans Beck replied. 'Instead they've skirted round, leaving us be.'

'For now that is,' Willy Zirnheldt pointed out.

Peter pulled out his cigarettes and lit up. 'Have they established a beach-head yet?' he queried.

'No one knows for sure. Information to date is sketchy,' Joachim Henchel replied.

If they did succeed then that was it, the war was as good as over, Peter thought. But, as Gerber said, they had Rommel to contend with first and his reputation was legendary.

As though reading Peter's mind Henchel went on. 'If the Allies do manage to land and establish a beach-head then they'll start pushing from the west while the Russians will be doing the same from the east. Which means we'll be in a vice that will squeeze and squeeze until finally both sides of the vice come together.'

'It will never happen, Joachim,' Gerber protested. 'Take my word for that, it will never happen.'

'I wish I could be so certain of that,' Henchel muttered.

'It would mean us being cut off from the mainland,' Peter stated. 'Which must be the Allies' intention as they've by-passed us.'

Zirnheldt suddenly laughed. 'All that construction and they simply sailed on by. It's funny when you think about it.'

'I doubt the Führer is amused,' Hans Beck commented wryly.

The room fell silent, each man engrossed in his own thoughts.

'All we can do is wait and see,' Peter said eventually. 'We should know the outcome of this attempted landing soon enough.'

'I have every faith in Rommel,' Gerber declared. 'He'll kick their arses back to where they came from.'

Maybe, Peter thought. Maybe.

Heather Aubin jerked her head at Holly, indicating she follow her. Heather bent to pretend and smooth a perfectly made bed awaiting a new patient and Holly did likewise.

'The Allies have invaded France,' Heather whispered excitedly.

'What!'

'Ssshh, keep your voice down.'

'How do you know?'

Heather winked at her. 'I just do, that's all.'

Well, well, Holly thought. This was momentous.

'Isn't it terrific?' Heather enthused.

'I should say. You're absolutely certain now, there's no mistake?'

'Not unless the BBC is lying, and why should they do that? According to them a huge force has landed and bitter fighting is taking place. There was no word about casualties but they're bound to be heavy.'

Holly could well imagine. There would be thousands killed on both sides, poor sods. Also, the Allies might be in France but the battle for the Islands remained to be fought. That's when they'd all be well and truly up against it.

Peter stared at the notice informing all German personnel that they were to be transferred to the new underground hospital which was due to be commissioned the following week. That meant an end to his seeing Holly on a more or less daily basis.

A contingent of German nurses had arrived in Jersey three days previously and they too would be installed at the new hospital. They'd come on one of the few boats to reach the Islands since the Allies' invasion.

Gerber had been wrong. Rommel had failed to drive the Allies back into the sea. Instead a beach-head had been successfully established and now the Allies were pushing inland. The western part of the vice that Henchel had described had begun to squeeze.

*

'Ah, come in, Nurse Morgan,' Sister Porthcarron said.

Holly was wondering why she'd been summoned. Special duties perhaps?

Sister studied her. 'You've been promoted to Staff Nurse. Congratulations.'

Holly's eyebrows shot up in surprise. Staff Nurse! That was tremendous.

'How do you feel about that?'

'I'm delighted.'

'Hmmh,' Sister murmured. Holly would make an excellent Staff Nurse, and Sister in time, but she had no intention of saying so. She'd always intentionally been scant with praise – she wasn't going to have any swollen heads on her ward – rebukes were far more in her line.

'On this ward, Sister?'

'That's correct. You'll start next Monday.'

Holly couldn't wait to tell Heather who'd be green with jealousy. And Elspeth of course. Not to mention Peter whom she'd be visiting that weekend.

It was frustrating that he'd been transferred but they'd both known for some while that was in the offing. Come the weekend, the first time she'd have seen him since his transfer, she'd hear all about the new hospital.

'That's all, nurse.'

'Yes, Sister. And thank you.'

'I just hope you won't let me down.'

'I won't, Sister. You can rely on that.'

Sister Porthcarron was certain Holly wouldn't, otherwise Holly would never have been promoted in the first place.

This place gives me the creeps, Peter thought. Miles of seemingly never-ending tunnels that echoed tomblike when you walked them. At least they were safe from Allied bombing down here, they could have been blitzed day and night and it wouldn't have made the slightest difference.

He wished he could have had Holly transferred as well, for the safety factor, but the staff was strictly German, as were the patients.

God alone knew how many lives had been lost during the tunnelling that was still going on. He'd heard stories that had made him go cold all over. POWs being trapped under rockfall, mangled and crushed beyond all recognition when finally dug out. Disposed of if still alive but badly injured. Limbs that had been torn from trunks, blindings, men blown to smithereens.

The other awful thing was that the anaesthetic had run out again and this time there wasn't any likelihood of replacement. The Islands were isolated for the duration of the war with the German army in retreat on the mainland.

Somewhere in the distance came the sound of a muffled explosion as the tunnelling continued.

Holly stopped to stare out over the Channel which was sparkling bright green in the sunshine. It was a beautiful summer's day, seabirds crying as they swooped and wheeled overhead.

It was so peaceful it was hard to imagine the fierce fighting that was taking place not all that far away. When she got to Half Hidden she intended asking Peter to tune into the BBC so she could hear the latest news.

She tingled at the thought of being with Peter again and knew he'd be eagerly awaiting her arrival. It would be bliss being in his arms again.

A rabbit broke cover and scuttled away. Once that had been a common sight, but no more as the vast majority of them had been caught and eaten. Her tummy rumbled at the thought of food. Rations had been reduced yet again, that now doled out was so small it was worse than pitiful. How a person was supposed to exist on it was beyond her. Things had been chronic before, now they'd become desperate in the extreme.

For a few seconds she held her face up to the sun, letting its rays wash over her, then continued on her way to Half Hidden.

Chapter 24

'Staff Nurse, that's wonderful!' Peter exclaimed when she told him about her promotion. 'You must be pleased.'

He kissed her on the lips. 'I've been champing at the bit, as you English so quaintly say, waiting for you to get here. Are you staying the night?'

'I've arranged for a neighbour to look after Jemima until I get back.'

'Good,' he smiled.

'How is it at the new hospital?'

His face darkened. 'Dreadful. I hate it.' He then proceeded to describe what it was like.

'Sounds appalling,' she commented when he was finished.

'I can't wait to get out at nights for a breath of fresh air. It's like being released from prison.'

'I can imagine.'

'But I wish you were there with me. When the British come it's going to be the safest place on Jersey.'

'And when do you think that'll be?'

He shrugged. 'The duration probably. None of us ever thought of them by-passing the islands. That was a complete surprise.'

'They must have their reasons,' she said.

'Must have. But one thing we can rely on is that come they will. It's only when that's the question.'

He lit a cigarette. 'Now I'm going to have to stop. Just as I'm going to have to move back to the Grand.'

She frowned. 'Why?'

'Petrol, Holly. It's still being issued for the present but that's bound to change, and soon. The issue will be for essential purposes only, which rules me out. It's hardly essential that I live at Half Hidden.'

'But what about our weekends together?'

'They'll still take place, only I'll be walking to and fro just as you've been doing. It's too far and inconvenient to do that on a daily basis.'

'I just hope it's not ransacked while you're not here,' she said.

He thought of the soldiers who'd broken in previously. 'I'll certainly take all the precautions I can.'

He moved to her and took her into his arms. 'Now about those fainting fits?'

'No recurrence, Doctor.'

'Excellent. I have a few bits and pieces for you to take home with you, but not much I'm afraid. Still, it's better than nothing.'

'They've cut our rations again.'

'I know,' he sighed. 'It's the same with us. There's going to be a lot of belt tightening on our side from now on.'

'Welcome to the club,' she replied, a hint of sarcasm in her voice.

He smiled. 'I suppose that pleases you?'

She didn't answer, confirming that to be so.

'At least we've got the vegetable garden. Pity I haven't been able to plant and sow as I've done previously, but there's a little there which'll help.'

She laid her cheek on his shoulder. 'I've been so tired recently. I have to drag myself from bed in the mornings and then for the rest of the day I'm like a limp rag.'

'It's the lack of food,' he said softly. 'Tiredness is only to be expected.'

'I know.'

'So why don't you sit and rest while I make us both a cup of coffee. It's ersatz I'm afraid, and there isn't any sugar or milk so you'll have to have it black.'

Ersatz was horrible, but marginally better than acorn coffee. And considerably better than beet tea.

She sat and closed her eyes as he was leaving the room. When he returned with her coffee he found her fast asleep and decided to leave her like that. The coffee would always reheat.

Peter emerged from theatre shaking like a leaf. How could he be expected to do this? It was unbelievable.

Willy Zirnheldt came up to him. 'Are you all right, Peter? You're white as a sheet.'

'I've been operating.'

'Oh!' That explained it.

Peter shook his head. 'I don't know if I can take much more, Willy. What we're doing is horrific, barbaric.'

'I sympathise with you, Peter, believe me. But what's the alternative? There isn't one.'

Peter sagged against the tunnel wall, the memory of what had happened in theatre torturing him. He'd have given anything not to have to go through that again. 'I could use a drink,' he croaked.

'I have a little brandy in my quarters. Why don't we have that,' Willy suggested.

Peter nodded. 'Please.'

He downed the contents of the glass he was handed in one swallow.

'We'll have to get rid of the cat,' Terry said.

Elspeth stared at him, aghast. 'We can't do that!'

'We'll have to,' Terry repeated. 'It's a luxury we can no longer afford.'

'I'll give it even less to eat, how about that?' Elspeth pleaded.

Terry knew he'd have to be hard hearted over this. His mind was made up. 'It's depriving us and that can't be allowed to continue. Good God, Elspeth, if the rations are cut again we could all literally starve to death. Which we might do anyway. It's only a cat after all, human life is far more important.'

Tears welled in her eyes. 'But he's so adorable.'

'That's neither here nor there. Look at the pair of us, we're skin and bone. And you're pregnant, don't forget.'

He played his ace. 'Do you want to lose the baby?'

That shook her. 'Of course not.'

'Then see sense. Needs must.'

Elspeth swallowed hard, brushed away her tears and looked over to where Tiddles lay curled asleep. 'How . . . I mean what will you do to him?'

Terry breathed an inward sigh of relief, she'd accepted that the cat had to go. It wasn't easy for him either, he was as fond of the cat as she was.

'Don't worry, he'll live. If he can adapt, that is. I plan to take him into the country and release him. From there on he'll have to forage for himself. Mice and other rodents, that sort of thing. He'll get by.'

'But he's a house cat,' Elspeth protested. 'He doesn't know how to hunt.'

'Then he'll have to learn quickly.' Terry paused, then added softly, 'It's the best I can do, Els. I'm sorry.'

She went to the cat, knelt and stroked him. Tiddles woke and purred. 'When?' she asked.

'Tomorrow after work.'

'And what if he follows you back?'

'He won't. I'll make sure of that.'

Terry left the room feeling like Judas Iscariot. But as he'd said, needs must.

'Have you considered inquiring about extra rations?' Holly asked Elspeth who'd just told her about Tiddles.

Elspeth frowned. 'How do you mean?'

'Well, you're pregnant after all. They might increase your rations on account of that.'

'It never crossed my mind to inquire, or Terry's.'

'Well, I would if I were you. What have you got to lose after all?'

Elspeth nodded, Holly was right. She had nothing to lose. 'I'll speak to Terry about it tonight,' she said.

Having got rid of Tiddles, wouldn't it be ironic if her rations were now increased, Elspeth reflected a little later. The thought made her feel ill.

'Rules are rules,' the German official declared. 'There can be no exceptions.'

'But my wife's pregnant!' Terry exclaimed angrily. 'Here's a letter from our doctor to prove it.'

The official waved the letter away. 'I repeat, Herr Le Var, there can be no exceptions. Your wife will have to manage same as everyone else.'

Terry fought back the urge to smash the man in the face. That wouldn't do anyone any good. But oh, he was tempted.

The official sat back in his chair, his expression one of supreme superciliousness. 'Next!' he barked.

Terry clenched his hands tightly as he turned and walked away.

Outside the building he swore vehemently. Still, it had been a good idea of Holly's, even if nothing had come of it.

'We will still win, you'll see,' Helmut Gerber declared to the others present in their new common room.

Willy Zirnheldt grunted. 'We've been driven out of Normandy, Helmut, that's hardly winning.'

'A temporary setback,' Gerber replied dismissively. 'Nothing else.'

'The Allies are still pouring men and equipment ashore,' Joachim Henchel pointed out.

Peter sat quietly listening, having no intention of taking part in what he considered to be a futile discussion. Gerber would still be proclaiming the same sort of fanatical nonsense when the Allies were in Berlin itself. Privately he wished someone would assassinate the Führer, which would save an awful lot of lives all round and finish the carnage. Little did he know there were others, including the great Rommel himself, of a like mind.

'They will all be dealt with in time,' Gerber replied. 'Once we regroup we will again advance and be victorious.'

The man is a moron, Peter thought. Regroup! There was little likelihood of that. It would be retreat, retreat and retreat again. If they hadn't been fighting the Russians as well it might have been a different story, but the fact remained they were. And Stalin, the man of steel, would hardly make a peace deal now. Not with so much still to gain by continuing the war.

'And what about our new secret weapons,' Gerber went on. 'The Vergeltungswaffe is causing terrible destruction in London. Furthermore we are assured, by the Führer no less, that there are even bigger and better weapons in the pipeline.'

'It said on Berlin radio that the Londoners are terrified of the Vergeltungswaffen which they've nicknamed buzz bombs and doodlebugs,' Willy Zirnheldt commented.

'*Terrified*, exactly!' Gerber exclaimed passionately.

'A few rockets aren't going to change the tide of the war at this stage,' Henchel said.

Gerber stabbed a finger at him. 'That's treason, Joachim.'

'No it's not, it's common sense.'

Peter rose, he'd had enough of this. He made his excuses and left.

Holly was still spending her lunchtimes in the park facing the hospital, and that day had been joined by Elspeth whose bump was now clearly visible.

Elspeth sighed. 'It's good to get off my feet for a while.'

'Is everything OK?'

'Oh yes. I only wish I could get more to eat, that's all. But who doesn't?'

Holly laughed hollowly. 'You're right there. You'd think you'd become used to being permanently hungry, but you don't. At least I don't. It's there all the time, gnawing away at you.'

'How's Jemima?'

'Thin, same as all of us.'

Elspeth's face lengthened. 'I do miss Tiddles, he was such fun to have around. Terry does too though he won't admit it.'

'Hardly surprising you miss him, he was a cute little thing.'

'I hope he's all right,' Elspeth said, a catch in her voice. 'I can't bear to think he may be lying dead somewhere.'

'I'm sure he isn't.'

Elspeth rubbed her stomach. 'I'd like you to be there when they deliver me. I'll need a friendly hand to hold.'

'I'd love that. Thank you.'

Elspeth shifted uncomfortably. 'I don't want to bring back bad memories, but have you recovered from your friend yet?'

'Friend?'

She glanced around to make sure they weren't being overheard. 'Your *doctor* friend.'

The penny dropped. 'Oh!'

'It's just you haven't mentioned him for ages.'

'I haven't seen all that much of you recently, that's why.'

'True enough. When I get home most nights I don't want to know about going out again. Or entertaining.'

'I understand. I should pop round more often but like you I'm usually incredibly tired after my shift.'

'Well?' Elspeth prompted.

'We've started up again.'

'What!' She stared at Holly in amazement. 'But you were so vehement about breaking it off. He being what he is.'

'I know,' Holly said softly.

'So what happened?'

'I love him, Els, despite what he is. He's simply the right man for me. I tried to keep away from him, tried my utmost, but in the end I couldn't.'

'Despite your father.'

'Despite my father,' Holly repeated. 'I'll never forgive the Germans for his death, they're a cruel despicable race. But Peter's different, you couldn't meet a kinder, more gentle man. As he said, he's never hurt anyone in his life. Quite the contrary, his life has been dedicated to saving and helping people.'

Elspeth placed a hand on Holly's arm. 'I just hope you know what you're doing.'

'We'll marry properly after the war and move away, though where we don't yet know.'

Holly covered Elspeth's hand with her free one. 'We're so happy when together, Els. It's . . . magic.'

Elspeth smiled. 'I understand, it's the same as Terry and me. It's as though we're the one person really.'

'Exactly.'

'Except, Terry isn't one of *them*.'

'The war will finish, Els, that's what Peter and I are looking forward to. Things will be different then.'

'He'll still be a German,' Elspeth stated softly.

Holly couldn't argue with that. 'I love him,' she repeated, and squeezed Elspeth's hand.

Elspeth upended hers and squeezed back.

Peter couldn't sleep because of his room-mate's snoring. He toyed with the idea of getting up, dressing and going down to sit in the lounge, then decided against it.

His thoughts drifted to Holly, making him smile in the darkness. How he wished she was there with him, without Hermann Eschenberg his room-mate of course. They would cuddle up as they always did, cheeks touching, the smell of her hair in his nostrils. Hair that was nicely growing back though it still had a long way to go to its former length.

They would be separated at the end of the war, he reflected. There was no way round that. He'd be returned to Germany while she would remain on the Island. He'd no idea how long the separation would be for, but it would be as short as possible if he had anything to do with it.

He wondered how his mother and father would take to the idea of his marrying an English girl? They'd probably be horrified. As would his brother. But they'd come to terms with it eventually, he was certain of that.

The thing was, where should he and Holly go to start afresh? His preference would be the United States or Canada, but would they let him in? There was also South America which should be far less difficult, there were many countries there with German sympathies. He'd discuss it with Holly next weekend during her visit. It was a subject they'd only briefly touched on to date.

Hermann suddenly snorted, shifted position, and the snoring stopped. Relief, Peter thought. Trust his luck to be landed with a room-mate who snored, and one as loudly as Hermann.

Being separated from Holly was going to be hell. It was bad enough now only seeing her every two weeks, but for months on end, perhaps longer! Still, it would just simply have to be endured.

Venezuela, he thought. He'd heard good reports of there. Maracaibo was supposed to be quite a place. It was certainly a possibility.

Not Bolivia though. That was dreadful from all accounts.

He was still going through the list of South American countries and what he knew about them when he dropped off.

Jemima mewed up at Holly, pleading for more food.

'I'm afraid there isn't any,' Holly said to her. 'You've already had more than your fair share.'

Jemima scampered to her empty bowl and gazed mournfully into it. She then slowly returned to Holly and pawed her leg.

Holly scooped up the kitten and stroked her, Jemima purring in response.

'I'm sorry, little one, I truly am. But Mummy can't give you what she hasn't got.'

Holly knew Terry had done the right thing in getting rid of Tiddles and perhaps it would be kinder for the animal for her to do the same with Jemima. She could take her out to Half Hidden and let her loose there. That way, hopefully, she'd still see her from time to time.

Jemima twisted round, presenting her belly for Holly's attentions, her two front paws waggling in the air.

Not yet, Holly thought. Jemima was still too much of a kitten. If she did release Jemima it would have to be when she was older. Or, and it was a dreadful prospect, if the rations were further cut in the meantime.

Peter and Joachim were deep in discussion regarding a case of Henchel's when a line of Russian and Lithuanian prisoners, distinguishable by the markings on the rags that were their clothes, appeared to go shuffling and stumbling past.

They stopped talking and gazed at them, Peter thinking he'd never seen more wretched human beings. One man stared directly at Peter, eyes huge in his gaunt face. The man's expression was one of pure hatred.

I don't blame him, Peter thought. Not one little bit. In the same place he'd have hated his captors.

'And you say they're not sub-human,' Henchel smiled.

Peter bit back a stinging retort. 'Now where were we?' he said instead.

They resumed their discussion, Peter forcing himself to ignore the POWs continuing to file past.

The stench from them was unbelievable.

Terry was in Halkett Place when he spotted his cousin Tony up ahead. Just the man! he thought, hailing him.

'How are you?' Tony smiled.

'Not too bad. Yourself?'

Tony shrugged. 'You know how it is.'

Terry found this extremely embarrassing, he loathed asking favours of anyone. But in the circumstances he just had to. 'You know Elspeth's pregnant,' he said.

'Of course.'

'The thing is, I'm worried about her.'

'Oh?'

'She's already miscarried one child and it would be calamitous if she lost this one as well.'

Tony frowned. 'Is there a problem?'

'It's the rationing. Elspeth desperately needs extra to ensure the baby's not only born alive, but healthy.'

'I see,' Tony murmured.

'I was wondering, you being a farmer, if you could help out? Not for me you understand, but Els and the baby.'

Tony rubbed his chin. 'It's not easy for us either any more. Not like it used to be. We've permanently got Jerries crawling all over the place poking their noses into everything, trying to make sure we're not trying to cheat them in any way.'

'Which of course, being farmers, you are.'

Tony laughed. 'You seem to have great confidence in us, old bean.'

'I know farmers, Tony, and they don't come any more conniving or crooked. You'll be hoodwinking the Germans some way or another.'

'We do manage a little here and there,' Tony admitted. 'But as I said it's nothing like the way it was. *We're* even going hungry at times.'

Terry simply didn't believe that. Tony and his family might be doing with less, but hungry? Never!

'Can you help? I'd be ever so grateful if you could.'

Tony knew what his father's answer would be. Help one relative and they'd all be clamouring at your door. But Elspeth, whom he was fond of, was pregnant and that made a difference.

'Tell you what, I'll see what I can do,' he said.

Terry grasped his hand and shook it. 'Thanks, you're a pal.'

'I'm not promising anything mind you.'

'I understand.'

'As long as you do. Now where are you off to?'

Terry told him.

'I'll walk part of the way with you.'

They'd only gone a few steps when Tony asked, 'How's Holly?'

And she remained the subject of their conversation until the two men parted.

A weary Elspeth arrived home to find the most delicious smell of cooking wafting from the kitchen. She stopped, frowning in puzzlement. Was she hallucinating?

'That you, darling?' Terry called out, having heard the front door shut.

'Yes.'

'Come on through. I've got a surprise for you.'

She hung up her cape and went into the kitchen where Terry was busy at the stove. She stared in amazement at the bubbling saucepans.

'Hungry?' he queried with a smile.

She found herself to be momentarily rendered speechless.

'It's duck. I hope that's all right,' he stated.

'Duck!'

'A big one too, we should get quite a few meals out of it if we're careful. Also mashed potatoes, cabbage and parsnips.'

Elspeth swallowed hard. This was a miracle.

'We're starting with watercress soup,' Terry announced. 'That's something of a favourite of yours, isn't it?'

She lurched to a chair and sat. 'How . . . how did you get all this?'

'Aha!' he exclaimed. 'I can see you're impressed.'

'I'm more than that, I'm dumbfounded.'

Terry opened the oven door to reveal the roasting duck. 'Told you it was a big one. I just hope it isn't tough because of that.' He was enjoying teasing her.

'How, Terry? How?'

'Cousin Tony. Bumped into him in the street the other day and asked if he'd help out, you being pregnant and all. Hated doing it, mind you, but felt it necessary. Tony hummed and hawed a bit, even tried to tell me they were going hungry as well which was a laugh. But he came up trumps and here we are.'

Tears welled in Elspeth's eyes, she was quite overcome. God, she was starving, and now this. She simply couldn't believe it.

'Tony's also promised to drop other items in from time to time. So there's that to look forward to,' Terry went on.

Elspeth couldn't restrain herself and burst out crying. Terry immediately crossed the room and put his arms round her. 'There there,' he crooned.

When she'd recovered he began dishing up. The duck did turn out to be a little tough but neither of them gave a damn about that.

Chapter 25

'Separated!' an appalled Holly exclaimed.

Peter shrugged. 'It's bound to happen once the British are in control of the Islands again. I'll probably be interned for a while and then shipped off home to Germany when the appropriate time comes. We all will, those of us who survive the fighting, that is.'

'Oh, Peter,' she whispered. 'That's going to be awful.'

'I know. It could be months, longer even, but there's simply no way round the fact that's what will happen.'

He went to her and took her into his arms. 'We'll just have to be brave about it, both of us. Brave and patient.'

She ran a hand over his cheek, then lightly kissed it, brushing her lips across his skin. How could she stand their being parted for so long, not seeing him, touching him, being made love to by him? It was a dreadful thought. As Peter said, she'd just have to be brave and patient.

'What do you think of Venezuela?' he asked.

'Venezuela?'

'Maracaibo to be precise.'

She laughed. 'Didn't that use to be the haunt of pirates?'

'Really! I didn't know.'

'Captain Morgan and his band of cut-throats. But then, you

wouldn't have heard of them, they were English pirates on the whole. I doubt they were mentioned in your history books.'

'I thought we might consider living there.'

She was intrigued. 'Sounds wonderful.'

'It's just a possibility which I thought we'd talk over.'

Maracaibo, how exotic it sounded. In her mind's eye she pictured whitewashed walls with pantiled roofs and headscarved men with big boots and cutlasses swaggering through narrow streets.

'Could you practise there?' she queried.

'I'm sure the Venezuelans would appreciate a good European doctor so undoubtedly it could be arranged.'

'You must have a brass plate outside,' she said. 'I'll insist on that.'

'Of course.'

'And only treat rich people whom you'll charge lots and lots of money.'

He laughed. 'I didn't realise you were so mercenary.'

'And when we're rich ourselves we'll buy a huge house which we'll fill with children.'

'At least ten,' he teased solemnly.

'Oh, at least.'

'Five of each.'

'Of course.'

'Nothing simpler.'

They both laughed, thoroughly enjoying themselves now.

'And my friends Elspeth and Terry, with their children, will come and be ever so jealous.'

'My my,' he mocked. 'I am learning about you today, Holly Morgan.'

A thrill ran through her to hear him call her by her full name. 'There's nothing wrong with having your friends jealous of you. Providing you don't rub in whatever it is they're jealous of that is.'

'Which you wouldn't do.'

'Which I wouldn't dream of doing. Certainly not where Elspeth and Terry are concerned.'

He loved her to bits he thought. If only they could get married properly straight away instead of having to wait. Damn this war. But there again, as he'd told himself in the past, if it hadn't been for the war they'd never have met. What did the English say? Every cloud has a silver lining and Holly was certainly his.

They fantasised some more about what life in Maracaibo would be like, Holly getting quite carried away much to his amusement.

It was a weekend of much laughter and lovemaking. Then all too soon it was time for them to leave.

'I'll be staying the next two nights in the hospital,' Peter informed her as they got their few things together. 'I hate that. It's like being buried alive in there.'

Holly sympathised with him.

'At least you won't have your room-mate at the Grand's snoring to contend with,' she said, Peter having told her about that.

He smiled. 'True enough.'

'So you must look on the bright side.'

He took her hand and kissed it. 'I'll miss you.'

'And I'll miss you.'

He hugged her tight, wishing it was the start of their weekend and not the end of it. Wishing the war was over and they were together in Maracaibo. Wishing all manner of things involving her.

She left first as had been agreed, pausing to wave at him standing in the doorway.

There was a lump in her throat that felt the size of a grapefruit.

Holly started in sudden alarm at the sound of a battery of shore guns opening up. She stared at Heather Aubin, both of them wondering what was happening.

'Maybe it's our boys coming back at last,' the patient they were attending, a Mr Morel, speculated excitedly.

Could it be that? Holly wondered as the battery, situated not all that far from the hospital, fired again.

Sister Porthcarron came striding on to the ward, the same thought having occurred to her.

Another battery, further away than the first, also fired, and then a third.

Holly went to a nearby window and stared up at the sky thinking she might see RAF planes, but the sky was clear.

The batteries continued firing for some minutes and then fell silent.

'Carry on as usual, Staff,' Sister instructed Holly, and left the ward.

Later they learned that a British warship had been sighted far out in the Channel which had caused the activity.

To everyone's disappointment, with the exception of the Germans that is, the warship didn't herald an invasion force. Why it had been there was anyone's guess.

'What will you do after the war?' Willy Zirnheldt asked Peter, the pair of them alone in the doctors' common room.

'Go back to my old practice, I suppose,' Peter lied, having no intention of telling anyone about his plans for Venezuela.

Willy sighed. 'This will all seem a bad dream one day. If we come through alive that is.'

'We shouldn't come to any harm while here,' Peter pointed out. 'And this is where we'll be during the fighting.'

'That's true.'

It was Holly Peter was worried about, not himself. If anything happened to her . . . Well it didn't bear thinking about.

The door opened and Helmut Gerber walked in. 'Have you heard that we've razed Warsaw!' he declared triumphantly.

'That'll make up for losing Paris,' Willy riposted drily.

Gerber glared at him. 'Why do you take such a defeatist attitude, Willy?' he bellowed.

'To annoy you if nothing else, Helmut,' Willy retorted.

Gerber harumphed and stormed out again, banging the door in his wake.

'Temper temper!' Willy called after him.

He and Peter burst out laughing.

Holly lay in bed feeling completely exhausted despite having had a full night's sleep. She was drained of energy, listless in the extreme. It was lack of food of course that was the cause of her tiredness.

She struggled on to an elbow. 'I must get up,' she told herself. She was due on duty in an hour.

She groaned as she swung her feet out of bed, her head suddenly spinning. She dropped her head and held it in her hands.

Many of the nurses had been taking time off recently because of the same complaint. Even the redoubtable Sister Porthcarron had missed a day, now that was something!

Must stand up, Holly thought, forcing herself to do so. Once upright she swayed and had to hold on to the bedside table to stop herself from toppling over.

Another fainting fit? she wondered. She'd had several during the past week which she had no intention of telling Peter about. Why cause him unnecessary anxiety when there was nothing to be done about them? A good square meal was what she and everyone else needed. That was the cure for this. And not only one square meal either, but a number of them.

She sucked in a deep breath, feeling steadier now.

She felt better after breakfast, a small chunk of bread washed down with cold water.

Peter's heart sank as he read the notice pinned up on the bulletin board. The duty roster had been changed and now his two days off came mid-week.

He mentally swore. This meant he could no longer see Holly, which made him feel sick.

I have to do something about this, he thought. Perhaps he could arrange a swop?

Holly returned home to a cold, cheerless house. It was September 1944 and what every Islander had feared might happen had finally come to pass. The gas and electric had been permanently cut off. That didn't apply to the hospital of course but to private dwellings.

She sank into a chair and laughed wryly. How could people possibly exist under such conditions? They simply couldn't. Already many had died, though, surprisingly enough, morale was still fairly high.

The Germans too were feeling the pinch. It was rare to see them laughing and joking amongst themselves now as hunger began taking its toll amongst their ranks.

Holly sighed. She had a little thin vegetable soup in a saucepan that she'd made the previous day, cooking it by using most of her week's allocation of wood. She would reheat it with the wood that was left, her fire already made up.

When she'd eaten and washed her few dishes she sat again in front of the fire till it died away, then took herself off to bed.

She dreamt of being with Peter at Half Hidden.

'Oh come on, Fritz, it can't make any difference to you.'

Fritz Mueller regarded Peter with amusement. 'But I prefer the weekends off.'

'Why? Saturdays and Sundays are no different from weekdays. It's not as if you can go anywhere special. There's nothing to do.'

'It's the idea though. And it'll give me the chance to go to church.'

Peter was desperate. 'Please, Fritz? I'm begging you.'

'If weekends are no different from weekdays then why are they so important to you?'

'I have my reasons.'

'Sorry, Peter. That's not good enough.'

Peter clutched his arm. 'If I tell you you must promise to keep it to yourself?'

Fritz raised an eyebrow and didn't reply. He was intrigued.

'Promise?'

'OK.'

'I have a girlfriend and that's the only time I can be with her.'

'Not weekdays?'

'Not unless she can get her days off changed as well. That is possible I suppose, but an awful lot easier for the pair of us if I can have those particular weekends off again.'

'A girlfriend,' Fritz mused. 'Now I understand.'

'She's a nurse at the General Hospital,' Peter confided quietly.

'You sound keen.'

'I am, Fritz, believe me.'

'Are the pair of you in love? Or is it a simple case of lust?'

'We're in love. Very much so.'

Fritz relented. 'An Islander, eh?'

Peter nodded. 'No one knows anything about us which is how I want to keep it. You've seen what these so-called Jerrybags have to put up with. I don't want that for her.'

'You really are serious,' Fritz mused.

'Again, in strictest confidence, we plan to get married after the war. I'm only telling you all this so that you appreciate how important those weekends are to me.'

'Then change we will, providing there's no objection from higher up. And your secret's safe with me. You have my word as a German officer and gentleman, not to mention fellow doctor.'

'Thanks, Fritz.'

'And good luck.'

Fritz paused, then added softly, 'I envy you, you know that. I wish I had someone similar in my life.'

Terry was at his wit's end. The supply of food from Tony had dried up for the simple reason that, because of the time of year, Tony rarely got into St Helier any more. Nor could he make a special trip as his petrol ration was even more regulated than it had ever been. Farmers were the only Islanders now getting a petrol ration because it was necessary to the Germans that they did. Even GPs, who up until recently had also been allowed a ration, now had to resort to bicycles.

Terry stared at Elspeth sitting slumped in a chair. She was so thin it terrified him. He was worried sick about her and the baby she was carrying.

There had to be a solution, he thought. Some way he could lay his hands on food. He'd do anything, even resort to stealing if he had to. Except who could he steal from? Everyone was in the same boat as themselves. The only exception being the black market, but that source, to his certain knowledge, had almost dried up. And what there was to be had was outrageously priced, far beyond his pocket.

Then he had an idea, something he'd overheard, that made him go cold all over just thinking about it.

Was it possible? The consequence of being caught would be inevitable, no doubt about that. It would be a firing squad.

He stared again at Elspeth. But he had to do something. He couldn't let things go on as they were. Not if there was an alternative.

'You must be joking!' Fred Parr, a long-standing friend of Terry's, burst out.

Terry shook his head. 'I'm in deadly earnest.'

'Raid the States Food Control Store? You wouldn't have a snowball in hell's chance of getting away with it.'

'I think we can. And I intend trying.'

'Well, not with my help you won't. It's crazy.'

Terry said patiently, 'I've come to you because you've got three children. How are they coming along?'

Fred's face clouded. 'Bloody awful. It breaks my heart every time I look at the poor little mites. And now Paul, that's the middle one, has a terrible chest that just won't clear up.'

'There's a lot of illness about,' Terry sympathised. 'All down to diet of course. Elspeth tells me that diphtheria has reached epidemic proportions with cases of jaundice not far behind. The hospital is chock-a-block and there's little they can do.'

'Things are bad, true enough,' Fred murmured.

'And getting worse.'

Fred chewed on a thumb for several seconds. 'It's impossible, Terry. That place is banged up like a prison. The noise you'd make trying to get in would alert every German in the area.'

'Who said anything about noise?'

Fred frowned. 'How else would you get in but through a door or window? I know for a fact the windows are barred and the doors heavily secured.'

'That's right.' Terry was enjoying this. 'But there is another way in. A silent way.'

Fred's eyes gleamed with interest. 'Go on.'

'It's obvious really. And simple, that's the beauty of it. There's a drain in the cellar connected directly to the sewage system. We enter through that.'

'A drain?'

'Connected directly to the sewage system. I've checked.'

'How?'

'At the library. All the plans are there for anyone to look at who asks.'

Fred was flabbergasted. 'It's simple all right, and obvious. So why has no one thought of it before?'

'Probably because it *is* so obvious. Anyway, whoever thinks of what's *below* the street? I know I don't. At least not until now.'

'I certainly never do,' a bemused Fred agreed. 'How did you guess there was a drain in that building anyway?'

'Because the building is very old and large, and at that time all the large ones were installed with cellar drains as a matter of course. My dad mentioned it once.'

'If the drain's been there that long it's probably all rusted up.'

'There is that chance. But it is possible we can dislodge it which is why I want you along, those buggers are heavy. I'd never lift it on my own. Certainly not in my present state. Even fit and healthy I doubt I could manage.'

Fred considered all that had been said, then laughed. 'You know it's crazy enough just to work.'

'You're on then?'

'I want to think about this, Terry. It's not something to be rushed into lightly. And I'll have to talk it over with the wife. If she says no that's it.'

Terry stuck out his hand. 'OK. Let me know when you've made a decision.'

'You're insane!' Elspeth exploded. 'It's far too dangerous.'

'Not really, if we go about it the right way.' Terry had just told Elspeth about his plan, Fred having agreed that they go ahead.

'It means breaking curfew and that alone would end you up in prison.'

'There is that element to it,' Terry agreed. 'But only on the return journey; we'll be going down in broad daylight.'

'Now I know you've gone off your head.'

He grinned. 'First of all the German curfew patrols are far fewer in number, nor are they nearly as diligent as they once were. It's over eighteen months since someone was last caught past curfew, which is why the Germans have relaxed in that respect. Also they know no one's got the energy or inclination any more to go charging around at night. As for going down into the sewers in broad daylight, that makes perfect sense. Who'll give a second glance to two workmen going about their job? It'll all look perfectly natural.'

'I still say you're off your head!'

He went to her and took her hands in his. 'I have to do something, Elspeth, we can't go on as we are. I'm thinking of you and the baby.'

'But, Terry, it's so dangerous.'

'We'll be careful, I promise you. It's worth a try.'

'I don't know,' she murmured, caving in at the thought of Terry and Fred being successful.

'What made you think of it?' she asked.

'I saw it in a film years ago. A bunch of crooks broke into somewhere the same way.'

'And were they caught?'

'No,' he lied.

The crooks were. But there again, the film had been a comedy. Unlike their situation which was no laughing matter.

Terry was wearing his work overalls, Fred his. Both were carrying bags with tools in them, Fred a sledgehammer.

'How do you feel?' Terry asked as they walked jauntily along the road.

'I'm shitting myself.'

'Me too.'

They arrived at the drain they'd decided would be their point of entry and set down their things. As Terry had said would happen none of the passers-by gave them a second glance.

'We could still change our minds,' Fred said nervously.

'Want to?'

Fred considered that for a moment.

'Let's get on with it.'

Fred carried both bags and the sledgehammer while Terry lit their way with a torch they'd managed – and that had taken some doing, batteries being like gold dust – to borrow. In his other hand he held a sheet of paper on which he'd sketched, from the plans in the library, their route.

'Christ, but it stinks down here,' Fred grumbled.

'What did you expect?'

It was a strange, eerie world they found themselves in. The river of waste that ran down the centre of the tunnel was a khaki colour with all manner of disgusting things bobbing around on the surface. As Fred had commented, the stench was appalling.

Moving along they occasionally heard rustling sounds which they presumed to be rats but never actually saw or encountered any.

'You could easily get lost down here,' Fred declared. For it was indeed a labyrinth, many smaller tunnels running off the larger one they were in.

'We won't,' Terry assured him. 'Not as long as I have this map anyway. We branch off here,' he announced a little further on, and they plunged into one of the smaller tunnels.

'This place gives me the creeps,' Fred said.

Terry laughed, which went reverberating away into the distance. 'You and me both, chum.'

Eventually they arrived at a spot Terry declared to be below their drain, the tunnel here only a little more than head high. The torch beam revealed the metal drain cover.

'Are you sure that's the right one?' Fred queried. It would be awful if they found themselves in the wrong place.

Terry studied his map intently. 'According to what I've got down here it is.' He was thinking that what had seemed relatively easy before had in reality proved far more difficult. He prayed it was the correct drain and he hadn't made a mistake.

'Now we wait,' he said. A glance at his watch told him it was twenty past four in the afternoon. They wouldn't attempt the drain until gone six o'clock.

He snapped off the torch and both men squatted, the steady drip of water all around them.

'Six-thirty,' Terry finally announced. It seemed to them they'd been there an eternity.

Fred picked up the sledgehammer. 'Here goes,' he said, and smacked the head upwards against the cover.

It didn't move.

'Shit,' Fred swore.

He smacked again with the same result.

'Keep trying,' Terry urged.

The drain cover had become rusty but eventually after repeated blows, Fred and Terry taking it in turn, their chests heaving from the effort, Fred felt it yield a little.

'Let's take a breather,' Terry said, arms trembling.

Fred leant on the sledgehammer. 'This is bloody hard work.'

'But worth it if we get in.'

If it *was* the right place, Fred thought yet again. When their breathing had returned to normal they had another go.

The rust gave, and the cover rose fractionally. Fred grinned at Terry

'That's it.'

They put the sledgehammer aside and attempted to lift the cover. It was extremely heavy, seemingly more so as they were lifting from below as opposed to pulling from above, but slowly the cover grated to one side.

'Success,' Terry huffed to Fred. He shone the torch through the now exposed drain to reveal a stone ceiling.

Fred went up first, Terry assisting him. Then Fred did the same for Terry. They found themselves in a large stone-walled cellar with a door leading off.

'Just our luck if that damn door's locked,' Fred said. But it wasn't.

Carrying their now empty toolbags, the tools having been left in the sewer, they progressed along a corridor until they came to a flight of stairs which they mounted.

'Oh, my my!' Terry exclaimed a few minutes later, playing the torchbeam over cases and cases of food, many of which had been opened and partially emptied. Above them were wooden beams from which various carcasses hung.

Terry swallowed hard, feeling he'd just walked into an Aladdin's cave. Which, regarding food, he had.

Their original plan, at Elspeth's suggestion, had been changed.

They now filled their toolbags till they were almost full, then retreated back the way they'd come, Fred dropping down the drain hole and Terry carefully handing him the bags descending himself.

'Like falling off a log,' a grinning Fred said when the drain cover was back in place.

Terry didn't quite agree with that but didn't say so. He'd only be happy when he was home safe and sound.

They covered the stolen food with the tools they'd left behind, and retraced their steps, Terry again taking the lead.

The further part of Elspeth's suggestion about the toolbags was that they not only go down in broad daylight but come out as well, her argument being that was safer than emerging after curfew. Why take unnecessary risks after all? The toolbags themselves would be an excellent way of transporting their stolen food even if it meant taking less than they otherwise might have done.

As earlier, no one gave them a second glance when they popped out of their entry point and strolled off.

Elspeth was out of her chair the moment she heard the front door open. In the hallway she flew into Terry's arms, sobbing with relief.

'Smooth as clockwork,' he declared with a huge smile on his face. 'Tonight we eat well. And the lovely thing is,' he said as, arm in arm, they went through to the kitchen, 'we can repeat the procedure on a regular basis.'

'Won't the staff there realise things have gone? They must keep a record, surely.'

'What we took is so infinitesimal I doubt it'll be noticed. And even if it is they'll think it's petty pilfering amongst themselves.'

And so it proved. Almost a dozen times between then and liberation Terry and Fred returned to the States Food Control Store by the same route without any trouble or difficulty whatsoever.

Chapter 26

'This is brilliant!' Peter exclaimed. 'Where did you get it from?' He was referring to a copy of the *National Geographic* magazine featuring a large article on Venezuela.

'Dad was a subscriber before the war and I remembered only the other day reading that article years ago. Sure enough, when I went through his pile of copies, he kept them because he liked to re-read them from time to time, I found what I was looking for.'

The pictures were filled with sun, the people in them happy and laughing.

Peter flicked from page to page, thinking how delightful the scenery was. 'I certainly wouldn't have any trouble about living there,' he declared.

'Me neither.'

'A population of around twelve million,' he read. 'That's interesting.'

'The principal industry is petroleum,' she informed him.

'That's interesting too.'

She stopped him as he was about to turn another page. 'Just look at those orchids, aren't they gorgeous?'

He nodded. 'Other major industries include gold and diamonds,' he further read.

'Oh, yes please! I'll have lots of both.'

He regarded her seriously. 'And you will, Holly Morgan, I'll personally see to that.'

'Will you?' she replied coyly.

'You have my word on it.'

Her eyes shone with pleasure, imagining herself decked out like a fairy princess.

'Once I'm established and successful that is,' he added. 'Which may take a little while.'

'I can wait. The important thing will be that we'll be together.'

'With our ten children,' he smiled, tongue firmly in cheek.

'Five of each.'

He kissed her lightly on the lips.

'And won't it be fun making them,' she murmured.

'Very.'

She indicated a house at the rear of the orchids picture. 'I knew they'd have white-painted walls and pantiled roofs.'

'And you were right.'

'I can't wait, Peter. I really can't.'

'And you won't miss Jersey?'

Her face saddened. 'Of course I will, dreadfully. But perhaps I can come back occasionally to visit.'

'I'll see you do. In fact I'll insist on it. And who knows, maybe I can even come with you.'

Holly wasn't sure about that. There was going to be a great deal of bitterness towards the Germans after the war. Germans might be extremely unwelcome on the islands for many years to come.

'Maybe,' she prevaricated.

He guessed what was going through her mind, and she could well be right. There were many countries where Germans wouldn't be greeted with open arms.

'I think we should call our first boy Morgan,' he teased, changing the subject.

'Why Morgan?'

'After your famous English pirate of course.'

Holly laughed. 'Idiot!'

'I'm serious. Morgan is a fine name.'

'Then Morgan it is,' she declared, calling his bluff.

And it would be too, she decided.

'Typhus,' Peter repeated.

Hans Beck nodded. 'There's no doubt about it.'

'Christ!' Willy Zirnheldt breathed. This was dreadful.

Peter had never encountered a case of typhus, having only ever read about it. Now he was going to have to deal with it at first hand.

'Communal showers are being installed,' Beck went on. 'They've been given grade one priority. Every prisoner has to shower on a daily basis from on.'

'Trust those Russkies to bring in a filthy disease like that,' Joachim Henchel spat. 'God knows what else they've brought in as well.'

'How many are down with it?' Peter asked.

'Three to date,' Beck informed him. 'And one of the nurses. It was only this morning that we were able finally to diagnose what was wrong with them. I'm sure we could have done so more quickly if any of us had served on the Russian Front, but none of us have.'

'What are the symptoms?' Peter queried.

'A rash similar to that of measles, which was what we at first thought it was,' Beck explained. 'That and severe headaches to begin with. Followed by coughing, constipation, high fever and confusion that can turn into delirium.'

Peter stared grimly at Beck, digesting this information which he'd look up later anyway.

Beck went on. 'Death can be from septicaemia, heart failure, kidney failure or pneumonia.'

'And we have nothing to fight it with, not even disinfectant,' Willy commented in disgust.

'Do the POWs know what's wrong with their three comrades?' Henchel asked.

'Not yet, as I said it was only diagnosed this morning,' Beck replied. 'But it won't be long before they do the way things quickly get round.'

'There could be mass panic,' Peter reflected quietly. 'With them all penned up like animals typhus could spread like wildfire.'

Silence descended on the group as they considered that.

'Those are the orders from higher up,' Henchel said to Peter.

He was appalled. 'But it goes against everything we believe in as doctors.'

'That may be so but orders are orders. And it does make sense if you think about it. We can't treat them anyway.'

'But to shoot those even suspected of having it, that's outrageous!'

'Shoot them and bury the bodies in quicklime. At least that way we may contain the problem.'

'And what about our nurse who has it, are they going to shoot her too?' Peter queried sarcastically.

'No, she'll be looked after as best we can manage,' Henchel replied in all seriousness. 'But I suppose it's possible it could come to that.'

The man was a monster, Peter thought. 'And what happens if *you* get it, Joachim?' he asked.

Henchel paled. 'Please God I don't.'

'Will we shoot you also?'

Henchel swallowed hard. 'Orders are orders,' he repeated. 'And they must be obeyed without question. If that was to happen then so be it.'

'Then let's just hope and pray it doesn't,' Peter said softly.

Peter passed the delousing station, as the communal showers were being referred to, these jam packed with POWs having their daily wash. Useless in itself, Peter thought in despair. Disinfectant was needed to kill the fleas, mites and ticks that spread the disease.

He shivered involuntarily. Seventeen POWs had now been diagnosed as either having, or suspected of having, the disease and all seventeen had been shot.

Their nurse continued to survive.

'Ten children,' Elspeth laughed. 'Isn't that a teensy bit ambitious?' Holly had called to visit while Terry was out seeing one of his friends.

Holly grinned back. 'It's just a bit of fun really. Two or three will be enough for me.'

'I should say. Any more would be greedy.'

'How's yours coming along?'

Elspeth patted her ever enlarging bump. 'Terry wants me to stop work but I don't wish to. As long as there aren't any complications it wouldn't be right somehow.'

'He has a point. There are so many infectious diseases in the hospital now. Why put yourself at risk?'

'I'm hardly doing that on the ward I'm currently on. I'll be safe enough there.'

'I hope so.'

Elspeth shifted herself into a more comfortable position. 'I must say this Venezuelan thing is exciting. It sounds a wonderful place.'

'We think so. And we're convinced we'll do well there.'

'It'll be sad without you, Hol. I'll miss you terribly.'

'And I'll miss you and Jersey. But what else can we do? If we're to make a go of it together we have to get right away from Europe. Peter did fancy the United States or Canada, but in the end we plumped for Venezuela.'

'You'll need money to get there,' Elspeth pointed out.

'There is that, but we'll think of something.'

Elspeth sighed. 'Imagine you marrying a German! It's incredible.'

'I find it that myself. But as I've told you, Els, we're very much in love. I adore him and he me.'

Elspeth thought of how different life would have turned out for Holly if Martin hadn't been killed, but didn't comment on the fact. He had been and now Holly, who'd been inconsolable over his death, had her German.

'I must say you're looking better than you have for a while,' Holly declared.

Elspeth smiled inwardly. Thanks to the States Food Control Store and what Terry was stealing from it. But that was one secret she was determined to share with no one, not even Holly. 'I suppose it's my pregnancy that's making me bloom,' she lied.

'I suppose so.'

'Don't forget I want you there holding my hand during delivery,' she said.

'I'll be with you. You can count on it.'

*

Willy Zirnheldt gazed at the fallen, gibbering, Lithuanian POW. Delirium, Willy thought. It might not be typhus, but his orders weren't to take any chances.

He gestured with his head to a pair of waiting, gauntleted, soldiers who instantly pounced.

God, he hated this, Willy thought wearily, as the POW was dragged away to his death and burial in quicklime.

Another POW standing watching these proceedings was certain he also had the disease but so far had somehow managed to conceal the fact. For how long though?

At least he'd have the satisfaction of taking one of these bastards with him, he decided.

And leapt at Willy.

'Killed?' Peter echoed incredulously.

'Strangled. He was dead when the man was pulled off and shot there and then.'

Peter had liked Willy, he'd been a good chap. This was horrible, and deeply upsetting.

'Now none of us is safe,' Henchel commented quietly.

Gerber snorted. 'An example will be made. You'll see.'

'An example was made,' Peter pointed out. 'The Lithuanian paid for what he did with his life.'

'A bigger, better, example. That's the only way.'

Gerber was proved correct. The following day thirty Lithuanians were executed by machine gun.

'It's true, I tell you,' Nurse Le Ruez said to Holly, her face ablaze with excitement. 'A Red Cross ship is entering the harbour bringing relief supplies.'

'Are you absolutely certain about that?'

Nurse Le Ruez nodded vigorously. 'It's going all round the hospital and a party is being organised by Matron to go down there and bring back what they can.'

The Red Cross, God bless and save them! Holly thought. It wasn't exactly liberation, but it was certainly the next best thing.

*

Peter almost whooped when he heard the news, thinking of the medicines the *Vega* would have on board, not to mention the anaesthetic so badly needed. Disinfectant also, he prayed, to help combat the typhus.

Several days later Holly queued for her ration of the supplies the *Vega* had brought. She was allocated two parcels which she immediately took home and opened.

She could have cried when she saw what each parcel contained. Six ounces of chocolate, twenty ounces of biscuits, four ounces of tea, twenty ounces of butter, six ounces of sugar, a two-ounce tin of milk, fifteen ounces of marmalade, fourteen ounces of corned beef, thirteen ounces of ham in one, the same of pork in the other, ten ounces of salmon, five ounces of sardines, eight ounces of raisins, six ounces of prunes, four ounces of cheese, a tablet of soap plus an ounce of pepper and another of salt.

It took all her willpower not to sit down there and then and gorge herself.

When the *Vega* sailed it was with the promise that she'd return with a similar load.

'It must be almost over,' Holly murmured, safe and warm in Peter's arms. 'With the Allies continuing to drive into Europe as they are it can't last much longer.'

He stroked a breast, thinking how contented he was being here with her. How he looked forward to these weekends with Holly. Those two days had somehow become his whole life.

'It won't be over for us before the battle to retake the Islands,' he replied. 'And that's going to be hell. Thousands and thousands, military and civilians are going to end up dead, maimed and mutilated.'

Holly felt sickened at the thought of her beloved St Helier in smoking ruins. On the other hand a city could always be rebuilt, but you couldn't bring a corpse back to life again.

'If anything was to happen to you I doubt I could go on,' he declared softly.

'Don't, Peter.'

'No, I mean it. You've become everything to me.'

'And you to me.'

'I'll be all right inside the military hospital. It's you that's the worry.'

She twisted away on to her side and gazed at him. 'If something did happen to me promise you wouldn't do anything stupid.'

He didn't reply.

'Promise,' she repeated sharply.

He sighed. 'I promise.'

'Good.' She believed him. He wasn't a man to break his word.

He drew her again into his arms. 'Now let's get some sleep. That's all I ever want to do nowadays.'

'All?' she teased.

He smiled. 'Not quite. But we've already done that.'

They had, she thought. Very much so.

'Goodnight, my darling. Sweet dreams,' she whispered.

'Sweet dreams.'

Holly sat up in bed as dawn was breaking, its pale light flooding their bedroom. She was still tired but for some reason couldn't sleep having been wide awake for the past hour and more.

She gazed at Peter lying beside her, he certainly wasn't having any trouble in that department. He was soundly asleep.

What a kind face he has, she reflected. And beautiful blond hair. The sort of blond that many children have but which darkens in time. Not so with Peter.

He is like a young God, she thought. A blond, blue-eyed Aryan God, a perfect example of the so-called master race. Except he had none of the ubiquitous German arrogance, that entirely missing in his nature. A nature as kind as the face she was staring at.

What would their life be like in Maracaibo? she wondered. She'd insist he wore a white linen suit which would be incredibly sexy on him, and a panama hat encircled with a thick black . . . No, not black, she thought, changing her mind, that was too sombre. Anything but that. A bright colour, red perhaps, or yellow.

How distinguished he'd look, doffing his hat to passers-by, stopping for a quiet word here, an exchange there. Taking coffee outside a café in the afternoon.

As for their social life, there was bound to be a great deal of that.

They'd have to entertain and be entertained. As he'd be a man of standing in the community they'd undoubtedly have servants. A thrill ran through her to think of that. A maid and a cook, maybe even a gardener to tend the beautiful orchids they'd have in their garden.

'Dr and Mrs Schmidt,' she murmured, smiling. She wasn't going to be called Frau. Not after all she'd been through during the past four and a half years. That was something else she'd insist on, *Mrs* Schmidt.

She wondered if there would be many English people in Maracaibo? There was bound to be at least some. That could be sticky, mind, on account of the war. But a bridge to be crossed when they came to it. She hoped there were at least some sympathetic English people to have as friends

British, she corrected herself. Mustn't forget the Scots, Welsh and Northern Irish.

She'd have to learn Spanish which shouldn't be too difficult, she thought. The fact she was conversant in French showed she could learn another language.

Peter, with his ear and gift for languages, wouldn't have any trouble there, he'd pick it up in no time.

And what about their children? Their first language would be Spanish but she'd ensure they were bilingual. She wasn't going to have any child of hers unable to speak her native tongue.

She sighed. What a wonderful prospect it was, a complete contrast to life under the Occupation.

'Holly,' Peter whispered, still fast asleep.

'I'm here, darling.'

He reached out and grasped her leg, making funny snorting noises as he did.

She snuggled back down again without displacing the hand on her leg. Moments later the hand moved up to her waist.

The Germans Holly now passed in the street were of a totally different calibre from those who'd first arrived on the Island. The originals, in all services, had been first-class troops, the crème de la crème. But gradually they'd been withdrawn and replaced, the replacements not only becoming younger and older but far poorer quality troops.

The majority of those now on the island were the scrapings of the Teutonic barrel and, in many cases, more dangerous to the civilian population because of that.

Peter hummed as he poured disinfectant into his bath, then climbed in, luxuriating in the warmth that enveloped him. It was the same with his clothes and of those belonging to everyone else in the underground hospital; they too were constantly disinfected.

The latter also applied to the POWs. Though in their case it had nothing to do with their well being, but that of their captors.

It was now three weeks since the last suspected typhus victim had been taken away and shot. The medical staff believed, and certainly fervently hoped, that the disease had been beaten.

After the second arrival of the *Vega* Peter had managed to acquire some cigarettes. For three days now he'd been in a quandary, should he or shouldn't he?

To hell, he thought, finally giving in to temptation. He opened the packet he'd been carrying around in his pocket, stuck one in his mouth and lit up.

'Aaahhh!' he exhaled as a thin stream of smoke hissed away.

But that was good.

'Jemima! Jemima!' Holly shouted. The cat had been at Half Hidden for several months now and, to Holly's great delight and relief, appeared to be thriving despite having to fend for herself. What had finally persuaded Holly to bring the cat to the cottage was hearing the story, which proved true, that cats and dogs were being abducted and turned into sausages.

'Jemima!'

Usually she came running to Holly's call, but on this occasion there was no sign of her.

She'll turn up, Holly thought. She must be out on a hunting expedition or something. Cats did like to wander after all and Jemima was no exception.

She went back inside to wait for Peter, who was due any minute.

Chapter 27

Holly looked on disapprovingly as Peter pulled out a packet of cigarettes.

'I thought you'd given up?' she accused.

He pulled a face. 'I had. Well, I couldn't do much else.'

'And now you've started again?'

'I'm afraid so.'

'You should be ashamed of yourself. Where's your willpower?'

'What willpower?' he joked.

'Exactly.'

He lit up and drew the smoke deep into his lungs. Next moment he was coughing and spluttering.

Holly laughed. 'Serves you right for being so weak willed.' She went to him and patted him on the back.

'It's this damned English tobacco,' he choked. 'I'm just not used to it. It's rough as old boots.'

He continued coughing for a bit, and then it gradually subsided.

'What a daft way to supposedly enjoy yourself,' she mocked.

'You wouldn't understand. You don't smoke,' he riposted.

'No wonder, it's a filthy habit.'

'Don't condemn something you've never tried.'

He tentatively had another draw. 'The first packet didn't affect me this way, but as soon as I opened the second I began coughing.'

He shrugged. 'As I say, it's the English tobacco and probably the fact I haven't smoked for a while.'

'I still think you're mad taking up cigarettes again. And I bet you paid a small fortune for them too.'

He looked sheepish.

'Didn't you?'

He nodded.

'Well, if you want to throw your money away like that it's your affair.'

'Quite so.'

'By the way, I brought my salmon ration with me so we can have that for lunch.'

'Salmon,' he smiled. 'Lovely.'

'And real tea, so we're in for a treat.'

'Not like the old days when I was able to lay my hands on all sorts, eh?'

'Nothing like. But at least things aren't as bad as they were, thanks to the Red Cross.'

'For the Islanders,' he pointed out. 'Not us.'

'We need it more than you Germans, we've been starving longer. Your lot are relatively new at the starving business.'

He laughed softly. She was right of course.

Halfway through the cigarette he had another bout of coughing which persuaded him to put it out.

Peter shivered.

'What's wrong?' Holly queried dreamily. They were on the couch and she was lying stretched out with her head on his lap.

'I'm cold.'

'Cold?'

She sat up and glanced at the roaring fire they'd laid, Jemima, who'd eventually shown up, lying in front of it. Having decent fires was one of the advantages of being at Half Hidden, regularly stocking up on wood which they gathered from round about.

'You shouldn't be cold with that fire on,' she frowned.

'Well, I am.'

Strange, she thought.

He coughed, which he'd been doing intermittently all day despite not having smoked the remainder of the cigarette he'd earlier put out.

'Let me feel your forehead,' she said.

It was warmer than it should have been, and yet he was cold.

'How do you feel?'

'Not all that clever actually now you come to mention it.'

She nodded knowingly. 'You're coming down with something, Peter, and my guess is flu. There's a lot of it in St Helier at the moment.'

'Blast!' he muttered.

'My recommendation is that you go straight to bed and get a good night's sleep.'

'Thank you, nurse,' he replied sarcastically. 'I would remind you I'm the doctor round here.'

'And what would you suggest, Herr Doctor?'

He pretended to consider that. 'I should go straight up to bed and get a good night's sleep.'

She playfully punched his arm. 'Clown.'

'And that I sleep alone as I don't want to pass it on.'

'Too late for that,' she replied brightly. 'Not only have we been together all day but there's been kissing and cuddling to boot. If I'm going to catch it from you I imagine the damage has already been done.'

He sighed. 'The logic of the female mind is astounding.'

'And invariably correct. Yes?'

'Yes,' he conceded graciously.

Holly woke to the sound of Peter coughing. He'd been restless all night, repeatedly tossing and turning. This was the third time he'd woken her.

She felt his forehead which was not only slick with sweat but even hotter than it had been on the previous occasions. There was now no doubt in her mind, it was flu. A little later, she still awake, he moaned, then spoke in German, pausing from time to time as if having a conversation with someone.

Holly wondered who with?

*

347

They both slept late the following morning, Peter waking shortly after Holly.

'How do you feel now?' she asked.

'Dreadful.'

He looks it too, she thought.

'I've got a terrible headache, a real blinder as you English say.'

'It's definitely flu, Peter. The symptoms are obvious.'

'Damn!' he swore.

'You did a lot of talking in your sleep last night,' she informed him.

'Did I?'

'All in German though so I can't tell you what you said. You seemed to be having a conversation with someone.'

He would have shaken his head if it hadn't been so sore. 'I can't remember, Holly.'

'And you did a great deal of tossing and turning.'

His expression showed concern. 'Did I keep you awake?'

'That's all right,' she said, stroking his stubbly face.

'I'm sorry.'

'There's no need to be.'

'You should have gone into another bedroom.'

'It wasn't that bad, honest. Anyway, I wouldn't abandon my man when he was ill. That's not the way I'm made.'

She pecked him on the lips. 'Now you stay there and I'll fetch us some breakfast.'

Peter sank back on his pillows. What a waste of one of their precious weekends together. Why couldn't he have fallen ill another time. Hell and damnation!

He watched Holly shrug into a dressing gown and disappear through the doorway. What a lucky man he was to have her.

'I can't eat that, I'm afraid,' he declared. 'I'm just not hungry.' The bread Holly had brought up for their breakfast was courtesy of the *Vega* which had landed tons of flour.

'Try, Peter, it's best to have something in your stomach.'

He picked up the chunk of bread, stared at it, then returned it to his plate. 'I can't. I'm sorry.'

Holly nibbled her chunk, after which she sipped her tea. 'I don't suppose there are any aspirins in the cottage?'

'None, I'm afraid.'

'Or anything else that might help?'

'Nope.'

She thought about that. 'I could go to the hospital for some but that would mean leaving you, which I don't want to do. Also they'd insist on knowing why I wanted them and I can hardly say for my German lover.' She was referring to the fact that the medicines and drugs that had arrived on the *Vega* were strictly controlled. Everything, but everything, had to be accounted for.

'I'll get by just as I am,' he said. 'A few days in bed will sweat it out of me.'

'That'll have to be it, I suppose.'

'What about you, you'll have to leave later as you've got work in the morning.'

She wagged an admonishing finger at him. 'You weren't listening, Peter, I said I wasn't the sort to abandon my man. I'm staying put and taking care of you. The hospital will just have to do without me for a while.'

She had another sip of tea, drinking it slowly to savour it. It was amazing how you appreciated everyday things when you'd had to go without. 'It's a pity the phone's been disconnected otherwise I'd have been able to ring and tell them I wasn't coming in.'

Peter had had the phone disconnected when he'd moved back to the Grand because, even when he was at the cottage, the phone wasn't a necessity in his new post as it had been previously.

'Pity,' he agreed.

Peter drank some of his tea, at least he was able to get that down.

They chatted for a few more minutes, then Holly cleared away their dishes before getting dressed.

'I'm so cold,' Peter complained, this despite the fact there were three quilts on the bed, two coming from the other bedrooms.

Holly wiped his perspiring forehead with a dampened cloth. His eyes were bright and feverish, his skin burning. 'It's certainly a bad dose you've got,' she sympathised.

'How about . . . you?'

'No signs yet. I feel fit as a fiddle.'

He managed to smile. 'Good.'

He was about to speak again when he suddenly burst out coughing, his entire body jerking with each cough. He muttered in German when it was finally over.

'Poor baby,' Holly whispered.

'God, I feel awful,' he croaked.

'You're bound to.'

His hand sought hers and squeezed it. 'You're a damn fine nurse, Holly Morgan.'

'Why, thank you, Dr Schmidt.'

'Why don't you work for me in Maracaibo? Until the children come along, that is.'

'What a marvellous idea!'

'We'll make a wonderful team.'

She smiled suggestively. 'I thought we already did?'

'Not like that.'

'Like what?' she queried, pretending innocence.

He chuckled.

In the midst of which he was racked with yet another bout of coughing and spluttering.

Rheumatism? Holly wondered, rubbing her right shoulder which had become painful. She didn't normally suffer from that. It must be the damp, she decided, for it had been raining off and on all day.

A little later her back began paining her as well.

It was a lovely dream, Peter thought, half asleep yet remaining fully conscious. He was home in Germany, a boy again, playing with his brother Manfred. They were flying a kite their father had made, the kite soaring high in the sky, its long ribboned tail trailing out behind.

Let me hold it, Manfred demanded.

Later. Not yet.

But you've had it for ages.

Have not.

You have so.

Manfred attempted to snatch the wooden frame he was holding but he shrugged off his much smaller brother, jostling him away.

I hate you! Manfred declared angrily.

Don't care. And I'm going to tell Dad.

Don't care about that either.

You will when he punishes you.

He laughed, which annoyed his brother even further.

Manfred fell into a sulk, sticking his hands deep into the pockets of his shorts.

He relented, he'd only been teasing after all.

All right, here you are.

Manfred accepted the wooden frame with delight.

Make sure you keep it up, that's all.

I know what to do.

Manfred gazed rapturously at the kite. I'd love to be up there with it, he declared.

You can't. That's impossible.

Would still love to be, though.

Peter recalled that was the first time Manfred expressed an interest in flying. An ambition he achieved when war came.

Peter grinned. 'I used to be acquainted with an old horse that on occasion had a bark like that.'

Holly shot him a filthy look over the hanky she was coughing into. She too had a raised temperature and felt chilly.

'What a couple of crocks,' she declared when she stopped coughing.

'A fine pair, eh?'

She sat on the edge of the bed when her head started to spin.

'If I was you I'd take my clothes off and get in beside me.'

'I'm not that bad yet!' she protested.

'You soon will be,' he chuckled. 'You can bet on it.'

'Old horse indeed. That wasn't very complimentary,' she admonished.

'Sorry.'

He wasn't at all, she could tell.

'How's the back?'

'Killing me.'

'And the shoulders?' Both were now hurting.

'More or less the same.'

He reached out and took her hand. 'At least we've got each other. If you'd come down with this at home you'd have been alone.'

'And if you'd come down with it in the underground hospital you'd have been stuck there for days.'

He pulled a face at the thought of that.

'Do you think you could manage some bread?'

'No. I'm still not hungry.'

'I'm not either. I know I should eat something but the thought of food revolts me.'

'Me too.'

She gave a sudden laugh. 'Dieting is the last thing either of us needs. Me in particular.'

He laughed as well.

'How's your water?' she queried, glancing at the cup on his bedside table.

'I've drunk it all.'

'I'll get you some more then.'

'Christ!' she swore when she stood up. 'I feel so weak.'

It was the same with him. He'd never felt so weak before in his life. It was as though a tap had opened and all the energy had drained from his body. 'Can you manage?'

'I'm OK.'

She took the cup and, head continuing to spin, staggered through to the bathroom where she refilled it.

Holly woke with a start to discover herself shivering all over. Despite the bedclothes and three quilts she was freezing. Beside her a sleeping Peter was muttering in German, the only word she could understand being Gretchen.

'Must have been my cousin, that's her name,' Peter croaked next morning when Holly told him.

'Are you sure?' she gently teased. 'It wasn't some past lover?'

'I only know one Gretchen and that's my cousin,' he assured her.

'You certainly had quite a chat with her.'

'We were quite close. She lived nearby.'

They both lay silent for a while.

'My nightdress is soaking with sweat,' Holly commented eventually.

'So are my pyjamas.'

'I should get up and change but doubt I could even make it across the room.'

They fell silent again.

That afternoon Peter began to rant. Eyes open, but seeing nothing, he sat up in bed and started to shout.

'Peter! Peter!' Holly croaked, trying to bring him round, to no avail.

Finally, eyes still open and staring wildly, Peter collapsed back on to the bed.

'You've got a rash all over your face,' Holly informed him.

'Rash?'

'It's quite distinct.'

He frowned. You didn't get a rash with flu.

'Oh dear God!' he breathed as the awful truth dawned.

Holly stared at him in horror. 'Typhus?' That was deadly.

'Yes.'

She bit her lower lip so hard she drew blood, and whimpered.

'Oh, Holly.'

'Are you absolutely certain?'

He tried to nod but couldn't because of his thundering headache. 'Yes,' he repeated.

Typhus, the word screamed in her brain.

'I've picked it up at the hospital and passed it on to you.'

He tried to concentrate, finding it difficult to think. Not that weekend, the incubation period was roughly twelve to fourteen days. He must have passed it on during their previous weekend together.

353

'What are our chances, Peter?' Holly asked softly.

Lie to her? No, he couldn't do that. She deserved the truth. 'Not very good,' he admitted reluctantly.

She tried to digest that.

'But there is a chance, we have to remember that,' he added.

Peter smiled grimly. Damn those Russians and Lithuanians, damn them all to everlasting hell! If it hadn't been for them, this would never have happened. If only the disinfectant had arrived sooner than it had. Or if the outbreak had started later than it did. Now he was as good as dead meat. But worse still, worst of all, so too was his lovely, adorable Holly.

But there was that outside chance, he reminded himself. They mustn't give up hope. And if it turned out one of them was to survive he prayed it was Holly.

'I'm scared, Peter. Really scared,' she said, voice trembling.

He was too.

'It seems so unfair,' she went on. 'To have been through so much and now this, almost right at the very end.'

'Yes,' he agreed. 'But I was once told that life is rarely fair. It just doesn't work like that.'

A single tear escaped her eyes and slowly trickled down a cheek. She was thinking of the children they'd been going to have, the wonderful life in Maracaibo.

'Whatever happens, you're my wife,' he said huskily.

'Yes. And you're my husband.'

'For ever and ever.'

Till death us do part? she thought. No, that didn't apply. They'd be together in death as they'd been in life. As they were at that moment. Their love *was* for ever and ever.

'Amen,' she said.

He waited till Holly was asleep before attempting to get out of bed. He groaned and clutched his head as his feet touched the floor. It was raining again, the soft patter of raindrops on the window panes. If he did manage to get outside he'd soon be soaked, but that didn't matter. All that did was to get help. With luck he might even run into someone before he got to the road.

He slowly stood, his legs trembling like a couple of shaking jellies. And drew in a deep breath.

If only the telephone hadn't been disconnected. If only he still had the car. If only . . . if only . . . if only.

He gasped when he attempted to take a step, a shaft of ice-cold fire lancing through him. The next moment he'd crashed to the floor, managing to break his fall partially by grabbing the side of the bed.

Head bowed, chest heaving, he sobbed with frustration.

'Peter?'

He was still by the side of the bed having been unable to get back in. 'Here,' he whispered.

Her neck seemed locked into position, but somehow she managed to turn it. 'Why are you there? Did you fall out?'

'Yes,' he lied.

His plight was obvious. Inch by inch she manoeuvred herself across the bed until she was able to grasp his hand. 'Come on,' she urged.

His forehead was beaded with sweat as he tried to raise himself, Holly assisting with all the strength she could muster.

His elbows were on the bed now, then a hip. In a supreme effort he flopped back on to the bed.

'Thanks,' he whispered.

It was ages before he was under the covers again and they were once more lying side by side.

Holly clawed at her body, the rash unbearably itchy. I must look dreadful, she thought, her face a hideous sight. Peter was either asleep or unconscious, she didn't know which.

'*Wasser . . . Wasser,*' he mumbled.

She too would have given anything for a drink. Her throat was parched and raw, her tongue swollen. Her lips had begun to crack.

She stopped clawing, too exhausted to continue.

The itching was driving her mad.

Peter couldn't remember any English. When he spoke it was in German. From the puzzled expression on his face Holly thought he was asking her who she was.

If she'd have understood German she'd have known she was right. Peter didn't recognise her.

The itching had mercifully ceased but now there was a dull, nagging pain in the region of her kidneys. In her mind's eye she was watching a waterfall cascading down from high cliffs. She quietly wept at the thought of standing underneath that waterfall with her mouth open.

The chance Peter had mentioned wasn't going to happen, she was certain of that now. The end couldn't be far away for both of them.

She'd often heard it said that your life flashed before you as you were dying, and so it was for her.

Pictures from the past kept popping into her mind. The time she'd fallen from a tree and broken her arm, the bicycle Dan had given her on her thirteenth birthday, she and Elspeth playing hop-scotch, playing rounders. Dear Miss De Freitas who'd been ever so kind to her at school and who'd suggested she'd make a good nurse. The gumboil that had been terribly sore. Her first real kiss. The first time she'd worn make-up, what a hoot that had been! And so on and so on.

'Holly?'

She opened her eyes. 'Hello.'

'How are you?'

'How do you think?'

There was a choking sound that was in fact him laughing.

'You've been muttering in nothing but German for ages.'

'I don't remember.'

'I think you even forgot who I was.'

His mind was numb, his body ethereal as though he'd already left it. He too knew the end was close.

'I love you,' he said.

'And I love you, Peter. With all my heart.'

He tried to make saliva and failed.

'I wish I'd never thrown away your ring,' she said. 'I'd like to be wearing it now.'

He smiled thinly. 'Just pretend you are. That's good enough for me.'

'OK.'

She listened to his laboured breathing, her own as tortured. 'That was a rotten diagnosis thinking we had flu,' she whispered.

'Yes.'

'I wonder who'll find us?'

'God knows. But someone's bound to eventually.'

'Just like bloody Romeo and Juliet.'

Again there was that choking sound that was him laughing. 'Just like bloody Romeo and Juliet,' he agreed.

There were further dreams, memories and periods of simply staring into space. There wasn't pain any more, or headache, just a state of being.

'Peter?'

He didn't reply.

Holly's hand edged sideways to touch his, a hand that was cold and stiff. Peter was dead.

She knew what she wanted to do, had to do. Somehow she summoned up the energy to twist herself over and lay her head on his chest.

A bird sang sweetly. Real or imagined? She didn't know. And then a shaft of bright light pierced the room to fall across the pair of them. Real or imagined? Again she wasn't sure.

'Wait for me,' she whispered, and closed her eyes.

The last words she was to utter.

Epilogue

A nd so it was finally over. At long last Liberation Day had arrived. Contrary to all former expectations and beliefs the Germans had surrendered without a shot being fired. There was to be no battle for the Islands after all. Hitler's suicide and the fall of Berlin had seen to that.

Elspeth stood with baby Holly in her arms watching the Tommies stream ashore. Beside her was Terry. They formed part of a throng that seemed to consist of the entire St Helier population.

'What a day,' a beaming Terry said into her ear.

She nodded. Truly it was.

Elspeth gazed down at her daughter and thought wistfully of her friend for whom she'd been named. Baby Holly gurgled back.

When Holly had gone missing, even murder had been suspected. But she'd guessed where Holly was, though not the circumstances in which she found her friend.

She didn't know what Holly and her German had died of although she suspected typhus. She had known they wouldn't be buried together as Holly would have wished. The authorities would never have allowed that.

A single match had provided the answer. A last act of friendship. A final goodbye.

Elspeth turned her attention again to the Tommies continuing to stream ashore while all around her the tumultuous cheering went on and on.